Of Fur and Ice

Andrea Marie Brokaw

Also by
Andrea Marie Brokaw

Pride,
Prejudice,
and
Curling
Rocks

I'd
Rather
Not
Be
Dead

Of Fur and Ice

A Werestory

by

Andrea Marie Brokaw

Hedgie Press

Of Fur and Ice

Printed in the United States of America
First Printing, October, 2014
ISBN 978-0-9847021-7-6
Hedgie Press

www.hedgiepress.com

Covert art by Melody Daggerhart.
Author photo by Andrea Brokaw.
Hedgie Press logo by Amanda Ulevich.

For Sommer,
the best near-sister a girl could
have.

Chapter One

Our footsteps echo through the empty halls as Mrs. Bentley drags me to the office, her hand so tight on my arm that my hand tingles from lack of circulation. She half-flings me through the door in front of her, loosing the bruising grip but keeping close in case I try anything. If I had any idea what she thinks I might do, maybe I would try it, but since I don't I let myself be yanked up to the reception desk, where I stand and look meek. I let my long brown hair fall forward to cover the sides of my face in an attempt to seem abashed.

Everyone pauses their work, amazed to see me here. They know me, but as an easy to ignore, Honor Roll student, not as someone expected to be manhandled into custody.

Folding her arms but not looking too alarmed, Principal Reeves nods to us. "What's going on?"

Mrs. Bentley puffs up in self-righteousness. "What's going on is that Michaela just desecrated a textbook with a knife!"

"A knife?" Principal Reeves stares at me, seeming to expect me to say something, but all I can do is shake my head in mute denial as I stand before her with my arms wrapped tightly around my torso.

"Don't you dare lie!" Mrs. Bentley waves the book in front of me like the prosecutor in a particularly melodramatic courtroom drama. "I have evidence!"

The part of me that would usually point out no one saw a knife is completely absent, leaving me fully controlled by the part of me in charge of blinking stupidly and the bit in charge of feeling nauseated, which is working extra hard.

"She looks like she's in shock," Mr. Weston, the school counselor, says in the most reasonable of voices. "And you're yelling at her in public."

"Did you see what she did?" Mrs. Bentley thrusts the book

1

toward him in a way that implies she'd rather hit him with it.

Principal Reeves chooses this as the moment to intervene. "My office. Now."

Mrs. Bentley gives Mr. Weston a disgusted glower before charging across the room to the principal's door, and the counselor puts a gentle hand on my back to guide me after her. "Someone get Michaela some juice, please?"

One of the office aides springs up to go find me something to drink, as though orange juice has the magical power to save me.

They have me sit down, and Principal Reeves waits until Mr. Weston closes the door to ask, "What happened, Michaela?"

Mrs. Bentley makes a sound like she's yearning to cut me off, but she falls silent fast when Principal Reeves shoots her a glare of intimidation.

"I got angry," I whisper. "I tore up the book."

"Tore?" the principal repeats. She holds a hand out for the book, which Mrs. Bentley hands over with a derisive snort and raises her eyebrows at its condition. "You're telling me you used your hands to do this?"

I swallow, knowing no one will believe me. My stomach swims in acid, but I keep breakfast down as I force my eyes to meet Principal Revees's. "Yes, Ma'am."

The adults trade looks and Principal Reeves sighs. "Michaela, it's obvious this book was cut. This will go a lot easier if you cooperate."

I consider telling them the truth. But they'd think I'm crazy. So, I just shake my head and repeat, "There was no knife."

This provokes a harsh laugh from Mrs Bentley. "Do you think we're idiots?"

Tears of frustration spring up in my eyes. "Of course not."

With a look of calm, Mr. Weston clears his throat. "Did you see her destroy the book, Yolanda?"

"No..." Mrs. Bentley admits. "But no one else could have done it!"

"Uh huh." Mr. Weston folds his arms. "And did you see a knife?"

"She won't give it to me!"

2

Looking to Principal Reeves, Mr. Weston raises his eyebrows. "Sounds to me like there's no evidence Michaela did anything."

"She admitted it!" Mrs. Bentley counters.

My self-appointed defender shrugs. "We'll leave aside arguing about the value of a confession made under distress for the moment and say she did admit she damaged the book. But she didn't confess anything about a weapon even with you harassing her."

The word *weapon* breaks through the wall of fog clouding my thoughts. Destroying a book is bad. It could get me suspended. But bringing a weapon to school? That's expulsion, if not arrest. "I want my dad," I blurt.

Principal Reeves sighs again. "Yes, I think he needs to come in."

She looks at Mr. Weston. "Gene, take her to your office, please?"

Dismissed, I rise on shaky legs and follow the counselor out of the room. He waves me to one of the plush chairs in his office and motions for me to open the bottle of juice I'd been handed when we walked back through the main office. "Want to talk about it?"

"No."

"Fair enough." He sits down across from me anyway and watches me as I drink. He waits a few minutes before asking, "What could have happened to make you so angry?"

I consider pretending the question is rhetorical, but it would be easy enough for him to get someone to tell him exactly what went down in homeroom. "Bad breakup," I condense. "Someone came to school wearing my boyfriend."

"Bad way to start the day," Mr. Weston comments sympathetically.

"No kidding."

"I can see why you'd be angry about that."

"Yeah." Angry isn't really a strong enough word. As I'd sat there watching Troy and Kim, a tsunami of aggression crashed over me. I tried to calm down – I really did. But there weren't enough mantras in the world to kill the rage.

3

"So you took it out on the book?"

I shake my head and stare at my juice. "It seemed like a better idea than attacking either of them."

"Probably," he agrees. "But did you really just tear it?"

"I don't even own a knife," I whisper, rubbing the label on my bottle and trying not to cry. The statement's true, though it doesn't really answer the question honestly. Because I didn't just tear the book; I cut the thing to shreds. With my claws.

Chapter Two

"It wasn't your fault I let myself get attacked," I tell Dad. His feelings of guilt over the incident have etched new lines into a face that isn't old enough to be wrinkled yet. His sigh brings his shoulder back to push into his seat, and his eyes hang around the speedometer. They're the same shade of hazel as mine, although his are partially shielded by glasses.

"Maybe not," Dad says, as close to admitting he wasn't to blame as he's gotten. "But what I've done since then is my fault."

Huh? I squint at his profile, at a loss. "What you've done since then? What do you mean?"

"I've tried to be there for you, but obviously I'm doing something wrong, Mike."

An affronted sound of disbelief rushes from my lungs. "You're not doing anything wrong! You have gone above and beyond the call of duty, Dad!"

He shakes his head, then ignores my words. "Your mother and I..." He turns into our subdivision, a characterless little community of cookie-cutter dwellings and white picket fences. "We've been talking. Before today."

"I do not want to go live with Mom," I state in the adamant tone I always say this in. "I belong with you."

The faintest of smiles crosses Dad's thin lips, deepening the faint lines around his mouth. "Thank you for that. But..."

"There's no but about it!"

"Micheala..."

It's never a good sign when he calls me by my full name. Never.

We make a left onto our street, and I see a massive SUV sitting the driveway. Jet black and with tinted windows, it looks like it could hold an entire secret government organization, though the mud on its tires and the dust coating its side suggest

5

it might be tougher than that.

No one in my family owns an SUV. Not even my mother's obnoxious fiancé. He has a cherry red BMW convertible. Its roof would come up to the bottom of this thing's license plate.

My dad curses. "I thought I had more time than this."

"More time for what?" I ask, a feeling of dread inching toward me from the distance.

The door of the SUV opens and a woman hops out, sticking a perfect landing despite being far too short for a vehicle as tall as this one. Red hair glistening in the sun, she beams at us, her freckles adding a level of cute she's never tried to hide behind makeup.

But what is Vivianne Fox doing here? Like my father, she works for the National Forests. Unlike my father, she spends most of her time actually in National Forests rather than typing data into the computers at the regional headquarters office. She should be wandering somewhere in the North Cascades right now, not sitting outside my house. Even if she's heard her co-worker was having a family crisis, why would she care?

Oh.

"You and Vivianne!" I blurt. "You're dating!"

Dad looks at me like I'm crazy, almost as if I'd just told him I was a werewolf. "We're not. We're just friends. She's here because..." He takes a deep breath, refusing to meet my eyes as he shuts off the engine. "You're going to boarding school."

My first impulse is to laugh, the statement is so ridiculous. "Yeah, right. Of course I am."

"I'm serious, sweetheart." Now he does meet my eyes, and I wish he wouldn't because the anguish in them cuts me.

"No."

He just looks at me, his lip trembling ever so slightly.

"What's that have to do with her?"

"Her kids go to the school you're going to."

"No, they don't." I saw them at the department minor league hockey night two weeks ago. They looked like a pair of mini-Vivians, though one was a boy.

"The younger two still live at home," Dad clarifies. "The older two... The older two go to North Sky Academy."

I stare at him, realizing he honestly means to send me

6

away. The tears that have managed to stay away all morning start to swell in my eyes, accompanied by a healthy dose of panic. "Daddy?"

"This isn't about today." He's not looking at me at all anymore. Dad could never stand to see me cry. "Like I said, your mom and I... We've been discussing this for a while now."

"And it didn't occur to you to ask my opinion?" How could they make a decision about this without talking to me about it? "This is my life!"

"I planned to talk to you about it soon, but then this morning..." His hands spread helplessly.

"Then this morning," I repeat. "I guess I finally gave you an excuse to get rid of me, huh?"

"Mike!" He grabs my hands with moist palms. "It's not like that. You know I love you. But this is what's best for you. You have to believe I think that."

There are so many things I could yell at him right now, so many hurtful words right there on the tip of my tongue. But I let the air flow from my body and wall the hurt away to deal with later. "Of course you love me." He does. I know. Mom, I'm not so sure about, but I've never doubted Dad. "So, what is this North Sky place? Military school in Siberia?"

"No. It's a really nice place." He's trying to get someone to believe that, but I don't know which one of us it is. "Vivianne is an alumna and, like I said, her own kids go there. She vouched for the place when the principal called us."

"Called us?" I ask, my nose crinkling up. "Why would the principal call you? Private school principals don't recruit, Dad. At least not students who aren't worth millions."

Dad looks thrown by that, as if it had never occurred to him something was strange. "Viv says they're on the level."

Great.

"Her kids go there."

Yeah, this is the fourth time he's said that. If he repeats it often enough, will I accept it as proof that North Sky's an academic version of Disney World and that every student in the world is dying to go there? "And where is there?" I ask again.

He takes another breath before answering, giving me time to brace myself for an answer I'm not going to like. "Alaska."

"Alaska!" I shriek.

"Don't freak." Dad looks at me now, his eyes widening at my expression. Freaked is understating my condition. "I've already applied to jobs up there, and the house will be on the market as soon as I can get the yard cleaned up some. I'm not exiling you. We're both moving. I just won't be going to the school."

He tries to smile at the little joke he slipped into his mad declaration, but it does nothing to calm me. Who picks up and moves without even having a discussion about it? Doesn't he see this affects me at least as much as him? I throw the door open. "Alaska!" I yell at the short little redhead, who doesn't seem half as adorable as she did a few minutes ago.

"Michaela, stop." Dad rushes out of the car after me, but I ignore him and advance on his dear friend Viv.

"So, what? You want me out of the way so you can put the moves on my dad or something? Because he's coming too." I grind out. She meets my eyes, not intimidated in the least. Oh, if only she knew how I destroyed my stupid text book. Then she'd be intimidated all right! "Alaska!" I bellow again in the face her calm, sympathetic, regard.

"It's a beautiful country," she says as Dad walks up behind me. Her voice is gentle, but it does nothing to soothe me.

"It's frozen!" I yell back.

"Not all the time. It's not as cold as people think. It's really hot in the summer." She starts reaching a hand toward me, and I let out a wordless scream of outrage, swatting her arm down.

"I do not want your comfort," I growl.

Her smile is sad as she nods. "That's understandable."

With a little cough to clear his throat, Dad commands, "Let our guest inside, please, honey. I'll get your stuff."

Our guest.

The same trembling anger I felt earlier shakes my body. The fingers that dig into my pocket for my house key are aching, starting to shift into weapons.

"Let me get that." Vivianne takes the key chain from me the second it's visible. She has to have noticed my hand is malformed now, but she remains cool as she slides the key into its hole. "Get inside before you shift in front of the neighbors,

8

and your dad's forced to spend his last weeks here avoiding the National Inquirer."

In an instant, the shock of her words halts my changes and returns my fingers in a flash back into those a completely normal American girl. My nails become their regular chewed-to-the-quick selves, which are about as capable of ripping someone apart as a plastic spork.

"What did you just say?"

She glances back at my father before answering. "The school is for weres, Mike. Weres. Like you and me." Her brown eyes flash for just a second, their shape shifting to something that isn't human.

Mind spinning, I let her into the house before me. "Weres?"

She holds out the keys with an apologetic air. "The thing that attacked you wasn't a dog."

"I know," I whisper back. "It was a werewolf."

Her teeth press down on her lip in hesitation. "I don't know. You don't smell like a wolf. We should know next full moon."

"No." I shake my head again. "I don't change at the moon." Last time the moon was full, I waited locked in my bathroom all night, but the only thing that came of it was that I failed a math test because I was so exhausted from sitting awake in the tub.

"Third moon's the charm," she says, her eyes behind me. "You'll change next time. But your dad can't know. That's important."

"What?" I stumble. "Why?"

But she doesn't answer me because he's made it to the foyer. "We should let Mike go pack," she tells him. "Michael's office faxed me the forms you need to sign. We can get a start on those while we wait for him."

"Wait for who?" I want to know as Dad hands my box of stuff over to me.

"Micheal Atherton," Vivianne tells me, her voice tinted with fondness. "He's the principal at North Sky and a good friend of mine. You'll like him. All the kids think he walks on water."

Gritting my teeth, I go up the stairs without bothering to acknowledge her any further. It's rude and bratty, I know that. But she's not going to tell me anything important with Dad around, and she's not exactly acting like my best friend in this if it was her idea to ship me off. Besides, her perfume wasn't doing my churning tummy any favors.

My brain struggles to catch up with the morning's events. Just to recap, today I lost my boyfriend to an evil bitch who hates me, grew claws, was expelled for bringing a weapon I didn't have to school, exiled to Alaska, and outed as a werewolf. Or... What did she mean about me not smelling like a wolf? Are there other options?

Without care for its contents, I toss the box on my bed and collapse beside it.

What in the world am I going to do?

My phone rings and for about half a second, I feel joy to think someone is checking up on me. Despite the fact that use of phones is prohibited in school, I would have expected someone, anyone, to have at least texted me by now wanting to know what was up. I would have been hiding in a bathroom stall typing away if any of them had been dragged out of class like I was.

But the ring tone is my mom's. It's the theme song from the old TV show LA Law. To be clear: Mom doesn't work in LA. However, she is a lawyer and she does belong on a drama. She was cheating on Dad with some guy from her firm for years before the divorce. And then she cheated on that guy with the one she's marrying. Not an excellent role model, my mother.

Knowing she'll just call Dad if I ignore her, I straighten my spine and accept the call. "Hey, Mom."

There's a silence.

"Mom? Are you there?"

"Oh, I'm here." And clearly not pleased. "I was just wondering if that was all you have to say for yourself."

"Yes, it is. Is that it, because I have a lot of packing to do." I pause for a quick breath before screaming, "I'm moving to Alaska!"

The faint sound of her breathing is all I'm met with.

"I'll be sure to send you a postcard," I assure her, preparing to jab my finger into the disconnect key.

"I'm sorry," Mom blurts, a crack in her voice. "I'm sorry, sweetheart. I knew things have been rough for you. I wish you'd felt like you could come to me instead of acting out."

"I didn't do it, Mom."

"I know how confusing it is to be a teenager," she tells me, completely ignoring my side of the conversation. "And to have someone you care about treat you that way... It's no wonder you were upset. Troy should have had more respect for you than that."

"Oh?" That's just too good to let pass. "So you're saying it isn't nice to cheat someone? I never knew you felt that way."

"That was uncalled for."

"Was it?"

She sighs audibly. "I know you're just attacking me because you're hurting. You're projecting the anger." Yeah, she's spent more than her fair share of time in therapists' offices. "And I deserve anger. But I deserve it from your father, not from you."

"Whatever."

"Mike..." Hushed voices creep into the edge of hearing. "Just a minute, Eli," Mom tells her assistant.

"You have an appointment," I say for her.

"You're more important to me."

"I know," I lie.

"I'm going to try to be at the airport to see you off."

Eli says something I don't catch, and Mom curses. "See if you can cancel it," she tells him. "Sweetheart, I'm going to try. And if I can't get out of this, then I'll fly up there and see you one weekend. Okay?"

"Yeah, alright." As if. She may mean what she says, but she's never going to follow through. That's just the way it is.

"Okay. Bye, sweetie. I love you."

My tone is flat as I mumble back, "Yeah. Love you, too."

Wrapping my arms around myself, I stare at the floor, and try to think. There has got to be a way out of this. My parents are showing rare solidarity right this instant, but it shouldn't be too hard to find a way to get them to disagree with each other.

I could call my grandparents in. I'm not speaking to my mom's mother, but my dad's folks... They met Troy over Christmas and told my dad he shouldn't let me anywhere near "the delinquent." They'd probably think Alaska is a great place to be. They probably think I should pick up some frontier work ethic and good old-fashioned values. Come to think of it, I probably shouldn't be speaking to them either.

11

My uncle told me once I could come to him if everything ever went wrong and I needed him. He meant it, too. But he's in the Navy. He's sitting on a ship somewhere in the Middle East. Not precisely somewhere I'd want to go, even if I could find a way to get there.

With a long expulsion of breath, I lay back on the bed, hoping the ceiling will give me more answers than the carpet did. Its pale face stares back unhelpfully.

Okay... My family either wants to send me away or isn't in a place to do anything about it.

My friends...

I laugh. What friends? The people who knew my boyfriend was cheating and didn't say anything? The ones who haven't bothered to message me since I was dragged out of homeroom, even though they've had plenty of chances to pull out their phones and type something? It's lunch time by now, isn't it? How can no one I know have sneaked somewhere to make a call?

They don't care, do they?

They don't even care enough to be curious, let alone concerned or worried about me.

Maybe going to another state isn't such a bad idea.

Yeah.

With one swift motion motion, I jump up onto my feet.

Screw my friends. Screw Troy. Screw my parents, and my grandparents, and the jerk across the street who keeps complaining about how I back into his driveway when trying to get out of mine. Screw the whole state of Washington.

Bring it on, Alaska.

Chapter Three

Almost before I know it, I'm standing on a runway at a tiny little airfield, looking at a plane not all that much bigger than Viv's SUV. The setting sun glints off the plane's wing like light on the edge of Death's scythe.

Vivian, AKA the party responsible for my sudden endangerment, gives me an encouraging smile. I used to think she was sweet. "He makes this run all the time. You're fine."

The "he" in question would be Mr. Micheal Atherton, who, in addition to being the principal of a school for were-kids whose parents don't want them around, is also a pilot. Alaska has more pilots per capita than any other state. And they brag about it on their official website. They also claim it isn't as cold as everyone thinks, but they're lying about that one. It's thirty degrees cooler there today than it is here in Washington, which is hardly a balmy state.

My dad is looking at the winged contraption in front of us, which doesn't look like it could fly the forty-odd miles to Canada, let alone the thousand and something miles to Anchorage. A sensible person would be objecting to his daughter being shoved into something so questionable – it has propellers, for crying out loud! But not my dad. He's looking at the death trap with an excited form of envy.

Disgusted, I grab the handle of my suitcase and yank it from him. "Nice knowing you," I mutter.

The man has the audacity to laugh. "I'll be joining you before you know it," he tells me.

Unlike my mom, my dad has always seemed to honestly want to be around me, so I believe he'll be up as soon as soon as he can sell the house. However, since I won't be living long enough to see the school in the first place, due to my tragic death in transit, this is of limited comfort.

Ignoring my glower, Dad pulls me into a long hug. "Call me as soon you get there." His voice chokes up, and there are tears in his eyes when he pulls away.

"Okay." I try to give him a brave smile, like a good little soldier heading to the front lines. "Love you."

His lips quiver as he nods. "I love you too, sweetie."

Vivianne is there at his elbow, touching it lightly. Maybe I wasn't so far off on my theory about her trying to get me out of the way. Except, before today I liked her enough I wouldn't have objected to her going out with Dad. "I just talked to my kids." She smiles again, giving me an urge to slap her. Luckily for her, I channel it into tightening my grip on my luggage. The plastic bends, evidence of my recently increased strength. "They're really looking forward to meeting you."

Somehow, I manage not to snort at her. I am so sure her kids are all excited to know I'm coming. Because we all know teenagers just adore it when their parents pick out new playmates for them. (I swear I never used to be this sarcastic. It must be a were-whatever thing.)

Her eyes go to Mr. Atherton, her expression shifting just a tad. There's a softness under the forced cheer now. Hmmm... Maybe it isn't Dad she's using me to get closer to. "You'll be back at break, Michael?"

His charming smile is perfect, making it less appealing than the smiles I've seen from him so far. Still, if I thought he had any interest in me, he'd be someone well worth moving onto a frozen wasteland for. Simply put, the man is gorgeous. If my mood were just an ounce less sour, I'd be thrilled at the prospect of spending the next several hours staring at him. Well, if I were in a better mood and if he wasn't escorting me to my death in Charon's airplane...

"Unless someone calls to tell me different." Something in his voice sounds off, but since I only met him few minutes ago, I can't make a guess about what it means.

Swallowing, Viv nods. With a gasp, her eyes widen. "I almost forgot." She digs into her purse. "This came for Tod yesterday, and I haven't forwarded it yet. Can you give it to him?"

The envelope she holds out is thin, pristine except for a

14

corner that must have crumpled from being carried in her bag. The writing on it is sharp and scrawled, impossible to read from here. From his frown, I would say Mr. Atherton reads it just fine. And doesn't like what he sees much.

Plastering a smile that is even more artificial than the last one on his face, he stuffs the envelope into a back pocket. "His father doesn't have the school address?" Compared to his previous ease, the question is downright surly.

Vivianne shrugs. "You know him."

Mr. Atherton doesn't say anything. I get the impression that if he did say something, it wouldn't be polite.

"Bye, Dad," I interrupt, not knowing what's going on exactly, but not wanting to see my pilot get distracted. I might need his help when we plummet into the ocean.

Taking his cue, Mr. Atherton hauls my stuff onto the plane and stows it between the seats in the back.

I only have two bags with me, and they aren't even full. It's sort of sad that my life fit into so little space, but I couldn't stand the thought of even looking at most of my clothes, which are too cheerful and happy and pretty. I grabbed everything black or dark gray and left the rest. And I didn't bring a single skirt. I prefer my refer my rear-end in a non-frozen condition.

Dad gives me one last hug, then hurries away before he starts crying. He goes all the way to the parking lot, but stands by his car instead of getting into it, waiting to watch the plane take off. He looks very, very alone.

Mom hasn't shown, of course. Not exactly a big shocker.

"Mike," Vivianne calls around me, addressing the elder Mike.

He looks down at her, waiting without saying anything.

She takes a nervous breath. "You are staying up there, right?"

His lips turn up ever so slightly as he nods. "Yeah. The bears can figure this out."

"Bears?" I blurt.

"You were attacked in territory claimed by a bear family," Atherton explains quickly, his first direct mention of anything not freakishly mundane.

"What, werebears?" Huh. No reason people can't turn into

15

bears. You know, once you accept that people can turn into other animals. "I'm a werebear?"

"No." Vivianne shakes her head, adamant. "You don't smell at all like a bear."

The other Mike puts his hand on my shoulder. "We don't know what you are yet. Usually, we can tell by scent, but yours is tricky."

I don't like the sound of that. "Tricky how?"

"I think you smell like a healthy young wolf," he tells me. Which doesn't seem very tricky to me.

But there's a loud sigh from Vivianne. "And you don't smell even slightly like a wolf to me. You don't smell like anything I've ever smelled before."

"You sniff a lot of people?" I have to ask.

She smiles faintly. "Enough to know how rare you are."

Removing his hand, Mr. Atherton clears his throat. "We'll have plenty of time to talk about this when we're airborne."

"Right." With a nod, Vivianne takes a step backward. She looks at Mr. Atherton like she wants to say something else, but in the end, she just waves and tells us, "Have a good flight."

As she goes to talk to Dad, I raise a hand toward him. Pretending I don't notice him wiping at his cheek before he waves back, I duck into the plane and climb to the front, hesitating a second before deciding to sit in what would be the passenger seat if this were a car.

I buckle myself in and take deep breaths of air that smells somewhat like a dog while Mr. Atherton flips a bunch of switches, grabs the wheel, and tells the tower he'd like to leave now. Closing my eyes, I wish I had more faith in God, because then I would have someone to pray to.

Humming to myself, I try not to notice the sounds around me or the acceleration that whips me back in the seat.

"You can open your eyes now," Mr. Atherton tells me eventually, his voice rife with amusement. "Unless you plan to keep them closed the entire flight."

The idea doesn't seem like a bad one, but he's already laughing at me. How much more ridiculous would I seem if I really did spend the whole trip refusing to open my eyes?

My breath takes when I see the view. On the left, the Puget

16

Sound lies at the feet of the sun, dotted with tree-coated islands and sea traffic of all descriptions. To the right, the Cascade Mountains reign, green and white and majestic. Mount Baker stretches up, higher than we are and even more impressive than it is from the ground. It's smaller than Mount Rainier, but when I've seen the more famous volcano from the sky, I was always in the coach section of a huge jet. The effect isn't the same.

"It's beautiful," Mr. Atherton agrees with my unspoken words. "I love it up here."

"So you're a werebird or something?" I ask, my eyes locked in awe on the scenery.

My companion laughs. "Hardly. I'm a wolf. Painfully traditional of me, I know, but we can't all be new species."

Dragging my eyes back inside the cockpit, I frown. "Is that what I am?"

"Maybe." He makes some adjustments while I think about that.

I don't think I want to be something new. I want to be something old. If I can't be human anymore, I want to at least have a new name for what I am, a new community....

"You're a were," Mr. Atherton tells me, firm but not aggressive. "We don't know what you change into, that's all." His smile is probably meant to be reassuring. "We'll know next full moon. It will be your third, right?"

"Including the one I was attacked on," I confirm.

A mummer of acknowledgment accompanies his nod. "Three moons is the waiting period. Next moon, you'll change. So, we'll have it all figured out in three weeks," he assures me, as if three weeks isn't an awfully long time to wait on knowing ones species. "And, really, it doesn't matter. I think you'll find North Sky is free of that sort of prejudice."

Why is it I don't believe him?

"So, what do the other students change into?" I wonder aloud, in the hopes of figuring out what I'm not will help me figure out what I am through the process of elimination.

"We have a lot of wolves, like myself," he says. "The Fox children are foxes, of course...."

"What?" I stare in disbelief. "Vivianne Fox actually is a fox?"

He grins at my outrage. "Not all families had creative founders."

I guess not.

"We have a few bears, of assorted subspecies," he goes on. "Some leopards, mostly snow leoprds. A few lions. Some tigers, including a pair of Siberians. A small pack of coyotes..."

"So, all mammals?" I catch on.

He nods. "There are those who change into other things, but you really need warm blood and fur if you want to be happy living as far north as we do." His head tilts to check a setting before going on.

"Most of the students were born weres...." Catching my confusion, he makes a backwards motion with his hand, as if rewinding himself, and explains further. "There are two ways to be a were. You can either be born to it, or you can be turned through an attack. You and I were both turned. If either of us have children, they'll be born to it."

Something about that seems wrong. "Shouldn't there be a lot of you? A lot of us, then?"

"We don't breed easily," he answers with a shrug. "Our dominance struggles tend to be to the death. And there are a lot of rules about who is allowed to reproduce, which vary by species."

I make a gagging sound at the idea of having to ask someone's permission to have children, but he rushes over it without pause.

"And we have a long history of strict punishments for weres who attack humans."

That strikes me as ominous. "How strict?"

"Usually, we kill them."

This is spoken with a complete absence of emotion.

My throat constricts as I swallow. "Is that what happened to the one who attacked you?"

He chuckles softly. "Worse. He had to marry the girl we were fighting over."

My expression must be funny, because he laughs harder when he sees it. "We were cousins. Through the non-were side, obviously. And she was his life mate. Not that she knew it at the time, or I doubt she would have been fooling around with me."

My nod of response is noncommittal. Something tells me he was pretty dazzling in high school. I can't imagine the girls around him were filled with chaste thoughts.

"He didn't mean to infect me, he was just too emotional, and too inexperienced, to control himself. His hands shifted to claws and ripped into me. He didn't even realize they'd changed until after it was too late."

"And they let him off because of that?"

Mr. Atherton shrugs. "And because I pleaded for his life. He was my best friend. And she was his life mate, even if he was the only one who knew it at the time."

I tilt my head. "And what did she think?"

More laughter meets the question. He laughs easily. "She realized when his life was in danger that she really did want to be with him. And in return for my role in their courtship, they named me godfather of their son."

He turns the plane, banking west and drenching us in the glare of the sun.

My eyes water in response to the light, then my mouth widens as a yawn overtakes me. My eyes feel really droopy, for reasons I don't think are related to not having brought sunglasses. My energy levels are plummeting as quickly as I had expected the aircraft to.

"I'm impressed you're still awake," Mr Atherton lets me know.

"Why?" I ask around a second yawn. "Excuse me...."

He gives my hand a pat. Apparently weres touch a lot. I would be freaked by that if I wasn't incredibly exhausted all of sudden.

"Changes take a lot out of a new were," he answers. "And partial changes can really tire all of us. Stopping the change before it's over takes more energy then changing the whole way. Part of what saved my cousin was that even enraged with jealousy over his mate, he still controlled himself enough to only shift his hands."

"But I can't change the whole way," I point out. "Less than three months. Um. Moons."

"Yeah..." The word is drawn out thoughtfully. "It is strange to shift at all before then."

19

Great. I'm strange in addition to smelling funny. I'm just going to be the hit of my new school, aren't I?

"Get some sleep," Atherton tells me, sounding sympathetic. "You can lay down in the back if you want."

But moving seems like too much of a bother, so I just lean against the window and close my eyes.

I should be thinking about all the information that's been dumped on me today or worrying about what a school full of weres is going to be like, but my concentration is back at my old school. Troy will be in computer lab right now. I'm sure he's received the e-mail I sent him. Wonder what he thought when he read it. There wasn't a special one for him; he was cc'ed with everyone else. I wonder if he recognized the significance of that. I wonder if he cared.

Chapter Four

A blast of chill slams into me when the door of the plane opens, forcefully giving me firsthand knowledge of just how insanely cold Alaska really is. Why would anyone ever volunteer to come here?

Drawing my parka tight around me, I grab one of my bags and make my way through the tiny plane hanger to start toward a large, well-lit building. It's two or three stories tall and wooden, with large balconies coated in snow despite their roofs.

Atherton swings the hanger doors closed, latching them with only a pin. Guess there aren't very many people out here to steal his toy, so there's not much need to lock it up. "Welcome to my home."

At least he has the sense not to try to call it my new home. I can deal with it being his, as long as it doesn't have to be mine.

My eyes sting. I would be crying, except my tear ducts are iced over.

"As you become stronger, you'll mind the cold less." Atherton walks past me with the other bag, grinning over his shoulder. "And for the record, this is an unusually cold night."

The door nearest us swings open as we approach. A skinny little girl with a brilliant cloak of bright red hair dancing around her stands in its light. "Welcome back, Mr. Atherton!"

The girl rushes forward and tries to take the bag he's carrying, but he shoos her away with laughter and clear affection. "I've got it, Sam."

The girl contents herself with holding the door for us as we pass through it. She ducks her head when I try to look at her, and her hair falls to cover her face.

I decide to look at the nice, warm room instead. It's really about what one would have expected from the outside, a mixture of wood and stone and thick carpeting. It's more like a ski lodge than a school.

The girl peeks at me through her thick shroud of hair, looking away quickly when I try to meet her gaze. She mumbles something I don't catch.

"I'm sure she'd appreciate it, Samantha," Mr. Atherton answers when I fail to.

"Yes," I second, wondering what I'm agreeing about.

Tossing her hair back with a flip, the girl grins at me. Inside, in proper lighting, and without her hair covering her, I realize the girl isn't nearly as young I first thought. She might be the height of an average ten-year-old, but her face is that of someone closer to my age. If she's younger than I am, it's not by much.

"This is Samantha, Michaela." Mr. Atherton smiles in fondness. "She's a sophomore."

One year behind me then. I wonder if this place is too small for that to matter. Back home, I never really noticed anyone in lower grades. With nearly a thousand kids in my own class, why should I have?

She titters nervously. "And one of the Fox foxes. Mom said I should apologize if you're still mad at her."

Oh. So that's why she's here: mother's orders.

"No problem," I grunt, wondering when someone will tell me where to put my stuff.

"Um..." Samantha pulls on a lock of hair and looks toward the stairs.

"Michael!" yells a new person. "Thank God you're here!"

A very harried, very loud, woman rushes into the room from a door featuring a brass plate with the name Michael Atherton etched on it. "Hello, Michaela. Welcome to North Sky. You need to come right now before that hyena does something else stupid."

She says all this in one big rush, so I don't realize I'm not the one to be interceding with the hyena until Mr. Atherton answers her.

"Alright." Giving me a warm smile, he nods once more. "Sam will take care of you tonight. Come see me right after breakfast."

He hands my bag to Sam, who isn't much bigger than it is.

If the thing were full, there's no way she'd make it up the stairs rather than toppling down them with it.

As it is, she's undoubtedly very glad to see a boy charge down to us after she's made it a few steps up. He takes the bag from her with a grin.

The boy is big enough he could easily carry both bags, Samantha, and maybe even me, all at the same time. Tall and broad, he has a strange combination of Inuit bone structure and Aryan hair. Dark skinned, so blond it's tempting to say his hair is white, and with amazing cornflower blue eyes, he looks like the result of a Viking breeding with an Eskimo. The combination sounds like it would be odd, but it isn't odd – it's yummy.

"Michaela, this is Bryce. Bryce, Michaela."

Snapping my jaw up to its usual place, I reposition the bag hanging from my shoulder. "Most people call me Mike. Except for my mom and people who are yelling at me."

"And I'm Sam," Sam says.

"And I'm Hey You." Bryce's whole face lights up with his smile.

I *tsk* at that. "No, I bet you're Sir."

He laughs, a deep and rumbling sound.

The laugh cuts off abruptly as he jerks forward toward me with a loud sniff. "Polar bear?"

He squints and takes a slow step higher, his head held to the side so that his hair sways with the motion. "I thought you were attacked in Washington. I thought you were a wolf."

With a sigh, I shrug. "No one seems to agree on what I am."

Sam makes a small sound of curiosity. "You don't really smell like anything to me. Nothing I've smelled before anyway." She's addressing me, but her eyes are on Bryce.

"I don't think I'm a polar bear," I tell them. "I don't like snow all that much."

Staring at me, Bryce shakes his head. "The only werebears down there are browns and grizzlies. There's only one clan of polars, and we're all in Alaska and Canada. But damned if you don't smell like one of us."

"How strange," says Sam, a little too coolly, as she dodges

23

around Bryce to start up the stairs without us. I jerk my chin upward to get the boy to move, since he's still looking at me without seeming to notice how much Sam doesn't like all the attention he's paying me.

Boys are apparently clueless even when they turn furry once a month. Go figure.

The room we follow Sam into is much nicer than any dorm room I've ever seen. It's more like a hotel. There's a full bed with an opulent comforter, solid wood furniture, and even a thirty-something-inch television. The color scheme is a blend of burgundy and cream, warm but not too out of place in the snowy wilderness that I assume is visible when the thick, floor length curtains are slid aside. A small door stands closed beside the window, presumably leading onto one of the balconies I saw from outside, and another is open to reveal a full bathroom.

"I'm sorry," Sam mumbles. "This late in the year, only the smaller rooms are empty. You should be able to upgrade for next year though."

Uh... "This room is a lot nicer than my room at home," I admit, opening a double closet and placing my bag on the floor. I'm seriously starting to wonder how Dad is ever going to afford to pay for me to be here.

"Mine too." Sam laughs softly. "And here I don't have to share with my sister." Catching my look of interest while Bryce puts the bag he carried up next to the other one, she explains, "The school figured out a long time ago that it's best to let us all have our own space. Cuts down on conflict."

In a place where conflict quite possibly doesn't mean bickering, but murder and mayhem, I can see how cutting down on conflict would be a priority.

"You two coming to dinner?" Bryce asks, moving back toward the door.

My stomach wouldn't mind some food, but I shake my head. "No, I'm fine. Tired. I just need to rest." I smile. "Thank you for helping."

"No problem." Bryce smiles back, a joyous beaming free of all pretense. "I'm room thirty four." His head jerks towards a slender phone sitting on the night stand. "Call if you need anything else." He starts to back towards the door. "What about you, Kit?"

Kit, AKA Sam, arches an eyebrow. "I already knew your phone number."

The bear looks puzzled. "I mean, are you coming to dinner?"

Sam glances at me. "I need to call my dad," I tell her. I tried to do it as soon while Mr. Atherton was parking the plane, but my cell doesn't have coverage up here.

"Alright." The fox moves towards the door. "I'll check up on you later?"

"Okay." I try to sound happy about the idea. I sag against the door the second I have it closed, though, and I bite back a grumble when she knocks on the door later.

I'm happier to see her when she holds up a huge bowl of popcorn and two cans of pop dangling from a six-pack holder.

An hour later, Sam and I sit on my bed watching a rerun of some British sitcom I'd never seen before. There's a woman trying to explain to someone on the phone that while her name is spelled like "bucket", it is not pronounced this way as the "t" is silent. According to Sam, she does this every episode.

"So..." Sam holds our second bowl of popcorn towards me so I can grab another handful of buttery goodness. "You honestly have no idea what sort of critter you are?"

"Not a clue."

"Cool."

"Cool?" I stare at the redhead.

"Yeah." Turning a wistful look my way, she smiles sadly. "That means you are the only person here who can't be told they're supposed to act in certain ways because of their animal." Her eyes go back to the TV, but her attention doesn't. "I'm supposed to both fickle and feckless, but also clever. Bryce, loyal and slow. The leopards are elite and all into appearances and speed. And the wolves..." She shakes her head. "If the wolves listened, they'd be a bunch of reckless hooligans."

"It's hard to imagine Mr. Atherton as a reckless hooligan."

Sam smiles fondly. "Yes, it is now. But I've seen pictures of when he was our age. And then when he was with the pack...." She leans in with an air of conspiracy. "Don't tell Warren I said this, because his parents are the alphas, but it's really just a motorcycle gang."

25

My mind boggles at the idea of smooth Michael Atherton in a motorcycle gang, but when I speak it's to point out, "Some motorcycle gangs are cool. Like those guys who dress up like Santa every year and bring kids gifts on their Harleys. Or the people who hold bike rallies to support cancer research and stuff like that."

"True," Sam concedes. "But there are also biker bars the cops are ex-ing afraid to go into. And the pack's more like those guys."

Interesting...

Wait.... "Ex-ing?"

"Oh." Sam blushes. "That's a thing Aliah and I do to avoid cursing. It's short for expletive, which we say sometimes too. Like, 'Hurry the expletive up!' You know, an all-use word that doesn't make her mom go ex-ing nuts. Foxes are supposed to be all about family, you know, so we can't upset our mothers."

I swig my soda and shove pondering were-society into the back of my mind for a while. My brain needs distracting. If I let myself think too much about my new world, I'll go crazy fast.

I'm not ready to be alone with my thoughts yet when Sam leaves my room again, sometime around midnight. This time, I'm sad to see her go. It's quite possible she's only being nice to me to make her mom happy, but her easygoing humor kept me from feeling too much panic.

Going to the closet, I pull the stuffed leopard out of my bag. Leo has been with me since I was tiny. He saw me through my terror the first day of school, he rejoiced with me when I lost my first tooth, was there the first time I came home in tears because of something someone had said to me.... I clung to him through my parents' divorce, and my dad brought him to the hospital when I was recovering from my attack. Holding him close to me, I think about how unfair I am to him. When I was little, he was there for the good times along with the bad, but now it seems like I only reach out for him when my world is crumbling apart.

I hold him extra tight as I go to my laptop sitting on my new desk and pull up my email. Nothing new from Troy, although there are a few short messages from other people, mostly things along the lines of, "Hey, good luck!" Only one of them sounds even slightly sorry to see me go. Maybe the others are trying to be upbeat and supportive. Or maybe they just don't care. I'm too scared to check my Facebook account, which still reports me as dating Troy and living in Washington, so I waste some time watching videos instead.

My stomach rumbles, complaining that popcorn wasn't a decent dinner. I could log onto a messenger and try to pester Troy into paying attention to me.... I don't feel up to cyber-yelling just now though, so I shut the computer down, grab my shoes, and head out the door.

Following Sam's directions to the dining hall under the assumption the kitchen is next to it, I wind through the darkened building. There's very little light, but that doesn't bother me anymore. Another side effect of my strange new condition.

The kitchen is huge, with a walk-in fridge and a whole line of cooking surfaces.

Aware I'm probably not supposed to be in here, I nevertheless open the fridge and peek inside. I grab one of the first things I see, a package of sandwich meat, and retreat hastily from the cold.

I turn, walk three steps, and then scream.

The sandwich meat smacks against the floor.

Staring at the boy in front of me, who stares back with a frown, I try to remember how to breathe. "You should be in bed," he says in a rough voice.

"So should you," I tell him, searching for bravado through a mire of fear.

Pale, ice blue eyes glare down at me from beneath a shaggy mane of light blond hair.

He lacks Bryce's size, but there's an electric intensity about him that is far more frightening than mere mass could ever be.

"Wolf," I whisper. The word catches in my throat and sends shivers through my body.

"Indeed."

The agreement's far from jovial, and the boy continues to glare at me. But for about half a heartbeat, I think I see one corner of his mouth try to jerk upward.

"Arctic wolf," I clarify, though I have no idea how I know that about him. The truth of it is inescapable.

"Yes." His breath floats gently across the space between us, bringing a faint scent of apples. "My name is Warren."

"I'm Mike."

The corner of his mouth succeeds in forcing a half smile this time. "I know."

Without saying anything else, or giving me time to so much as open my mouth, he turns and leaves, his long strides taking him out of the room almost instantly.

The kitchen feels a lot colder now.

Chapter Five

Haunted by thoughts of the strange wolf, I don't manage to fall asleep until almost four, so it's no shocker that I sleep straight through my seven o'clock alarm. Some part of me must be aware of the time though, because exactly five minutes before I'm supposed to meet with Mr Atherton, I jolt awake.

I spring out of bed immediately, grab the top sweater from my bag, toss it on over yesterday's jeans, and run into the bathroom. Pausing just long enough to drag a brush through my hair, which isn't terribly happy not to be getting a shower, I hit the door only a minute late.

Sam's coming up the stairs as I barrel down them. "There you are! I didn't realize how late it was, or I would have gotten you earlier." She falls in behind me and follows me into the principal's office.

If he notices we're two minutes late, Mr. Atherton doesn't say anything about it, starting instead with, "Good morning, girls. Sit down." He waves us toward two black leather seats on the opposite side of a huge mahogany desk from his winged office chair.

The desk is free of clutter, housing only a sleek black laptop and a wooden organizer with two trays and a pen holder. There are no photographs or other decorations, although the walls contain a vast assortment of pictures featuring a variety of people, none of whom seem to be related. I assume they're pictures of past students. Several of them have signatures and written messages on them, but I can't read any of the writing without getting closer.

"How are you, Michaela?"

The question brings my attention back to Mr. Atherton, who wears a gray sweater over blue jeans. I had assumed he was going for a casual look yesterday because of the flight, but apparently he just doesn't see the need to wear the business type clothes my other principals have embraced.

"Fine," I tell him. "Maybe a little tired."

He nods agreeably. "You'll sleep better when you get used to the place."

Can't really sleep worse. In addition to not falling asleep at all until a few hours before I was supposed to be getting up, what sleep I did have was plagued by nightmares of being hunted down by an angry wolf. Leo had to transform into a real leopard and defend me. It was fairly messed up.

"I'm sure you still have a lot of questions about weres," Mr Atherton continues. "But I'm thinking you're probably still processing what you've already learned, and the best thing to do today is just to go out and meet your fellow students. Are you comfortable with that?"

I take the time to think about the question before answering, "I think so."

"Okay." He gives me a dazzling smile. "If it gets to be overwhelming, you can go back to your room or come here, and no one will hold it against you." He waits for me to nod my understanding. "We have a counselor who comes in during the afternoon. She'll want to talk to you. She was turned as a teen, too, and I think you'll like her. If you're not comfortable with her, you don't have to keep seeing her, but I would like you to meet her."

Again, I nod, starting to feel myself shut down. I'll think about spilling my guts to a stranger later, but I'm not going to worry about it this morning. I'm not even going to think about not worrying about it. I'm too busy not letting my stomach tie itself in knots over the prospect of being stared at by the entire school all day.

"Samantha," Mr. Atherton switches his attention away from me. "You're willing to show Michaela around? Make sure she can find everything and isn't too freaked out by us?"

Sam immediately responds with a cheerful, "Of course." And we're on our way out of the office in a matter of moments.

"See you tomorrow morning," Mr. Atherton tells me. "Same time. Unless you need me before then."

"Yes, sir," I answer, wondering if I should be freaked out

30

that he's giving me so much personal attention. Sam doesn't seem to think anything of it though, so maybe he's like this with everyone.

As I close the door behind us, Sam reads over my schedule. "You have classes all over," she tells me. "I'll just show you everything."

With a grin, she starts her tour, waving a hand at the foyer. "This is the main entrance. Our rooms are all upstairs." She heads away from the principal's office. "This is the Rec Hall. TV lounge, game room, and social area combined. That door goes to the parking lot, which is indoors because of all the snow. There's a student kitchen off through this other door here with snacks and a microwave."

"Really wish I'd known that last night," I mutter.

"Why?" She stops to look at me, her red hair swishing from the momentum shift of her halt. "What happened last night?"

"I found the big kitchen," I tell her, swallowing awkwardly. "And someone saw me there. That's all." Avoiding the rest of the story, I go to the student kitchen, more of a kitchenette really, and find a carton of powdered donuts sitting on the counter. I grab one and take a bite while I try to figure out where the cups that go with the coffee pot are.

Sam goes to a cupboard and pulls out two Styrofoam cups. She pours coffee into them, but holds mine just out of reach. "Who?"

I play dumb. "Who what?"

Her look is impatient, though in a friendly way. "Who found you in the kitchen?" She goes ahead and gives me the coffee before I answer, but I can tell she views my taking the cup as a pledge to spill.

"Warren." Dumping a generous amount of the toffee-flavored creamer I find in the fridge into my cup, I wait for her to say something about that, expecting a shocked inhalation followed by commiseration.

"Why do you wish he hadn't found you?" Sam asks, her look one of quiet bewilderment.

I stare back at her. "Because he's so freaky he gave me nightmares? He scared me half to death."

"Warren?" she asks, her nose crinkling. "The wolf? Tall guy,

31

blond, nice muscles? Laughs a lot?"

"Well, he was blond," I admit. "And he was certainly a wolf. But I'm not sure he even knows how to laugh."

Studying her coffee, Sam looks thoughtful. "What exactly did he do? Because Warren's usually a pretty normal guy. Really nice. For a wolf."

"Well..." Leaning against the counter, I go over the scene again. "Maybe I was just freaked out so bad because it was the middle of the night."

Sam nods. "That does do strange things to people's perceptions," she says slowly.

"The way he was staring at me though..." Shuddering, I push off and take several steps to the door. "I'm putting that back in the file of things to obsess over later."

Sam chuckles. "I should make one of those."

"They're useful."

I wait for Sam to catch up outside the kitchen door and we take our coffees for a walk around the rest of the building, passing all the interior classrooms. There are only a dozen of them, a side-effect of the student body totaling a mere forty eight combined with several classes being held in outbuildings.

Done with the indoors, we walk outside into the snow. Technically, the door leads onto a stoop, but only the top step is visible. Since I don't know how high the stairs are, I have no idea how deep the snow must be. I do know it's all packed though, which is why I only sink a couple of inches when I step out. I want to ask about that, but before I get a chance we're greeted by a pack of very vocal huskies. They scamper eagerly around, sniffing me and giving playful barks of welcome. They're remarkably comfortable with being around people who smell like predators, making me wonder what my scent is like for them.

"They're pretty smart," Sam tells me. "They know none of us are going to hurt them in human form, so they get along even with the scarier species. Except during the moon. They hide then."

During the moon... That seems to be the common way of talking about the nights the moon is full. I can see why the dogs wouldn't want to be around wolves or bears. And I can see why the foxes wouldn't want to be around them.

"Do the different weres separate during the moon?"

She laughs. "Yes, we do. Especially those of us who are younger. Older weres have more control over themselves in animal form, but we still tend to stay with our kind. Just in case, you know."

Yeah. Bryce could snap Sam in half in human form easily enough, but in bear form a fox would be less than a mouthful. And Warren... He's scary enough human.

"By the way, feeding and cleaning up after these guys are on the list of chores."

"List of chores?" I ask, wondering why I would want to volunteer to bag canine poop.

Sam gives the closest dog an extra scratch behind the ears before waving me toward a nearby building and answering. "You're probably safe for now, but eventually you'll have to sign up for an hour a day of maintenance. I usually work with the dogs or in the rink, but there are plenty of things to do inside the main building. Like cleaning the fridge and vacuuming."

"But we get to decide what we do?" I ask.

"If it's open when you get to sign up, which is on the first day after the moon."

Okay. So with luck no one will bother me with that for another three weeks.

My guide stops outside a barn. It's large, and its wood is painted a dull gray that makes it look older than its condition would suggest. "And this is my favorite place here."

Swinging a side door open, she leads me into darkness. A light flickers on revealing a full-sized ice rink surrounded by bleachers.

"Year-round ice." She grins and goes quickly to a locker room. "You skate?"

I shrug, wondering once again how much they were charging Dad to send me here. "I can skate."

"Figure or hockey?"

"Um..." Blinking, I try to figure out what she means. "Neither? Recreational."

She opens a locker and takes out two pairs of pink ice

skates, which she holds up so I can see them clearly. "Figure skates." She indicates one. "Hockey skates." She indicates the other. "I've also thought about getting some speed skates. I'm really not very good at racing, but maybe I'd get better if I had the right skates, you know?"

"Sure." Up until this second, I had no idea there was more than one type of ice skate. The people at the rental desk had never asked what style of skate I wanted, just what size.

Sam glances at her watch. "They start serving lunch in ten minutes though, so I guess we should go back in." With a slight sigh, she puts the skates back in her locker and closes the door. There's no lock on it. There aren't any locks on the outside of our rooms either.

"Why isn't anything locked?" I ask.

Laughing, the fox shakes her head. "Why would they be? No one here would steal."

My eyebrows go up. "That seems very trusting."

Sam snorts. "We're not fully human, Mike. A lot of us would kill someone who tried to rob us. Possessions are sacred."

"Oh." That's... good to know. I guess. Not that I was planning on stealing anything.

There's a tendril of emotion trying to get my attention, wanting me to panic about the fact I am now part of a society where theft can be punished by murder without anyone getting upset about it. I refuse to give into it, focusing instead on getting to the dinning room, which Sam lets me find without help.

There's a line there already, full of people who take a break from glancing from the serving counter to their phones and back again to look at me. They have features from a variety of ethnicities, although their hair tends toward reds and blonds. In an attempt to encourage them to stop looking at me, I send my own gaze to the floor.

"They're just curious," Sam tells me. "We haven't had a new student other than freshmen in two years."

"Really?" I ask, looking up to squint at her. "Two years?"

How am I supposed to break into that?

"Lots of people are really jealous of me," Sam says, then laughs at my expression. "Your novelty makes you the center of attention. And I am the person everyone is going to be asking about you."

"Sam?" someone asks, as if fulfilling Sam's prophecy.

The girl is about my height, but willowy thin. Her hair is nearly as long as Samantha is tall and is a pure, snowy white. Her eyes are huge, expressive, and... pink?

"Hey, girl!" Sam grins at her. "Mike, this Aliah."

I don't have to be told Aliah is a fox, even though she lacks the vivacity Sam has me expecting from the species. The information of one's beast really does seem to be carried on scent. It's hard to put into words how it works, though, any more than one could easily explain how one knows a chocolate chip cookie from smell. One can get into how it smells sweet and like something with flour in it, but when push comes to shove, the thing just smells like a cookie.

"Hi, Mike?" the new fox questions. "Welcome to North Sky?"

Um... "Thanks? It's nice to meet you."

She beams at me, her pale skin lighting up. It's almost as if she expected me to insult her or something instead of saying hello.

"Aliah's in my class," Sam tells me. "And her sister, Alysia's a year ahead of you." Her tone is colder when she speaks of the older girl.

"Aliah and Alysia, huh?" I shake my head. Their parents probably thought they were being cute using such similar names. At least the sisters aren't twins.

"Mom swears she never noticed the alliteration?" Aliah tries as the line finally starts to move.

Chuckling, Sam shakes her head. "Maybe it's because she thinks of Alysia as 'That Bitch' the way I do."

"I don't think so?" Aliah whispers, sticking with her streak of making questions out of statements.

"She should," Sam contests. "Honestly, I have no idea what my brother sees in her." She looks at me. "They sort of have a thing. I can only hope the insanity isn't genetic."

Nodding, I think of my mother's fiancé. I can relate to the sentiment.

"Everyone calls her Lyly?" Aliah whispers. "So it's really not confusing?"

We shuffle forward. There doesn't seem to be a menu

35

posted. Maybe there are too few of us for there to be any choices?

"Cooked or raw, dear?"

"What?" I stare at the lady behind the counter. I can't smell what she is because the odor of grilled beef is too strong, but my hunch is bear. She has the same facial structure and pale blond hair as Bryce, although she is much more petite and her skin is a deep ebony.

"Your meat, sweetie." Her smile is kind. "Do you want it cooked or not?"

Uh... Okay... Not the sort of choice I was expecting to make. "Yes, please?"

The lunch lady, who I will take this opportunity to note is a lot prettier than the lunch ladies I am used to, shrugs as she starts to load a plate. "I have to ask the new students. Most people do like it cooked, but there are a few who just can't stand it."

Trying not to look appalled at this information, I nod and take the plate she holds out to me – potatoes, carrots, and a huge slab of steak, cooked. The steak's not very cooked to judge by the little pool of blood that sloshes around the plate as I move it, but my stomach rumbles anyway.

When I first started craving extremely rare meat, I thought something was seriously wrong with me. But this was before I lived in a world in which saying, "Actually, I would like my steak raw, please," happens often enough people ask beforehand if you want it that way.

I wonder if the raw meat crowd eats the carrots or not, and if theirs are steamed like mine are.

Bryce the Polar Bear waves me over towards him when I look up from the meal, his motions big, as if he's worried I'm somehow not going to notice a mountain trying to get my attention. Grabbing a jug of chocolate milk from the beverage fridge, I start towards him, glancing to make sure Sam and Aliah are coming this way too.

There's another guy across the table from Bryce. He doesn't seem to notice my arrival, being too absorbed in his tablet. Judging from the bright red hair, I am guessing this is Sam's brother, a senior by the name of Tod. Sam told me last night that it's a family name always given to the oldest male in the generation, but she looked confused when I asked her why her name wasn't Vixen.

Aliah and I sit on either side of Tod, leaving the seat by Bryce free for Samantha. Giving me a shy smile, she takes it. Instead of talking to Bryce though, she directs her first words to her brother.

"Tod, stop staring at that stupid machine and say hello to Mike."

"Hello to Mike." He doesn't even glance at me.

"Lyly just broke up with him again," Bryce says softly, apologetic for his friend's behavior.

"Oh, is that all?" Sam sounds bored.

"It's nearly two weeks early." Tod doesn't sound heartbroken, merely confused. He glances at me finally, doing a mild double take but then going back to his display. "She wasn't supposed to break up with me until the Saturday after next."

"She has a schedule," Sam tells me with an eye roll. "He's programmed it into that thing so he can better predict her behavior."

"Seriously?"

That is so messed up.

"Yes." Sam cuts a bite of her meat, chewing it while I turn to stare at her brother's profile. Why on earth would anyone put up with being dumped on schedule?

"I might know what it is?" Aliah whispers, sitting up suddenly, unbalancing her soda in the process. Sam grabs it before it can tip all the way over and Aliah smiles gratefully. "Remember prom last year?"

This school has a prom? I would have thought it was too small. Even assuming it's all grades, I don't know how they manage.

Tod scowls at his tablet. "Yes."

"Oh!" Sam claps. "You're right!"

Looking between the two, Tod makes an impatient gesture.

"She stayed with you an extra week so you'd be together for prom?" Aliah prompts.

How sweet of her.

Tod spreads a hand in confusion. "And you think she's making up for it now?"

37

"No." The albino shakes her head. "But it indicates she'll change the schedule for special events, doesn't it?"

"Oh, right!" Smiling suddenly, Tod turns off the tablet, puts it down, and grabs a huge bite of potato.

"There's a dance right after the next moon," Sam fills me in. "If she stayed with the schedule, they'd be in the middle of their breakup for it. Then she'd have to go to the trouble of making someone else take her."

"Oh." I use my steak as an excuse not to say anything else because I really don't know what to say to that.

"So, how's your first day?" Bryce asks me.

Shrugging, I swallow my food and tell him, "Just got the tour so far."

"Is it a lot different from your old school?"

I laugh, then take a drink before answering him. "You could say that. Some of my classes back home had more people in them than this whole school. And we definitely didn't have our own ice rink." I add the second part quickly, lest they think I was complaining about the school's size.

"You probably had a football team though," Tod guesses, much more attentive since the mystery of his girlfriend's abandonment has been solved.

"Yeah, we did." I shrug. "I prefer the NFL though."

Tod smiles. "Well, you had the Seahawks then."

I'm going to respond to that, but a series of chills down my back makes me start to shiver. Thoroughly distracted by the sensation, I look around, finding the source of my unease sitting near the windows.

Warren is there, alone. His eyes are on me, cold and hostile.

When he sees me looking, his eyes narrow for several seconds before he looks away. Staring now at the plate before him, he cuts a piece of meat.

It would seem Warren belongs to the raw camp.

I shiver again.

"What's wrong?" Bryce asks.

"Nothing."

"He really is staring at you." Sam raises her eyebrow towards Warren. "Are you sure you don't know him from somewhere else or something?"

I glance back toward him, watching as a drop of blood falls from the huge chunk of flesh on his fork. "Positive." My head snaps back as he starts to look up again.

"Who are we talking about?" Bryce asks, squinting.

"Warren," Sam answers thoughtfully.

Tod makes an interested noise. "He's been moody all day. I thought he and Seth were going to get into a serious fight in class."

"They're always fighting," Sam dismisses.

"Yeah, but usually it's play fighting. This would have been the serious throat ripping sort of fighting."

"So what's wrong with him then?" I ask. "Does he just hate me that much?"

"Why would he hate you?" Tod gapes at me in astonishment.

I fill the others in on what happened last night. "Weird," Tod echoes his sister's sentiment. "And he's still staring at you. Extremely weird. Even for a wolf."

Well, that's just great. I'm weird enough to turn normal people into freaks. Go me.

Chapter Six

Tuesday and Thursday afternoons, everyone has the same class. If you want to call it a class. What happens is this: we are all dragged up a mountain and told to either ski or snowboard.

Of course, in my case, this is an actual class because I ski about as well as I ice skate. I've done it before. I can usually get down the bunny slope without falling. But show me a slope that isn't aimed toward absolute beginners, and I tremble in fear. Then I fall down.

Everyone else has their own equipment, which they keep in a locker room at the slope. Mr. Atherton takes me to the slope-side store, where the employees fit me for boots. While they're doing that, he picks out a pair or skis for me and tells the workers to charge them, the boots, and any clothing I need to the school account.

"No!" I protest as I latch onto his arm and pull him away from the sales counter. "I thought I was renting. I can't afford to buy all this stuff."

He smiles softly. "They're putting it on the school account."

"Right." I give him a look meant to convey that I'm not lacking in intelligence. "And then you'll bill my dad for it along with my tuition. Do you have any idea how little park rangers make?"

"Michaela..." He leads me to a more secluded part of the store. "There's no tuition. Your family is paying for your meals and that's it. Anything academic is completely covered by a trust, including this. Call it a perk of our curse."

I stare at him. "For serious?"

He raises his eyebrows at the skepticism. "For reals even."

I stop arguing and go back to the cash register to tell them to do as Mr. Atherton said.

While the skis are being adjusted for my boots, I browse the store, picking out a new jacket and a pair of pants with lots of nifty zippers and pockets. I go ahead and pick out some things to go under them too, hoping they'll also be covered by this mysterious trust. An hour later, I trudge out the door into the brisk smell of cold air, clad in my new gear and trying to remember how one carries skis. The things are long and difficult, and I keep dropping them.

"Need help?"

I look up from the skis, which lay on the ground again, to see a boy about my age watching me with amused, impossibly light blue eyes – eyes the exact same color as the bright sky above.

"Do you need help?" he asks again, his voice warm and somehow comforting.

"I forgot how to carry skis," I confess, feeling like a complete idiot. If an avalanche rushed down the mountain to bury me right this instant, I would consider it a blessing.

The boy's smile widens, showing off predictably perfect teeth. "I think I can help with that."

Bending gracefully, he stands the skis up, then slides them together so the bindings interweave with each other. "You want to make sure you hold them like this." He hoists them onto his shoulder and points at where the bindings meet. "Because if you hold them like this..." He turns them over. "Then they'll slide apart like they're doing now." With an agile motion, he flips them back the right way and aligns them again. "Where are you taking them?"

"Um... I'm supposed to be having a lesson?" That shouldn't have been a question, but I find myself uncertain about what I am supposed to be doing. Maybe Aliah is contagious.

Nodding, the boy starts to walk away. I clunk after him, awkward in my boots.

"Is this your first time?" my savior asks over his shoulder.

"No." I smile, wondering if I should have lied so my lack of grace would seem more excusable. "I'm just not very good."

He laughs. "No one thinks they're any good."

Shaking my head, I laugh along with him. "Yeah, but some of us are right."

He grins back at me, and I nearly trip from the impact of it. "We'll get you sorted out in no time, I'm sure. I'm Seth, by the way."

Seth. I've heard of Seth. The foxes told me about him at lunch, when I asked who it was that Warren nearly got in a fight with. Seth is one of the snow leopards. And the snow leopards are what passes for the cool clique at North Sky. My friends said he's really not bad for a leopard, he gets along with just about everyone who isn't Warren, and he's one of the best skiers in Alaska. But why the heck didn't anyone warn me that he's got the most amazing eyes on the planet? A girl needs to be prepared for that sort of thing.

"Mike," I hear myself say back. I didn't think about speaking, of course, because Seth is still looking at me, and I am finding it difficult to form coherent thoughts when he does that. "But I guess you figured that out already, huh?"

"I had a hunch," he admits, his amazing eyes sparkling like snow in the sunlight.

He walks me up to a chalet-like building with several people lounging on its porch. "Good," he tells me. "Claire's here. You'll like her."

Claire is in her early twenties, athletic in build, and scented like a cat. She doesn't seem at all chilled despite standing around outside, but I don't know if that's because she's a were or because ski instructors develop cold weather tolerance. Her companions, who all smell human, don't seem terribly bothered by the conditions either.

Seth leaves me with her, and she goes through a series of questions about my experience before asking if I'm comfortable going up the lift on the beginner's slope or if I think I need some work before that. Feeling cold enough to just want to get this over with, I opt for the lift.

The first decent isn't great. I fall and everything. "Don't worry about falling," Claire tells me as she helps me up. "If you go through a day without falling, you just went through a day without learning anything."

Easy for her to say. She isn't dying of hypothermia.

Claire gives me several tips on the lift back up, and several runs later she takes me over to one of the more advanced green slopes. By the time we're done, I'm feeling comfortable and thinking maybe one day before I graduate, I'll be able to tackle the blue intermediate slopes. The difficult blacks are still outside of my dreams, let alone the double black diamonds or the out-of-bounds stuff a lot of the kids from school are into, but I'm starting to think Claire can achieve anything, so maybe...

Seth grins at me as I complete my last descent of the day. "Hey, that run looks two hundred percent better than the one I saw earlier."

"Thanks. I think." Blushing warms my cheeks, and for once I'm grateful to be turning pink, since it means my face no longer feels like its coated in ice.

"He's right," Claire agrees. "You're doing a lot better. You should work some more on your own Thursday, then I'll see you again next Tuesday."

"Okay." Rubbing my gloves against each other in the hopes of warming my hands, I nod in response to her wave goodbye.

"Want some coffee?"

I blink stupidly. I'm not sure, but I think the most amazing pair of eyes on the planet just asked me to have coffee with them. Not trusting myself to speak, I nod dumbly.

The responding grin sends my stomach reeling. "This way then. I'll show you where to store those skis first."

I may make a sound acknowledging that, but it's more of a gurgle than a word.

He takes me to the building I left my street shoes in and helps me struggle out of my boots. He hangs the skis from a rack behind me while I put on my sneakers. The only people allowed in the room are people who can swipe a school ID to get in, so leaving things out here is as safe as leaving them in a school building.

My feet rejoice to be back in real shoes and tingle happily as I follow Seth over to yet another little building, this one housing a deliciously scented coffee shop. Dozens of people stop what they're doing to watch us as we walk in, but I try not to let it get to me. Seth ignores everyone completely, striding confidently to the counter to order a large cappuccino before asking what I want.

"Mocha?" I ask the barista. "That size?" I point at a cup on the display, not sure what they call the medium size here.

"Medium." She smiles and enters the order into her

computer.

"And half a dozen brownies," Seth adds, handing over a debit card before I can even remember what pocket my wallet is in.

He takes the brownies and his cup to an empty table near the windows, where we have a great view of the terrain park. "Hey, look!" He jerks his chin toward outside. "Tod's trying to kill himself."

"What?" Alarmed, I slam my drink onto the table, send coffee sloshing over the sides, and gaze with frantic urgency out the window.

Seth laughs at my panic. "Sorry to scare you. He was just inverting off a jump. And there's Ski Patrol to yell at him for it." I follow the highly visible red jacket to Tod. His helmet covers his hair, which was what I was trying to use to identify him.

"Why would he want to do something stupid like that?" I ask, grabbing some napkins from the dispenser in the middle of the table to lap up my spill.

After a shrug, Seth starts to take his jacket off. "Probably because he saw me doing it earlier." He grins wickedly. "I'm a corrupting influence."

My mouth opens to try to say something witty and flirtatious to that, but all that comes out is a little gasp as Seth takes off his hat and shakes out his hair.

Okay, to not mention his eyes to me had been a major oversight. But the fact that no one said anything about his hair is just criminal.

There are two very obvious things about Seth's hair. The first is that it cascades nearly all the way down his back with a healthy enthusiasm my hair will never achieve. There's not a single girl on the planet who wouldn't kill to have hair of that texture.

The second thing is... His hair is the color of a raven's wing. And his hair is the color of pure opal. At the same time.

"Should have warned you." Self-consciously, his finger touches a strand of hair. "It's sort of freaky."

"Freaky?" I gasp, shocked. "It's the most gorgeous hair I've ever seen."

Okay, I so did not mean to blurt that. But, my God, how

44

could anyone think it's freaky?

Still not in possession of good sense, I reach out to touch it. It's warm and soft and so very, very inviting.

His breath catches.

His hand folds gently around my wrist, pulling my fingers from his hair. "To touch someone's pelt is a highly intimate thing." His voice is a gentle caress, highlighting the intimacy.

Instantly, my cheeks start to overheat.

"I..." I stammer. "I didn't..."

"I know." He flashes me a smile and flings himself into a chair. Lounging easily, he nudges the plate of brownies towards me. "Hungry?"

My hand darts out to grab a brownie, shoving it towards my face to give me an excuse not to talk for a while. I sit across from Seth, trying not to stare at his hair or his eyes or his... well, anything belonging to his person.

Shifting to sit up straighter, he makes an interested grunt. "Warren's going to do the half-pipe." He flashes me a quick grin that makes something inside me roll over in submission. "He's better than me when he's on skis. And on his board... If the elders would let us draw attention to ourselves by competing, that wolf would have an Olympic medal."

Intrigued by this praise despite Warren not being terribly friendly to me, and disregarding that I've never seen the appeal of doing the sort of things that make the X-Games, I grab my mug in both hands and look out the window again. Anyway, it gives me something to gawk at besides Seth.

I don't know the names for any of the jumps and spins and twists and turns Warren makes, but I do know enough to be very, very impressed. And if I didn't, the a crowd gathering near the window to watch him might be a tip off, as would the applause he receives at the end.

Unstrapping his board, he stands it upright and leans on it, shaking his head at something one of the people near him says.

And then he looks at me.

No, he's not looking at the café or the window or the people up here who haven't drifted away yet. He's looking right at me.

Then he glances toward Seth. Then he looks at me again. And he turns abruptly, stalking off toward the lift to the more difficult terrain at the top of the mountain.

"Well, hello," says a new voice, not very nicely. The room falls into an unnatural silence while people poke each other and point out the pretty blonde glowering at me. They meander back to their seats, watching us while trying not to look like they're doing it.

"Simone." Seth smiles at the girl. It's not the smile he's been giving to me, but a strained and thin corruption of that smile. "How's the backside?"

"About to be contaminated by wolves."

Looking at me, Seth sighs softly. "Mike, this is Simone." He doesn't sound particularly thrilled to be introducing us. "And here comes Amber and Katerina. Rina's the other blonde."

None of the girls so much as glance at me. "We're ready to go, Seth," Simone whines. The other two come up behind her and nod. I catch both of them looking at me for a second, but then they immediately look away again like people under orders to ignore me. The blonde is noticeably shorter than Simone, but her hair style and fashion sense seem identical except for the fact that she's one of the few weres I've seen in glasses. The third girl, Amber, is taller than the other two and has short black hair that is spiking up in a disheveled punk sort of way. "Too bad there's no room in the car for your new friend."

"That's alright," I say calmly, smiling sweetly at Seth. "I'm not ready to leave yet anyway."

He shifts, uncomfortable.

"Come on, Seth."

The girls walk away, the shorter blonde glancing back for half a heartbeat.

"Um..." His gorgeous eyes are filled with an adorable form of uncertainty.

"Thank you for everything." I give him a soft smile. "For saving my skis and all. I don't know if I would have found Claire before giving up if you hadn't been there. And thanks for the coffee."

He looks at me as I raise my cup toward him. "I'm really sorry."

And he does seem miserably apologetic.

"It's okay," I assure him.

He shakes his head. "No, not really."

But he gets up and puts his coat on.

"It's just the girls, they're..." Letting out a heavy sigh, he shakes his head. "Well, they're complete bitches."

With a rushed, "See you later," he runs away.

Sipping the last of my mocha, I gaze at the spot now so painfully devoid of Seth. Should I be worried about him? I know we just met and all, but I like him. A lot. And for reasons other than his incredible eyes and amazing hair and breathtaking laugh. But he's not happy. And who could be happy being bossed around by people like Simone all the time? Why put up with that?

The guys I've met here really don't seem to respond to events like normal people do. A normal person in Seth's position would tell those girls where to take themselves, wouldn't he? And what about Tod? Who in the real world would let a girl treat him the way Tod's girlfriend abuses him? He tried to explain to me that it isn't her fault she can't stand being in a relationship for more than three weeks in a row. He says it's a fox thing. So maybe Seth's problem is a leopard thing. But, it doesn't seem right. We may turn into animals once a month, but we're not those animals all of the time.

Are we?

"So." Tod plops himself in Seth's seat. "I guess he thought you smelled like a leopard then?"

"What?" I pull myself out of my thoughts to squint at the fox. "What makes you think he thought I was a leopard?"

He shrugs. "I doubt he'd risk the wrath of his harem being nice to you if he thought you were, say, a vixen."

My head shakes as I think about that. "So I smell foxy to you?"

"Oh, yeah." He draws out the words, and his voice drops significantly.

I hide behind my coffee, hoping I'm not blushing.

"Everyone seems to think you smell like whatever they are," he goes on quickly. "Except the girls."

"Yeah," I agree, "they just think I stink."

He laughs. "They do not. They just don't have any idea what you are."

47

"You have a theory?" I wait expectantly.

"I look like I have a theory?" His head tilts playfully to the side.

I grin. "Yes, you look like you have a theory."

"Not yet, but I'm working on one." He looks out the window, and I notice the tips of his ears turning a shade more pink. "It has something to do with mating."

Coughing overtakes me. "What?" I squeak.

"Interspecies couples exist, but they're rare and are hardly ever fertile."

Breathing deeply, I try to act like a mature person. "But what's the point in making people think they can breed with me if they can't?"

"I don't know." He shrugs sheepishly. "That's what I'm stuck on." Laughing softly at himself, he offers me a small smile. "The other option is this is normal and all converted weres go through it. Seems like that would be documented though."

Yeah, it does. And Mr. Atherton's confused by me, so the answer can't be so easy.

I'm about to mention this when I realize something is very wrong with Tod. He's glaring at the table, a low growl rumbling in his throat. "What is it?" I gasp, but he just shakes his head at me.

Staring at him and wishing I had some idea of what I should be doing, I bite on my lip and wait, slowly letting the tension out of my shoulders as his growl turns to a hum. "Sorry," he says at last, a quiet mumble that sounds a lot like a continuation of the humming. He looks up, tears glistening unshed in his eyes, and tries to smile. "That's Lyly over there. With some human."

Feeling rather like growling myself, I turn to look where he's indicating. The human, a male of roughly collegiate age, beams merrily at a slender girl with pixie cut white hair and tight fitting jeans. She is possibly the most beautiful woman I have ever seen in real life.

"Shit," I hear myself whisper. "She's gorgeous."

"Yes."

The word is filled with longing and hurt, and it makes me remember to hate her.

At least the mystery of why he puts up with her is solved.

Chapter Seven

After dinner, I go to meet with the counselor, knocking on a door next to Mr. Atherton's office.

"Come in!" a bright voice calls, prompting me to slide the door open and peek into a room overflowing with pillows and aromatherapy candles. The smell of the place takes a few seconds to get used to, and my eyes spend the time finding a dusky-skinned girl who is busy typing something into a computer in the corner.

"Um... I was told to come here and meet Ms. Stanly?" I say to her when she flips her screen off, and looks up at me.

Her thin-rimmed glasses reflect the candle light as she comes over to me, laughing. "That's me. But call me Becky." She holds her hand out for me to shake, then motions me into the room so she can close the door.

"Oh." She looks like a student.

"You were expecting someone older." She smiles pleasantly. "Don't sweat it. This is my first job out of college, but I do have a degree."

She goes to an electric kettle sitting to one side of the room, the side without a fireplace. "Would you care for some tea?"

"Sure." Why not?

She fills a teapot, then brings it and two cups over to a low table near the hearth. "Sit." She waves to two plush chairs by the fire, then sits in one of them herself. "I wouldn't survive without my fire," she tells me. "When I was first turned, people kept telling me I'd develop this super-metabolism, but I never did." She shrugs. "Never put on the extra fifty pounds that would get me up to average bear weight either, so maybe I shouldn't complain."

"You're a bear?" I ask. I wouldn't have pegged her as one. She is at least fifty pounds too thin, several inches too short, and missing a certain attitude the other bears here all have. Maybe it's because she wasn't born a bear. Maybe the things about Mr. Atherton's personality I find so wolf-like were all there before he was attacked.

If I could have smelled her, I guess I would have known. But all I can smell is ash and lavender and tea.

"Yep. Spectacled Brown." She grins impishly. "And a brown girl in spectacles too. I'd hoped I wouldn't need the glasses after I turned, but if anything I need them more now because I can't stand contacts anymore. And, sadly, animals can have vision problems too. You should see my bear form someday. It's a miracle if I go through an entire change without walking into a wall."

"When were you changed?" I ask her. I'm not sure if it's rude to ask, or to ask that quickly, but she seems to want to talk about it.

Her eyes get a little cloudy, and her voice goes timid. "I was fourteen. Camping trip. I woke up in the middle of the night and tried to walk to this stream we were camped near, but I got lost. Some noises scared me into losing my footing. I tumbled down a hill, and smacked right into a werebear who was in labor. Her change had triggered it. Her mate never even thought about what he was doing, just swiped at me. Ripped huge gashes in my stomach..." Taking a deep breath, she rubs her arms. "He was so scared he'd killed me. He hasn't gotten over the guilt yet."

"But he wasn't executed?"

She shakes her head. "No. You're not going to find a were who wouldn't have acted the exact same way in that spot. When your family is threatened, the rules go out the window."

"Makes sense," I murmur. Then, louder, I ask, "What did your family think happened? I mean, the bears obviously didn't just leave you there like whoever attacked me did."

"No, they didn't. They took me into town in the morning and told the authorities they had found me mauled."

Nodding, I stick my nose further into her business. "Did they tell you what was going on? Were you aware of all of it?"

Taking the lid off of the teapot, she fishes out the bag and puts it onto the tray. "I passed out for a while. When I came to, the male had changed back to human. He explained all of it and

51

gave me the choice of being like them or dieing." She smiles faintly. "Being a bear isn't so bad."

I pour a splash of cream into the cup of tea I'm handed. "Being whatever I am is better than being dead too," I agree. Then I laugh. "I think."

"I can't imagine not knowing," Becky admits, curling into her chair with her tea against her chest. "That must be very unsettling."

What an obvious lead. I'm tempted to leap up and shout, "I object, Your Honor! Leading the witness!" Instead, I shrug and take a sip of the tea. It's pretty good.

Becky switches track. "I hear you've been spending time with the foxes."

I shrug again. "They're nice."

"They are," she agrees with a smile. "Most of the people here are."

I think about dinner, the unsettling way Warren stared at me and the hostile glowers given to me by Simone. But I keep my mouth shut.

Becky watches me closely. "My first week here, I was a mess. I didn't know anyone. People thought I should be hanging out with the bears, but most of them were polar bears and cousins. I was a different kind of bear and not family."

"Sounds hard," I agree. "I'm okay though. No one knows what I am, so everyone's talking to me."

She nods and waits for more, but I drink my tea rather than give it to her.

Trying to do her job, she refuses to just sit silently. "I heard you were expelled from your old school."

"Yeah," I admit. "I got upset. Destroyed a book. They thought I did it with a knife, and, of course, having a weapon would be a major bad. Then when I didn't give it to them..." I shrug. "It was lame. But I sort of wanted out of there anyway."

"Is that related to why you were mad?" she asks, making me shake my head at myself.

"Yeah, it was." I put the now-empty tea cup down. "I don't want to talk about it, though. No offense or anything."

Smiling kindly, Becky inclines her head. "It's alright. I'm just trying to get a feel for you. I want to help you if you need it."

"I'm okay," I tell her, meaning it. Maybe I'm still in shock or denial or something, but for someone who's changed species and moved hundreds of miles from home, I'm remarkably fine. "Everyone here is being really helpful." Okay, slight lie. But the vast majority of people here have been great.

"Well, any afternoon you do want to talk to me, I'm here. From one until about seven, later if you need me to be." She gets up and grabs a card. "This is my cell. Call it whenever."

"Thanks." I stick the paper in my pocket, feeling envious that she has a cell that works up here. Mine still doesn't get a signal. When I complained of Dad about,it, he said he'd sort it out when he got up here.

Becky looks uncertain as I start toward the door, but she lets me go without trying to stop me. The sound of Warren's voice approaching from the Great Room spurs me up the stairs without regards for what Becky must think hearing my sprint.

Hiding in my room, I stare myself down in the mirror. "You're being ridiculous," I tell me.

Okay, so the guy has gifted me with no small amount of directed brooding. Has he done anything that actually seemed dangerous? No, he hasn't. He hasn't threatened me in any way, and everyone I've talked to about him is certain he wouldn't hurt me. Of course, they seem surprised to find him staring at me, too. But there's out of character, and then there's drastically out of character. It's one thing to stare. It's something else to... Well, I don't know what it is I'm afraid of him doing.

A knock on the door makes me jump. "Get a grip, girl," I mutter to myself, creeping up on the door, at least half-convinced I'm going to find Warren on the other side of it.

Cracking the door just enough to peer around it, I laugh at myself.

Sam gives me a funny look, then glances down at herself. "I'm pretty sure my clothes match."

"I'm not laughing at you," I tell her, opening the door wider. "I'm laughing at me. What's up?"

She seems to want to ask about the laughing, but after a long pause, she shrugs it off. "I think you need to watch *The Cutting Edge*," she tells me.

53

Leaning against the door, I frown slightly. "*The Cutting Edge?*"

Enthusiastic, she bounces as she nods. "It will explain to you the difference between a hockey skate and a figure skate."

"It's ... a documentary?" I hazard.

Her eyes give a martyred roll. "No, it's a movie. One of the best movies ever made. Come watch it with me."

Why not?

Turning off my light, I close the door to my room, feeling weird about not locking it. Warren is up the hallway, talking to someone I don't know. He looks down at me, and I shiver, wishing I could secure my door.

Sam doesn't notice anything. "I can't believe you've never even heard of *The Cutting Edge*," she's babbling. "It is seriously one of my favorite movies. Ever since I was a little girl."

"I only watched cartoons when I was little," I tell her. "Then I never really had any friends who were willing to watch things more than a year old."

"Bizarre," she says, cringing. Maybe she's right. I never really thought about it before.

Warren's eyes are on me as I slide into Sam's room, and I remind myself again that he isn't a threat. The community here is tight enough people would know if he was psychotic. I'm sure he's just curious about me, like everyone else. I'm reading the sinisterness into things because I have an overactive imagination, that's all.

Still oblivious, Sam takes a DVD from a shelf of them and pops it into her player while I make myself comfortable on the couch in front of the TV. Her room is about twice the size of mine, large enough for a futon sofa and coffee table to form a sitting area my room lacks.

The film turns out to be a romance centering around a pair of bickering skaters preparing for the Olympics. It's cute and does, indeed, explain the difference between the skates. Figure skates have claws on the end, toe picks, and hockey skates do not.

The movie says absolutely nothing about speed skates.

As the credits roll and we discus what to do next, there's a frantic knocking on the door. "I think you should answer your door."

She laughs at me. "You know what? I think I should answer my door!"

She stops laughing once the door is open, and a banshee runs through it. Slamming the door shut behind the newcomer, Sam shoves her body against it to hold it closed a second before another pounding starts. "Go away!" she screams over her shoulder through the wood.

"Give me my sister!" comes the answering demand.

"No!"

"You send that brat out here right now!" bellows the girl in the hallway.

"I'll call Mr. Atherton!" Sam counters.

"This isn't wolf business!"

"Fine!" Sam snaps. "I'll call my brother then. Do you want me to call my brother?"

The other person doesn't answer.

Interesting. It never would have occurred to me that Tod could be used to threaten people. He's about as scary as a stuffed animal.

There's another bang on the door, and then the person moves off down the hallway, yelling at other people about her evil sister and her evil sister's allies.

"Thank you?" The banshee, who is no longer screaming – thank God – peers out from behind the bed, looking like Aliah now that she's stopped wailing.

"No problem." Sam smiles at her friend. "Your ex-ing sister is heading my list of least favorite people today anyway. Don't hold Alysia against her, Mike."

"That was Lyly?" I try to reconcile the ugly rage-filled voice with the overtly attractive body I saw earlier and have difficulty doing it. That figure's voice should be sultry and sophisticated, not harsh and grating.

"Yes?" It's Aliah who answers, in a timid whisper. "We fight sometimes?"

"You should tell Tod." Sam has the air of someone who has said this many, many times in the past.

Aliah shakes her head and curls up one of Sam's pillows.

55

"He's in love with her," she whispers sadly. For once, she doesn't make the statement into a question.

"Yeah, I know he's an ex-ing idiot." Sitting beside her, Sam runs a hand through the other girl's hair. "But it's his job to protect you, even from her."

With a soft sniffle, Aliah pushes her head into Sam's hand, rather like a pet would. "It's not stupid for him to want to be with her. Considering they're destined to be together anyway."

Destined? I frown toward Sam, who scrunches her face and lets out a huff of air. "Destined, smestined. He doesn't need to mate into the east; he can have the west. I don't want it."

Huh?

"You should," Aliah whispers.

Sam ignores her to give me a shrug. "It's just politics. We're in line for a throne, so to speak." Her hand motions in a dismissive wave as she quickly adds, "But it doesn't mean anything."

Aliah shakes her head, but instead of arguing asks, "Can we talk about something else?"

"Sure, sweetie," Sam coos. Her eyes go to me. "I heard a rumor one of us was seen hanging out with Seth today."

"Oh?" Aliah looks eagerly at me.

Turning to my side to fully face my companions, I shrug. "We had coffee."

"You had coffee?" Aliah asks, trading a look with Sam. "You and Seth?" she clarifies.

"Why is everyone so surprised?" I want to know. "He's nice. You guys said as much at lunch."

"Yeah..." Sam admits before taking a deep breath. "But he's nice in a distant sort of way. Doesn't mix with the commoners much."

"Or maybe you don't mix with him." Folding my arms, I find myself glaring, wanting to defend Seth. "He's not even remotely snobby. And I think he's lonely. Maybe if people gave him a chance, he wouldn't be so distant."

Sam's staring at me. "Lonely?"

"Yeah." Putting my feet on the sofa, I pull my knees up and hug them to me while I think about it. "He doesn't like the other leopards much, but they're the only people who try to hang out with him. Because everyone else is all, 'Oh my gosh, it's a leopard!' aren't they?"

"You may have a point," Sam admits slowly, looking thoughtful. "That's kind of like what I was saying yesterday about how lucky you are not to know what you are, isn't it?"

"But you had coffee with him?" Aliah asks me.

Nodding, I smile. "And he helped me get to my lesson when I couldn't remember how to carry my skis. He was incredibly sweet the whole time."

Then I remember I had something to complain about. "And why didn't anyone warn me how gorgeous he is?"

"His eyes are great," Sam admits.

"And his hair!" I'm annoyed anew that no one mentioned that. "He has the most amazing hair I have ever seen!"

"His hair?" Aliah sits up to blink at me. "You like his hair?"

"Of course I like his hair!"

The other two girls look at each other.

"Oh, come on," I moan.

Sam clears her throat. "It's just... Well, everyone's hair is related to their fur. Aliah's fur is white, mine's red... But to have marking show through is unusual. I mean, my ears are black in fox form, but you don't see streaks of black in my hair now."

Streaks of black would look unbelievably cool in Sam's hair, but I get the feeling saying so will get me labeled insane.

"It's something like a birth defect?" Aliah tries with a tiny wince. "It's not exactly gross or like it makes you a bad person, but it's not something to be proud of?"

"Then why does he have so much of it?" I ask instantly. "If he's ashamed of his hair, why grow it so long? Why not go with a crew cut? Or dye it? Why leave it natural and so unavoidably there?"

Aliah's head tilts to the side and her eyes narrow in thought. Sam frowns in a very similar way. "That's a good question. I never thought to ask about that."

The question is the first thing that pops into my head when I see Seth the next morning, sitting in my English class, but I keep it to myself. I just can't look at something that glorious and say something that implies there's a problem with it. That would be like asking a supermodel why she lets people take

57

pictures of her. Besides, there's something timid in the way he looks at me when I walk in, something almost frightened. I think he expects me to yell at him, or at least snub him, because of the way he left yesterday. Instead, I smile and ask if it's alright to sit next to him.

The smile he gives me in return does all sorts of interesting things to my insides and it occurs to me that sitting near Seth is probably not conducive to learning anything in this class. But at least if I'm directly beside him, I can't spend too much time looking at him, right?

Luckily, Simone is not in Junior English, on account of being a sophomore. The leopard Amber is there, but she sits quietly on the other side of Seth. She even gives me a tiny smile before she sits down. She doesn't say anything to me, or to anyone else. I can see how people could find the behavior aloof, as if she thinks she's too far above everyone else to talk to them, but something in the way she looks at me makes me think she's just shy.

Simone, who is not at all shy, is in my afternoon class on Wednesday. As are both Sam and Aliah. And a lot of other sophomores. Chemistry is a sophomore class here. I had biology my sophomore year. Oh, well.

My first week passes in a rush, until Friday afternoon hits, bringing with it my hunting and tracking class. Then the tempo crashes to a painful form of slow motion.

Warren is in my class.

Well, not exactly in it. It's a freshman class. He's the instructor's assistant. So, yeah... Warren is teaching my hunting class, and gets ordered to tutor me the instant class starts. Great.

He shuffles over, his eyes snapping between my face and his toes in a pattern that repeats for the whole time he's walking toward me. When he approaches, he grunts in the direction of the ground, "Michaela."

"Warren," I answer, proud of my voice for not shaking.

His gaze goes up to my face, and I do my best to meet it. His eyes are a different blue from Seth's, although they're also pale. Where Seth's eyes remind me of polished gems, Warren's are more like less precious stones. There are no glittering facets,

58

but blended veins of purples and aqua.

There's something in them that chills me more than the air or the snow covering my boots up past the ankle, something that reaches straight into my heart and coats it with ice. But it's not normal, lifeless ice. It's a living, breathing form of it. Like winter personified.

"Let's do a tour," he mutters, melancholy. Like he doesn't want to be doing this, but he's sad about it rather than angry. "Put your feet in my footprints. That way you won't hit a drift and sink down."

Without making sure I leave with him, he starts away from the class and begins to tell me about the grounds.

The wolf is talented. He manages to ignore me for two hours straight, while talking to me the whole time. I follow, numb and cold, and try to listen to his words while ignoring him back. But I'm not as skilled as he is, so I spend more time watching his back and wondering what's going on in his thoughts than I do listening to what he's saying.

What I wouldn't give to know what's in that wolf's head....

Although, then again... Considering all the things that could be in there, maybe I'm better off not knowing.

Chapter Eight

Saturday morning, I wake up completely lost. The sense of urgency that propelled me through the week has evaporated, leaving me floating without direction.

What am I supposed to do all weekend?

A bunch of people have headed up to the ski slopes, but I slept too late to go with them even if I wanted to.

Sam's skating, but I don't feel like flopping about like a fool on the ice while the others perform art.

Cuddling Leo, I bring up my email. There's a message from my dad, nearly identical to the email I get from him every morning, saying he misses me and hopes I'm doing well. I write back and try to sound cheerful. I miss him, too. I'd call, but I'm too scared I'd wind up crying, and I don't want to put him through that.

My mom wrote too, babbling about the wedding and complaining about how much more difficult my dress fittings are going to be with me way up here, hundreds of miles from the seamstress handling the wedding party's dresses. I consider writing back that I wouldn't mind being dropped from the list of bridesmaids. In fact, I would dance around in cheerful bliss if she let me off the hook on that. I feel weird as anything being part of her wedding and only agreed to it because Dad told me it would hurt her feelings if I didn't. The main motivation was to not disappoint him. When I do respond to Mom's message, though, I manage to keep myself from volunteering to be fired and from ranting about how, "Oh, you caught me. I got expelled from school and shipped off to Alaska just to inconvenience you." Instead, I calmly point out that I will be home for a whole week at the end of March and then again for an entire month before the wedding, assuming Dad doesn't get the house sold.

There's still nothing from Troy. Not that I've written him either. Outside of my dreams, I've been doing a good job of not even thinking about him. Inside my dreams... When I'm not having nightmares about wolves, I'm dreaming about Troy. Sometimes we're back together. Sometimes I'm killing him. Either way, I'm left feeling bad.

There's only one mail from anyone at my old school. I was cc'ed on something about going to the mall today. They're probably still there. I'm not sure if I was cc'ed by mistake or if the sender hasn't noticed I'm gone.

I'm still not willing to check my Facebook account. Seeing posts about the mall trip or who asked who to what movie wouldn't make me feel any better.

Wading through a mire of angst-riddled apathy, I put Leo down with a pat and slink into the shower before forcing myself into jeans and stomping off to the library to find something to read.

The library is smaller than the one in my old school, but much larger than the size of North Sky would usually warrant. It's also somewhat higher on the the fantasy and mythology scale than most libraries I've been in. The walls are decorated with scenes from lunar myth, the largest space being given to an original painting of a pale man driving a team of dogs across the sky. The plaque under it identifies the driver as Mani, the Norse god of the moon. The artist's name causes me to blink in surprise – Michael Atherton. My eyes go over the painting again, taking in the brush strokes and composition. I don't know much about art, but it seems really well done for a high school principal.

Wanting to escape into make believe, I drift over to the fiction section to hunt out something fluffy. But before I can settle on anything, my attention is grabbed by a sound drifting down the hall.

Haunting music calls to me from a room I haven't been in yet. I follow the rich, Gothic melody along the corridor, but stop at the doorway it leads to, scared to step in lest I break the magic spell Seth is constructing.

He doesn't notice me watching him as his fingers charm sound from the piano. He's too focused on his song, which flows from him without the aid of sheet music.

No one ever bothered to mention he was musician. There's

61

a lot of things no one ever says about Seth. Surely they aren't all shallow enough to think driving a cool car and being feline is more important than being able to make people cry with music.

And there literally are tears sliding down my cheeks.

The song goes on and on, never becoming dull.

When Seth's fingers fall still, I sniffle to control my nose, then clap slowly.

He whips to face me, startled and embarrassed.

"That was beautiful," I whisper, my voice choked with emotion.

Eyes wide, he pales noticeably. "Thank you."

He lowers the cover over the keys, staring down at it. "I didn't know anyone was there. I usually don't make people listen."

"Make people listen?" What world does this guy live in? "Seth, you could charge people. Go on tour. Sell t-shirts and everything."

Laughing, he rises from the stool and takes a few steps towards me. "I don't think pianists sell much swag."

I shrug. "Well, they have people to do it for them, sure...." Trailing off into a grin, I find myself staring into his eyes yet again. The grin falters and fades.

Seth looks down to his feet. "So what are you doing today?"

"Reading." I wave down the hall. "I was in the library looking for something when I heard you."

He frowns slightly. "Are you completely sold on the idea of reading all day?"

My eyebrows go up. "Not really," I say slowly, my stomach rolling in waves of nerves.

Looking up to meet my eyes, he takes a breath and asks, "Have you seen town yet?"

Swallowing, I try to keep my wits about me even though all I can clearly focus on are those eyes. "There's a town?"

Seth laughs. "Yes, there's a town. There's a city too if you want to go all the way to Anchorage."

"Town sounds fine," I say. Then, realizing he didn't actually offer to take me to town and had merely asked if I'd seen it, I start to feel myself blush. "Um... I mean..."

"Great." His grin sweeps down and masters me. "Let's go

then."

"Okay," I say. Or I think I manage to say it. Like always, it's possible I just made a completely unintelligible noise. He acts as if I said it though, waving me through the door ahead of him and running upstairs to find his coat while I search for mine and my shoes.

Seth's car is red and sporty and rare enough that I can't name the model. It's likely European and certainly worth a small fortune. It has a backseat, but barely. Simone wasn't just being mean when she said there wouldn't be room for me in it. There was hardly room for the four people already riding in it.

The leather seats are heated, of course, so it's easy to pretend all the snow and ice we pass, like all the gorgeous white on the mountains rising so majestically around us, is just decorative graphics. Inside the car, it's warm as spring.

Which makes it all the colder when we step out downtown and the wind hammers into me.

The town is comprised of two streets, a high street and a low street, with a few smaller roads connecting them. The low street has an excellent view of a river. I don't know which one, just that it's mostly frozen. The high street sits up a steep incline and backs onto a small cliff.

Despite the weather, we leave the car parked across from the water and start to walk along the storefronts. There are still a lot of small businesses here: tiny clothing stores, stores for camping supplies, and even a general market.

"I guess Wal-Mart hasn't made it here yet," I muse, mostly just to have something to say. We've fallen into a silence that isn't exactly uncomfortable, but isn't warm and fuzzy either.

"What do you mean?" Seth asks, squinting at me.

My hand waves at the nearest store. "All these small businesses. In most towns, if you want to survive downtown like this, you need some kind of gimmick going. I don't think I've ever seen a general store that wasn't trying for retro. You know, a 'Grandpa, tell me about the good old days' kind of thing."

"When penny candy was a penny and dime stores sold things that cost a dime?"

I grin. "Yeah."

A cell that isn't mine starts to ring, and Seth curses. He

takes a vicious step away and flips the phone open, hissing into it. He faces away from me, and the wind is blowing. It seems like I shouldn't be able to hear him, but his voice still carries to my newly enhanced ears. "What?"

Not wanting to crowd him, I look at the window we've stopped next to. It belongs to the sort of gift store that only carries things people's grandmothers would buy, like angel statues and dolls with huge eyes and panes of painted glass with Biblical verses on them.

"If she's not dying, I don't care," Seth tells whomever called him. "And even then, you'd have to sell me on it."

His teeth grind together with enough force that I can hear it as he listens to the response. "I'm busy, Amber. Tell her to call the frigging shuttle."

Biting my lip, I move my eyes along the store front, trying at least not look like I'm eavesdropping.

"Yeah, I know." There's a very unhappy and aggrieved sigh. "If I do this, it's not for her. It's for you. And you owe me." Whatever Amber says produces a sound that's part *tsk*, part snort, and part laugh. "Yeah, I love you too. Bye, brat."

I keep my eyes forward as he snaps the phone closed and steps up behind me. "Mike..."

"Yeah?" I kneel beside the glass, pretending to be examining a figurine of a polar bear.

"Simone twisted her knee." In the window reflection, I see him rake his fingers through his hair in exasperation. "She needs to go back to school. And my sister is threatening suicide if I don't go get her right this second and shut her the hell up."

"Your sister?" It's more of a whisper than anything. Something inside me that had tightened, loosens.

"Yeah, Amber." He chuckles. "Spoiled senseless, of course, but I seem to be attached to her."

"I didn't realize you were siblings." I suppose now I think about it, both their scent and their appearance have certain similarities. She lacks his distinctive hair, of course, and if her eyes are even half as amazing, I've never noticed. Haven't spent much time gazing into them though.

"Yeah. Amber and I are twins." He shuffles his feet. "The

other two are foster sisters."

Oh.

"I guess this is when you ride off to save the damsel in distress, then." I smile. "It's your duty to save her."

"In short," he answers with a snort. "Although, damsel isn't the first word I think of when I think about Simone." His hands stuffed in his pockets, he asks the pavement, "Do you want to come with me, or do you want me to drop her off and then come back here?"

Laughter spits out of me. "I don't think it's a fantastic idea for me to go with you. Simone's not exactly a big fan of mine."

"Yeah..." His eyebrows slide slightly upward. "She doesn't seem to like you too much."

No shit.

"Not that she likes most people," he adds with a little curvature of the lips. Head still down, he gives me an uncertain look. "You want me to come back and get you later?"

"It was a long walk," I tell him, smiling at his look of confusion. "Yes, please come back and get me when you're done."

"You'll be alright here?" he checks.

Nodding, I look up the street. Just walking up and down the whole thing would take less than five minutes, but if I start going into places I'm sure I can waste an hour or so. "Yeah, I'll just explore."

"If you get done before I get back, there's a place at the end of the street called Denali's," he tells me after a long breath. "Wait there?"

"Italian?" The end of this street doesn't appear to be a likely place for international cuisine.

"No." He laughs at the thought. "Bar."

I blink at him. "I'm not old enough to get into bars," I point out dimly.

"They won't card." Seth gives me a teasing grin. "If you don't want to think of it as a bar, think of it as a restaurant. They have excellent chili. You should try a bowl."

"Chili," I repeat. "Right."

"And, so you know... That really big hill over there is named Denali too." He jerks his chin toward the looming monster in the distance that I thought was Mount McKinley, the

65

largest "hill" in North America. Dimly, I recall the natives had a different name for it. Denali, I assume.

"You sure you're okay with this?" His look is uncertain. I wonder what all the people who think he's too cool for the rest of us would think about the expression, the fear and certainty of rejection in it. "I could take you back to school and then go get her."

Shaking my head, I smile. "No. This is good. Stop worrying about me and go rescue your sister."

"Okay." With a grin and a deep breath, he turns and trots to his car, waving before he climbs in. He pulls out of the space and drives back to me, stopping and rolling his window down.

"Just go," I tell him before he can ask again if I'm okay with being temporarily ditched. "I'll see you soon."

Laughing at himself, he nods sharply and drives off, leaving me to wander the streets of...

What is the name of this town, anyway? Great. I don't even know where I am.

Trying to make the best of it, and reminding myself I did have the option of going back to school but chose to stay here for some reason, I push open the door of the nearest store.

The place is far too warm and scented with some truly obnoxious scents. I never liked the sorts of candles you find in places like this when I was human, and I like them even less as a were. Fleeing the smell of potpourri and cinnamon clashing in battle, I slide through the cold into the next store down.

Even going into places, it takes twenty minutes to see everything downtown has to offer, so I find myself heading somewhat reluctantly to Denali's. I doubt my dad would be terribly happy with me if he saw the place, a rustic two story building with peeling paint and smudged windows.

At least there are windows, though. So it could always be worse.

The interior is much in keeping with the outside. A few beer signs flash in dim neon, a faded mural shows a wolf pack running under the Northern Lights, and the floor hasn't been swept in recent memory, if at all.

But the place is open, which puts it above the closed family grill up the street. And it does have chairs, which makes it better than the general store, even if the seating does look like it could give a person splinters from ten feet away.

Summoning my courage, I walk towards the bar, wondering if it's manned right now. Since I seem to be the only person here, I could understand if it wasn't.

There's a clattering from behind a door... a curse... a thump... and someone pushes his way into view.

His eyes lock onto mine, widening in startled recognition. "Michaela," he grunts, wrestling a keg through the doorway.

"Warren," I whisper, fighting the urge to run.

Never run from an animal you're afraid of. Everyone knows that. Run and it'll chase you.

The wolf places his hands on the counter, leaning forward, his eyes still unflinchingly on my face.

"I was told to come here and have chili," I babble.

I wonder if that sounded as inane to him as it did to me.

"Told by whom?" His head tilts, his nose flares slightly, and his eyes narrow. "Told by your leopard?"

Forcing myself to meet his eyes again, I try to look dignified. "It was recommended by a leopard, yes."

"And where is this leopard now?" the wolf wants to know.

Suddenly tired, I sit on a barstool. "Simone hurt her knee. And Amber swore she would die if she had to listen to her go on about it for one second longer than it takes her brother to drive up to the slope."

Warren snorts softly. "I suppose hurting her knee is code for hearing he was somewhere with you."

"Probably." I smile as I nod.

He's staring at me again, but it's not hostile this time, more curious than anything. Straightening abruptly, he asks, "You wanted chili then?"

For reasons that are completely beyond me, the question, or the look that goes with it, makes my heartbeat skyrocket. "Sure. If there's any made."

The grin he gives me knocks the breath right out of me. "There's always chili."

I don't breathe again until the kitchen door swishes shut behind him.

Chapter Nine

To my surprise, when Warren returns, it's with not one, but two bowls of chili. And two glasses of chocolate milk.

My eyes widen at the sight of the milk. Is he admitting to staring at me every meal I've eaten at North Sky? Or does he simply share my weakness for the stuff?

"Thanks," I say, instead of asking about that.

"You don't mind me joining you?" he verifies, his voice cautious and in no way frightening.

"Of course not." At least, I don't mind it if he's going to act like a normal person.

He's completely relaxed as he sits down, acting as if the last week hasn't happened. It's surreal, but I play along as I wonder what sort of game this is.

"So, you know why I'm here," I look down at my chili, stirring it as I speak. "Why are you here?"

"Here in Denali's?" He squints at me as I try a bite of the chili. It's remarkably good. Not so spicy I can't taste it, but not bland either.

"Yeah."

He's looking at me like I've started piling the chili onto my head instead of eating it. He answers slowly, drawing out the words, "Probably because my family owns it."

"Oh." Alright, now I feel stupid. I don't remember anyone ever telling me his family name though. In fact, I think the Fox siblings may be the only kids I've met here whose last name I do know. And they only mentioned it so I'd know who their mother was. "Hence the wolves, huh?"

The smile he's giving me, I'm shocked to realize, isn't at all mocking. "Hence the wolves."

Aware he's watching me, I look down at my bowl. "So I guess you come here often, then?"

He laughs. "Yeah. Several times a week and most weekends." He waits while I take another bite of food, then asks, "Do you like it? It's an old family recipe."

I look up without moving my head, trying to see if there was a joke in that or not. His gaze seems to be teasing, but unless the stuff comes from a can, I can't imagine why. "Yeah. I like it." Nice, noncommittal answer.

"Good." Spooning up a huge bite of the stuff himself, he watches me with a look of great amusement while he chews. He swallows and gets up as the phone behind the bar starts to ring.

"Denali's," Warren says into the phone, his voice smoothly professional and years older than he is. "Oh, yeah, she made it here alright." He nods to the caller. Is it Seth? Seth should be back by now. Unless his car fell off the mountain or something. Are they talking about me? "Sure, I can tell her..." I eat some more chili, wondering about my new habit of listening in on other people's conversations. "Don't worry about it. I'm sure she'll understand.... I'll take her back up when I get off.... See you later."

He raises his eyebrows at me as he hangs up the phone, not buying that I wasn't listening. "If Simone's knee injury was on your account, then she's even more psycho than everyone thought."

That would have to be pretty darn psychotic.

"She's really hurt?" I ask, more confused than distressed by the information.

Giving me a shrug, Warren starts back towards the table. "Seth says her knee is roughly the size of a grapefruit, so they're taking her to the city for x-rays. She probably tore her ACL. Big problem for humans, but she should be fine in a week or so."

Putting down my glass of milk, I nod. "That's good."

His responding look is somewhat droll. I think uncertainty of the goodness of Simone's quick recovery shone through my words.

"So," I go on quickly, "I'm stuck here until you get off work then?"

He shrugs. "You can take my truck if you want. I can run back." He doesn't look at me as he waits for the answer.

"You get off before midnight, right?" Sure, it's a bar, but if

69

he's here now, they can't expect him to stay until closing, can they?

There's a flicker of a smile. "I get off at six. Mom doesn't like me manning things when there's a point to being open."

"Okay." I scope up some more chili. "Then I'll wait for you."

"Okay," he repeats quietly, sitting down to finish his food in silence.

Amazingly enough, a group of other people come in before we've cleared off our table. Gathering the dishes as Warren goes to handle them, I reflect on how different the wolf is today. I'm starting to understand why everyone's been so confused about his response to me. If this is the real Warren, then freaky staring Warren is... What? A sign of mental instability? A multiple personality?

I take the things into the kitchen and rinse them out in the sink before putting them in a massive dishwasher. I'm humming softly to myself when someone starts talking behind me and startles me nearly out of my skin.

"What is it with you and kitchens?"

Slowly, I turn, afraid its going to be Evil Warren behind me, but find Nice Warren smiling at me. I grab the counter behind me, leaning back on it to preserve my balance. "What do you mean?"

"The door clearly says, 'Staff Only.'" Walking toward me, he captures my eyes with his and refuses to let them go. "You're not the one who works here." Maybe this is Evil Warren after all. His gaze bores into me. His scent, traveling before him, threatens to drown me.

He stops inches from me, his eyes electric with intensity. My tongue runs along my bottom lip, and his focus shifts to watch it.

My heartbeat sounds loud in my ears.

Abruptly, Warren takes a large step backwards.

"You play pool?" he asks.

Unable to speak, I settle for nodding.

"Come on, then." He opens the door, holding it for me while I force myself to pass by him, rather than hiding in a cupboard like I want to do.

It somehow fails to surprise me that, although I'm a pretty

good shot, I'm not nearly as skilled a player as Warren. He easily beats me in the first round. I do manage to win the second, but I attribute my victory entirely to luck.

The wolf runs out to grab another round for the bar patrons while I set up in the back room for our third game. He returns quickly, saying as he strolls back into the room, "Let me guess! You want to place money on this game, having allowed me to win the first round and almost beat you in the second just to give me a false sense of hope."

Giving him the expected laugh, I shake my head. "No, I have to let you win this time too so you'll be willing to place a decent bet on game four."

"Right." He gives me a grin that I am rapidly become fond of seeing. "Smart girl."

My break is decent, but he gets four in a row after it before handing the cue ball over. "Is it always this busy here?" I ask him as the other people leave.

He watches me sink one of my solids, waiting until the shot's over to answer. "We're pretty much open during the day to be nice to the regulars. It'll start picking up by dinner and be packed tonight."

"Do people know it's werewolves running the place?" I wince as I narrowly miss my shot and wave Warren toward the table.

"The weres do. But, no, the local humans don't have a clue." He easily gets two more, but then gets a disgusted look as the third shot goes wrong. With a head shake, he steps back to make room for me.

"Then what do the locals think about you working here?" I feel compelled to ask. He gives me a completely baffled look as I set up and asks what I mean. "I mean, it's not legal for minors to run bars in most places. Alcohol licensing and all."

He snorts derisively. "Sheriff's were. And the mayor. And the head of the licensing board."

"And just like that we don't have to follow laws?" I ask, making a shot I honestly thought I'd missed.

"Not human ones," Warren grumbles, folding his arms and looking appalled. "Can you imagine what would happen if we thought we could get away with the things they do?"

"What?"

That question is so strange it makes me hit the ball all wrong. Which turns out to be a good thing since the target goes in now.

He watches me quietly for a few seconds before trying to answer. "We ignore their little rules when we can, yes. But the big rules? Theft? Murder? Rape? They do that stuff and get slapped on the wrists. We do it, and our own families execute us."

I shiver. That seems so harsh and unyielding. What about due process and the right of appeal? But I've also been told multiple times weres who attack humans are killed, even though I know of two who weren't. So there is leniency somewhere in the system.

"Nice shot," Warren says with genuine enthusiasm as I pull off a miracle to sink the eight and gain my second victory.

"Thanks." I smile slightly at him and start taking the balls from pockets, rolling them down to him so he can put them in the triangle.

"So how did you learn to play this well?" he asks, dropping the balls into place with decisive clicks as he changes the subject. "Are you the daughter of a pair of professional players?"

"No." I laugh, but the sound turns sad. "It was Troy who taught me."

Damn. I would never have let myself think of him right now if wondering about justice in the world of shape shifters hadn't thrown me off my mental balance.

"Troy being?" Warren's hands are still on the edges of the triangle.

My throat hurts as I swallow. "My ex-boyfriend."

It's the first time I've had to describe him as such. The phrase send a knife of pain through my heart.

"Who is good at pool despite being a complete idiot?"

Huh? I squint at Warren as he bends to hang the triangle in place. Oh. Right. Troy is an idiot because he was my boyfriend. My jaw locks tightly.

Warren squints back at me as he straightens. He stares at me for a few seconds, as if confused by my change in expression. "He's an idiot because he broke up with you. It was an attempt

72

at a compliment."

He rolls the cue ball to me.

"Oh."

I trap the ball in my hand.

Trying to aim for the break, I realize my entire body is shaking.

I pull the stick back, make my shot anyway, and manage to miss every single ball on the table.

"Michaela?"

"He didn't technically break up with me," I whisper to the beer stained felt. "He just started going out with someone else."

There's a growl from across the table. "Then he's a coward, too."

The trembling gets even worse and my hands start to tingle with lost circulation. A wave of dizziness hits me.

Warm arms wrap around me.

My pool stick clatters onto the ground.

Dry sobs slam through my body.

Warren draws me against him, leads me into another room, and sits me on an old sofa with fluffy pillows and horrible floral fabric. He kneels in front of me, smooths my hair back from my face, and gives me the softest of looks. "What happened?"

"I don't know." But despite the fact I haven't said a word about this to anyone else, I find myself telling Warren everything I do know, starting with the way Troy started to distance himself after my attack. I didn't realize it at the time, but it seems obvious in retrospect.

Tears roll down my cheeks when I get to the part when he started answering his phone less and less, until eventually he wouldn't take my calls at all.

I end with him not even bothering to e-mail me since I've been here. "How could I have meant so little to him?"

There's a short silence and eventually a whisper. "I don't know."

The door opens in the front room and he glances back.

"You can go," I tell him, trying to smile.

He gives me a very long look as he thinks about whether he should leave me alone or not.

"Honest, I'm not going to hurt myself or anything."

73

His head shakes. "Not what I was worried about."

Oh. What was he worried about?

The front door opens again and a loud party comes through it. Warren looks torn.

"I'll just lay down," I offer with sniffle. "Try to take a nap..."

He doesn't look convinced, but he gets up when someone up front yells out for attention.

"We'll leave the second I can get my relief in," he tells me.

Nodding, I hold back on crying anymore until he closes the door behind him, at which point I break down again, letting giant sobs tear their way through me.

I do lie down and try to sleep, but my brain won't stop thinking about Troy, dwelling on my hurt. I can't even make myself be angry, I'm so miserable. I've been repressing so much without even knowing I was doing it. And now it's all caught up with me in one sudden blow. In front of Warren, of all people!

With a growl of defeat, I grab the remote on the coffee table. Turning on the TV, I flip channels until I find a show I can stand.

The couch smells like wolves. Somehow, that comforts me, and I start to calm down, eventually falling asleep until Warren wakes me by gently saying my name. "Michaela?"

He squats in front of me, smiling and stroking my hair. "Good morning."

The TV is off and the lights are on. A mug of something steaming sits on the table.

I open my mouth to say something, but all that comes out is a yawn.

Chuckling softly, Warren picks up the mug. "Hot chocolate, sleepy girl?"

"Thanks." My fingers wrap around the cup, brushing against Warren's. His hand zips away hastily, almost making me spill the drink. Looking at the beverage, I try a small sip to hide the unreasonable hurt I feel at his reaction to my touch.

"I need to bring another keg up from the basement, then we can go, alright?" He neither looks at me nor waits for an answer. In fact, he's out the door before he even finishes the sentence.

What a strange wolf... a strange wolf that makes very good hot chocolate. Made with real milk and marshmallows, it is quite possibly the best cocoa I've ever had. I wonder with a tiny smile if it's a family recipe like the chili.

"You ready to go?" Warren asks right after I drain the last of the drink. It's almost as if he was waiting outside for me to finish before he came in. And maybe he was.

"Sure." I bring the cup with me, taking the time to put it in the dishwasher on our way to the parking lot. My ride watches me do it with a hint of humor playing on his lips and tiny wrinkles around his eyes. My breath catches when I see the look. When he's not busy scaring me out of my wits, Warren really is something to look at.

The ride back to school is much less chatty than my ride down was. Warren doesn't say a word from the time we leave the kitchen until we pull up at the school, and I can't think of a thing to say to him. Should I thank him for being so nice about my little breakdown? Apologize for it? Mention that I wish he'd spend more time smiling at me and less time glaring because I like his smile?

He pulls into the drive rather than the parking garage. "I have to run an errand for my mom," he offers as explanation.

"Alright," I respond, aware he'd just as soon I get out of the truck without saying anything. My hand goes to the door, but I don't climb out yet. "Thank you. For earlier. For listening."

I move the door handle towards me, but halt when he whispers my name.

"Michaela." He leans over, placing his fingers on my cheek and turning my face toward his. "Please don't cry over that jackass. He's not worth it."

Sniffling, I lean into the seat. The worn cloth is soft and cool. The skin of Warren's hand is warm and comforting. "I know. I think I'm crying more for me."

He removes his hand, letting the cold air chill me again. "That's different then."

He turns back to the steering wheel, placing his hands on it, but then he looks back to me. "I would prefer you not cry over anything."

I wish I could find the strength to smile. "I'll try not to."

I very nearly ask if I can go with him, and he must sense that because his features turn hostile again quickly. "It's pack business," he says with clipped, terse words.

Nodding, I brush the fresh tears away from my face and whisper a goodbye, jumping quickly from the vehicle and running straight inside before the moisture on my cheeks can freeze.

That night, I dream again of a wolf. One that is kind to me, but then attacks. And poor Leo has to rescue me again.

My subconscious isn't very subtle, is it?

Chapter Ten

Seth strolls into the mini-kitchen as I am stirring some creamer into a cup of coffee. I wish I had a real mug, but I didn't think to bring one with me.

"I am so sorry about yesterday," he starts before he's even though the door. His hair is pulled back against the nape of his neck and the sapphire blue sweater he wears really brings out his eyes.

"It's alright." Smiling, I pick up the silly little Styrofoam container. "How's Simone?"

He rolls his eyes as he opens the donut box and pulls out a powder-coated selection. "She's fine." He doesn't exactly radiate concern for her well-being.

"Glad to hear it," I offer in the same tone.

"I'm getting out of here before she wakes up." He grins before stuffing about a third of the donut into his mouth.

Laughing, I lean against the counter beside him. "Don't blame you." Blowing on the coffee, I breathe in its aroma, appreciating the little nuances that I never noticed before. My senses are continuing to sharpen.

"Wanna come with me?"

The cup pauses just before my lips. "Skiing?" I ask, making an assumption based on the pants he's wearing.

"Yeah, skiing." His lopsided smile warms me more than the coffee.

Skiing with Seth? There is no way I could keep up with him. "Can't," I demure. "I'm supposed to go snowshoeing with the foxes." Not that I'll do great at that either, having never before put snowshoes on my feet.

Eyebrows rise over the most amazing eyes on earth. "You're joining the den?"

Huh?

Laughing, Seth shakes his head. "Nothing. It's just that the outing sounds like a den activity. And you're not, technically speaking, a fox."

"For all we know, I am," I argue, threatening to spill my drink with the sharpening of my posture that goes with my words.

"Really?" He leans back and gives me a taunting smile. "So a fox mauled you badly enough that you spent a week in the hospital?"

It wasn't a full week.

But he has a point. Of all the creatures here, the one I am least likely to be would be fox.

"Maybe I pissed it off," I theorize.

Seth laughs again. "Yeah, could be." He grins at me and wipes his hands together to get the last of the donut powder off of them. "I'm going to run before anyone can beg me not to."

"Won't they just call you?" I ask.

He gives me a mischievous look. "The phone only works at base." Starting to the door, he waves cheerfully. "See you, kit."

Kit: (noun) An endearment for a young fox. Or, possibly, for a young leopard if it's short for kitten.

I finish my coffee and have a donut myself, then head upstairs to find my boots and my guide. Sam approves of what I'm wearing before leading me down to one of the nearest outbuildings. It's made of the same gray wood as the skate barn, but is maybe a tenth of the size, if that.

We enter to find several of the foxes inside, standing in two different groups and talking to one another. Sam goes to a wall where the snowshoes are stored, pulls down a pair, and hands them to me as if she thinks I have any idea what to do with them.

I sit down and try to figure out how to get the things on, making Sam laugh at me. Not in a mean way, more in an aren't-you-the-cutest-thing way.

Tod walks over to see what's happening and shakes his head. "You don't put them on inside. That would damage the grampons on the bottom. Take them out."

He grabs another pair of shoes and motions for me to follow

78

him out. Sam trails behind us, still looking amused.

It's not nearly as cold outside as I feared it was going to be. It's still somewhere shy of freezing, but the wind has died. Constant freezing is so much easier to handle than being ravished by uneven gusts of ice, and I suspect once we start exercising, I may actually approach comfortable.

Tod tosses all of the shoes onto the ground, two of the smaller ones directly before me, and kneels in front of me without seeming to notice the snow. Taking my foot in his hands, he guides it onto one of the the shoes and then fastens the straps that will hold it to my boot, talking me through the process as he goes. "See? Easy! You try the other one."

As he sits back watching, I slide my foot into the bindings of the other one and fuss with them until they close. The heel strap requires ratcheting, which throws me off balance, but I somehow manage to stay upright. "Like that?"

"Like that." He smiles up at me. "You're a natural."

"Yep," agrees his sister. "Although, it does beg the question of a natural what."

She grins at me to show she's just teasing, and I smile back. "A natural something. Let's leave it at that."

As Tod wanders off to round up the others, Aliah, decked out in a large woolly gray sunhat, picks her way over to us. She carries half a dozen poles, two of which she holds out to me when she comes to a stop. "For balance?"

To demonstrate how much I need help with that, I nearly fall reaching over to grab them. The shoes don't seem like they should be causing problems, especially while standing still, but putting anything on my feet without being used to it tends to give me issues. "Thanks! I have a feeling I need them."

Aliah smiles her shy smile. "Me too?"

"I don't need them at all," Sam says. However, her claim is a bit on the suspicious side as she makes it while grabbing a pair off her friend. "I just carry them so people who do need them don't feel bad."

"Uh huh." Aliah lowers her sunglasses enough to wink at me. "She doesn't need a calculator in geometry class either? She just doesn't want me to feel stupid?"

"Of course I don't." Sam puts an arm around her shoulders.

79

"I can't have my bestest friend thinking she's lacking."

Aliah just shakes her head at that and starts putting her own snowshoes on.

Everyone else must be ready because Tod returns to us. "Aliah, you got your sunblock on?"

"No," Sam answers for her. "She decided white is unfashionable, and she'd rather be bright red."

The albino in question shakes her head. "Yes, I have my sunblock on. And extra in my inner pocket where it won't freeze."

"Good." Tod smiles like he's checking something off a mental checklist and a few minutes later, we're trudging across a field. We sink less than in just boots, although there's still some slipping into the snow. It's both surprisingly easy and surprisingly awkward.

"So..." I struggle along between Sam and Aliah, whom I suspect of going slower than they usually would on account of me. The half of the group ahead of us is steadily gaining in their lead, although Tod and one of the freshmen are only a few yards up. I get the impression the adorable Japanese girl he's helping isn't much more experienced with this than I am. "Last night..."

When I got back yesterday, Sam stopped by to invite me on this hike, but didn't hang out for long because she was going out with her favorite polar bear.

"Where did you and Bryce go?" I ask.

Sam's eyes narrow in annoyance. Did he do something, or was I not supposed to mention she was with him?

"We just went shopping." Her voice is matter-of-fact.

"Shopping for what?" Tod asks without turning around. Dang it, I'd thought he was far enough away not to be paying attention to us. I have got to get used to how well weres can hear.

Sam glares at his back. "He wanted a present for his sister's birthday. Thought a girl could help him."

"So he didn't ask you to the dance?" one of the younger foxes behind us asks.

"Don't be ridiculous," she snaps. "We're just friends." The look she gives me borders on petulant. "I would rather hear about why you smelled so strongly of wolf."

Okay. Guess that's payback for me asking about Bryce in front of everyone.

"I should have smelled like leopard too," I tell her.

Tod makes a sound somewhere between a laugh and a cough.

A blush heats my ears. That sounded sluttier than it should have.

"Seth was showing me what there is of the town when he got a call about Simone blowing out her knee," I tell the den in general. "He thought he'd be right back, but I wound up at Denali's for a few hours until Warren could bring me home."

Tod glances back again. "You do know we have a car, right? That you could have called us?"

I blink. "Yeah, of course." Saying it never occurred to me to call Tod would be the truth, but I'm not sure it's a polite one. "It's not like I was in a hurry, though, and Warren was being civilized. Let me beat him at pool and everything."

"So he's not scaring you anymore?" Tod asks.

"Not too much," I answer, my lips tugging upward. "Most the time."

He glances back again. "And the rest of the time?"

I shrug. "He got a little weird at the end, but..." I nearly say I gave him reason to be, but thinking back I'm suddenly not sure it was me. His mood changed when I wasn't around to see why. "He said he had wolf business after he dropped me off."

Aliah makes a sympathetic noise. "Wolf business can be upsetting, you know?"

"Can it?" I ask her. "More so than other were business?"

"Oh, yeah," Sam answers.

Tod protests, "Hey, dealing with fox stuff is stressful!"

"Of course it is," his sister agrees with syrupy sweetness. "But when's the last time you had to condemn someone to death for eating people?"

"What?" My jaw drops as I stare at her. "You're not serious?"

"Last summer?" Aliah nods. "There was a rogue?"

"Yeah." Sam's expression grows even darker. "And Warren's dad made him issue the sentence."

"Why?" I ask, appalled that someone would do that to his

kid.

His head is bent as Tod nods. "It's part of leading wolves. Part of leading any weres, but Sam's right. Foxes just don't do the shit wolves do."

"We could!" someone behind me objects, apparently offended.

"Yeah, right." I can almost hear the sneer the person answering must be wearing. "You could kill somebody? You can't even slaughter a rabbit."

"What do you know?" the first voice asks. "You're a vegetarian."

Which sort of makes the point, really. A fox that won't eat meat is odd, but I can't for the life of me imagine a vegetarian wolf.

The topic of conversation switches off of me and wolves, moving on to the little dramas and comedies that make up school life. The foxes banter easily with each other as I listen in amusement. I can see why Seth was surprised they would be taking an outsider with them. The atmosphere is much like a family outing, the jokes frequently inside ones that they don't explain except when I ask them to. I don't have to do anything to be included; just by being there, it's like I'm a fox.

The mood is shattered when we get back to the storage shack and find Lyly waiting for us, her arms folded and her features pinched. The glower she wears should make her ugly, but somehow fails to. She must have sold her soul to Satan to be able to pull off that sort of expression and still look gorgeous.

"Oh, expletive," Sam mutters as her brother's sometimes-girlfriend bares down on us.

As Tod bends down to remove his snowshoes, Lyly plants herself before him in a way I can only describe as menacing. "You left without me!"

He blinks at the onslaught. "We didn't think you were coming."

"I said that I was!" she snarls.

He looks closely at her, his face lacking in all expression. "You said that last weekend."

"So?" Her arms are crossed so tightly it's amazing she can breathe.

82

He just looks at her, silent and wooden.

"Oh." She doesn't even have the grace to look embarrassed by the reference to their breakup. When Sam asked me to come on this, the first thing I asked was if Alysia would be there. I was assured she wouldn't be because she never hangs out with the den when she's abandoned Tod. Apparently, a long time ago she put it to them that they would have to chose between him and her. They chose him. "Well, I was still going to come."

Tod picks his snowshoes off the ground and turns toward the building. "Sorry."

I'm not sorry.

And as the others busy themselves with their own equipment, I get the impression no one else really is either.

Chapter Eleven

Predictably, Simone makes a big production of needing to be helped everywhere she goes, even though the swelling in her knee has disappeared, and despite how she doesn't actually look like she's in much pain. Poor Seth has to follow her around toting her things and letting her lean against him while she pretends to be off balance. Which is probably why he rushes off to the ski slope the second he's out of class Monday and skips Calculus to go straight there on Tuesday.

Also predictably, Warren is back to staring at me from afar. That bothers me a lot more than Simone's behavior.

He's the teacher's assistant in my camouflage and flight class, just like in tracking, but this instructor chooses to let me struggle behind the freshmen in peace, without inflicting Warren with the odious task of tutoring me. That leaves him free to alternate at will between ignoring me and glaring at me without having to bother with pretending to be civil.

Yet... Sometimes, out of the corner of my eye, I can swear I see him smiling at me, laughing when I'm silly and nodding in approval when I get something right. But he always stops before I can focus on him. Always.

He would probably frown at my senselessness if he saw me now, standing at the top of my first blue slope on Thursday afternoon. Or at the top of the slope that would be my first blue if I were actually good enough to survive going down it, I should say. I could have sworn I was ready to move on to tackle intermediates, but I didn't realize how steep they are.

Clearly, my fantastic ski instructor was off her rocker to suggest I should come up here. I'll have to tell her after I walk down.

"Need help, kit?" Seth glides to a rest beside me and gives me a heart-stopping grin.

I stifle a sigh. Not only am I standing here like a nitwit, but here is between a lift and the slopes my friends do. Like I wasn't humiliated enough without people I know seeing me. "Yeah," I mutter. "Is there a green way down?"

"Green?" He shakes his head. "No, not from here. But that's an easy blue."

"Which is not the same thing as being an easy slope." I twist around, looking for my binding release.

"What are you doing?" Squinting at me, he looks absolutely bewildered.

"What do you think?" I roll my eyes. "I'm taking my skis off so I can walk down this stupid cliff."

He laughs, and suddenly, I like him a lot less than I usually do. "You can do this slope. I bet you could even do it with your eyes closed."

Yeah, right. I can't even manage to get my stupid foot out of my stupid binding.

"You can follow me. Go where I go. You'll be fine."

Biting my lip in consideration, I stop messing with my ski. It'd be embarrassing to have to walk down. Not to mention the fact it will be tiring and painful and will take a very long time. I'm already half frozen; can I even handle staying out here long enough to trek to the base?

"Trust me, kit."

I look into the most wonderful eyes in the world and feel myself nod.

Seth grins. "Great."

Glancing at the slope, he turns around and creeps towards the lip.

"What are you doing?" it's my turn to ask.

Slowly, he slides downhill for a few feet. "Showing you the way to the kiddie slopes."

"Backwards?"

The laugh is gentle. "Don't worry about me, worry about you." He pauses. "No, don't worry about you either. Just keep your eyes on me, and you'll go where I go, alright?"

Lovely. I'm stuck on the side of a mountain, freezing to death, with a madman. "Sure," I grumble.

Locking my eyes onto his, I hope he's not overconfident in me.

His eyes move further away and with a yip of dismay, I dig my poles into the snow to push off after him.

"It's alright," he calls up, starting a wide turn.

I watch his eyes... And I turn!

He leads me in a lazy snake downhill, taking up the whole slope with a traverse pattern that keeps our speed slower than what I would do on an easier slope.

"See?" He reaches an arm around my waist when I pass him at the very bottom. "I told you so."

"You did," I admit, my heart racing from either the thrill of getting down or from being held. The difficulty I'm having breathing is almost certainly all Seth's fault.

His eyes are very close to me now. Very, very close.

"Go again?" he asks, his tone light, but his expression seeming to hold the promise of something that isn't at all related to skiing.

"Sure," I whisper.

The wind hits me when he pulls away, but I'm strangely warm despite it. Even sitting on the lift fails to chill me, not with Seth so close beside me. Our bodies almost, though not quite, touch. The gap between us seems to thrum with energy.

Riding a lift has never been half this interesting before.

We take the slope he found me on another three times before heading into the coffee shop. The first time, he lets me gaze into his eyes again, but the other two he actually forces me to go first. He says some helpful things though, and I have more fun than I have any other day I've skied here.

No one bothers us while we sip coffee together. And even more luckily when Seth offers me a ride back down, no leopards appear to steal my seat. I thank him before hitting the shower back at school. I wash as quickly as I can, eager to head to dinner. But as I'm debating if I'm brave enough to try to sit with Seth or not, my landline rings.

"Hello?" I answer, confused. I just talked to my dad last night, and no one else has called me since I've been here. Possibly because I didn't bother giving anyone else the number.

"Michaela!" comes a hysterical sob.

Shoulders slumping, I resign myself to the possibility of missing dinner. "Hey, Mom. What's wrong?"

"It's Grandma."

For a half a second, I think my grandmother is dead. It doesn't upset me half as much as I feel it should.

But then my mom goes on, "She's threatening not to come if we have an open bar!"

Oh, good grief. Another wedding crisis. I sit in my desk chair and pull my feet up onto the seat. "Why?"

"She says it will just encourage people to drink," Mom whimpers.

Um... Isn't that the point of having an open bar?

"She says alcohol is sinful," Mom goes on. "And I'd be playing into the devil's hands."

"That sounds like Grandma." I can't say I'm surprised either. Every time I see her, she tries to give me a new pamphlet about how my entire generation is evil. Don't get me wrong, I'm happy she has a religion that makes her happy. I just wish she'd stop using it to make everyone else miserable.

"I knew she wouldn't approve. But not coming at all?" She sobs. "And Chaz says there's no way he's giving in to her."

Mark it down in the record books, I seem to be agreeing with my future step-dad on something. "It's your wedding, Mom. And Chaz's. It's not hers."

"But I want her there!" Mom whines.

"I know." Closing me eyes, I take a deep breath. "She's probably bluffing. Like when she swore to cut you off if you got divorced."

Which is when I stopped talking to the old bat. I wasn't happy about the break-up either, but Mom didn't deserve to be treated like that by her own mother. By Dad, sure. But not by her mom.

"Maybe..." She doesn't sound like she believes me, but I can't hear her crying anymore.

"You really think she's going to give up the chance to feel all superior to Chaz's family?" I ask.

Mom laughs. "True."

"And now she can tell all her friends how awful her daughter's fiancé is because he's willing to let his friends drink Scotch."

"She'll enjoy that..."

At least we're able to laugh about it.

"Michaela?" The timidity in Mom's voice makes me nervous. "Do you think you could ask your dad to talk to her? She's always listened to him."

"Mom..." Does she not see how awkward that would be for me? Does she actually expect me to call Dad up and ask him to smooth over the wedding arrangements of a woman whom I'm pretty sure he's still in love with? Does she just not realize how he feels, or is she really that insensitive?

"Please?"

"No, Mom." I feel bad about it, but if I have to chose which parent's emotions to be worried about, I'm siding with my dad. "Leave Daddy out of it."

"Alright. I have to go."

And just like that, I'm dismissed.

My appetite gone, I curl up in bed with Leo and my English assignment. Nothing will put a person to sleep faster than depression and Dickens.

Mom might not need me if I'm not actively helping her, but my new friends here do. The Foxes have me cheered up within the first minutes of breakfast. The happy mood sticks until I make it to hunting and find myself alone with Warren again.

"I saw you with Seth yesterday."

"And?" I follow him through the forest. He's supposed to be finding tracks for me to look at, but he doesn't seem to be paying much attention to the ground.

"He's not a trained instructor, you know."

"Yeah, I know." Chuckling softly, I dunk under a branch. "I kind of got in over my head, and he helped me out." I shrug. "Then he hung around to help me out some more."

A grunt is all the response I expect to get, and the only one I do receive for about two minutes. Then Warren suddenly asks, "You ever tried boarding?"

Stumbling a little, I answer hesitantly, "No. I've never gotten around to it."

My guide stops and looks down at me, his eyes unreadable. "Would you like to?"

Would I like to snowboard? "Sure."

He blinks ever so slowly. "Now?"

"Now?" I repeat, startled. "We're in the middle of class."

Looking around, Warren raises his eyebrows meaningfully. No one's going to notice if we take off now. There's no one to see us. And if they do notice, no one's going to worry. It's not like Warren is going to get lost in his home territory.

Still... Do I really want to leave with Warren? I can't even tell if he's being Nice Warren or not.

On the other hand, I'm already alone with the guy and pretty far away from the others. So... "Yeah, alright."

My stomach rolls at the boldness, but the grin Warren gives me more than makes up for any discomfort.

Although two hours and uncountable falls later, I'm seriously second-guessing how much discomfort that grin was worth. Particularly as Warren keeps bouncing between his nice mode, which I am growing rather fond of, and his freaky mode, of which I am not in the least bit appreciative. The wolf needs medication.

"What are you so scared of?" he asks.

Squinting at him, I accept his hand to get up. "What do you mean?"

He pulls me to my feet, then waves at the slope. "You get scared, you panic, and you fall. Why?"

Um... I stare at him. "Because I'm careening out of control?"

An eyebrow goes up and the rest of his face scrunches in disbelief. "Careening down the bunny slope?"

"Beginners' Area," I correct, feeling a sulk come on.

"Michaela, you're a were." His tone is steady, but his eyes are reasonably kind. "If you break your neck, it will hurt for a few days. If you gripe enough, you can probably make people carry your books for you. You're not going to die on anything groomed."

Nice not to die. But extreme pain doesn't sound fun either. "I don't have the full benefits package yet."

Warren rolls his eyes. "You're on the bunny slope, Michaela!"

"Why do you keep calling me that?"

He was all puffed up to escalate our argument, but he slumps in confusion at the question. "What?"

"Everyone else calls me Mike. My mom is the only person

89

who has ever called me Michaela."

I leave out the fact people also tend to do it when they're angry. It would be too easy, and typical, of him just to say he's always angry with me.

Shifting uncomfortably and keeping his eyes on the snow, Warren shrugs. "If I agree to call you Mike, will try a real slope?"

"A green one?"

A soft laugh shifts the mood again. "Your pick even."

I stick my hand out. "Deal."

He shakes the hand, then holds onto it so he can start my motion toward the lift, letting go once I get going, but then grabbing me again when I threaten to fall at the lift loading area.

How can it be so hard to stop a snowboard? Only one foot is attached to it when you're not going downhill, so the other can go wherever it wants. It should be a snap to stop. It is for everyone who isn't me.

"You're over-thinking your balance," Warren explains, even though I don't ask him about it. He helps me get on the lift, pulling down the little bar even though he made fun of me wanting the one on the last lift. Most humans don't bother pulling down the safety bar, let alone super-healing weres. "You need to start listening to your instincts."

"My instincts tell me to go home," I mutter gloomily, making him laugh for some reason.

We go the rest of the way up without speaking, and Warren follows me quietly to the slope I picked out. He doesn't say anything until after I've spent at least a minute surveying the thing in dismay.

"Go." The command is amused, but firm.

Looking down the slope, I hear myself whimper.

"You ski this slope," he points out with annoying calm.

"I'm not on skis!" I protest. "This isn't the same."

Letting out a hefty sigh, Warren shakes his head. "You can walk if you'd rather."

My eyes narrow at him. "You're not qualified to teach this, are you?"

"I never said I was." He flashes me a smile. It's not as good

90

as the grin that got me here, but it does make me shiver less. He gives me a gentle look. "If you go first, I can help you up when you fall. If you come behind me, you'll be on your own."

I puff up. "You mean if I fall."

"No." He grins. "I mean when you fall."

My teeth grit together.

Why I am letting him goad me like this? It's not as if it's a mark of shame to lose one's balance the first day of snowboarding. In fact, it was pretty darn ambitious to leave the bunny slope, whatever Warren's making out.

"You still have the reflexes of a human," the wolf commiserates. "It's not your fault you can't balance any better than a drunken monkey. Don't feel bad about it. I'll help you get up when you inevitably sprawl to the ground."

With a growl and a hop, I start down. Warren's laughter follows tight on my heels.

It is not the world's best run by any stretch of the imagination, but I do manage to get all the way to the bottom before I sprawl onto the snow. And I only do that because I'm not very good at stopping yet, and the area has gotten kind of crowded.

Warren absolutely beams at me.

"Damn you, wolf!" I yell up at him. "You did that on purpose!"

He's grinning as he helps me up. "It worked, didn't it?"

I move to smack his shoulder with a playful sort of swat, but lose my balance. If it wasn't for him lashing out to grab my arm, the same one that was trying to hit him, I would fall.

His hand wraps around my wrist as I lean towards his body.

His scent flows over me.

His eyes, wide and filled with something unnameable, search mine.

He drops my arm, slides down the hill a bit and informs me he needs to go to work.

"Alright," I mumble, feeling lost.

The board is somehow off of his feet, and he's walking towards the lodge.

Miffed, I bend over to release my boots, knocking myself off

91

balance again and falling face first onto the snow.

"Stay still!"

Out of nowhere, Seth is here, working to free my legs from their board of bondage. "Serves you right for messing with the powers of darkness."

"What?" I blink stupidly. "Warren?"

"No." The leopard laughs. "Snowboarding."

Free of the dark power, I roll over and accept the hand Seth offers to help me to my feet. "Why is it I'm always having to save you?"

Softly, I harrumph with as much dignity as I can muster. "Being grateful for help is different from actually needing rescue."

Seth smiles. "True. You clearly have no need of me whatsoever."

"Clearly," I agree. But I grin immediately afterwards so he'll know I don't mean it.

Bending over, he grabs the board. "Rental?"

"Yeah." I make a grab for it. "But you don't have to carry it."

"Already doing it." Easily dodging my attempt at reclaiming the board, he starts towards the rental shop, leaving me to trudge along behind him.

"So, is Warren planning on taking you back to school, or did he really just abandon you here?" There's something I can't pin down in his voice. Something tense lurking below the easy-going surface. One of those prospects seems to upset him, but I can't tell which one.

"I don't know," I answer honestly. "He said earlier he'd take me home before he went to work, but then he just stomped off for no reason."

"He had a reason," Seth assures me. "Warren always has a reason. It's just usually not a reason a sane person would understand."

"You know..." I draw out as we walk into the rental building. "I can't really tell if you two like each other or not."

Seth gives the board to the attendant and comes to sit beside me as I take off the boots. "Well, cats and dogs frequently get along. But deep down, they're cats and dogs."

Oh. "I hadn't thought of it like that." I struggle to get the first boots off, so Seth moves in front of me to pull it off. He moves onto the other boot without giving me a chance to fight it.

"That's because you still like to pretend we're human." He looks steadily up at me. "We aren't human, Mike."

"We're not our animals either."

Sadly, his head shakes. "I'm not as sure of that as you are."

I slip on my sneakers while Seth takes the boots over to the counter. Quietly thanking him, I walk out the door wondering if I have been left up here or not.

"There he is." Seth jerks his chin to a form lounging moodily on the corner of the lodge closest to the parking lot. "You know, if you'd like to stay longer..."

I give a serene smile. "I've figured out what I morph into, Seth."

He jerks to complete attention, eyes bright.

"A popsicle."

It takes about a second for him to realize that was a joke.

Smiling sheepishly, he lets out a sigh. "Go curl up by the fire, you house kitten."

"Meow!"

Chapter Twelve

It's another speechless ride back to school. I thank Warren for teaching me to play on a snowboard, but the only response is a moderately civil grunt of acknowledgment and an increase in the volume of the stereo, which is playing some sort of bizarre blend of country and metal.

Defying prediction, Warren pulls the truck into the community garage. "I thought you were going to work?" I blurt thoughtlessly.

The truck shuts off with a slight sputter. "Need to get some stuff. For the weekend."

I climb out of the truck, wondering what happened to Nice Warren. Did he get trapped in his ski locker with his board? "You spend most weekends with your family?"

"The ones I work Saturdays on."

So diving me home last weekend would have been out of the way even without the mysterious errand for his mother.

A gust of wind rips through me as we walk towards the entrance to the building. Even in a covered parking structure, the wind can be wicked here – Arctic.

Warren studies me. "You okay, Michaela?"

Sniffling loudly, I nod. "Of course. Just cold." Making a big production of it, I give in to a dramatic shiver. "Anyone who would volunteer to live here must be crazy. Explains a lot about you, I suppose."

My companion slows to a halt.

I didn't mean for the last sentence to come across in an accusatory fashion. I meant it as a joke, but it did sound hostile.

"Michaela?"

I stop, wrapping my arms around myself, and turn around to face him, even though the thing I want most in the world right now is to get into the building a few short feet away. "Yeah?"

"I'm sorry."

Confused by the declaration, I move my eyes up from the ground to Warren's face. He's watching me carefully, but his expression appears honest. "The last two weeks have been beyond weird for me, and I haven't been treating you well. And I'm sorry."

Holding my hands in front of my face, I blow air onto them, warming them to buy myself a few seconds of thought. "Actually, you've only been a jerk about half of the time. The other half of the time, I kind of like you."

If I were being more honest, I would have to say I really like nice Warren. Maybe even really, really like him.

Nodding, Warren starts toward the door, moving as he passes me to make sure we don't touch. "I'll put more effort into being a jerk then. Liking me probably isn't good for you."

Dramatic much? I catch up with him before the door shuts, and ask, "So why have the last two weeks been weird?"

"I don't want to talk about it."

At least he says that without sounding like he hates me. The words just seem tired.

Sam is in the Great Room, talking into a slender phone on the wall. "Wait, she just walked in. Hold on for a second." She presses a button on the wall and waves the handset in my direction. "Mike! It's some guy named Troy?" She doesn't even attempt to look as though she isn't curious as to who Troy is.

I feel a little guilty for the fact I never told her about him.

Sensing my hesitation, Warren reaches out to take the phone. "I can tell him to go away for you."

It's tempting, but I shake my head. "I went out with him for six months."

Warren gives me a calm look. "You don't owe him anything."

"No," I agree. "But I owe myself the satisfaction of telling him to go away." I try to smile. "Besides, if I don't, then I'm just as much of a coward as he is."

Smiling back with a smile that isn't happy, but is supportive, Warren hands me the phone.

Neither he nor Sam go anywhere, although they do retreat a few steps so as not to crowd me while they listen to my end of the conversation. Sam whispers something to Warren as I take a deep breath and press the button to bring the call off of hold, but instead of spilling the goods about Troy, he shakes his head at her and stays silent.

"Hello?"

I have to say the word twice before he responds. "God, it's good to hear your voice, Mike."

The same cannot be said of his. He sounds strained. Worn. It wrings my heart. Even though a huge part of me wanted him miserable, hearing evidence of it doesn't make me happy. It just makes me feel bad for him, which is something I don't want to do.

"Mike?"

The yearning in his voice slices through me and my eyes squeeze shut, fighting back tears. Warren was right before; Troy isn't worth crying over... or for.

"Why did you call me?" I want to know.

He sputters. "Why did I call you? Because I miss you so much it's driving me crazy."

"Well, I don't seem to miss you."

Oddly enough, that seems to be true. I had thought I missed him, but what really upset me was the fact he hadn't tried to contact me. Now that he's called, I find I'm not bothered by the miles between us.

"I love you, Mike." The declaration is scarcely a whisper.

"No, you don't," I whisper back, saddened. I lean forward, feeling the cool wood panel against my skin. My stomach rolls and my breath is shaky. "If you did, then you wouldn't have been messing around with Kim."

"Kim." He spits the name like it's a curse. "I don't know how she did it. I got so confused, and I made a huge mistake. I'm so, so sorry, Mike. She never meant anything to me. I swear."

Does that make it better? Or worse? And do I care?

He sobs, sounding like he honestly is crying. "You have to forgive me, Mike. I'm going to go crazy if you don't."

I sigh. "Alright. I forgive you."

"Really?" The word is cautious, like he expects to be slammed now. The forgiveness was too easy to trust.

"Yes, really," I confirm. It makes me feel better to say it, although my insides are still a nauseous tangle of emotion.

"Really?" There's more belief then. "Oh, God. Thank you, Mike. God. Things will be so much better this time. I'll make it up to you. As soon as you get home, I'll-"

"I'm not coming home," I cut off his mad dash of words.

There's a long pause. "What?" Genuine confusion is evident in the question.

"I'm staying here." I take a deep breath. "And I said I forgive you, not that we're getting back together."

"What?" Anger is starting to blend into the bewilderment now.

"I'm not mad at you anymore," I tell him. "But I don't want you to call me again, Troy."

"So you're moving to Alaska to punish me?" he demands, incredulous.

"I'm not here to punish you." Shaking my head miserably, I sigh. "Me being here has nothing to do with you."

He snorts loudly. "You expect me to believe that?"

"I don't care if you believe it or not," I state. And, once again, it's the truth.

"Why are you being such a bitch?"

"I'm not!" Straightening, I keep my face turned to the wall.

"What am I supposed to do?" he demands. "I said I was sorry. You said you forgive me. What else am I supposed to be doing here, Mike? You want me to be miserable? I'm miserable. I have been since I got that damned form letter from you! You didn't even personalize it! You just left me without anything!"

"You're the one who was cheating on me." Trying to calm down, I stuff my anger down as deep as I can get it. My stomach churns with it, but I don't rip the phone off of the wall. And I don't cry.

"I know," he admits. "And I deserved to be treated like shit for it. But I've been punished enough, Mike. And you said you forgave me. I don't understand what you want from me."

Taking a deep breath, I try to be kind while still being firm and not giving him a chance to think that maybe I don't mean what I'm saying. "I want you to have a very nice life and to stay out of mine."

"Mike... I can't do that."

"I mean it, Troy. Go away."

My hand is shaking too hard to hang up the phone, so Warren does it for me, just before he wraps me into a tight embrace and whispers, "It's okay, Michaela."

It's okay, Michaela....

The assurance sweeps over me, breaks the dam that was holding back my emotions. But I'm not going to cry. I'm not going to attack anything. The violence of suppressing my urges takes hold of my stomach, twists and won't let go.

Wrenching away from Warren, I lurch toward the nearest wastebasket. Oh, God. My entire body quivers as I vomit. I can't believe I'm doing this now, in front of Warren. If I wasn't being sick already, that would push me over the edge.

Sam's eyes are huge as I pull back. "Wow. I've been so upset I wanted to spew before, but I've never done it."

I smile weakly. "Sorry."

"You done with that?" she gestures toward the trashcan.

"I think so." Taking a deep breath, I get a whiff of the can's contents and very nearly need it again.

"You should lie down," the fox tells me gently, moving to take the mess away. Her hand gives mine a sympathetic squeeze as she leaves.

"What just happened?" Warren stares at me in clear concern. "Do you have a virus?"

Wishing my toothbrush wasn't a whole floor away, I laugh without heart. "No. I used to do that a lot when I was little," I admit. "When normal kids would cry or throw tantrums, I puked. The first month of my parent's separation, I couldn't keep anything down." I walk by him and head for the stairs. I'm sure I would be wearing a furious blush if my blood hadn't all drained from my face.

"You didn't throw up last week."

I glance at him, wondering about the tone of his voice. There's a strange uncertainty, almost fear, in it. "I wasn't as stressed last week."

Nodding, he follows me up the stairs, hovering behind me as though frightened I'm going to plummet backwards, break my neck, and be moderately inconvenienced for a few days.

"I'm fine, Warren."

"You don't sound fine."

My stomach heaves again in aftershock, keeping me from answering, but I thankfully manage to keep down everything that's left in me. Not that it's much.

Warren backs off when I go into my room, throw myself on the bed, and curl up into a ball. He stands in the open doorway, just watching me, worried and only slightly freaky.

"What is that?" he asks, his eyes narrowing on the stuffed animal I clutch against my chest.

"This is Leo." I smile sheepishly. "He's been my best friend since preschool."

The wolf grunts.

"You have to go to work," I remind him. The revolting taste clinging to my mouth reminds me I had wanted to brush my teeth, but I don't feel like moving again.

"Yeah."

He hesitates to leave though.

"I'll be fine," I assure him. "It's just my nerves."

Nodding, he nevertheless stays where he is.

"There's a building full of people who can help me if I need anything." Although it is kind of sweet that he doesn't want to leave me.

"Right," he grunts. "See you later then."

"That is one of the strangest people on Earth," I tell Leo a second before leaping up and dashing to the toilet to finish emptying the contents of my stomach. Ugh. Why am I still doing this? Didn't the first round calm me enough?

After I flush the most recent evidence of my emotional unrest, I grab my toothbrush and try to erase all reminders from my mouth. The girl looking out of my mirror hardly looks like me. Pale as a Gothic dream, she looks too vulnerable and frail to be me.

There's a knock on the door as I crawl under my comforter. "Come in," I call out weakly.

"Mike?"

The voice I hear isn't the one I was expecting. "Hey, Tod. I thought you were Sam."

He shuffles, looking like he's going to leave and take the

tray of whatever he's holding with him.

"You can stay," I tell him, and he smiles as he moves forward some more.

"The grapevine says you don't feel so well."

I sigh. "For once, it knows of which it speaks."

"Sorry to hear that." The tray, which he sits on the bedside table, holds a teapot and a dainty china cup. "We made you some tea," he informs me, somewhat needlessly. "It's ginger and mint," he adds, more helpfully. "It's supposed to help with nausea. My grandmother swears by it."

Sitting up, I smile with as much energy as I can put into it, which is remarkably little. "Well, if your grandmother thinks it will help..."

He pours some of the liquid into the little cup and hands it over to me. It radiates comfort, both with its heat and its scent.

"So, other than the vomiting, how's your day been?" Stuffing his hands into his pockets, he watches me investigate the tea. The sip I take is calming, soothing. "Sam said you were somewhere with Warren," he digs unabashedly.

Motioning him to sit on the edge of the bed, which he does with only slight embarrassment, I tell him the basics of what happened. "He wanted to know if I'd ever been boarding, then if I wanted to try it. Then, when I said sure, he was all, 'Now?' And next thing I knew, I was skipping school to learn how to snowboard."

Tod makes a noncommittal noise. "The falling isn't so bad. But the getting up's a bitch."

Bitch... Troy said I was a bitch.

"And the hopping," I reply in a rush, not letting myself think about my ex. I think about snowboards instead and about how snowboards don't come with poles like skis do, so if you need to start moving from a stop, you have to do it with a series of annoying little jumps.

Frowning at the panic in my words, Tod adds, "And the way you have to fiddle around with the bindings before and after every lift."

We nod, both convinced boarding is fine, but in no way superior to skiing.

Tod shifts. "But, anyway... The big bad wolf decided to teach you?"

The big bad wolf? Have I called Warren that out loud, or is it just an obvious thing to call him?

"Yeah." I hold out my cup for a refill. The brew's helping. "Except he wasn't acting like the big bad wolf most of the time. It was like at Denali's last weekend. He was nice, friendly... Likable even."

"And it was his idea to go?" he verifies.

"Completely." I narrow my eyes at my friend, who won't look back at me. "What do you think's up with him?"

"I don't know. But something is." He shrugs. "That wolf business maybe?"

"He said the last few weeks have been weird," I acknowledge.

"So maybe he's just stressed over something."

I frown at my beverage. "He didn't want to talk about it." The last of the tea slides down my throat, and I hand the cup over. "Thank you. I think it's helping."

"I'll send Grandma your thanks."

Smiling, I laugh softly. "Do that."

"So..." Tod watches me as I curl around Leo. "The guy on the phone..."

My eyes close. "Not someone I enjoy discussing."

"But Warren knew who he was?"

I look at Tod, taking in the details of his expression. He doesn't seem hurt by the observation, or jealous that Warren knows things he doesn't. It was just a fact.

"He sort of witnessed my last Troy-related breakdown," I admit. Swallowing, I decide continuing to bottle up as many things as I have been probably isn't healthy. Witness my stomach's recent rebellion. "Long story short, Troy and I went out for about half a year. Then he started seeing someone I hated behind my back."

Tod scowls. "And you're still willing to talk to him?"

"Not really." I sigh. "I just took the call so I could tell him to leave me alone."

"Good."

His vehemence strikes me as odd. "Funny you of all people

101

would be so upset on my behalf."

"What do you mean?" He squints at me, then rolls his eyes as he figures that out on his own. "Lyly's never cheated on me. She always breaks up with me before..." He ends the sentence without finishing it, taking a deep breath and making me feel guilty for bringing up his sometimes-girlfriend. "It's a fox thing, Mike. My parents are the same way. They've been together forever, but Dad's only around a few months every two years or so." He smiles a little. "You may have noticed the spacing between my siblings."

"And your mom is okay with it?" I ask, confused by the idea she could be.

He shrugs. "She was. About four years ago, he showed up, and she wouldn't let him in the house."

I snort. "Good for her."

Tod's eyes narrow at me. "Don't judge him by human standards."

"You know, I'm getting so tired of people using their animals as excuses for bad behavior."

Sighing, Tod looks at the carpet. "You just don't understand. Your animal doesn't speak to you yet."

I open my mouth to argue.

"I'm going to dinner," he cuts me off as he stands. "Do you feel well enough to eat anything? Or do you want me to bring you something?"

Considering my condition, I try to decide. "I think I'll come with you. If the smells make me sick, I don't need to be eating."

With a sharp nod, Tod grabs the tea tray and leads the way out the door.

We make it only a few yards before being attacked by a shrill demand. "What are you doing?"

In response to the shrieking, Tod stops, gazing calmly down at his erstwhile girlfriend. "Going to the dining hall."

"You were in her room!" Lyly yells.

Tod's eyes shift to me for half a second. I slink toward the wall, wishing there was room to easily get around the couple and continue on my way. "Yes," he says simply.

"You were in her room!" The declaration is even louder this time.

"Yes." This response is just as calm as the last.

"Alone!"

Tod sighs. Yes, he was in my room unchaperoned. That isn't against the rules here unless the door is closed, which is wasn't. "Do you have a point?" he asks, still calm to the point of being eerie. She sputters at him. "No? Could you get out of the way then? You're blocking the entire hallway."

Taking a very jerky breath, she nods, moving aside to let Tod pass, which he does with a somewhat majestic air.

But as soon as he is by, she jumps in front of me. "You stay away from him, you stinky harlot! You're stupid and you're ugly and you smell like a sewer! You're not half-good enough for him!"

The teapot crashes against a wall.

Lyly spins to stare at it, then to stare at Tod, who is wearing an expression of absolute fury.

"I'll grab a roll later," I say hastily, running back to the safety of my room.

The door shuts on the sound of Tod yelling at Lyly, blocking most of the racket. The rest is drowned out by my renewed retching.

Chapter Thirteen

"It's Aliah?"

The fox in question sticks her head around the door, looking for confirmation that my bid to enter would be extended to her. "I brought some rolls? And a baked potato? And some broth? If you think you can eat any of that?"

One day, I would like to figure out why Aliah has such a distinct tendency to make even the most obvious of statements into questions. My initial assumption had been that she was nervous, but surely she shouldn't still feel shy around me.

"It sounds great," I tell her. "Thank you."

She tiptoes into the room, balancing a cafeteria tray loaded with the aforementioned items, a container of chocolate milk, and another pot of tea. The new teapot is metal, presumably a statement on the fate of the last one to get sent to my room. Which is totally not fair since I wasn't the one to break it.

"Sam and Tod said to tell you they had to leave early for the meeting?" Putting the tray down on the desk, she looks down at it as if wondering what she should do next.

"What meeting?" I get off the bed and walk to where she stands. My stomach cramps, but I don't feel too sick.

"Den meeting?" She looks surprised I didn't know. "Tod's the Father of our little den here, but it's just the kiddie den? He still has to report to the grown-up one every Friday? And let them know what's going on? It's kind of intrusive, but they only do it because they care, you know?"

I pick up one of the rolls and start picking at it as I sit on the end of the bed. "Do you all go?"

"Sometimes." Shrugging, she leans against the desk. "I usually only go on holidays? But we're allowed anytime. Sam goes a lot. She's going to be our Mother when Tod graduates..."

Aliah pulls a hunk of hair over her shoulder and combs it

with her fingers while I eat my bread. "I think my sister's going? But I don't know why?" She twists her hair, frowning down at the carpet. "She's always been uptight, high strung? But she's gotten really unbearable lately?" Her startling pink eyes look up to me. "Tod wouldn't tell us what started the argument today, but I've never seen him so angry with her before? You know why."

Funny. Now she actually does want to ask a question, she made a statement.

I tear apart the last of my roll, focusing on it, rolling it into a little ball with my fingertips. "She was just jealous because he was spending time with me. It's probably good news for him when he calms down."

"Oh."

The syllable is mournful. She doesn't seem to think it would be good for them to get back together any more than I do. Maybe I haven't seen Lyly at her best, but if anyone isn't half-worthy of Tod, it's her. I don't care how gorgeous she is.

"So..." Aliah tugs her finger through her hair some more. "If you need me to take the tray down later, call me?"

"I'd rather you just stay. If you aren't busy."

"You would?" The shock on her face makes me incredibly glad I made the offer.

"If I stay alone any more, I'm going to start moping."

Her laugh is timid and shy, but still beautiful. When she smiles, her whole face changes. All of a sudden, she's at least as pretty as her sister. Not in Lyly's runway sort of way, but in a way that's much more genuine and valuable.

She doesn't say much as we sit in front of my television, but she looks comfortable and content. By the time the *Buffy the Vampire Slayer* marathon we stumble across is over, she's almost fallen asleep curled up on my floor.

Morning comes without me noticing, and I sleep until it's nearly lunch, not emerging from the shower until the kitchen is serving. In a sweatshirt that needs introducing to a washing machine and my most comfortable ratty pair of jeans, I go downstairs expecting it to be deserted.

It is not deserted.

The entire den, minus Lyly, sits in the dining room. And all of them watch me as I enter. Suspiciously, none of them have any food. Meals are made to order on weekends because so few people come into the hall, and the cook on duty today is sitting with the foxes, looking very relaxed.

They try to give me encouraging smiles, but the effect of all dozen of them doing it at once isn't exactly comforting. It's almost exactly the opposite.

My eyes rove over them, looking for a hint of what's going on and coming up empty. "This is like one of those dreams where you have the lead in a play, but you realize on opening night you've never even read the script."

"You're not the one with lines," Tod assures me, nodding to one of the freshmen, who blushes a crimson to match his hair and stumbles to his feet. His sister hisses something to him, handing him a box and an urgent look. "You're doing fine, Nate," Tod whispers, looking toward me.

Except, Tod's lying. Nate is doing nothing other than gaping at me. His eyes are frantic and his lines, whatever they may be, are clearly forgotten.

I smile, trying not to look frightening.

"Michaela Alexandrovna Miasnikov," Aliah whispers to the boy. Relieved, he repeats my full name as several of the others struggle not to laugh. She goes on with Nate echoing her, "We offer you our friendship eternal and our love unconditional. We beg you to accept it. And we hope you will meet us with friendship and love."

"The ring!" someone hisses.

A box is thrust towards me.

Trying not to shake too noticeably, I take the box, opening it to reveal a small gold ring with a fox running along it. It's beautiful. But... What does accepting it mean?

My attention slides up to Aliah. She smiles softly. "You'd be a friend of the den." Her voice is quiet, but steady. There's no hint of uncertainty in it. "It's like being an honorary member."

An honorary member of the den?

I cast my gaze around the gathering. The foxes watch with growing tension as my response time stretches out.

I go back to Aliah. "You all want me to do this?"

106

"The vote was unanimous."

Bet her sister didn't vote, though.

Looking over the faces waiting for my response, I realize how stupid it would be to hurt all of these friends, and myself, to avoid upsetting someone I don't even like.

A grin breaks forth as I take the ring from its little box, sliding it onto the ring finger of my right hand. The fit is perfect.

The foxes clap.

"To Anchorage!" Tod cheers, leaping to his feet.

"What?"

He grins as I squint in bewilderment.

"The elders said they wanted to meet you if you said yes," Sam tells me before aiming a mild glare at her brother. "She needs time to change first though."

"Why?" Confusion mars his features. The eyes that run over me seem completely oblivious. "She looks fine." He smiles towards me. "You look fine."

"Five minutes," I reply, sprinting up the stairs.

Grabbing a pair of corduroys and a clean sweater takes about three minutes. I dash down the stairs slightly ahead of schedule to find Tod sitting at the foot of them, watching the carpet with mild bemusement. "You looked fine," he tells me as I sit beside him.

My reaction is a combination of a laugh and a snort. "Not fine enough for meeting people described as elders."

His head tilts to the side. "But they're family."

Chuckling softly, I shrug. "Yeah, well, I wouldn't let my blood relatives catch me running around in stained clothing, so I don't see why my adopted relatives should get to do it."

A smile spreads across his face before he rolls his eyes. "It must be a girl thing. Sam and Aliah ran to their rooms, too, and they knew we were going somewhere."

I shrug again. "Maybe they assumed I'd say no."

"I thought you were going to for a few seconds," he confesses.

With a soft smile, I shake my head. "And make poor Nate go through all that stress for nothing?" I ask. Absently, I twist the new ring around on my finger. "Why did you make him ask me, anyway? I was afraid he was about to pass out."

"He's the youngest." Eyes on his boots, Tod goes on, "Usually it would have been the den leader, but we figured if I were to come at you with a ring babbling about unconditional love, you would understandably flee into the arctic never to be seen again." He offers me a rueful smile.

"Yeah... Probably..." I laugh. "Because, you know, then I would have been even more scared of Lyly's reaction."

His eyes narrow some. "That's what the hesitation was about?"

"She wasn't part of that unanimous vote," I state with confidence.

"No, she wasn't." His sigh is heavy and heartfelt. "I don't know what's wrong with her. It just isn't like her to be this malicious."

"I know it isn't."

He squints. "You know?"

Shrugging, I look down at the floor. "You love her." I attempt a smile even though the statement fills me with dismay. "So there has to be more to her than what I've seen."

"Unless I'm just stupid."

"Unless you're just stupid," I agree with a series of nods. He's clever, to be sure, but that's not the same thing as smart.

"What do you mean unless you're stupid?" Sam asks, bouncing down the stairs with Aliah behind her. "It's a given you're a moron."

"What would I do without you to keep me humble?" Shaking his head, Tod climbs to his feet, then puts a hand down to help me up so we can leave.

We stop at the town's general store, which is also its only gas station. Tod and Aliah go inside to pick up some snacks while Sam and I put gas into Tod's battered little car. "Is there anything special you want?" Tod asks, walking backwards toward the building, the bitter wind playing with his bright hair.

"I'm sure anything you pick out will be special."

He laughs. "I consider that a challenge."

Grinning, I square my shoulders. "I'm not scared!"

"Hey!" Sam hits the roof with a dull thump. "Stop flirting with my brother and close the door. You're going to let all of the heat out."

There's not much heat in it to begin with, but I close the car door anyway. "I wasn't flirting with your brother."

"Were too."

I consider. Really, honestly, consider the idea. "No."

"Why not?" Her hands fly to her hips, and her foot makes a diminutive stomp. "What's wrong with my brother?"

"Nothing!" In warding, I fling my hands in front of me, palms toward my friend. "Nothing is wrong with your brother!" I pause briefly. "Unless you count his psycho girlfriend."

Sam grins and gives her hair a toss. "I'm just messing with you. We're sisters now, so I can do that."

I start to laugh. Then the hairs on the back of my neck stand up, and my glee dies as I turn my head, looking for the source of my discomfort.

It's not terribly shocking to find Warren watching me, an unhappy expression on his face.

"Be right back, Sam."

She rolls her eyes. "Yeah, sure. Just abandon us."

Smiling, I wave her off and walk over to the wolf. He shuffles as if thinking to leave without talking to me, but stands his ground.

"Warren," I say.

"Michaela," he says.

We blink at each other.

Slowly, he reaches out and takes my chilled, ungloved hand into his warm, ungloved hand. He brings it up toward his face, his touch ever so gentle. My heart races. His thumb rubs against my new ring. "It's pretty," he whispers.

How did he know it was there?

"I'm glad you're feeling better," he says, louder. He starts to move away, starts to drop my hand, but my fingers instinctively latch onto his. I tug gently against his motion of retreat.

"Warren?"

His eyes wide with surprise, he looks down at our hands and then up to in question.

"We're going to Anchorage. Do you want to come?"

The offer is impulsive, but feels right.

Dizziness starts to creep up on me as I wait for his answer

without bothering to breathe.

The corners of his mouth tug upwards. "Are they taking you to the mall or to see their parent den?" he asks.

My thumb rubs against the back of his hand. It tingles. "I'm to be presented to the elders."

"And you want to take a wolf into a den of aging foxes?" There is soft, affectionate, laughter in his voice.

Shrugging, I smile through my nerves. "For all we know, I'm a wolf."

The grin he has been holding back breaks out.

"So?" I prompt.

The grin fades, and I know the answer before he shakes his head. "I can't. I have to stay here and keep my dad from killing someone."

Okay, I knew half of the answer. Is it too much to hope the rest was a joke?

His fingers squeeze my hand. "Good luck though."

"Yeah, you too..."

My hand is suddenly freezing as he moves away with a sad smile and a nod. "See you Monday."

"See you," I repeat, somewhat fuzzily.

He turns, shoving his hands into his pockets and taking a few steps away. He stops and turns, blinking when he realizes I haven't moved. "Michaela?"

"Yeah?" I can hardly hear the word over the blood rushing around in my ears. Or maybe that's the wind...

"You should be wearing gloves."

Gloves?

This time when he turns, he doesn't turn back. At least not before Sam calls me back to the car.

"What was that?" Tod asks with a playful look as I climb into the passenger seat beside him.

"I have no idea." And I'm not being evasive. I have no idea what just happened.

In my pocket, there's a pair of gloves I hadn't thought of before. I pull them out, sliding them on as Tod pulls out of the parking lot.

Warren stands in the doorway to Denali's as we pass by and I raise a now-gloved hand to him, wriggling my fingers in a wave.

The amused smile he gives me warms me more than the extra gear.

The feeling lasts all the way to Anchorage, helped along by foxes who sing merrily along with the satellite radio feed and give me an endless stream of sugary candies.

I try to get them to talk about the den, but all Tod will give me is an annoying, "You'll see."

"They aren't scary," Aliah calls over the stereo. Which means a lot, coming from someone as timid as Aliah. "Don't worry about it."

Still, my insides are a trembling mass of paranoid worry as I walk into a cute little restaurant to find the Mother of the elder den waiting for us in the corner.

Huge windows let in a view of the water behind her, the sunlight reflecting off it with a brittleness that somehow implies cold. The woman smiles at us with Tod's smile, and I give his arm a light smack. "You didn't say your aunt was the den mom."

"She's not," he hisses into my ear. "That's my grandmother."

Sam rushes forward to hug the older vixen, even though they must have seen each other at the meeting last night. Grandma Fox looks younger than I expected, appearing to be closer to thirty than to the upper-side of fifty, where she should logically be, at minimum. Honestly, she doesn't look anywhere near old enough to have an eighteen-year-old grandson. When you get down to it, she doesn't even look old enough to have an eighteen-year-old son.

"You must be Michaela," she greets me, her arm around Sam's shoulders. She's just as short as my friend, telling me where Samantha got her lack of stature from. She smells of cigarettes, the first were I've met who did so. "I'm Emma. And, yes, you should call me that."

Still nervous, but feeling better due to the fact she's so obviously related to my foxes, I hold out a hand to her. "Hi, Emma. Call me Mike."

"Mike." Her smiles widens while she shakes my hand. Her eyes go to Tod. "You're right, I like her."

"Tod was right about something!" Sam exclaims. "Write it

111

down!"

Emma gives her a light smack and motions her to sit. Sitting herself, she turns her smile to Aliah. "It's good to see you, Aliah. How've you been?"

"Alright?" Despite her assurances I shouldn't worry about any of the den, Aliah looks awfully uncertain as she perches herself on the edge of a chair and gives Emma a wavering smile.

"And your family?"

There's a visible wobbling of her posture. "Mom just got a promotion. And Dad's..." She smiles fondly. "He's got a hold of a 67 Mustang GT."

"Really?" Emma laughs and smiles at the waiter as he appears to fill up water glasses. "In good shape?"

"Falling apart." Aliah follows the report with a happy grin.

"Good." The elder nods. "Then it will keep him busy for a while."

There's a short silence. I'm not the only person who is painfully aware Aliah has another family member she isn't mentioning. I'm also not alone in not wanting to be the one to say her name.

Pointedly, Emma looks at the waiter, "Another barley wine, please."

We order drinks, and the waiter goes to fetch them while we read over the food menus.

"I want to speak to Michaela alone," Emma informs us as soon as the waiter leaves again with our meal orders. She grabs her new glass of beer as she gets up. "We'll be outside."

I would rather the others have been sent outside, but Emma isn't the sort of person one argues with.

Frigid air hits us when we slip through a side door into a small stone yard. There's a fountain in the middle of it, completely drained. I wonder what percentage of the year the thing is operational.

Emma lights a cigarette, leans against the edge of a concrete table, and regards me with steady eyes. I don't know how she can stand the smell of her tobacco, let alone the burn of it. The second hand smoke hurts much more than it did when I was human. "How is my grandson really doing?"

Not what I expected her to ask.

112

"I've only known him for two weeks." I sit on a bench near Emma's perch. Upwind of her. She nods and waves me on, smoke trailing behind her hand. "He's hurt. But surviving."

Again, she nods. "That girl..." The words are filled with venom and can only refer to Lyly. "She is..." She sighs instead of finishing. Holding her cigarette carefully between two fingers, she grabs her glass in the same hand and takes a long sip of the dark beer. "What do you think of her?"

"Didn't you order wine?" I blurt, panicking.

A long laugh answers me. "Barely wine is a style of beer, dear. And I'm sure you didn't expect me to give up that easily."

No, I guess I didn't. Sighing, I opt to go with the truth. "I can't stand her."

"Neither can I," she admits baldly.

"There has to be more to her than we see though." I search her face for some clue that she agrees with me, but don't find one. "Something Tod sees..."

She snorts and puts the beer glass down. "Tod's a teenage boy. I know exactly what he sees in her."

Ah... Well... Lyly is inarguably hot. However, "I don't think Tod's that shallow."

Emma doesn't look convinced of it herself, but she shrugs and takes a drag off of her cigarette rather than arguing. "He seems different this breakup," she tells me thoughtfully. "It used to be when they were having troubles, he was depressed. The first time she dumped him, I think he cried for the whole three weeks they were apart." And I'm so sure he'd want his grandma telling people about it. "But then he stopped caring so much. And now, there seems to be an anger boiling under the surface."

I've noticed a hint of that too, but I'm not very comfortable with this conversation, so I don't volunteer my observations. Emma flicks some ash to the ground, her eyes intent on reading my expression.

She takes another swallow of beer before asking a new question. "Do you know why you were invited to join with the den today?"

That's more a topic I was expecting to be broached.

"Today," Emma clarifies. "Rather than after your change proves you're a fox and due admission anyway?"

113

Now that she mentions it, it would have made more sense to wait, even though the odds are severely against me being a fox.

I shake my head. "No, I don't."

"It's because of that girl." She covers a snarl with another puff of her cigarette. "Lyly is bringing a complaint against you."

"A complaint?"

Emma's eyes roll, making her look exactly like an older version of Sam. "She thinks you're a threat to the den's well-being."

"How?" I ask.

"You're sowing contention."

"Bullshit!" My eyes widen as I resist an urge to slam my hand over my mouth, but Emma smiles at the exclamation.

"You are making waves," she states calmly.

"She's jealous because she knows I've been spending a lot of time with Tod. But she hasn't been paying enough attention to know there's nothing to be jealous about."

"Nothing at all?" Emma's voice is quiet, and she watches me very closely.

"No," I whisper back.

She sighs and picks up her beer. "I didn't think so." Despite expectations, she doesn't go on to ask me why not. "But it isn't just Lyly. There are others who are worried about you."

"Why?" What about me could possibly be worrying anyone else?

Emma takes another drink before she answers. "It's your scent. No one can identify it. That makes them nervous."

"And justifies a complaint?" I shake my head. "What is a complaint anyway?"

The cigarette dances in little loops. "A call for action against you."

"Action?" I squeak. I've been shivering for a while now, but now there's more reason for it than being cold.

"We're not wolves," Emma states with gentle calm and an extra pull of nicotine. "No one's going to eat you. If she proved her case, which doesn't take much against a non-den member, it would be more a question of banishment." She tosses the butt of her cigarette onto the ground, crushes it out, then picks it up again so she can throw it into a trash bin. "And, no, we can't send you anywhere. Banishment would just mean none of us are supposed to talk to you. She'll have to do a lot more to prove you're deserving of it now that you're a den member, though. Banishing a den member requires some very serious harm being done. Don't eat anyone, and you should be fine."

Chapter Fourteen

"That wasn't so bad, was it?"

Tod beams at me as we pull away from the party where I was introduced to and welcomed by the parent den.

"No." For being on display for two hours straight, it was remarkably low on the stress scale. "And I like Emma a lot."

Sam pipes up, "Everyone likes Emma!"

I don't know about that. People who find themselves on her bad side probably don't like her in the slightest.

"And everyone liked you," Tod says merrily.

Which seemed true for the most part. A few of them acted confused as to why I was being embraced so quickly and there were one or two people who seemed worried about it. Nobody came across as antagonistic, though. Even the people who were mentioning my scent appeared more curious than anything.

I consider mentioning I know what Lyly is up to. But when I look over at Tod, who has started singing along with the radio like he did on the way in, I find I just don't have it in me to slaughter his good mood.

Snowflakes start to drift down as we drive, and they continue to float down overnight. Despite the fact there has been snow on the ground the whole time I've been here, this is the first storm I've seen. Not that it's much of a storm by local standards. Just two feet of accumulation. The roads aren't even closed.

Sam pokes her head around my door about lunchtime, telling me to get out of bed and come to the rec room for a movie marathon. Obediently, I trudge down, sitting on the floor between Bryce and Seth, letting my friends and the movies lift my spirits.

I can't say why the snow has depressed me. It's not as if I dislike snow. I suppose it just drives in that I'm trapped somewhere far from home. It's not a bad place to be trapped, but...

Drawing my knees up, I wrap my arms around my legs and try not to feel the urge to cry.

"What's wrong?" Seth whispers.

Shaking my head, I concentrate on following the movie. The tears fade into the background as Seth places an arm around my shoulders. Letting myself be drawn against him, I soak up his warmth and his scent, which is part boy and part cat and all wonderful. And I start to feel content again....

At least until the door opens and Warren walks into the room. His eyes fall heavily on me. He nods once in greeting, not smiling even though I smile at him. Then he continues on his way to the stairs, leaving me wanting to weep again, even though I don't know why.

I go up a while later, telling everyone I don't feel very well, even though I doubt they buy it. If nothing else, I'm sure I don't smell sick.

There's a gift basket sitting outside my room: a collection of little bottles from Bath and Body Works swimming in slivers of pink paper. The assortment, which reeks of leopard, comes with a note card. "Please, we beg you, hide your stench."

Interesting. When Seth smells feline, it's comforting and sexy. When Simone does it, it's gross.

I take the present inside, and I use a few of the bottles in the morning. Lavender and rose. No point in letting them go to waste.

There's another gift when I wake up, slid under the door. It's a letter from Mr. Atherton asking me to stop by his office. I assume he can smell the scents when I pop in, but I don't mention anything about them before sitting in my usual seat.

"You wanted to see me?" I ask him.

He gives me the same gorgeous smile he always uses. "How was your weekend?"

"It was all right..."

He nods. "I hear you were adopted."

Holding up my hand, I show off the ring. "Yep. I'm officially a fox."

He studies me for long enough that I start to feel nervous and lower my hand, letting it clasp the other hand and go to my

117

lap. One thumb taps against the other while I wait to see why he's looking at me like that. "What?" I ask when the silence drags on too long.

"I like the foxes. I think they're good for you." He takes a breath.

"But..?" I lead, knowing there's a "but" in the sentence.

"But I'm worried about what the pack will say if you turn out wolf."

My thumb stills as a cold hand grasps at my stomach. "They haven't shown any interest in me," I whisper.

"Not yet," he agrees. "Because you aren't wolf yet. If you are..."

"What will they do?"

He takes his time to answer. "Most likely, they'll force you to chose between breaking with the den or being shunned by the pack."

"Shunned?"

"No one in the pack would be allowed to associate with you," he clarifies.

I bite my lip as I process that. "Would that mean I'd have to leave school?"

"Of course not." He seems confused by the question.

"But if you're not allowed to associate with me..."

Folding his hands together, he smiles sadly. "I haven't been a member of the pack for ten years."

"Really? Why?"

I regret blurting the question as I watch a wave of pain pass over Mr. Atherton's face. It was intrusive and obviously brought up bad memories. And it just wasn't appropriate. I'm one of his students. "I'm sorry. I didn't mean-"

"No," he cuts me off. "It's alright." Leaning back in his chair, he gives me a long look. "The pack is a very controlled society. The leaders have a lot of rights that people raised human can have trouble accepting." His gaze falls nowhere near me, nor anywhere in this time period. "Let's just say they asked for something I wasn't willing to give them."

Maybe I don't want to be with them anyway...

"So, if I'm shunned, I can stay, but the other students..."

"They wouldn't be required to ignore you in class," I'm told.

"But they wouldn't be allowed to socialize with you."

"Not that any of them like me anyway," I mutter.

Mr. Atherton's eyebrows go up. "What do you mean?"

My head shakes. "Nothing."

"Has someone been giving you trouble?" he wants to know.

"No, not really." Warren was sullenly glaring at me through breakfast, but that hardly seems like something to tattle to the principal over.

"If someone does, and you don't want to tell me about it..." he says slowly, his gaze steady. "You could go to Warren. They listen to him."

I can't help it, I burst out laughing.

"What?" Mr. Atherton watches me in incomprehension.

"Nothing." Folding my arms, I lean back in the chair. "Hey..." Something occurs to me as I stare at the edge of the desk, bringing my eyes up to my companion again. "How well do you know Warren anyway?"

Mimicking my pose, he studies me for a while before he replies, "He's my godson."

"Your cousin's kid?" I ask, remembering what he told me about his cousin the day we met.

"The same."

Probably knows him fairly well, then. Maybe well enough to know why Warren seems torn between liking me and barely tolerating my existence. I open my mouth to ask something about that, but Mr. Atherton silences me.

"Let me cut you off before you start," he says. "If you have questions about Warren, then you're going to have to ask Warren."

But I don't want to ask Warren.

Glum, I nod and look down at the desk again.

"Is there anything else you want to talk about since you're here?" Mr. Atherton asks.

With a grunt, I shake my head. Yeah, I'm being bratty, but I can't seem to help it.

We sit in silence for several moments before his phone rings. "I'll let you take that," I mumble, rising to my feet.

I'm through the door before he's through telling me goodbye.

119

There's a vial sitting at my desk when I get to class. Perfume. "Anti-skunk Medicine," a handwritten tag proclaims. I smile. It's not a cheap perfume. Way too much money is being spent on me. And the leopard girls must have devoted the whole weekend to thinking up presents. How sweet.

I try to focus on class, but the teacher is a wolf; and that makes me think too much about what Mr. Atherton was telling me. There's no way I'd turn my back on the foxes for the pack. Which means, if I turn out to be wolf, there's a decent chance I'm going to find myself ostracized from every wolf in school.

Remembering what Warren said about having to stop his dad from killing someone, I hope that shunning really is all they'd do to me.

I wonder if Warren would stop staring at me if I were to be shunned. Or would it only be Nice Warren I'd lose?

My eyes go to his usual spot in the dinning hall when I go to lunch, but I've beaten him in.

As I walk by Simone on my way to my table at lunch, she brings out a can of air freshener and makes a dramatic display about spraying it behind me. Her sidekick Rina keeps her eyes on the ground, but waves her hand through the air like she's shooing away a bad odor as I pass. Maybe she's playing along with Simone, or maybe she just can't stand the aerosol; it's hard to tell.

"What the hell was that about?" Bryce asks me as I sit down. The bear's the only member of my group who is here already. In fact, there are only about half a dozen people in the room period. Were I Simone, I would have waited until later to try to ridicule me. Or maybe waited a few days. Spreading all these attacks on my scent out over a week or two would probably have been more effective than throwing everything at me all at once. It would have made her seem less unhealthily obsessed too.

"Insecurity," I tell him, opening my milk jug with a sharp twist.

"Is it bothering you? Should I go smack them around some?"

I laugh. "Only if you're going to do it anyway. It's not bothering me." Oddly enough, this is true. "It's almost a

120

compliment really. I'm important enough to Simone that my very existence is driving her crazy."

The bear chuckles, a deep and rumbling sound. "I suppose that's one way to look at it." His eyes watch her dubiously though.

Hastily, Simone hides the can in her backpack and kicks it under the table as Seth and Amber walk into the room. Rina stares down at their table, not even looking up at her friends as they sit.

Ah. That's why Simone didn't wait. She has the sense to hide her actions from Seth. And Rina is obviously cowed enough not to tell on her, but Amber wouldn't be.

"Hey, Bryce?" I put my forearms against the table and lean over them. "Do you know why Mr. Atherton was kicked out of the wolf pack?"

"Something about an arranged mating I think."

"Arranged mating? Do you mean what I think you mean?" Staring at him, I marvel how calm the bear is about the concept.

He shrugs. "They figured the world needed more little baby wolves from his line. So they picked out someone for him to mate with. But he was all, 'She's not my life mate.'" His eyes give a dramatic roll. "Not sure what difference that makes. It's not like they were asking him to marry her, just to..." He clears his throat. "You know. Make little baby wolves."

"Yeah..." So he got kicked out of the pack for refusing to breed with the woman they picked out. "Who's his life mate?"

"How should I know?"

I shrug. "Just wondering if his objection was because he knew her."

Bryce shakes his head. "Never been any hint of a woman around him." He stabs his fork into the pile of mashed potatoes on his plate. "More likely he's gay."

That would explain it. And maybe he just didn't want to tell me because he thinks staying in the closet would be healthier for his career. Or it's simply none of my bee's wax. But for some reason, I just don't peg him as gay. And something in his expression earlier gave me the impression he was thinking about someone.

"I can't believe you," Sam proclaims from behind me. "Did

121

you really just imply that the only reason for not doing a random female is homosexuality?"

Bryce shifts a little. "I didn't say he couldn't have met his life mate."

Our friend puts her tray down and pulls out the chair next to mine. "Wolves mate for life," she tells me. "And when the males meet their mate, they know it. Instantly. And don't usually have much interest in anyone else afterward."

"And the woman?" I ask. "Does she know it?"

"Nope. Not fair, is it?"

No... Although I'm not certain who it is more unfair toward, the woman who doesn't know what's going on, or the man, who has no choice whatsoever. The woman can presumably walk away. And in Mr. Atherton's case, may have.

Talk shifts to chemistry when Aliah shows up with questions about our current assignment and when we're done eating, she and I go to the library to work on it some. Because of that, I'm running a tad on the late side for my afternoon class and am the last person to make it to the meeting place by the skate barn. I get there to find everyone staring at the side of building.

Drawing nearer, I realize Warren is literally growling about whatever everyone's gawking at.

The instructor is nowhere to be seen.

Finally rounding the building to get to the point were I can see the main attraction, I stop dead in my tracks.

Written in letters five feet tall are the words, "Micky is Stinky."

"Oh, come on!" I exclaim, appalled. "She can't possibly think that rhymes!"

Warren's eyes snap from the barn to me. "Who can't?" he demands.

A shiver spills down my spine as I look at the wolf. He hasn't seemed this wild since the night I met him. It scared the hell out of me then, and it scares me now.

"Michaela..." He takes a step closer to me. "Do you know who did this?"

If I thought the anger simmering in his voice was directed at me and not Simone, I would die of terror on the spot.

"Someone with no talent for using the English language," I banter, trying to stay calm. "I could think of fifty worse things she could have written, all of which would have sounded better. And that's just on the spur of the moment. If I took the time to actually try to write something..."

He's gotten so close that one more step would have us pressed against each other. His breath is warm on my face, the mist from it floating around my cheeks.

"Warren..." I whisper.

"What?"

"It's not worth being upset about."

"I beg to differ."

I don't know how long we stand there, our eyes locked together and the rest of the world nothing but a curious blur on the edge of my notice.

"Michaela!" the instructor calls, walking briskly in our direction. "Mr. Atherton wants to see you."

My mouth twists. "Someone defames me, and I'm the one getting called to the principal's office."

"Are you going to tell him who did it?" Warren wants to know.

"Probably not."

He follows me as I start toward the building. "Why?"

"I'm not bothered enough to care if she's punished." I shrug. "I'd rather have something to blackmail her with."

"You're going to blackmail this person with the threat of telling Mr. Atherton who she is?" I'm not sure, but I think there may be some admiration in his tone.

"What makes you think I'm not going to threaten her with telling you?"

"Me?" He squints at me.

I laugh. "You're a hell of a lot scarier than Mr. Atherton."

A frown meets the statement. "So you're going to threaten to rat her out to me?"

"Nope."

"You're starting to get annoying, you know."

"Sorry. I didn't ask you to follow me though," I point out. "Or to ask questions."

There's a soft growl. "Who are you going to threaten to

123

tell?"

I give him a soft look. "If I told you that, then I would have told you who's doing it."

His responding sound is one of sheer frustration.

"What are you going to get her to give you?" he asks as he opens the front door for me.

"I don't know," I admit. "But I'm sure I'll think of something eventually." I shed my coat as soon as I step into the warmth of the building. "It's better to have enemies who owe you favors than enemies who don't."

"True."

He goes into Mr. Atherton's office with me, something the principal doesn't bother to comment on. "How are you, Michaela?"

"I'm fine," I answer truthfully, folding my arms lightly over my coat and giving the older wolf a smile. "The barn might need a new coat of paint though."

"So I hear." He smiles back. Leaning back in his chair, he tilts his head as he watches me. "Any idea who would be plastering graffiti on my buildings?"

I could lie, be all, "No, sir." Warren wouldn't narc on me. But somehow I don't think Mr. Atherton would believe me.

"I might," I hedge. After all, I can only prove the soaps and the air freshener stunt. I have no evidence Simone was behind the idiocy with the barn. And even with the soap basket, it would be my word I'd smelled her on it versus her plea of innocence.

"Do you want to tell me who you think it is?"

Shaking my head, I let my eyes drop to the floor. "No, I don't."

There's a few seconds of silence in which I'm certain I'm being studied.

Then Warren makes a movement. "She's handling it."

"Handling it?" Mr. Atherton repeats back to him.

"Much less aggressively than I would."

Glancing at Warren, I catch a slightly rueful but fond smile.

"Alright." Mr. Atherton drums his hands on his desk. "You handle this, Michaela. But if she damages any more school

124

property, I'm going to have to do something."

"I'll let her know."

He nods, waves his hand toward the door. "Get back to class then, Mike."

My wolf shadow starts to follow me out the door, but Mr. Atherton stops him. "Warren, one minute, please."

Warren takes more than a minute to get back to class, though, showing up over half-way through.

It's none of my business what Mr. Atherton wanted to talk about, so I force myself not to ask. Not that I get close enough to Warren to ask him anyway. He seems very content to stay on the other side of the class from me.

Based on that avoidance, I'm surprised when he catches up to me on the way back inside and falls into step at my side. He doesn't say anything and neither do I. My mind tries like anything to give me a line, just one line! But I can't think of a thing to say.

At least not until we get to the building to find a dozen people milling around near the foot of the stairs talking about me. Then I have something to say. "I don't want to talk about it."

"But-" someone starts. The kid cuts off abruptly, literally cowering before the vicious look Warren gives him.

Warren stays with me as I go up to my room, stopping just shy of my door. It wouldn't have surprised me too much at this point if he followed me in, but he doesn't.

"Michaela..." He takes a deep breath and gives me a long look without quite meeting my gaze. "If you change your mind about how you want to deal with Simone... And you want me to do something... Let me know." His eyes finally touch mine. "Please?"

I make myself squint as though confused. "Simone?"

He smiles softly, ironically, and takes a step backward. "Just let me know if you want anything from me."

Turning quickly, he rushes down the hall while I stare at his back.

When did he figure out it was Simone? And is he not going to do anything with that information?

I do my homework and write an email to my parents, not saying anything about the hazing. My stomach argues with me when I try to watch TV instead of going to dinner, so I make my way downstairs, regretting the decision when Lyly pounces on me before I reach the ground floor.

"Mike!"

Astonishingly, there are tears in her eyes.

"You have to tell them it's not me!" she wails.

Coming off of the bottom step, I fold my arms across my chest and regard her calmly. "What are you talking about?"

"I didn't paint that stuff about you! I swear!"

My eyes roll. "I know that."

She blinks. "You do?"

"Yes." I give her a glare. "I know you've been trying to get me disassociated from the den, but this isn't your style."

"You have to tell Tod! He thinks I did it!"

"Oh, gee," I wheedle sarcastically. "Why ever would he think that when you've been such a good friend to me?"

"Mike!" she gasps.

I sigh. "I'll tell him."

Only it turns out I don't have to tell him, because when I walk into into the dining hall, it's to find the rest of the school watching Seth and Simone yell at each other about it.

Exactly one pair of eyes notices when I walk into the room. Warren's. They look at me with quiet sympathy, but his jaw is tense with some other emotion.

Sighing, I resign myself to not having anything I can hold over Simone anymore, and I grab a snack from the student kitchen to take upstairs.

126

Chapter Fifteen

There's another note summoning me to the principal's office when I wake up in the morning. "You rang?" I ask him, sticking my head into the room.

He smiles back. "Good morning."

Sitting in the usual chair, I lean back and wait.

"I suspended Simone," he tells me. "I thought you'd want to know that."

I give a snort of laughter. "And you didn't think the gossip lines would tell me that soon enough?"

"Well..." With a half smile, he shrugs. "I thought I should tell you since I told you that you could do things your way."

"It obviously didn't work," I admit. "I never even had time to try."

Mr. Atherton nods. "As soon as I couldn't deny knowing who the vandal was, I had to do something about it."

"Understood." Stretching my spine out, I yawn. "Anything else ,or can I go get coffee now?"

"No, that's it."

I grab my coffee and donuts in the student kitchen. Warren finds me there and takes a pastry without saying anything. He doesn't do anything other than give me a small smile and a nod of his head before he goes again, but I feel better after he leaves than before he wandered in.

I keep low the rest of the day, skipping skiing in the afternoon and watching movies in Sam's room with her and Aliah in the evening.

Seth isn't in English the next morning, and I realize that I haven't seen him since his argument with Simone, a fact which makes me very nervous. I spend most of the class trying, and failing, to stop myself from darting glances at his empty desk. When the teacher finally dismisses us, I wait for Amber, asking without lead, "Where is he?"

Amber's skin looks eerie against the darkness of her hair. Her eyes are a lot like Seth's, similar enough that seeing them filled with pained uncertainty bothers me. "I am unsure. He left sometime the eve before last."

I shiver. "What do you mean left?"

She shrugs. "He took the car, and drove off without a word."

"And he didn't tell anyone where he was going?"

"No..." Amber sighs. "Or he didn't confide in me anyway." Her lips move into a sickly imitation of a smile. "But he's well. We're twins, so I'd know if he wasn't."

She manages to sound pretty confident about that, but she turns to go up to her room rather than going into the dining room.

"None of you know where Seth is, do you?" I ask my table as soon as I sit down.

The foxes trade looks. Sam shrugs. "If any of us knew, wouldn't it be you?"

"I've sort of been in hiding."

"We noticed," Tod mutters.

"Are you mad at me?" I ask him.

"No!" He shakes his head and looks at me like I'm crazy.

His sister waves her fork around. "Never mind him. He's just upset that it didn't turn out to be Lyly."

Tod glares at her. "Am not."

"Are too," she counters.

He glowers rather than continuing the volley.

"Are you worried about him?" Aliah asks me, ignoring the siblings.

"A little," I admit.

She gives me a sympathetic look. "Sometimes people just need to get away, you know?"

"Yeah."

"Especially males?"

Sam snorts. "Wish more of them would."

"What is your problem?" her brother demands.

She stiffens defensively. "I don't have a problem."

She clearly does, but she won't tell me about it, even when we get ready go ice skating after class.

128

"It's been repainted already," I observe as we come up to the skate barn.

"Of course it has." She smiles. "You thought we'd leave it up there?"

I shrug. "It's awfully cold to be painting. I'm impressed she got the words up there. A whole new coat..."

"It took two," Sam informs me.

"Two?"

She shakes her head. "It didn't take long, though. There were more volunteers to help than there were brushes."

Wow... My eyes prickle with what might be tears.

Sam helps me find a pair of skates to borrow, then Bryce rushes over as I'm putting them on. "You're going to cut yourself," he grumbles, falling to his knees in front of me and helping me into the skates.

"She was fine," Sam contends, rolling her eyes and making me laugh.

"Come on." Bryce holds a hand out to help me up, catching me when I start to fall.

"Okay, maybe fine was optimistic," Sam drolls. She goes to my other side and helps me remember how to walk while balanced on little wedges of metal.

They get me up onto the ice, then pick me up when my feet slide right out from under me.

"I thought you knew how to skate." Sam stares at me, perplexed.

"I do!"

Breaking away from my keepers, I start off, making it around the rink in a way that is very unskilled but which does not re-introduce my still-sore bottom to the ice.

I haven't been ice skating since middle school. None of my friends were serious skaters, and I guess we just decided at some point that we were too old to do it as play. I'd tell the weres about that, but they wouldn't understand. I love that about them.

Gradually, I start to loosen up, and my body remembers what it's supposed to be doing. I can't do the little jumps and spins that Sam's showing off with, or even the surprisingly graceful weaves of Bryce, but I start to look like maybe I wasn't lying when I claimed I knew how to skate.

Just before nightfall, a third of the skaters leave the building.

"Interesting," Bryce drawls.

"Are we missing something?" I ask, slamming to stop against the railing next to him.

The bear shakes his head. "They were all wolves. There's not a single wolf left here."

Sam stops beside us, spraying ice chips around her ankles. "Want to go see if there's any in the main building?"

"No point," Bryce tells her. "We know there won't be."

"So..." I cast around for clues. "They're having a party, and none of us were invited?"

"A meet." Sam bites her lip. "But why in the middle of the week?"

"Something must be going on," Bryce deduces.

"Obviously." I don't think I've ever heard Sam sound so sarcastic towards Bryce before. "But what?"

Bryce gives her a long, hard look. "You are not allowed to go after them."

Sam whimpers at that, but nods. She may be vixen enough to be more curious than Pandora's cat, but she isn't suicidal.

"You don't suppose it's related to what Atherton's doing?" she wonders.

Bryce shakes his head. "Don't see how."

"What's Mr. Atherton doing?" I ask.

"You haven't heard?" Sam squints at me.

"Obviously," Bryce grumbles, grinning at Sam's glare.

"Mom called him this morning," Sam tells me. "He left in a real big hurry after that."

"Why?"

She looks around, then leans forward like she's telling me a secret. "Rumor has it that there's going to be a new girl."

Suddenly, the cold rolling off of the ice starts to get to me. "A new girl?"

Bryce takes a deep breath. "Someone else was attacked near Seattle."

"Who?"

The bear gives me an exasperated look. "Do I look like a

reporter to you? I don't know who. I haven't met her yet."

"But she's probably coming here," Sam adds. "At least, that's what Mom said when I talked to her."

"Oh," is all I can think of to say.

"But I'm not sure how that would tie into the wolves," Sam admits thoughtfully.

I shrug. "Unless they care about events in Seattle."

"They don't," Bryce assures me. "Different pack down there."

"But if that pack is just letting people get attacked without doing anything..." I lead.

The bear grunts. "Then the other local weres will take care of it."

Sam nods her agreement. "Yeah. The bears down there have things under control." She sighs. "Or they did."

Our mood pretty well killed, we step off the ice and get out of our skates. My ankles are sore, telling me that I wasn't skating right after all. I try not to let on about that as we walk back to the main building, even though I feel like I'm wobbling.

Dinner is noticeably wolf-free, but the lupines start to wander in while I'm watching repeat coverage of the latest X-Games event with the foxes and Bryce. None of them say anything, or even acknowledge that they see us sitting in the great room while they walk through it.

"Why are they so quiet?" I ask my friends.

"They're not allowed to talk about the meet," Sam hisses back. "Never are."

After a few more wolves file through, the sound of a small prop engine is heard. Mr. Atherton is back.

I wait for Sam to go meet the new girl like she did for me, but she stays sleepily cuddled next to Bryce. "You aren't going to go greet her?"

"Let one of the wolves do it," she mutters. "They're already up."

"You don't want to be the first person to meet her?" Bryce asks, sounding confused by what is clearly not typical Sam behavior.

She snorts. "Expletive no, I'm not getting off the couch. Mom doesn't like her. That's enough for me. Besides, I don't want to lose my spot."

Tod climbs to his feet. "You're such a brat," he informs his sister before looking to me. "You curious?"

I shrug. "Sure."

Quietly, Aliah gets up and follows us to the door. We wait in the warmth, watching the plane through the window as it pulls into the hanger. The anticipation builds as we wait for Mr. Atherton to walk into view. Weighed down by five massive suitcases, he looks grateful to have us open the door for him. He gives Tod a tight smile. "There's another five in the plane."

"Another five?" Tod mouths to me, aghast. The bags our principal has already wrestled in aren't exactly petite.

A group of freshman wolves wander in. One of them runs out to help Tod. The others hover around waiting on a figure bundled in enough arctic gear to climb Mount McKinley. Er... Mount Denali.

I shuffle to the back of the group, not curious enough to fight over seeing the newcomer. I feel I should be helping Tod, but my boots are up in my room, and I am not running into the snow in my socks. Aliah, her feet likewise unshod, hovers beside me silently, her paleness reminding me of a ghost.

Tod stumbles back inside, his cheeks flushed from the cold and his breathing quick. He carries three bags, each one larger than his sister.

The wolves scurry away before anyone can ask them to help carry anything, suddenly more worried about that than eager to meet the newbie.

The girl pushes back her hood and gives Tod her largest, most becoming smile. Dazzled, he smiles back, not seeming to care anymore that she made him carry heavy things through the cold.

Oh, expletive. What are the odds of the new girl being someone I know? Odds that I not only know her but despise her boyfriend-stealing self?

Feeling my dinner threaten to rise, I turn and sprint up the stairs before Kim sees me.

Turning the corner at the landing, I run toward my room.

...And slam straight into a wall.

"Michaela?"

Why is the wall I ran into talking to me? And why is it using Warren's voice?

"Michaela?"

Oh. Because the wall is Warren. I should have known him from his scent, but I suppose the tears that have blurred my vision are blocking my sense of smell too.

Strong, warm hands grip my shoulders in a hold that is both firm and gentle. "What happened?"

He sounds really, really freaked out, so I make an effort to sniffle my sobs quiet and whisper, "New girl. Kim. From my old school."

My archenemy. The one my friends prefer to me. The one my boyfriend left me for.

"Really?"

That question was way too enthusiastic. I start to sob again.

"No!" Grabbing me tightly against him, Warren strokes at my hair. "I just meant it was an odd coincidence, not that I was happy to hear she's here."

Sniffling is the closest I can come to responding.

"Come on." Shifting so only one arm holds me, he walks me to my room. "Can I come in?"

Managing a nod, I rush into the room. He closes the door behind us. Against the rules, but I don't care.

I sit on my bed, grabbing Leo and clinging to him as Warren sits beside me. "You still have the leopard, I see."

I use Leo's ears to wipe at my face.

"I could get you some tissue," Warren says softly, his voice lilting in mild amusement. Tenderly, he strokes my hair.

Someone bangs on the door a second before Aliah calls my name. "Come in!" I call back. My breathing will not settle down, but I seem to have stopped sobbing for now.

"What-" She stops over the threshold to blink in surprise. "Hi, Warren?"

He grunts at her, his attention still focused my way.

"I know her," I whisper.

"The look of horror when you saw her face kind of made me suspicious?" Aliah creeps further in, leaving the door cracked. "I take it she isn't a friend of yours?"

133

"No," Warren answers for me. Because I can't answer for myself due to the resumed sobbing and trembling and general blubbering.

A timid hand rubs the back of one of mine, Aliah's fingers tender and soft as they stroke me. "It'll be okay, Mike. Whatever she did to you, you're fine now." Warren puts his arm around me, squashing Leo as he pulls me against him. "What did she do to her?" Aliah whispers to him.

He doesn't answer, not even to tell her that it isn't his business to tell her. Wolves are pretty good at not blabbing everything they know.

The door opens again, its creak accompanying Tod's voice, "You would not believe-" he cuts off sharply. "What's wrong?"

"She knows the new girl," Aliah fills him in with a quiet voice.

"Yeah, that would make me cry."

I sniffle, looking up at him. "It would?"

"You expect your friends to like her?" Warren asks me softly.

"They usually do." Misery coats the statement.

Tod tips my chin up, his eyes narrowed with concern. "If it means so much to you that we dislike her, we'll all despise her."

"I hate her already!" Aliah chimes.

Warren squeezes my shoulder.

"What's wrong?" asks yet another person as Sam makes her way through the door.

Aliah answers her. "She's worried we won't hate the new girl."

"That's pretty stupid," Sam jumps onto the bed on the vacant side of me. "Everyone hates her. Which is odd because she smells just like you, but everyone loves you."

Everyone other than Simone. And Lyly. And all the other people who hate me but have never bothered mentioning it.

"She smells like Michaela?" This is from Warren.

"Definitely the same animal."

He curses. "They knew each other in Washington, and they've been turned into the same beast, something no one has ever encountered before." His grip on me tightens.

"Yeah," I sniffle. "She hates it when I have something she

134

doesn't. I caught lycanthropy, so she had to go catch it, too. It's like when I had bird flu."

"Well, she's going to have to find her own friends," Sam says. "She can't have yours."

The blind loyalty is enough to make me start crying again.

"Now look what you did." Tod bumps his foot against Sam's.

Smiling through the tears, I shake my head. "It's okay. This is good crying."

Warren's hand rubs against my arm. "We strongly prefer you not crying at all, you know."

"It's a girl thing," Tod tells him, sounding very much like a guy with sisters.

"You want to go back to the games?" Sam asks.

My head shakes some more. "No... I think I want a bath. And sleep." I look around at my friends, feeling very lucky to have them. "If that's okay."

"Of course, it's okay," Tod tells me.

Warren gives me another squeeze before he lets go of me and stands up.

The world's much less warm and secure than it was a second ago.

135

Chapter Sixteen

I wake up feeling amazingly foolish. For the first time since I've been here, I ignored a call from my dad last night. I hope it doesn't freak him out too much. It's just that I've never been good at lying to him, and I don't know how to explain how Kim's family even knows where this place is, let alone why she'd suddenly show up here. In theory, I could have told him everything except the bit about me being a were-something, but then he'd have questions the were community might not appreciate him asking. I should have just said I had a virus. He'd have believed me on the phone. Probably.

My walk to breakfast is slower than normal. I'm not sure if I'm afraid of my friends being mad at me for causing drama or being disappointed in me for my weakness, but I think the main problem is I'm worried they're going to treat me like I'm fragile now. Emotional and fragile are different things.

"It was accumulated stress," Tod brushes the breakdown off when I try to apologize for it. "You've been through a lot in a really short period of time."

"You were bound to crack eventually," Sam agrees cheerfully, gathering a huge spoonful of Fruit Loops.

Bryce gives me a kind smile. "And the week before the full moon is always rough."

I suppose if Kim were going to show up and wreck my new life, she might as well do it while I'm insane anyway. Maybe that way it won't hurt as much as when she destroyed the old one.

Kim isn't at breakfast, and if she's in my first class, she doesn't come in. I assume she's getting the tour I was given my first day. Part of me is surprised there wasn't a note under my door asking me to see Mr. Atherton about being the new girl's guide. If it was anyone else, I would have been volunteering.

Either someone tipped the principal off, or he's just smart enough to know a personality clash when he sees one.

Kim is present at lunch. She sits at a table with Lyly and a pair of werelions. The leopards are usually there too, but Simone's still suspended, Seth's still MIA, and both Amber and Rina have taken to eating in their rooms all of a sudden.

"Lyly's not going to try to bring her over here when she comes back, is she?" Sam's taking her duty as my friend to loathe Kim very seriously. "Tod?"

Her brother looks up, as if surprised the question was addressed at him. His response waits until after Sam asks the question again, and then it's a bewildered, "How should I know? That's like two weeks from now anyway."

"That's Monday," comes the instant correction.

"Monday?" After a few taps on his ever-present tablet, Tod shakes his head. "A week from Monday. Okay, it's a week and a half then."

Sam raises her eyebrows at me and tilts her head to the side. "Dude..." says Bryce. "She broke up with you a week early, remember? That thing's off."

"Really?" Tod squints at the display. "Oh, yeah. Weird."

Aliah bites her lip, Sam and Bryce exchange a look, and I stuff my face with food to hide the smile that's trying to form. If her sometimes beloved hasn't missed her at all, does that mean there's a chance she won't be coming back?

A girl can hope, can't she?

A few hours later, I'm not sure if it feeds my hopes or dashes them to see Tod smile politely at Kim as she jumps from her seat on the bus to slide next to him before one of us can claim the spot.

Yeah, he's not sitting with, or appearing to think about, Lyly. But he doesn't look too upset over the way Kim's blatantly flirting with him, either.

I start to say something about it to Aliah, who sits beside me staring out the window, but then I realize her earbuds are playing music too loud for her to hear me anyway.

Sighing, I try not to worry about it. Tod and Kim separate as soon as they're off the bus, Kim going with Mr. Atherton to the ski shop and Tod showing no sign whatsoever that he wants to follow her.

I hang out with Aliah on the slopes. She's a lot better than I am, but unlike Sam, she's modest enough she doesn't mind staying on terrain I can handle. Sitting in the coffee shop afterwards, we watch Tod and Warren play in the terrain park.

"You miss your leopard, don't you?"

I shrug. "This is sort of our place. Not that Seth's my leopard."

Gentle laughter answers that. "Of course not. But you do miss him? That's why you're upset? It's not because Kim managed to snag the seat next to Tod on the bus?"

So, she noticed that too.

"Well..." I sigh. "I can't say that has me all thrilled either, what with Kim's history of messing with guys I care about and with Tod's complete idiocy concerning pretty girls."

"Yeah," Aliah agrees softly. "How can someone so freakishly smart be so terrifyingly stupid?"

"I have no idea." Shaking my head, I tap my fingers against the side of my mug. "But I'm more worried about Seth right now. I know everyone says he's just off thinking... But I have this incredibly bad feeling about it."

"Like how bad? Have you had any visions?" Aliah leans forward expectantly while I blink at her.

"Visions? No..." I run a finger around the top of my mug. "A couple of bad dreams though. Last night, I dreamed he was locked away somewhere dark and something was about to happen."

"But you didn't know what?"

I shake my head. "Only that it was bad."

She makes a thoughtful sound.

"I'm sure it's just my imagination."

"Maybe?" She sounds even less convinced than usual.

"What, do weres usually have a lot of visions?" I feel compelled to ask.

"Not a lot..." She shrugs. "Sometimes our animals know things they can't explain to our human parts? And when they tell us, it's like it's something metaphysical?"

Nodding, I think about that. "Human dreams are similar. But, no, I think they're just telling me I'm scared. Letting me

138

visualize things my conscious mind would label crap and ignore."

"Maybe," she whispers. "Still... I would pay attention to them, you know? Just in case?"

"Yeah... Just in case..."

I'm thinking about that when I fall asleep. But even if the dreams I have are somehow real, they aren't helpful. I just see darkness and pain. Violence. Anger. The idea it could be real terrifies me, which I'm sure is why I'm having the dreams.

He's just taking a vacation, that's all....

I wish Kim would take one, even though she just got here. My luck at avoiding her wears itself out Friday afternoon, when she appears at the edge of my hunting and tracking class. Scowling at the other students, probably because they're freshman, she stands several yards away from any of them, shifting whenever someone looks like they might possibly try to address her.

But then Warren appears, and suddenly she does want to talk.

She runs up to him, brandishing a broad smile. Meeting the advance with a polite nod, he stops and waits expectantly. Her hand reaches out to touch his arm. Something rumbles deep in my throat.

Warren takes a half step backward, freeing his arm. As Kim's hand drops, he glances towards me.

Quickly, I look away.

Claws break through my gloves.

Gasping, I look back toward Warren. He's laughing and bouncing on the balls of his feet. He shakes his head and then starts to walk in my direction. His stride is very nearly a skip.

Cursing at myself, I turn to hide my action, then bend my neck to slide my ruined gloves off of my hands with my teeth. Frantic, I shove both the gloves and the clawed hands into my pockets.

"Hello, Michaela." He sounds more chipper than I have ever heard him sound.

"Warren."

A long, wolfish laugh responds to my uncivil growl. "You're in a bad mood." He looks down at me with sparking eyes, his

139

mouth twitching as it curves.

"And you're not," I observe dryly.

"Nope." The grin wins its battle to appear. My narrowed eyes do nothing to daunt its enthusiasm. "Michaela..."

Presumably, he was going to say something after that, but class starts. When the instructor tells Warren he's going to be tutoring Kim along with me, his humor flees.

"I told him not to do this," Warren hisses at me as the class breaks into its assigned groups. He makes like he's going to go deal with the issue, but I grab his arm.

"Where are your gloves?" he demands in a rough growl.

"I lost them." And thank God I've managed to lose my claws now too. "But I'm fine with Kim joining us. Hiding from her just gives her more power over me."

The wolf watches me for a few seconds, then nods with approval. "Alright."

He takes his gloves off and hands them to me. "Wear these though."

They slide on loose. They're are several sizes too large for me, big enough there's a chance they'd fly off if I were to wave my hands around in the air, but they're full of comforting warmth – warmth from their fleece and from Warren's heat clinging to them. They're a lot warmer than the pair I just slaughtered.

Warren ignores Kim as she comes up to us, instead filling me in on the day's objective without bothering to explain what we're doing to her.

If it wasn't cold enough my tears would freeze, I'd be tempted to cry. I wasn't expecting him to be so unwelcoming of her. That he is being this much of a jerk is incredibly sweet of him.

He wasn't exactly friendly to me on my first day either, but thinking back on it, all that comes across more like shyness now. This... This is what Warren's like when he wants to be antagonistic. He doesn't say anything out of line, but the looks he gives her makes those early sullen glares he used to give me seem like cheerful overtures.

It all slides right over Kim though, who continues to bat her eyes at him and purr her stupid little lines. Warren may well be the first guy she's met who wasn't instantly crazy about her, and it confuses her too much for her to even process it.

"I'm cold," Kim whines for the twentieth time or so, sidling towards Warren, clearly angling for him to share some of his body heat with her. He counters the move perfectly, almost as if they're dancing. Dancing some sort of dance that keeps him a perpetual ten feet away from her, with me between them the whole time.

Inside Warren's gloves, my fingers wiggle. They aren't quite warm enough to make me not relate to Kim's complaints. It's one of the coldest days we've had since I've been here. I'm not altogether certain it's safe to be outside.

I wonder, if I were to bat my eyes at Warren like Kim is doing, would he put his arm around me?

More likely he'd just laugh. I'm sure I'd look like a wounded bird, or possibly a deranged otter.

"Is that what we're looking for?" I ask, pointing a finger of Warren's glove at some markings near a fallen tree.

He smiles proudly. "Yes."

"Those gloves are way too big for you," Kim sneers.

"I know." I smile sweetly. "That's what I like about them."

Warren chuckles and moves closer to the tree. "These-" he starts, only to be cut off by a loud burst of harsh, antagonistic, laughter.

"You're growing fur, Mike!"

Forgetting about the animal tracks, Warren whips around to face me. "And ears," he says with as much awe as Kim's taunt contained disgust. "You must be shifting to try to keep warm."

Wincing, I guide my hands to my head.

Sure enough, inside the hood of my parka, big, fuzzy ears sprout from my hair. Hair which has a completely different length and thickness than usual.

"That is so hideous!"

"Actually..." Warren inches towards me with an intensity sharpening his gaze. "They're beautiful ears." His eyes meet mine. "Wolf ears."

"Wolf ears?"

The panic must have come through in my voice, because Warren's face shuts down and he turns to start stomping back towards the school.

"Warren!"

He stops, looks back over his shoulder, and raises his eyebrows.

"It's not that I wouldn't like to be a wolf. I'm just..." Turning all the way around, he watches me closely. "I'm just afraid of the pack. Silly, right?"

With a deep sigh, he shakes his head. "Not really. They aren't exactly the sort of family you're used to." He takes a step back towards me, but is stopped by Kim's body as she flings herself in his path.

"But you'll keep them from hurting me, won't you?" she simpers.

Warren's lip curls back. "Why should I?"

Kim gasps at the effrontery, and I'm certain my eyes are about to pop out of my head.

The wind shifts, a new blast of cold causing my fur to spread further over my exposed skin.

Sweet Jesus, I must look like a complete freak.

Warren frowns. "What's that scent?"

Kim screams and bolts towards the buildings.

I look after her in confusion, then turn back to my remaining companion. "I don't look that bad, do I?"

Warren narrows his eyes at me. "You look fine. It's impressive you can do that already. Most of us who were born weres can't." But his attention isn't on me, his eyes are roaming around the forest and his nose is actively sniffing.

Taking a deep breath, I try to figure out what he's concerned about. I turn. I sniff the air. And I know what has Warren on edge. My knees weaken, and it's suddenly hard to breathe.

"Male," I whisper. Forcing a swallow, I move closer to Warren. "It's a male whatever I am."

Warren starts to curse.

Nausea sweeps over me, and I bend over by a tree, supporting myself with a hand against its trunk while I lose lunch.

"Michaela?"

Why am I always puking in front of him?

142

"I'm fine," I gasp. "Just a really strong scent."

Except I realize it isn't that strong. It's just that permeating. It reaches straight into the core of me, clenches its fist, and twists.

"Come on," Warren urges, putting an arm around me and turning me back toward school. His walk increases in pace until we're jogging through the snow.

Without stopping for longer than it takes to open a door, we go straight to Mr. Atherton's office.

The principal smiles at me. "Nice ears."

"There's an intruder," Warren jumps to the point. "And he doesn't smell like anything I've ever smelled."

Mr. Atherton's face stills. "What do you mean?"

"She's says it's a male..." He trails off, not knowing a word to use.

"He's whatever I am," I finish weakly, moving away from Warren to lean against the back of one of the chairs.

"Where is he?" Mr. Atherton asks swiftly, on his feet.

"We caught the scent about half a mile south," Warren responds.

"Take me."

They're heading out the door before I can turn around.

"Not you," Warren snaps as I try to fall in with them.

"Excuse me?"

With an aggrieved sigh, he looks to Mr. Atherton, who backs him up, "Stay here. We don't know how dangerous he is yet."

Dangerous?

My stomach heaves again. "If he's dangerous, why are you going?" My eyes are on Warren.

"Because he might be dangerous," the wolf replies, with a bit too much amusement.

Mr. Atherton rolls his eyes. "Please, Michaela. Just stay here until we know what's going on."

Not liking it, I nod.

Then they're gone.

With an aggrieved sigh, I retreat to my room to brush my teeth and start a shower. Scalding water and several little bottles of body wash try valiantly to get the scent of the male out of my nose, off of my skin. They fail.

Still feeling somehow dirtied, I leave the bathroom to pull on a pair of freshly cleaned sweats. The fabric softener's gentle aroma should make me feel better, but it doesn't. I retrieve Warren's gloves from out of my coat pocket, sticking my nose inside one in an attempt to catch his scent. Finding it comforts me some, so I lay on the bed and concentrate on allowing the wolf scent to remove the memory of the other's smell.

Someone knocks on my door, and I pull my nose out of the glove to tell them to enter. Feeling silly and probably blushing, I stuff the gloves under my pillow.

Tod, Aliah, and Sam slide into the room. "You alright?" Sam asks. "Warren said you were totally freaked."

Aliah pours me a cup of the tea they brought with them. "Another of Emma's?" I guess.

"Chamomile." Tod holds his head to the side as he studies me. "Calms the nerves."

I take a sip of it. My nerves do not instantly calm. In fact, they're getting worse. Trying not to get more upset, I put the cup on the bedside table. At that point I lose the battle to act like a sane person, and I rush forward to fling my arms around Tod as I bury my face against his chest.

"Mike?" He wraps an arm loosely around me, his other bring his hand to stroke my wet hair.

"I can't get the smell of him out of my head." The statement is a whimper.

"He smelled like a normal fox to me." Sam puts a hand on my shoulder, brushes her fingers against my neck.

"No," I sigh. "He smells like... like everything and nothing."

I feel Tod nod. "That's a good way of phrasing it."

"That's what you smell like, Mike," comes Aliah's soft voice. "Pretty much?"

I whimper. "How can you stand me?"

Tod pulls away so he can look down at my face. "They're not saying it's a bad smell. Just unusual."

Aliah puts her hand on my shoulder. "It's like a blended perfume to someone who's only smelled flowers."

My whole body starts to shake. "No. It clings and ravishes. I feel violated just having smelled it."

144

Very still, Tod searches my eyes. "Almost like being raped by a scent?"

"Yes!"

Tod moves away completely, giving me over to Aliah so he can go to the door and call for Warren and Bryce. Aliah wraps her arm around my waist, letting me lean against her shoulder while Sam reaches out to hold my hand.

The boys whisper quickly to each other at the door, then Warren starts swearing and walks into the room, Bryce following him with a bemused expression.

"What?" Sam asks, not patiently.

Bryce shakes his head and answers slowly, "If this guy were a she, I would say it sounds like she's in heat."

"Males don't go into heat?" Aliah states.

"No," Warren agrees.

"But that's exactly what it sounds like," Tod finishes unhappily.

Chapter Seventeen

My evening is spent curled beside Bryce in front of the television in the lounge. The smell of polar bear is much more to my liking than the scent that continues to plague me when left on my own.

Warren went into town to fill the pack in on what's happened, and Tod likewise journeyed to his grandmother's house. Bryce's clan is based too far north to be involved in anything as local as our mystery beast.

It seems unfair for me to cuddle up to Bryce when I'd really be happier next to one of the others, but he doesn't seem to mind being used as an olfactory distraction. And Sam doesn't even act like she minds sharing him, watching me with huge, worried eyes right up until the time I close my door on her to try to sleep.

My dreams aren't exactly untroubled. I stumble through snow-coated forests, freezing while I try to avoid being tracked by creatures I can't identify. Bad things are happening, just outside my field of vision. I hear the attacks, know what the sounds mean. Warren... Tod... Seth... Bryce... One by one, all die trying to keep me safe.

It's a relief when the clock finally tells me it's late enough to get up.

I make it downstairs before the dinning hall opens and go into the student kitchen. My fingers gradually shred the donut I pick up without putting any of it into my mouth. I got it out of habit, not because I'm actually hungry.

"You don't look so good," Warren tells me, going straight for the coffee on arrival and for once ignoring food.

"Thanks," I mutter. "You have such a way with compliments."

The smile he gives me in return is small and exhausted.

"You learn anything last night?" I ask.

Leaning against the counter, he stretches his feet in front of him and stares down at his boots. "Nope." He shakes his head. "No one's ever heard of anything like this."

"Like me, you mean."

He sighs. "Yeah."

"Has anyone talked to Kim?" I ask.

"Atherton did. She says she doesn't know anything."

Which doesn't mean she doesn't know what's going on, just that she doesn't want to tell an authority figure about it. "Maybe you should try."

His eyes slide up. They're tinted with red, implying he slept even less well than I did. If he slept at all.

"She likes you," I justify.

There's a ghost of a smile. "No. She's just under the mistaken impression you do."

Mistaken impression? Awfully early in the day to be starting a fight, isn't it? Or am I supposed to flatter him at this point? It's too early for that, too.

"That's ridiculous," claims a new voice, insanely chipper for the time of day. "You're completely unlikeable, wolf."

Warren's mouth twists into an approximation of a smile for Sam as she breezes into the room. The vixen instantly takes command of our attention with her typical dramatic flair.

"Why are you eating in here?" my friend asks me. "You aren't hiding, are you?"

"Dinning hall's not open yet," I point out, earning myself a confused look. My eyes go to the clock on the wall. "Oh. Guess I've been here longer than I thought."

Sam grunts, her eyes focusing on Warren for a second, as if she's blaming him for me loosing track of time. "Well, come on," she urges me. "I haven't grilled Tod about last night yet."

Standing up, I look at Warren, but since he pushes himself away from the counter like he's coming with us, I don't don't bother to say goodbye to him.

Without a word, the wolf follows us to the dining room, grabbing the extra chair without anyone commenting on it.

"So..." Sam waves a hand at her brother, then grabs a handful of bacon off of his plate.

"So, get your own food," he tells her.

Sam rolls her eyes. "What happened last night?"

"Nothing." Glaring down in annoyance, he jabs his fork into the pile of eggs in front of him. "No one has a clue." He glances at Warren. "Wolves?"

Lips pressed tightly together, our token wolf shakes his head.

In the doorway, I see Kim hesitate on entry. With her hair untidy, her face lined from lack of sleep, and her complexion pale with exhaustion and worry, she looks almost like the little girl I used to know. The one I was friends with. My hand starts to rise, to wave her over to my group.

Then her eyes see me watching and her expression changes, a bitter hatred tightening her features. Lyly can pull off looking beautiful through an expression like that, but Kim can't. On her, it's just ugly.

"Do you think she knows something?" Sam asks me.

"I don't know." I sigh. "It's not like she'd tell me if she did."

And she doesn't tell anyone else either, or the grapevine would be on it in a heartbeat as rumors fly all day.

We have something new to talk about by nightfall though.

Shortly after dinner, Aliah and I stop on our way from the rec room to upstairs to watch one of the most sophisticated women I have ever seen waltz into the building. Without so much as blinking in our direction, she approaches Mr. Atherton's door with the practiced ease of a runway model, not bothering with knocking before she enters the room and closes the door behind her.

"Who was that?" I ask, awestruck.

"Seth and Amber's mom?" my companion offers.

My eyes snap to her, then back toward the principal's office.

It takes self-control to walk up the stairs instead of placing my ear to the door, but I manage.

Aliah leaves me alone, citing an essay she needs to write. If she were Sam, I'd tease her about doing homework on a Friday afternoon, but if she were Sam, she wouldn't be doing it.

Trying not to obsess over Seth, I sit down and type an email to my dad. It feels absolutely fake. There's just so much of my life I can't share. Not that I ever told him all that much before I

148

became a were, or anything. It's just I used to keep things private out of choice. Being literally unable to tell Dad about vast and important chunks of my life feels unnatural and restrictive.

There's a pounding on my door just before I hit send, preceding Sam running into the room by about two seconds.

"Guess what happened to Seth?"

Images from my dreams flash through my thoughts, but I shake them off. They were just dreams. Seth wasn't ripped apart by a wild animal. Not in real life. "What?"

"He's challenged Simone's dad! I always thought he would, since the alternative's marrying Simone, but-"

"What?" I blurt over her story.

"They were betrothed when she was born. You didn't know?"

Uh... No! He described her as a foster sister, not a fiancée!

I shake my head and motion for her to go on.

"Anyway, the only way out of it would be to challenge her father to combat. Which could be lethal, but being dead is better than being married to Simone. I always figured he'd wait longer though. Gain more experience. Let the guy get old and frail. Simone's dad is supposed to be the most powerful leader the leopards have had since moving to this country."

Ice terror clutches at me. "Is he alright?"

"Well, yeah, they haven't fought yet. Simone's parents are in Europe right now, and it can only be done under one of the spring moons anyway." She plops onto my bed as my heartbeat starts to return to normal. "But he made a formal declaration when he was gone."

"He's back?" I ask.

"Almost. His mom was here to make sure he's allowed to come back."

She seems oblivious to how annoying her incomplete answers are.

"Why wouldn't he be allowed back?" I prompt. No one has said anything to imply he could be expelled for running off like he did. The general attitude appears to be that it's better to let people get away when they need to than to trap them here until they explode into violence.

149

"He's on probation from the family," she tells me in a bored voice, sounding like that should have been obvious.

By family she doesn't mean his parents and sister. It's what the leopards call their community. Just one of the ways the group is like the mafia.

"Why?"

Sam squints at me, then remembers I was born human. "He's challenged his alpha. Until that's resolved, he isn't part of the group anymore."

Oh. Okay... "But what does that have to do with school?"

"Seth doesn't have any money," Sam tells me. "The car belongs to the family, the same people who've been paying his tuition. If he stays, he'll have to be on scholarship like you."

Scholarship? That must be what Mr. Atherton meant when I said I was here courtesy of a trust.

"So why's he doing this now? Why not wait?"

The vixen on my bed gives me a lopsided look. "You tell me."

Her meaning is pretty clear to me. "I didn't have anything to do with it."

Her smile mocks me. "Of course you didn't."

It's a subject that keeps me up most of the night.

The reason he had that last big fight with Simone was because of me. If it hadn't been for that argument, wouldn't he have continued to put off breaking his engagement?

And it's not just the sudden lack of money he has to deal with. There's the pesky little issue of upcoming mortal combat.

He'd have to do it anyway, even if he'd never met me. But would he have waited until later?

I hide in my room the next day, crawling deep under the covers and whimpering in answer to Sam coming in to invite me to go to Anchorage with her and Bryce. I stay there until I'm hungry for lunch, then make myself a sandwich in the student kitchen before heading to the library.

When I leave a few hours later, a half-read novel in my hand, piano notes welcome me to the hallway.

It's a familiar tune. The one Seth was playing last time I heard him.

Standing in the doorway, I wait until he's done. Just like

150

last time. Then I clap, grinning as he looks over at me. He doesn't act half as startled this time though.

"Good to see you." I walk into the room, my eyes surveying Seth's face. He's more relaxed than he ever has been before, though his answering smile is tired.

"Good to be seen."

Timidly, I sit down beside him, touching a few keys with my finger tips. "I was pretty worried about you, you know."

"Sorry." He looks down at the keyboard. "I needed to clear my head space."

"So I heard."

His fingers dust along the keys. "Rumor has it, there's a new girl."

"Yes," I answer slowly, not pleased with the direction he moves the conversation, although the beautiful dance of amusement in his eyes in response to my tone makes up for a lot.

"Rumor also has it you don't get a long with her too well."

"You could say that," I acknowledge. "Lyly adores her though. And I suspect Simone will think she's just awesome."

A dramatic shudder follows this. "So, was it hate at first sight or do you know each other from before?" Yeah, I knew he'd ignore the opportunity to shift the subject to Simone.

"We've known each other since third grade." I sigh."And we've been fighting since sixth, when her dog bit me and had to be put to sleep. As if I'd wanted the dog to die. Or to bite me. Or for people to see it happen. It's not like I ran crying to the adults about it or anything."

"Hmm." He tilts his head, his hair swaying softly with the motion. "Does this mean she's a dramatic clue to deciphering your past? Since she was there through it all?"

"Deciphering my past?" I chortle. "She was a part of my pre-Alaska life, if that's what you mean."

A lazy smile plays on his lips, lights his perfect eyes. "What was your life like before here?"

"Boring."

"Boring?" He leans backwards, folding his arms as he gives me a crooked look. "That's it? Just boring?"

I shrug. "Yeah, pretty much. I went to school, spent way too

151

much time in the mall, and hung out with people who I thought were my friends, but who probably weren't." The black keys dance together, blurring to cover up much of the white as I stare at them. I spread my fingers out, letting them blend into the pattern. "I mean, I've had exactly one phone call and maybe a dozen emails from them since I left. They don't seem to have noticed I'm gone, and I don't miss them much either. I've only been here three weeks, but there are already so many people I'd miss if I left..."

My eyes drift to Seth, and I'm hyper-aware of the heat he gives off beside me. He's looking at my hands, his breath paused.

"Yes, you're one of them." I smile.

His eyes slides up to mine. "My insecurities are that obvious?"

"Sometimes."

He looks down again, saddened for some reason.

I lean toward him. And I kiss him.

Pulling back in surprise, he blinks at me. Then he pulls me forward, and he kisses me.

Our mouths come together, lightly then more firmly. His tongue brushes against my lips and they part so my tongue can reach out to meet it. My hands grasp his shoulders and his hands run along my hips. Then something shifts...

And now we're still trying to kiss, but we're laughing too hard.

"We should have done that as soon as we met," Seth says.

"Yeah," I agree. "Then we would have known it wasn't going anywhere."

We grin at each other.

"At least we can say we tried," he tells me, sweeping a chunk of my hair back behind my ear.

Turning, I fold my legs on the bench and just look at him for a while.

He's still beautiful beyond words. So why wasn't I more into kissing him?

"Can I ask you a question?"

He plays a quick series of notes. "Shoot."

"What's with your hair?"

152

Slowly, he turns his head to stare at me.

I shrug apologetically. "I was scared to ask before."

"And now you're not?"

"Nope." It's hard to explain why, but I guess it boils down to me figuring that if we can get past me throwing myself at him, we can get past just about anything.

He looks at me for a few seconds before asking, "What about my hair?"

Without me telling them they have permission to do it, my fingers reach over and stroke through the hair in question, which is so, so soft. "I love your hair," I whisper.

Clearing my throat, I force my hand to my lap. "But everyone else thinks it's..."

"Weird?" he suggests. "Disgusting? Repulsive?"

"They're not that upset by it." I take a breath. "But, yeah, they think there's something wrong with the coloring. Which has always made me wonder why you flaunt it." My fingers jerk as I struggle to hold them still. "You're not the kind of guy to be telling them to take their prejudices and screw themselves with them. So what are you saying?"

"Maybe I just don't care what they think."

"Maybe." Biting my lip, I tilt my head and watch him look back at me. "Except you're awfully insecure about it."

He plays a few moments worth of music while he thinks about his answer. "I don't want to be insecure about it. I'd like to learn not to be." He smiles faintly. "But, really, if I'm telling anyone anything, I'm talking to my sister."

"Amber?" I haven't picked up on any sibling rivalry between them. "She harasses you about it?"

"She harasses herself about it." He gives me shrug. "Her hair's exactly the same as mine. She dyes hers."

Oh. "So you grew yours to tell her there's nothing wrong with her being the way she is?"

"In a nutshell."

Something inside me goes all squishy, and I suddenly want to cry. "That's so sweet, Seth."

He shakes his head. "If I'd really been looking out for her, I'd have gotten rid of Simone a long time ago."

"Hey," I reach out to grab his hand. "As I heard it, it took a

153

lot of guts to do it now. You wouldn't have stood a chance when you first realized you needed free of her."

His laugh is self-deprecatory. "True." He takes a deep breath. "Of course, I'm not sure how much of a chance I stand now."

Shivering, I swallow and try not to feel all the fear that statement summons. "Can you back out?" I ask.

"No."

"Then you can't think like that, or you'll poison yourself."

His mouth twists. "Are you telling me to believe in myself?"

I smack his shoulder. "Yes."

He sighs dramatically. "Alright then. I'll keep a positive outlook."

"You do that."

I stand, stretching a little.

Something catches the corner of my eye, and I turn toward the door, running several feet forward in alarm as the scent of what I'm seeing hits me.

"Seth!"

"What?"

Quickly, he's behind me.

My arm reaches out to point. "Please tell me that isn't blood."

He lets out a breath and when he walks around me, there's no hint of tension in him. "Yeah, it looks like blood."

The fact there is a pool of blood laying in the doorway doesn't bother him in the slightest.

With a light hop, he moves over it and into the hallway, his nostrils moving as he smells the passage. "Can't tell who it was," he says. "Too many people come through here, and I don't think this person stayed very long."

"Seth!" I protest his easy tone. "Someone's hurt."

"Not very hurt." He shrugs and frowns thoughtfully at the blood. "Probably a small cut. Maybe a shallow stab wound."

I gape at him. How can he be so uncaring that one of our classmates is injured?

"If they needed help, they would have made noise," he tells me.

Well... I guess that's true. Whoever it was just stood calmly

154

bleeding well within earshot of us. Sure, we were distracted, which would be why we didn't notice this person anyway, but we would have noticed someone saying, "Excuse me, I appear to be bleeding. Could you help?"

"I'll go get something to clean it," Seth offers, still completely nonchalant.

"I'll help," I tell him, even though looking at the spill is making my stomach do all sorts of unpleasant things.

The leopard shrugs and walks to the nearest bathroom to grab a spray bottle of lavender-scented cleaner, a sponge, and a bunch of paper towels.

Taking some of the paper towels, I blot at the floor, feeling my face go pale as I watch the dark liquid spread across the towel. Some of the warmth touches my hand, and I nearly gag.

"You okay?" Seth squints at me in concern while he presses down with his own handful of towels.

"I've never cleaned blood before."

He smiles softly. "Whoever it belonged to is okay," he assures me. "People are just weird this close to the moon."

Weird enough to bleed in strange places? Or to make other people do it? In silence?

Tossing his towels into a plastic bag, he leans over and pries mine from my hand. "You're not ready for this, kit."

"No," I admit, wondering if I ever will be. Or if I would want to be.

Standing quickly enough to send little light bursts across my vision, I take several steps backward, trying not to look at the reddish pool despite the fact that my eyes keep going back to it. "I'll see you later," I blurt, turning and literally running away.

Good grief. Seth must think I'm a complete wuss.

I don't stop running until I get to my room, though.

There's a gift bag sitting in front of the door, and I laugh at it, thinking someone has picked up where Simone has left off. There's no way that sort of thing is going to get to me right now.

But when I bend over to pick it up, I realize the bag doesn't smell like Kim or Lyly like I thought it would. It smells like wolf.

There's no card, but when I move aside the tissue paper

155

and see my gift, there's no doubt in my mind who left it. Even without his scent, it could only have been him.

I was wrong about whatever was in the bag not being able to get to me. This reaches deep inside of me and squeezes something, bringing tears to my eyes.

"Thank you, Warren," I whisper, pulling the plush wolf free of the bag and pressing it tightly against me.

Chapter Eighteen

Monday is decisively lacking in Warren.

Sunday was too, but it didn't click in my head he had disappeared because I expected him to be with his parents in the day.

But then he's not at breakfast or lunch Monday.

Still, I don't get seriously concerned until he fails to turn up for class in the afternoon. "Where's Warren?" I ask one of the freshman wolves.

The kid shrugs stupidly, shaggy brown hair falling into his face. "Dunno."

None of the others are any more informative.

I go by Warren's room after class, but he doesn't answer when I knock. His scent isn't terribly fresh in the hallway either.

"Mr. Atherton?" The principal looks up from his desk as I stick my head around his door. "Do you know where Warren is?"

I don't want to snitch on him for ditching class or anything, but a lot of people are seriously worried about the prowling whatever-we-are, so now isn't exactly an auspicious time to be disappearing.

"Yes."

Blinking several times, I wait.

"Is that all, Michaela?"

I stare at him. "Where is Warren, Mr. Atherton?"

The older wolf gives me a steady look. "I'm not at liberty to say."

Not at liberty to say? What, is he on a secret mission?

"He's safe, though," he assures me. "You don't need to worry about him."

You know what would get me to worry less? Knowing where he is.

But no one I corner has any clue where Warren has gotten

off to. "It's nearly the full moon," Bryce soothes at dinner. "This is not the first time someone has had to run away for a few days during a moon and been perfectly fine."

Staring at Warren's usual table, I poke at food I have no appetite for. No one else is worried. Maybe I shouldn't be. But how do I stop?

The worry coats my waking thoughts, keeps me from being able to finish the simplest of my assignments. It keeps me up for hours, then gives me new nightmares where I'm hunting a wolf, but can't find it anywhere.

My eyes go straight to Warren's table at breakfast Tuesday, but it's just as empty as it was on Monday.

My friends trade concerned looks and talk gently around me, although no one says anything directly about my mood or about Warren's continued absence.

I'm not the only person in a strange funk this morning, but we're outnumbered by people who thrum with new energy. Tonight is the moon.

The schedule is different on days of the full moon. It's only at night that young shifters are forced to change. Older weres generally do, but can usually control it if changing form would be inconvenient. If they put enough effort into it, mature weres can go for as long as a year without succumbing to the need to change, which is the only way a female were can hope to carry a child to term. However, tensions are usually high and people tend to be tired. So there are no classes for the next three days.

There is a ski trip this morning though, and I trudge from breakfast to the bus.

It isn't until after Kim and Lyly file on board, glaring towards me with all of their might, that my thoughts take a break from obsessing over Warren to let me realize today is Tuesday. Or, more specifically, that yesterday was Monday. Or, even more to the point, that something important was supposed to happen on Monday.

"Tod?"

"Yeah?" The fox looks up from from his tablet, which he's using to play a game with his sister, who sits beside him.

"Today's Tuesday, right?"

"Yeah." He squints at me. "Why?"

"No reason. Just checking." I turn to face the front again, hiding my grin from him.

Beside me, Aliah's eyes have gone wide. A smile spreads across her face, bringing a pretty sweetness. She nods at me when she sees me looking over, and she's dancing with the mountain as she rides the snow on our runs. There's a playful joy in her motions today, lending her a most unusual and high-flying form of grace. Watching her is like seeing someone with paralyzed legs suddenly rise and start performing the lead from Swan Lake. The word 'amazing' just isn't strong enough. I can only wish the moon affected me like it's affecting her.

After a morning of cold and activity, we return to the nice warm school for lunch and then have the afternoon off to rest up. Most people, even the suddenly giddy Aliah, go to their rooms to nap, although a few gather in the rec room to watch movies. I decide to play detective.

Trembling, I creep into the boys' side of the living area, a story prepared about how I need to ask Tod a den question should anyone catch me. It's not Tod's door I ease through though. It's Warren's.

The room is remarkably neat, with very few personal touches. That strikes me as sad. He's been living in this room for four years, it should have more of him embedded in it even if he is only here during the week.

I glance through the drawers of his desk, finding nothing but old essays and exams papers. The book shelves are bare save for a few books, mostly texts and nonfiction. The worn Stephen King novel tossed negligently on the nightstand doesn't have any bookmarks with convenient notes or addresses on them. Nothing under the bed, not that I thought there would be. Nothing helpful in the trashcan like there would be if this were a film.

I spend about half an hour nosing about in Warren's things, but don't learn anything I didn't already know. He didn't even leave his laptop for me to try to hack into.

With a dispirited sigh, I get up to leave.

Before I open the door, something catches my eye.

The sweatshirt, left uncharacteristically balled up behind the door, doesn't strike me as a clue. Unless you were wondering which college football team Warren sides with, in which case you'd now know it's the University of Alaska's. But it does smell of Warren.

Thinking about Aliah's belief that I should be having visions if people close to me are in trouble, I fold the shirt over my arm. Maybe if I have something with his scent to focus on, I'll be able to open a psychic link to him, or get my subconscious to pay attention to details I already have, or something. It can't hurt to try.

Going back to my room, I curl up on my bed, Wolfgang, the wolf Warren left me, hugged to my chest and Warren's dirty sweatshirt under my cheek. Closing my eyes, I let his scent envelope me, hoping I'll be sucked into a vision that will let me know what's going on.

The only thing I wind up sucked into, though, is sleep.

When I open my eyes again, it's an hour until moonrise and a strange new vibe thrums through the building.

Walking into the dining room is like passing into a wave of excitement and power. The energy is raw, tense, and intoxicating.

My steak seems bloodier than usual, its flavors more vibrant. The red of it pops out against an otherwise gray world, reminding me of the special effects in the film *Sin City*.

"Just think," Sam chirps, "after tonight, we'll finally know what you are."

I shiver, not sure I want to know.

"You'll be fine." Tod gives me a gentle smile, and I nod in response.

I don't want to talk about my change. Or think about it too much. I've been doing a pretty good job of not thinking about it until now, not allowing myself to feel the fear that nibbles at my insides or the panic that makes it harder than it should be to breathe.

Warren's not at his table. Not that I expected him to be.

Lyly's here, but she's not sitting with us, thank goodness. I think we're all too grateful of that to ask Tod about it and risk him remembering to get back together with her. Assuming, of course, the problem's that he's forgotten about her. Surely if he simply refused to take her back, he'd have told us, right? So we could stop wasting brainpower worrying about it? Unless he's doing it to give me something other than changing and Warren to ponder.

The meal is over far too quickly, and I find myself walking through a bit of a haze down to sickbay, where Mr. Atherton is waiting with the counselor Becky and the school nurse.

The nurse's office is a little strange. It has the usual tables and collections of needles. It has the same diagrams of body parts that were in my old school's medical rooms and the same little charts about common illnesses. It has a few beds, for students who are too sick to stay alone in their rooms. None of it's unusual.

No, the odd thing about this sickbay would be the cages.

There are three of them in a line.

I've been briefed on what to expect tonight. I'll be locked up, but only as a precaution. The first turn is usually more stressful than the others, and a lot of people react with high levels of violence. Therefore, it seems safer for everyone if my first change occurs in a controlled environment. Particularly when we don't know if I'm going to change into a vole or a saber-toothed tiger.

"You ready?" Becky asks, sounding excited.

"Don't have much choice," I mutter, walking past her into the first of the cages. As cages go, I suppose it isn't so bad. The bars are strong and daunting, and the door closes with an ominous clank. But the bed I plop myself onto is soft and the comforter is fluffy.

"I hope I don't try to become a woolly mammoth," I tell the adults. "Because I don't think one of those would fit in here."

"I don't think you're a mammoth," Mr. Atherton tells me with a smile.

I start to smile back, but then remember I'm mad at him for refusing to tell me where Warren is. "Is Warren still okay?"

He nods.

"And you still won't tell me where he is?"

He shakes his head while Becky gives him a curious look he ignores.

"If I do become a mammoth, I'm going to squish you."

The mumbled threat makes him smile.

My eyes go to the window, and I wonder how much longer I have to wonder what's going to happen to me.

"Just a few minutes," Becky answers the unspoken question.

We wait in silence. Sitting there with people watching me, eager to see what I'm going to do, makes me feel like I'm in a zoo, waiting for the keeper to show up and run me through a series of tricks.

The moon rises.

I don't see it. It's behind the trees. But I feel it deep inside of me. So do my observers; I see it in their tension.

My limbs start to tingle, my senses heighten. Every little sound becomes enormous, every flicker of light a painful sun.

Mr. Atherton turns the lights off, and I whisper a thanks. The whisper sounds like a shout. The blood in my ears becomes a torrent of noise. The creaking of the walls is a riot of sound.

Pressure builds inside me.

And builds.

And builds.

And then bursts.

Leaving me sitting on the edge of the bed, feeling perfectly normal.

The adults look at each other. They look at me. No one says anything.

"Sorry," I whisper. "I don't think we're going to have a show today."

"What happened?" Becky asks. "You were shimmering... Then... Nothing."

My mouth twists through a surge of irony. "Maybe I'm a werehuman."

Her eyes widen as if she's considering the idea.

"You're certain it's been long enough?" the nurse verifies.

"Yes," Mr. Atherton answers her.

The nurse nods thoughtfully. "And her scent was doing something."

"What?" Mr. Atherton demands.

"It sort of shifted too. To a series of things. Bear, wolf, leopard, lion, fox... Something I couldn't identify."

"Might have been woolly mammoth," Becky offers, sounding serious.

"And how do you feel now?" the principal asks me.

I shrug. "Fine. Normal. Kinda confused."

He meets the last admission with an understanding nod. "You're not alone. I've never seen someone not change on their third moon." He looks to the others, and they shake their heads.

Becky tilts her head. "I don't understand how you could control it when you can't control your partial shifts."

The nurse makes a light snorting sound. "I still don't understand how she's making partial changes before her third moon to start with. I've never heard of anyone doing that. Let alone a kid too young to partially shift at all."

I didn't realize the skill was quite that rare, although Warren had hinted it was. "Can Kim do it?"

Mr. Atherton's eyes narrow. "Where is Kim?" he asks.

We all shake our heads. "Go find her," Becky is ordered. "But be careful. It's possible they shift on earlier moons than we're used to."

"No," I tell him, as Becky sprints off. "I was paying attention last moon. I didn't change."

"And the one before it?" he asks.

I shrug. "Okay, I don't remember that one."

I'm not sure if Kim is on her first or second moon, but she looks just as human as I do when Becky leads her into the room a few minutes later.

They put her in the middle cage and she lays down straight away, turning her back to all of us without a word. She doesn't bother to answer when she's asked how she feels, just tenses and huffs.

Whatever.

I trade shrugs with Mr. Atherton. He doesn't look hurt by Kim's response to his concern for her well-being.

He turns on the room's TV, finding a marathon of ancient Star Trek episodes that no one objects to watching.

I fall asleep around midnight, as Kirk rips his shirt fighting a guy in a lizard costume, and wake up to find the TV off and Kim already gone. My door is open, so I walk out and go upstairs, happy to find it's still breakfast.

163

"So?" Sam asks, not waiting for me to put my tray down on the table.

Sitting, I sigh.

"That bad?" Tod asks. "Tasmanian Devil?"

A tiny smile forms on my lips. "No."

"Poodle? Mouse? Guinea Pig? Please tell us you're not an insect."

I laugh. "No. Nothing like that." Not looking at anyone, I sigh again. "Nothing at all actually. I didn't change."

Not looking at them doesn't mean I don't know they're all staring at me. "You didn't change?" Tod repeats. "At all?"

"Nope."

"How is that possible?"

"I have no idea." There are tears in my eyes. Stupid eyes.

Aliah reaches over and rubs my hand. "You've done things you aren't supposed to be able to do yet before. Like the ears Friday? Maybe you subdued it without meaning to? Maybe because the nurse's office just wasn't a good place to change?"

"Yeah," Bryce supports the concept with eagerness. "That could happen. I hate that room. My bear wouldn't want to play in there."

Everyone nods now. "Maybe we just need to get you outside," Tod concludes.

"Maybe." Should the idea should make me feel relieved or distressed? I realize I'm looking at Warren's spot while I think about it and give myself a mental slap.

I stay behind with the ice skating crowd today rather than going with the skiers. Bryce gets me into some hockey skates and starts teaching me some new movements. Sprinting back and forth is distracting. I work up a sweat and manage to forget to worry about Warren for thirty straight seconds at least a dozen different times. But when I stumble out of the shower, exhausted, before heading down to lunch, the wolf is the only thing on my mind. I hug his shirt tightly, focusing on his scent and trying to summon an image of him, but there's nothing.

For a moment, I consider wearing the shirt, but shove it under my blankets instead.

I mean to go to lunch, but I fall asleep in the few seconds I let myself curl up on the bed, launching quickly into an awful dream.

Warren stands in front of me, bleeding. It was his blood in the hallway Sunday, spilled by the beast that took him away. He tells me to leave, begs me to flee. With a snarl, he turns, accepting the attack of a fierce wolf. The wolf knocks him over, mauls him with its claws, bites at his throat.

The beast's teeth sink into Warren.

Blood is everywhere.

I leap out of bed before the dream fades, going straight for my shoes. My hands are trembling as I tie my laces. Sprinting, I return to Warren's room.

He isn't there, but I notice something, something I saw last time without understanding what it meant.

I grab his truck keys, and I run to the garage.

Chapter Nineteen

I curse when I spot the truck sitting in its usual spot. I was hoping to be wrong about that. Why couldn't the keys in my hand just be his spare set?

If Warren left without his truck, doesn't that imply something is wrong? Seriously wrong? Mr. Atherton is acting like there's nothing to worry about, but is he just sparing me?

My parking job at the end of my drive into town, during which I stall the truck's manual transmission only three times, is not the best the lot behind Denali's has ever seen, but I leave the truck near the rear entrance, where it's unlikely anyone who doesn't work here will be inconvenienced by it. Taking a deep breath, I open the door and step into the biting cold, letting it fortify me for the task at hand.

The bar is warm and deserted save for a bored-looking woman reading a magazine behind the bar. "Where's Warren?" I ask without preamble.

The woman doesn't look up, just points towards a door marked, "Private."

Ignoring the sign, I open the door and walk up the flight of stairs it reveals.

The stairs dump out into a living room. A battered brown couch, two reddish recliners that have seen better days, and very nice television sit amongst handmade wooden tables, dream catchers, and a vast assortment of forest-themed paintings.

Classic heavy metal comes from behind an archway, and I follow it into a kitchen that was obviously decorated in the nineteen seventies and not touched since.

At an olive green stove, stirring a pot of something, stands a very shirtless Warren.

Well, obviously, he's fine. His throat has not, in fact, been ripped out. There's is not a single mark on his back save for a tattoo of Celtic knotwork on his shoulder blade. He's even singing.

About half a heartbeat before I run away, he turns.

"Michaela?" Holding a large wooden spoon, he takes a step closer to me. "What are you doing here?"

A blush rushes over my cheeks. "I was worried about you."

"I'm fine."

Nodding, I feel like a complete looser. I recognize I should be relieved, but there's too much humiliation for me to feel happy about Warren being safe and healthy.

"You could have called, you know." He steps back again, leans against the counter, and folds his arms across his bare chest, the spoon lying against one of them. There's a hint of amusement in the creases on his face, but his eyes are distant. "I have a phone. Seth even has its number."

"And it's probably in the student phone book, huh?" I stare down at the ground to keep myself from staring at Warren's partially hidden pectorals. "I'm sorry. I wasn't thinking."

"Michaela?" The concern in his voice causes me to realize I'm shaking.

"I had this dream," I blubber. "This wolf ripped your throat out. And there was blood all over the place. And Mr. Atherton said you were alright, but he wouldn't tell me where you were. And then I found your truck sitting in the parking lot, so I was scared, and-"

Suddenly, Warren is wrapping his arms around me, pressing me against his bare skin. I stop trying to talk and concentrate on trying to remember how to breathe. His scent flows into me, comforting but, at the same time, making me struggle all the more to figure out how my lungs are supposed to work. "It's alright, Michaela. I'm fine."

A few moments of trembling later, I finally relax enough to draw a normal breath. My arms slide around Warren, hugging gently back. My eyes are closed as my cheek presses against his chest and I let myself swim in his warmth. His heartbeat is fast, but its deep timber comforts me. Warren is fine.

He pulls away from me. "I think I need a shirt."

I think he doesn't, but I don't argue.

His room here is nearly the opposite of his room at school. He doesn't have piles of dirty clothes and old dishes on the floor, or anything. The room is still clean, but the adjective 'cluttered' springs to mind. Three walls are covered in shelves, which are crammed full of books and wooden carvings. The carvings cover everything from kittens to the Grim Reaper. The books include a wide selection of fantasy and horror novels, a decent collection of graphic novels, and a full section on wolves and werewolf myths.

He appears to have the complete works of Stephen King, Neil Gaiman, and Poppy Z Brite. The entirety of Laurell K Hamiliton's Anita Blake series. And... I find myself grinning inanely. He has a whole shelf of Sherrilyn Kenyon.

"Okay, I'm not going to give you a hard time over Anita Blake, because she's fairly violent and from what I've been told, the later books are fairly pornographic, but the Dark Hunters series?" I turn as Warren drags a long sleeved t-shirt over his head. It's a shade of blueish gray that seriously sets off his eyes, a fact that distracts me from what I was saying.

Warren raises his eyebrows. "What about it?"

What about what? Oh, yeah.

"Well, those books are pretty solidly in the romance genre."

He pulls a pair of boots from under the bed. Apparently he's decided if he's going to get dressed, he's going to get all the way dressed. "Your point being?"

"Well..."

"It's a stereotype that only women read romance novels." He quickly ties a lace and moves onto the other boot. "Sherrilyn Kenyon has an interesting take on were-culture. It intrigues me. Even if she is incredibly sentimental and optimistic."

"Romances wouldn't be much fun if they were realistic."

He smiles sadly at his boot. "No, they wouldn't be." Standing abruptly, he leaves the room. "Are you done invading my privacy yet?"

Sheepishly, I follow.

In the kitchen again, Warren turns off the stove, his eyes narrowed at the overcooked oatmeal on it. Shaking his head, he takes the pot from the stove and dumps its contents into the trash with a dull bang on the bottom of the vessel. "Is whoever brought you waiting down stairs?"

"Whoever brought me?" I mimic mindlessly.

"Yeah. Seth? Tod?"

"Me."

He runs the spoon around the edge of the pot, dislodging the last of the ruined oatmeal. "You?"

"Yeah. I sort of borrowed your truck." Pulling the truck keys from my pocket, I hold them up with fingers that are suddenly tingling from lack of blood circulation.

"You borrowed..." The pot slams down hard in the sink, the spoon hurled angrily after it. Flames in his eyes and his nostrils flaring, Warren bears down on me with long, hostile strides, a growl in the back of his throat.

"I'm sorry," I whimper. "I-"

"Michaela!" Fingers dig into my arms, bruising the flesh. "It isn't safe for you to be out alone! What the hell were you thinking?" My teeth rattle as he shakes me.

"I was thinking you were in danger!" I yell back.

He stills. His next line is a whisper. "Even if I were, you should have gotten someone to come with you."

He sighs and walks away.

He picks up the pot again, then starts to scrub it. "Do you like oatmeal?"

What? Oatmeal? I rub my arms sulkily, but answer, "Sure."

"Good. I'll try not to burn this batch."

"You do that," I grumble.

Stopping, he looks at me for several long moments, until well after the point were I start to feel ashamed of my churlishness.

"I'm sorry, Michaela." He makes his eyes meet mine. "You scared me."

"You scared me first," I whisper back.

Nodding, he acknowledges that with solemnity. "I know. I'm sorry about that too."

"Why did you do it?" I ask. "What's been going on with you?"

In answer, he turns away again and puts the pot on the stove, starting the water to boil.

Okay. Not going to tell me. I could try harder, but I've already forced my way into his home, being even more invasive

169

would be wrong.

"Could we have apples in it?"

He squints at me, then a look of relief skirts over his features. "Sure." Grabbing one from a bowl on the counter, he tosses it to me. I'm a bit worried when he gets out a knife that he's going to throw it, too, but he slides it along the buttercup yellow counter instead. It stops exactly on target, right in front of me.

"Are you going to ask me about last night?" Carefully, I start to peel the apple, preparing it for dicing.

Warren sighs. "Don't have to. Mom called the school this morning. She wants to know what it is the pack is hunting."

The fruit knife moves slowly around the apple. "The pack is actively hunting the male whatever-I-am?"

My companion gives me a slow nod. "He's been slaughtering livestock, breaking into barns in human form, and then eating what he lures out." His lip curls in revulsion. "Not even eating all of it, letting most of the animal go to waste."

I can't tell if he's more disgusted by the stealing or the waste, but his repulsion is clear.

"So you left school for a while so you could help your pack find this monster?" I guess. So maybe I'm not willing to let that go completely...

He shrugs, not meeting my gaze.

"What are you going to do to him if you find him?"

"Do you remember when you invited me to go to Anchorage, but I couldn't because I had to stay here and defend someone?"

Coming to the end of the apple skin, I consider tossing it over my shoulder to see if it spells out the name of the man I'm going to marry like the old wives' tale says it should, but I drop it quickly in the trash instead while I answer Warren's question. "Yeah. I wasn't sure if you were joking or not."

He gives me a pained look. "Not."

"Alright." I take a deep breath. "So you didn't want your dad to kill this guy..." Angling the knife, I start to cut wedges.

"He'd taken a chicken."

"A chicken?"

Warren nods, taking the apple slices and starting to dice them into a small bowl. "It was his third chicken, but he'd never

170

taken anything more noticeable." He gives me a long look. "His crime wasn't so much that he had taken the birds. The crime was doing something that could draw unwanted attention to our kind."

"Right." I nod my understanding. "But a chicken here and there wouldn't draw much attention, would it? The farmer would just think a fox had gotten in or something, right? Or a the mundane kind of wolf?"

"Right. Or maybe the chicken had escaped. Even if he thought it had been stolen outright, he'd have no reason to think it was a were."

"Okay." No longer having a task to perform, I put my little knife in the sink. "But your dad wanted to kill him anyway?"

"No, not really," he says, weary. "But some of the pack did, and the rules were on their side."

I shiver. "So you had to defend the guy so it looked like your dad wasn't going against the will of the entire pack?"

Warren nods and puts down his knife. Picking up a bottle of cinnamon, he shakes some powder out onto the apple before putting the bowl in the microwave and going to check on the oatmeal. "Right."

"Did it work?"

"He was sent on a Trial." Stirring the pot, he glances at me to see if I understood that word. I shake my head. "He was sent into the wilderness to try to survive alone for three days. He's the one who first smelled the Mystery Beast."

"Mystery Beast?"

Warren shrugs. "They didn't know to call him the 'whatever-Mike-is' when the pack first started talking about him." A teasing smile is flashed my way before he turns serious again. "Although I'm not sure why not. They'd been told about you, that no one knew what your beast is because your scent is different to everyone and females always say they've never smelled anything like it. I was pretty sure you were connected; I just hoped I was wrong."

"Why?" I ask softly.

Warren looks down at my hand on his arm. When did I put that there? "Why what?"

"Why..." I move my hand away, wondering what possessed

171

me to put it there in the first place. "Why did you hope we weren't connected? People don't think I have anything to do with the dead animals, do they?"

"I don't think anyone seriously thinks that, no." Watching the pot closely, he stirs the oatmeal some more. "Would you get the apples?" he asks as the microwave dings.

"Would I get the apples?" I mutter under my breath, going to get the apples despite resenting the way my companion likes to evade questions. Telling myself I'm being unreasonable, that he doesn't actually owe me answers to anything, I open the door to the microwave. The bowl is hot enough I drop it almost as soon as I touch it. Drawing my sleeves down to act like oven mitts, I pick it up again and take it over to Warren, who doesn't seem to notice how hot it is when he picks it up.

Silently, he mixes in the apples and then divides the cereal into two bowls, putting mine on the table for me rather than just handing it over. He puts his in front of the chair furthest from mine, then pours two glasses of milk, stirring chocolate syrup into mine.

"Thank you." I smile when he brings the milk near, but the expression falters when he ignores the hand I hold out for it and puts the glass down on the table instead. Is he trying to avoid the possibility of touching me? Considering that he was pressing me against his naked chest not half an hour ago, that's kind of strange.

But then, what about Warren isn't strange?

The silence as we eat isn't exactly an easy one, although its not as uncomfortable as it could be.

"It's good," I offer, but he meets it only with a quiet thanks.

We're both finishing up when the door from downstairs bangs open. "Michaela!" Mr. Atherton's voice storms into the kitchen. Then Mr. Atherton himself storms into the kitchen. "You did not have permission to leave the school."

Permission? Since when did I need permission? "My understanding," I state calmly, and as officially mature as I can manage, "is that as long as I return at a reasonable hour, my movements are unrestricted."

Warren informs me in a grumbling, gravel-filled voice, "That was before something interested in hunting you moved into our territory."

"Precisely." Mr. Atherton glares down at me, and I realize his anger was based on fear. "Do you have any idea how worried everyone is about you?"

I blink. It hadn't occurred to me people might be upset to find me missing.

"No, you don't, do you?" Shaking his head, Mr. Atherton lets out a not-so-gentle snort.

The sound rankles, and anger tightens my spine. "If you'd just told me where Warren was, then maybe I would have been happy to stay locked up!"

"That wasn't his fault," Warren interjects quickly. "I didn't tell him he could tell you, so he didn't know I wouldn't mind. Besides, I wasn't hard to find. Would have been even easier to find had you remembered how to use a telephone."

"Mike..." Mr. Atherton sighs softly and squeezes his eyes shut for a breath. "I'm sorry I made you more worried about Warren than you needed to be. The fact remains, though, that if you honestly felt a need to search for him, you should have taken others with you. At least half the school would have done it in a heartbeat." He shakes his head at me. "Hell, I would have brought you down here if you'd just asked me."

"You wouldn't tell me where he was." I squint at the principal, thrown more by that one little curse word than by his blustering. "Why would you bring me to him?"

Mr. Atherton shrugs. "Simply giving you a lift to a place you specified wouldn't be betraying a confidence."

Wolves. Will I ever understand them?

Warren clears his throat. "You need to be going if you're going to make it back before moonrise."

"You aren't coming with us?" I ask him. The question sounds like half of a plea.

Warren shakes his head.

I get up, trying to keep my head from drooping but failing. "Well, thanks for the food. Sorry I bothered you... and scared everybody... and all."

"Michaela?"

Warren's watching me with a quiet expression. "I'll be back after the moon."

Nodding quietly, I decide not to wonder why that comforts me so much.

Chapter Twenty

Mr. Atherton doesn't speak to me on the way home from Denali's. Which is fine. I don't want to talk to him either.

When we walk into the building, I'm instantly faced with a glowering version of Tod. With Mr. Atherton's cell phone, I called him from the car so he could tell people to stop freaking out over me. He didn't sound very happy then, but the disgruntlement in his voice had nothing on his expression. Aliah stands beside him. She gives me a teeny smile of welcome, but Tod himself only narrows his eyes. His arms are folded moodily in front of him, and the manner in which he leans against the wall is far from nonchalant.

My head dips, and a whimper threatens to voice itself as I start to understand exactly how upset my den father is with me. The feeling of worthlessness goes beyond what I would expect to feel for distressing a friend. This is closer to how I felt when Dad walked into the school office back in Washington.

"Tod, we have finished this discussion," Mr. Atherton states firmly.

"No," the fox replies, just as firm. "We have not."

So... A flicker of hope tries to come to life. Was Tod not staking out the door to get a chance to lecture me before I go to my cage? Is it Mr. Atherton he's so angry with? My eyes go to Aliah, hoping she'll give me a clue, but she's watching the carpet too closely to notice my questioning gaze.

Wearily, the principal sighs. "I know she's one of your den children. But she's also one of my students."

"That doesn't take precedence."

Under an intense, hostile glare from someone who outweighs him by at least a hundred pounds of pure muscle in human form and turns into much more impressive beast, my favorite reynard squares his chin and refuses to budge an inch

175

from his position.

"She's not going to change in a cage." Tod's voice remains calm, although his eyes are another matter. "We all know that."

"We don't know for sure."

Tod and I just look at him. Aliah shuffles her feet, clears her throat, but doesn't say anything.

"If she doesn't change this month, we'll try your idea next moon," Mr. Atherton offers.

"But it's not just a matter of learning what I am." Shaking a little, I enter the conversation. It is about me, after all. "The wolves have no idea what they're hunting."

Catching the look Aliah gives me, my stomach rolls over in misery. "The parent den's involved in the search too?" I ask her.

She gives me a solemn nod.

Stupid foxes. They're supposed to be oh, so clever. Shouldn't they be smart enough to leave the dumb, potentially dangerous stuff to the wolves?

"They have to know," I tell Mr. Atherton. Turning to Tod, I ask, "What's your way involve?"

"You changing," he states simply, his eyes on our principal.

They glare at each other as I look to Aliah. She takes a quick breath. "You go outside."

"Alone?"

Her head shakes. "No, but with a smaller audience? Because we don't know if it was the room or the company?" Her eyes start to go to Mr. Atherton, but then fall to the floor.

"I'll be with you," Tod tells me.

Aliah opens her mouth, shifting Tod's glare to her. Her eyes wide, she closes her lips again with instant obedience. "No," he says to her. "Just me."

Miserably, my friend nods.

"We don't know what you're going to be," Tod explains to me. "Or how dangerous you'll be."

Mr. Atherton nods. "Which is precisely why I can't go along with it."

Shivering, I rub my arms and try to think. "If I'm going to be a danger to people..."

"You're not," Aliah whispers. "They're just being over-protective."

176

Tod glowers at her, but doesn't bother to debate the issue.

"This isn't up for discussion," Mr. Atherton declares, motioning me toward the sickbay cages. "I'll leave you alone, but I can't leave you free."

But when he places me in the cage and closes the door, his hand hovers over the lock... which he leaves hanging open.

I stare at his back until he's out of view, then stare at the open lock. He saw me to the cage, then put me in it. No one can say he didn't. But he also very clearly had no intention of trying to lock me up.

Tod and Aliah are exchanging harsh whispers in the foyer when I get back to them. Aliah squints at me. "What happened?"

"He put me in my cage," I tell her. "Then I left it."

No need to say in as many words that he meant for me to do that. Everyone will think it, but I wouldn't want people to try to prove it.

"Well..." Tod pushes off the wall and gives me a grin. "Let's go then."

"Where?"

"Courtyard?" Aliah answers. She lets out a breath and looks to Tod. "You still have the rifle?"

He shakes his head fondly. "Now who's being overprotective? I thought she wasn't dangerous."

Pink eyes roll, then focus on me. "Good luck?"

"Thanks."

She swallows. "I don't think he needs the gun, you know? Because if I did..."

"Yeah, yeah." Tod moves toward the door. "You'd be scared of what my sister would do to you if you let me get mauled." He waves her off. "Stop worrying so much."

She meets my eyes before I turn to go, but I'm not sure what I'm seeing in them. The color is so strange, it makes reading emotions hard.

"We'll be fine," I tell her, accepting her nod as agreement.

She slumps up the stairs as Tod and I leave, going to the stables to pull a rifle from hiding. "What are you doing with that?" I ask.

"It's just a precaution."

I snort. "Yeah, but where did you get it?"

"Oh." He gives me a faintly sheepish smile. "Aliah took it from the supply cupboard earlier today."

"You had Aliah steal it?" I stare at him as he shrugs and leads me back outside into the dimming evening.

"We borrowed it." He walks to a bench that I suspect plays the part of a table in warmer months. It sits about halfway between the school and the kennels, under a huge pine tree that keeps some of the snow off it although Tod still has to brush several inches off. After clearing enough space for both of us, he sits down and takes out a box of bullets that look like little syringes.

"What are those?" I ask.

He glances at the bullets, as if checking to make sure. "Tranquilizer darts." He grins. "You didn't think I was going to aim something lethal at you, did you?"

"The thought had crossed my mind," I admit dryly.

His head shakes as he slides darts into the weapon. "It's just a sedative mixed with a tiny amount of silver to make it work on a were."

I blink. "The silver thing's true?"

Slowly, he nods. "Yep. The silver thing is true. You may have noticed, no one here wears any." He snaps the casing closed. "But there's not nearly enough in here to kill you. It would just knock you out and leave you with a migraine."

"Yippee."

He laughs at me. "Do I need to point out this is only for the off chance you're trying to kill me?"

"Kill you?" My cheeks go from cold to frozen.

Tod rolls his eyes. "I don't think you're actually going to."

"Oh, I don't know." Heavily, I sit beside him. "You can be awfully annoying sometimes."

"Thanks."

My eyes on the horizon, I wonder how much time I have until the moon rises. "What if I don't change tonight either?" I whisper.

My companion reaches out to take my hand. Since I haven't been able to replace my good gloves yet, I wear my backup pair. They're too thin, so my hand really welcomes being held. "It won't be the end of the world, Mike."

178

Nodding, I try to accept that. Tears prick at my eyes though. "But what if someone dies because I couldn't tell them what that creature out there is?"

"That's a pretty big if, kit." Tod gives my hand a squeeze. "And it's not your fault if you don't change tonight."

I nod again. It is not my fault if I'm too stupid to do something that everyone else does instinctively. Right... "And you'll be alright?"

He smiles softly. "I've been able to control my shift for about a year now."

Which is pretty impressive, according to the stuff Sam and Aliah were telling me earlier in the week. While females frequently learn to manage their changes in their late teens, males usually don't develop the ability until sometime in their twenties. Foxes are usually early learners though. Either because of their superior intelligence, as they claim, or because the fox just isn't as difficult a beast to reign in, as the other weres maintain.

"And..." Tod whispers. "I won't let anything bad happen to you."

My fingers tighten around his as I hope he can keep that promise. I know he'll try.

I take a breath, my gaze again on the skyline. "I'm sorry I didn't tell you where I was going earlier. I had this weird dream, and then I just panicked."

"It's alright." His breath warms my cheek as he looks at my profile. "A lot of people do strange things during the moon."

Shaking my head, I let out a sound that merges laughter and crying. "I don't think it was the moon, Tod."

"Well, maybe you're just strange all the time then," he suggests, making me smile.

"You're one to talk," I banter back, leaning my head against his shoulder.

His arm goes around me. "You make a good point." He gives me a squeeze. "So are we going to talk about why you let yourself get all panicked over the wolf?"

I sigh. "No."

"You sure?"

"Are you back together with Lyly?" I counter.

179

He stills and takes his time to answer. "I don't know."

"You don't know?" I twist my head to look at his face. "How can you not know?"

A hint of a sheepish smile traces the edges of his mouth. "I've been avoiding her since Monday morning." The sound following his words is conflicted, half a sob and half a bolt of laughter.

I make a thoughtful murmur and lean my head down again. "That sounds like a no to me."

He shrugs under my cheek. "I guess." Moving his hand along my arm, he plays with the fabric of my coat. "I'm just not sure what I want to do, so I haven't done anything. You know?"

"Eventually doing nothing is doing something," I point out.

"I know." He sighs and rests his head against mine. "I don't suppose you're going to tell me what I should do?"

Guess I walked into being asked for advice. "Do you love her?"

It takes him several moments to answer that. "I've always assumed so."

"Well, if you do..." I find his hand and wrap my fingers around it, entwining them with his. "Then you have to find a way to break this pattern."

"What do you mean?"

"It's not good for her," I say. "She's turned into a spoiled brat, and it's largely because you let her walk all over you."

He's silent, presumably thinking about that.

"You told me once I shouldn't hold your dad's behavior against him because he was a fox," I say softly. "And I know that's what you use to justify Lyly. But, how many times did your mother tell your dad to leave? How often have you looked at Lyly and told her you felt it was time to take a break?"

Cold air moves against me as he moves his head away. Which is answer enough for me.

"Right," I breathe. "Their problems aren't in their better halves. They're in the human halves."

"Maybe." The admission is a weak whisper.

Sitting up, I turn so I can look at him, keeping his hand held against my arm. "Did it bother you and your siblings that your dad was always coming and going?"

For a while I think he's not going to reply, and he won't meet my eyes, but eventually he nods.

"The whole den feels that way over Lyly."

His eyes go quickly to mine. How could that news have startled him?

"So..." I take a deep breath. "My advice is that you can break up with her for good. Or you can take her back, and fight to keep her. But you can't keep this up anymore, Tod. You deserve better. Lyly deserves better. And our den deserves better."

He stares at me with wide eyes, looking completely shocked at my words.

His lips move, like he's trying to get them to say something, but before any words form, the pressure of the moon rising comes over me again, the same heightening of the senses as last night, the same sensations.

Wiggling out from under Tod's arm, I get off the bench and take a few steps away from it as the urgency mounts.

My body tingles again like last night, the pressure building in the same way as before. The world thrums with energy. The colors around me pop out in dazzling effects. The wind against my skin feels like a million touches and the scents riding it wash over me in a dizzying aromatic display.

Tod leans forward, anxious.

The night presses down on me, harder and heavier, until I'm certain I'm going to burst under its pressure.

And then the world pops. And the feelings reside. And I could be any girl standing out in any yard in the world.

"And that's it," I whisper through a colossal sense of failure.

Tod smiles sadly. "It's alright, kit."

Tears form in my eyes as I shake my head at him, slumping in defeat. "I want to change."

My companion shrugs, clearly not having any idea what to say to me.

I'm a were who can't were. What a freak.

"Don't cry!" Tod lays the gun on the bench and rushes to me, hugs me tight. "It's okay, Mike. Really."

"I've never even seen a change," I whine.

Tod pulls back, wipes at my face with the edge of my scarf.

181

"Do you want me to change for you?"

Sniffling, I blink at him. "Would you?"

"Of course." Smiling, he walks a short way from me. He stops, takes a deep breath, and gives me a nervous laugh. "Not used to this being a performance."

I smile at him, even though I want to cry some more. "I'm sorry. You don't have to do it if it's weird."

"Not weird." He shakes his head. "Just..." He trails off into a shrug. "It's not all that impressive."

Not impressive? "You change shape. Where I'm from, that's impressive."

"Not where I'm from." Holding his arms out dramatically, he bows. "But I'll try."

Eyes closed, he pulls in a breath, and with it he seems to draw in the moon. He starts to shimmer, the dance of light moving in a rhythm matched by the night.

It's hard to follow what happens next. He blurs into a fog that isn't bright, but is somehow blinding. Then, he just sort of rearranges into a new shape. Then he's looking at me from much closer to the ground than usual, the personality in his eyes still the same but everything else different.

And then the pressure of the moon presses on me again, molding me into something new. The whole world shimmers with that strange fog, slamming my eyelids shut.

And when I open them again, Tod is at eye level.

The bright red fox lets out a yip of pleasure. Barking, he darts forward and tries to bite my tail.

What the expletive? My tail? Twisting away from him, I look back to see a fluffy brown fox tail bobbing behind my rear legs. I have rear legs too. And front ones with paws on the bottom.

"I'm a fox?" The question comes out as a bark.

Tod barks back, then pounces on me. I meet the attack, and we roll together on the ground like a pair of kittens. He pins me beneath him and makes a series of merry little noises.

I'm a fox.

And Warren had me more than half convinced I was a wolf.

Tod yips again, but this time the sound is more frightened than happy. He leaps off of me and back peddles, his eyes huge.

The fog swarms in to cover my vision again. Through the glistening veil, I see Tod grow smaller. And not because he's gained distance.

There's a blinding flash and when I can see again, I'm looking down at my paw. It's bigger. I look back. Yep, my butt is bigger now too. And my tail is different. Lowering my head, I move my front paws up to feel at my head.

I'm a wolf.

I think maybe I would rather have been a guinea pig.

Tod swells in size and after a second of loosing my sight to mist, I see my tail has all but disappeared.

"What's going on?" I squeak.

I try to become a Tasmanian devil, but stay stubbornly in my shape as a cavie.

Kitten.

Glancing back, I see a long, slender tail.

Dog. Cow. Bear.

Every animal I picture clearly, I become.

Human.

"Michaela is a human."

I hug myself tightly. Then Tod's arms fall around me, and he hugs me, too. "You're everything," he whispers in awe.

"I'm nothing," I whisper back, my voice choked with unshed tears.

Chapter Twenty-One

Tod and I enter Mr. Atherton's office together first thing in the morning. We skip over going into how I left the cage last night and get straight to the point. "We know what I am." I sigh as I sit down. "Sort of."

"Sort of?" the principal asks, frowning slightly and leaning forward over his desk.

Coming up behind me, Tod places his hands on the back of my chair. "I've never heard of anything like it. But she's not one animal. She's all of them."

"All of them?" Mr. Atherton redirects the frown to the fox behind me.

"Anything I can think of, I can be," I clarify. "I went through a series of things. Fox, wolf, bear, cat... Guinea pig."

"Guinea pig?" He doesn't even try not to stare at me.

"Yeah." Drawing in a long breath, I meet his eyes, trying to battle the disbelief I see in them. "At first, I didn't change at all. But after Tod shifted for me... It was like seeing it helped me figure out what to do, or something."

"But you weren't compelled to do it?"

I shake my head. "No. It was just like the first night. The pressure came, but I rode it out."

"And then you could be anything you wanted?"

Closing my eyes, I try to tap into the energies I used for my transformation. Reaching it, I concentrate on changing form. I open my eyes and wind my lemur tail around my body as Mr. Atherton gapes openly. "How is that possible?"

I snort, not needing words to convey I have no way of knowing.

"She wants to demonstrate for the den and the pack," Tod says on my behalf. "Do you think we could get them together, or will she need separate meetings?"

It takes a while for Mr. Atherton to respond because he's

too busy trying to wrap his mind around the concept of someone who can be anything. "I think we can get them together. I'll call your grandmother."

Tod makes a sound of agreement. "We figured there's no way anyone's going to believe this without seeing it."

"No..." Mr. Atherton shakes his head, then stops and clears his throat. "I don't think you should tell anyone here about this. Wait until after we panic the adult community, okay?"

I nod, then realize there's no point in staying furry. Summoning the fog again, I shift back to fully human. Still stunned, Mr. Atherton shakes his head.

Behind me, the door slams open, and I turn to see a vaguely familiar girl sprint into the room. She stops, takes a half-second to catch her breath, and then throws herself at Tod. Instinctively, he scoops her into his arms, grinning down at her. "What are you doing here?" he asks, obviously pleased.

Catching something in the girl's expression, his smile fades. "What's wrong?" Fear radiates off of the question. I find myself on my feet as I wait for her answer, realizing where I know her from. She's the third of the Fox siblings, and really should be back in Washington.

"Toni?" Mr. Atherton stands too and walks around his desk, looking at the visitor with mingled curiosity and concern.

"My mom's in the car," the girl tells him with a tremble in her voice. "Scot's trying to get her to come in, but she's scared."

"Scared?" Mr. Atherton's face takes on a mask of adorable confusion. A hint of pain breaks through. "Of what?"

Toni's look is pitying. "Just scared in general, I think."

"Antonia Marie!" Viv Fox calls dramatically down the hallway. She stalks into sight, stops just outside the door.

"Hello, Vivianne."

Mr. Atherton's simple greeting is deep, warm and yet cautious. As if he's the one frightened of her, but not for anything physical she might do to him.

She blinks, blushing. It's almost as if she's surprised to see him in his office. Or if she didn't realize where she was going when she chased after her errant offspring. "Michael."

All at once, we notice her bruises.

"What happened?" Tod and Mr. Atherton demand, in sync.

185

Another young Fox, the mirror image of Tod eight years or so ago, creeps into the room around his mother. His attempt at going unnoticed fails, and his brother narrows his eyes on him. "What happened, Scot?"

Toni's the one who answers though, not Scot. Scot just cowers under his brother's disapproval. "Daddy."

"What?" Tod stares at her.

Mr. Atherton starts to growl.

"Michael, don't," Viviane says quickly. "My mother's handling it."

"How?" he demands.

The abused vixen looks down at the carpet. "It's a den matter."

The wolf stares at her for several heartbeats, and a new growl adds itself to his.

"Then why are you here?"

Oh, expletive. I'm the one growling with him.

"Mike..." The warning in Tod's voice is my tip-off he's trying to control me rather than answering the question. His hand wrapping around my arm would also be a clue.

My fingers twine around his where he holds me, using the contact as a grounding force. I have no idea why I am so angry right now, but I can feel the claws trying to form.

Tod's siblings stare at me, but neither his mother nor Mr. Atherton pay me any mind at all. The latter is too busy watching the former, who focuses on the floor as if praying it will open up and swallow her. I know the feeling well.

After a few very tense moments, Tod says in a remarkably quiet voice, "It was a good question, Mom."

Vivianne's eyes shimmer when she looks up, timid and terrified. The stress in Mr. Atherton's jaw starts to relax as his gaze softens. "What do you need, Viv?"

"I don't know. I just..." Tears flow freely down her marbled cheeks now. She gives up trying to communicate as Mr. Atherton rushes to her, crushing her against him, and running his hands down her back.

"It's alright," he whispers.

Several pieces of information slide together in my head. The tone he uses for her. The fear and longing when he looks at

186

her. Even the way he treats her children, which is ever so slightly different from the way he acts around the other students. He's fond of most of us, but there's an extra affection and concern around the Fox kids I never stopped to consider before.

Jerking my head at the Fox kid holding onto me, I pull him out of the room. "They need some time alone," I whisper to him. "And we should find Sam."

The other two trail after us to the dinning room, where Sam and Aliah sit with an open textbook between them. They start when they notice the extra people with us, and Sam lets out a happy squeal before jumping up to embrace the pair.

"Mom brought them," Tod tells her, his voice ominous.

Aliah and Sam follow us to the food line, wanting to know more. "When?" Sam demands. "And why? And where is she?"

Toni wraps her arms around her sister's. She grabs a plate of pancakes from the serving counter before answering. "Just now. Something bad happened. She needed to be with Michael."

My friend's eyebrows knit together. "How bad?"

"Daddy showed up." Toni swallows with a barely perceptible shiver as she moves away from the counter to let me take a plate. "He didn't like not being let in. He..."

Scot finishes for her. "He beat her up pretty bad. I dialed 911."

Tod's teeth are gnashing together loud enough for people around us to hear them. Aliah puts a hand on his arm, trying to be soothing, but it doesn't break his tension at all.

"And now Mike's probably going to kill him," Toni states, not sounding too distressed by the idea.

Tod frowns at her, confused.

"Well, she is his life mate," I respond, going to grab my chocolate milk.

"What?" Tod blurts behind me.

"Life mate," Sam repeats. "It's something wolves have."

"I know what a life mate is!" He follows me to the table with short, rapid steps. "But what the hell makes you think my mother is his?"

Toni rolls her eyes and takes a seat. "Because it's obvious."

"To who?" he wants to know.

187

Settling into the chair she vacated, Sam lets out a grunt of frustration. "Oh, come on. You never noticed? He's been in love with her since the dawn of time!"

"It's not his fault," Toni puts in with kindness. "Tod can't help being a boy." She gives her big brother a mocking little smile, which he counters with a sneer.

"Remember the day Kim got here?" I ask, ripping off a sliver of pancake with my fingers. "Your mom called him some time after breakfast, and he was in Seattle, which is over four hours from here, by lunch. As in, she called, and he jumped." I run the pancake through a puddle of syrup, but don't eat it yet. "He hung up the phone and then ran to the airplane. Didn't even think about it." The pancake goes to my mouth.

"Because she was tied into the mystery of you."

I shake my head as I chew my food. "No," I state when I'm done. "It was because of who called. Your mother could have been calling to ask for help with a splinter. The response would have been the same."

Tod looks miffed about this while Scot, sitting beside his elder brother, appears to be confused. Okay, fine, Scot is ten. Scot has room to be unconvinced. But surely Tod should recognize the symptoms of a hopeless romantic entanglement.

Then again... I think about about Lyly and remember how Tod had said not that he was in love with her, but that he had always assumed he was, and I have to wonder.

"I don't understand," Scot says, sad and hesitant. "Why wouldn't she want to be with him before now? This isn't the first time Daddy's hit her, and he was never around anyway."

Yeah, alright. That's a decent thing to be confused about.

"This isn't the first time?" Tod demands.

"He's a wolf," Sam tells Scot gently. "They're pretty..."

"Violent?" I wager.

"No." She gives me a disapproving look. "Intense."

Toni makes a sound of agreement. "I mean, how freaky is it to be told, 'Hey, I don't know you, but you're my life mate, and the only way you're going to get rid of me is by dying.' Seriously?"

"But he loves her!" I protest.

Aliah nods. "And, she did get away from him, didn't she?"

188

"She moved to Seattle," Sam acknowledges. "And he just let her."

"As far as we know," Tod qualifies. He doesn't sound like he's accusing Mr. Atherton of anything, though, it's just he is so thrown by events he honestly has no idea how to react.

Sam waves a dismissive hand at him. "And it's all impressive that he loved her enough to let her go. But, I don't know, maybe the problem was how he just let her go," she proposes. "Maybe he was supposed to throw a fit and drag her back home by her hair."

"That's stupid," Tod tells her.

"No," Toni counters. "That's feminine thought."

"Same thing," mutters Scot.

Sam rolls her eyes. "Eat your breakfast, smarty pants."

Scot sticks his tongue out at her, but digs into his food with remarkable zest.

Tod just stares at his plate, too deep in shock to eat.

He still hasn't said anything new when we all finish up and go to change for skiing, the younger foxes borrowing stuff because they didn't think to bring their ski things when they left Seattle. Apparently, they left almost immediately once their mother made her decision to come up here.

We go up to the mountain in Tod's car, to give them more freedom about when they come back than if we'd taken the bus. It's too small for both me and Aliah, so she stays behind to come up later, thus saving me from a ride spent being stared at. The foxes may have reason to be distracted from the mystery of what I changed into last night, but the rest of the school is going to want to know.

Tod stays virtually silent, but Toni and Sam more than make up for his reticence with wild gossip about people they know back in Washington. Things will be interesting next year with Tod gone and Toni at school.

I find I don't like to think about Tod leaving. Not that I suppose he'll be completely out of my life when his sisters will be so much in it. Still, the concept leaves a cold pit somewhere inside of me.

Putting on my too-thin gloves, I think sadly about Warren's pair. He wasn't at breakfast today, but he'll be back tomorrow. I

189

suppose I'll return them to him then. But what am I going to do about his shirt? If I just put it back in his room, he's going to smell me on it. If I wash it, will he realize something is up with it? Even if I get the right detergent, maybe he'll notice it was supposed to be dirty. And if I keep it, then I stole it.

"Earth to Michaela!" Sam moves her hand moving up and down in front of my face. "We asked if you wanted to hit the backside with us."

Unconsciously, I look towards the lift that would take me to the top of the mountain. "No," I say slowly. "My brain's pretty fried. I'll stay on the easier stuff. You guys have fun."

Shrugging, the three younger foxes push off towards the lift line. Tod stays in place, watching me. "You alright?"

"Yeah." I give him a smile that I hope is reassuring before narrowing my eyes with concern. "Are you?"

His head shakes. "Other than being a blind idiot, you mean?"

"You are not an idiot," I state with firm insistence. "You're one of the smartest people I know, fox."

An eyebrow goes up. "Thanks. But I notice you aren't arguing against the blind part."

I use the fact I haven't gotten my skis on yet as an excuse to look at the ground. Clicking my first boot into its binding, I sigh. "There are a lot of things you don't see."

"So it would seem." He sighs. "What else am I missing?"

I slide the second boot onto its ski and give my friend smile. "The point of life is figuring that out."

His eyes roll. "Right." He waves, then skates away after his siblings.

Much more awkwardly, I push my poles into the snow and move toward a lift that only services green slopes.

Three runs into the morning, I realize this isn't the distraction I'd hoped it would be. My form is off. I keep falling. I need new gloves. And I'm just not having fun today.

After taking my ski things back to their locker and picking up a replacement pair of gloves that costs me all that's left of my birthday money, I go over to the coffee shop and borrow one of their collections of short stories to curl up in an armchair with near the fireplace.

"What, all alone? Couldn't find anyone else's boyfriend to keep you company?"

Sighing down at the book, I don't look up at Lyly. Last time I talked to her, she begged me to help her. Guess her gratitude over me being willing to do that wore off.

"Too bad you can't find and keep one of your own," snarks a second voice.

My fingers clutch the edges of the novel. "I had Troy for six months, Kim. He broke up with you after, what, a week?"

"Three. We were together for two weeks before you ever found out about it." She brags of this as though it is something to be proud of. "And I broke up with him."

"Very sensible of you," I tell her, still gazing at the text before me. "Boyfriends who cheat on the girl before you frequently become boyfriends who cheat on you."

"No one has ever cheated on me," she claims, her tone inarguable and assured.

"Bill Stevens. Ninth grade."

"Yeah, but that girl went to another school," Kim defends instantly. As if what school the girl had gone to could possibly make a difference.

"Whatever." Sticking a finger in my place in the book, I yawn and stretch. "Did you two come over here for a reason?"

"Yeah." Lyly strikes a dramatic pose. "Tod's mine. You need to stay away from him."

"Ah." I put the book face down on the side of the chair and fold my hands demurely in my lap. In all honesty, I've been expecting this confrontation for weeks. "So, Tod's not allowed to play with me anymore?"

"No, he isn't." Her features contort into an ugly visage of hatred. Interesting. I guess she can be unattractive if she tries hard enough.

"Have you told him?" I ask reasonably.

Her eyes narrow into slender daggers. "I'm telling you."

I smile. "I'll keep your opinions in mind. But you need to keep in mind I'm his friend, not yours."

"I don't trust you." The words lack emotion, more a statement of fact than an actual attack.

Which begs the question, "Do you trust Tod?"

She absolutely glowers. "You already stole Seth from Simone. Do you have to ruin every relationship in this school?"

There's a growl from behind me. "She did not take my brother from Simone. He was always going to challenge to be free of her."

Lyly glares at Amber. "Yeah? Well, he never said a word about it until she showed up." Her finger jabs at me in accusation.

"He spoke plenty of it to me," Amber states with calm alacrity as she places her hand on the back of my chair. "Since we were in preschool, back when he first realized what he had been committed to, he's been telling me he'd fight it. If Mike had anything at all to do with it, then all she did was give him an extra push. And I thank her for that."

The other two watch her with stunned expressions, dropped jaws and all. "Simone is your friend," Lyly whispers, astonished and appalled.

Amber's face goes cold. "Simone is a member of my community," she says with a complete, and frightening, lack of warmth. "But she was never my friend."

The leopard leans over me. "But Michaela is my friend. And if you desire to remain healthy, little fox, you will leave her alone."

Lyly just stares.

"Mike's not worth fighting over," Kim drawls, trying to sound bored. If I couldn't hear how fast her heart is beating, I might have believed it. But Amber managed to scare her, too.

"Yeah," Lyly mutters in agreement.

"And she's not a threat to you and Tod anyway." Kim tosses her hair and gives her hips a little shake. "She's way too freakish."

Freakish. She doesn't mean I'm a freak for being a new kind of were either, or because of my scent. If that's what she meant, then she'd be a freak too. No, it's just a word she's been tossing at me for years. Once upon a time, it hurt my feelings. Back before I realized that if she was normal, then I wanted to be a freak.

My tormentors saunter away, acting as if they won our little battle. Whatever.

"I'm sorry," Amber whispers.

"For what?" I turn in the chair so I can see her.

"For claiming the right to name you friend." Her eyes, the same color as her name, drop to the floor and refuse to meet mine. "I know I don't deserve the honor."

"Sure you do." I smile at Seth's strange sister, wondering if it's normal for her to talk like she lives in a fantasy novel. I've never heard her say enough to know for sure. "You just defended me against my arch-enemies. Usually people stand in line to stab me in the back and get on Kim's good side."

"Why?" Her eyes move up to squint at me. "Are the people in your old school unusually dimwitted?"

I never did figure that out, actually. Yes, she's prettier than I am. Yes, she's wittier than I am. But she's mean and petty and shallow too. What is the attraction? And why don't the weres echo that draw? Is it simply that animals are good judges of character?

Instead of getting into that, I laugh softly. "See, spoken like my friend." Waving at the chair next to mine, I invite her to sit down.

At the door, Tod and Aliah pass by Lyly on her way out of the shop. There's a slightly panicked look on Tod's face when he first sees her – first realizes he's completely trapped into, at minimum, acknowledging her existence. They're too far away for me to hear what's said, but it's a very brief exchange that leaves a lost confusion hovering over Tod's features.

His face is scrunched as he continues into the building toward the barista. Before he gets to the counter, he notices me and alters his course to come stand behind Amber. Aliah trails him quietly, sadly. In animal form, her tail would be drooping right now.

"She said her dress is lavender," Tod tells me, absolutely bewildered.

"Yes," says Amber. "So you can obtain for her a suitable corsage."

He looks as clueless as ever.

The leopard shakes her head with amusement. "It is certain you know what corsages are, Tod. You've taken her to dances before."

"But not this one." A hand runs through hair already mussed by the helmet now grasped in his other hand. "There has been zero discussion about going to this dance."

"But you did get back together?" Amber gives him a sideways look. "And you usually go to these dances. So it's a reasonable assumption you're going to this one."

"I guess," he admits. Behind him, Aliah slides towards the counter. "But..." Tod draws the thought out. "I'm not sure back together is really what we are."

Amber makes a sharp sound of surprise.

I sigh. "But you haven't told her you aren't either, have you?"

The abashed way he starts to study his helmet is sufficient answer to the question.

"Well, you'd best hurry," Amber tells him. "The dance is the night after next. You've already waited long enough for not taking her to be somewhat morally ambiguous."

"Morally ambiguous?" he repeats with disbelief, looking up to gawk at her.

"Yes." Amber turns to kneel backwards in her chair, wrapping her arms around the back of it. "If you ignore her thinking you're going together until Saturday, then don't take her, then you have fundamentally stood her up. Even waiting until tomorrow would make you an ass because it's roughly the same thing as breaking up with her the day before a dance. The only reason you're not clearly one already is because you lacked understanding of what was occurring." She pauses to look thoughtful. "Although that does seems a very high level of cluelessness for someone who got a perfect score on his SATs."

Tod stares at her like she grew a second head. "When did you start talking so much?" She starts to blush. "I think that's more than you've said to me in the whole three years we've known each other. And it was to tell me I'm an idiot and an asshole."

"I... I... I didn't mean..."

"She was trying to help," I say softly. Tod narrows his eyes at me, redirecting his disgruntlement. "Lyly thought the two of you were going to hook up again because you always have before. If this time is different, you have to tell her, or you're

194

stringing her along. Which isn't nice." Of course, I don't necessarily think being nice to Lyly is a high priority task.

He glares balefully at me for a few seconds, angry and at least slightly hurt. "I'm going to get coffee." Turning sharply, he takes a step away, but then stops. Scanning the room, he lets out a quiet sound of confusion. "Where did Aliah go?"

"I don't know," I tell him.

He looks back at me, and I shrug. "I thought she was going to go get a drink, but she disappeared when I wasn't looking."

"I never saw her leave," Amber seconds.

Unhappy, Tod goes to the barista alone, returning with only one cup of coffee, but enough cookies for several people. He nudges the plate toward Amber with an air of silent apology, and she takes one with a small smile.

It's about fifteen minutes later when Seth stalks past us in ski boots, issuing a command in passing. "Come here."

Tod and I raise our eyebrows at each other, but join Amber in following her brother to the windows.

"There she goes again!" The long-haired leopard points at someone in the park.

"There who goes?" Tod squints down at the figure starting in the half pipe. She gets a good amount of air, crosses her skies, and spins before nailing a perfect landing.

"You don't recognize your girlfriend's sister?" Seth taunts without animosity.

"Aliah?" Tod whispers, staring as the skier launches into the air again, doing a tail grab and another spin.

"Since when does Aliah hit the park?" I ask, thinking of how she knew all the beginner slopes so well and never tried to get me onto anything harder, never acted even slightly bored with my choice of terrain. I always knew she was worlds better than I am, but it didn't occur to me she could hold her own competing against anyone on the mountain.

"She's always liked it," Seth tells us. "But I've only seen her there at weird times, like at opening or just before close on a deserted day when we were the only two people around. She's always had too much stage fright when the rest of the school was up."

Tod, mesmerized, doesn't take his eyes off of her, or even

195

blink. "What changed?"

Seth gives the fox a short look. "All I know for certain is she showed up with her jaw set and flames in her eyes to ask me if she could drop in before I did." He looks back down at the show, which is attracting a fair amount of attention from other people. A group collected down on the snow applauds and cheers as she comes to a stop. "But whatever it is, this is as hot as I've ever seen her."

Tod frowns and when she gets to the end of her run, he turns sharply and leaves without saying anything to us.

Seth smiles as he leaves. "She'd kill me if she knew I sent him down there."

"You didn't send him down there," his sister dismisses.

Seth laughs, the sound rolling easily off of him. "Didn't I?"

"No." The response is automatic though, she doesn't seem to have much faith in it.

The most perfect eyes in the world look over to me. "Good work," I tell him, accompanying the praise with a quick hug. Over his shoulder, I catch a glimpse of someone walking quickly away.

"I'll be back," I tell the leopards. Then I sprint to the door before my prey can fully escape.

"Warren!" I run up behind the wolf.

Cautiously, he looks down at me as he stops. He's not dressed for boarding, unless he's hit himself really hard in the head and decided jeans are appropriate apparel. "Michaela."

"Why are you here?" I ask.

For several seconds, I think he's not going to tell me.

"I was looking for you."

The admission is quiet and pained.

"Why?"

He shrugs. "There are a lot of rumors going around about you. About what happened to you last night." His eyes flit around my face, never catching my gaze directly. "About why it is a girl who's been in town less than a month is calling a joint meeting of the pack and the den."

"And you wanted to ask me about them?" I hazard.

"No." The denial is swift, but heartfelt. His hand reaches to capture some of the hair being ripped in the wind back behind my ear. "I just wanted to make sure you're alright."

His hand, bare despite the weather, sends little slivers of warmth down my whole body. "Now who's forgotten how to use a telephone?" I joke, trying to distract myself.

"I called the school." He smiles faintly. "They said you were here."

"Which did imply I wasn't dead."

"Implied it, yes." His remaining hand reaches out to cup my free cheek. His eyes softly roam over my face. "I wanted to be sure."

Heart fluttering, lungs trying to figure out how to obtain oxygen, and thoughts scattered to the far corners of the world, I look back up at him. "Do you want to know what I am?" I whisper.

An eyebrow cocks. "Isn't it a secret?"

"Yes," I confirm, my voice scarcely audible. "But I'll tell you."

He shakes his head. "No, Michaela. My father would order me to tell him, and I would have to either do it or leave the pack." One hand moves to brush through my hair. "I'll be there tonight, though."

With a sad smile, he steps backwards, turns, and leaves me standing there staring at his back.

Part of me runs after him.

My body stays put.

Chapter Twenty-Two

"I think Aliah's mad at me."

Tod seems to be incredibly, adorably one might even say, confused by this. On a normal day, I would probably say something along the lines of, "Well, duh," and proceed to tease him about it, but the poor guy is starting to look seriously battered.

"She's just having a rough moon." The were-equivalent of the PMS excuse.

"Who isn't?" He watches her closely, even though she isn't doing anything more interesting than sitting on a bench with her phone's music app set to a volume too high for a normal human, let alone someone with enhanced hearing. After she put in her earbuds while Tod was trying to talk to her, she hasn't so much as glanced toward him. Which is pretty much the opposite of the way she usually reacts to his presence.

"Why are you at the bus stop?" Sam wonders, leading her other siblings up to Tod. "Did our car get stolen?"

"No." Tod doesn't elaborate on the humorless mutter.

Shrugging at Sam's glance to me, I tell her, "He's hoping to see Lyly."

"Why?" The question is cautious. Sam's eyes drift towards Aliah, narrow in concern, and then switch to her brother. "Why are you hoping to see Lyly?"

"Need to talk to her."

"Need to talk to her," Toni repeats the statement as a mocking grunt. "Tod so articulate. Like talk a lot."

Her brother glares at her and the rest of us roll our eyes.

"She already left." Sam looks for a reaction. "She rode down with the lions."

The bus pulls up, its brakes letting out a faint whoosh.

"Oh." Tod takes his keys from his pocket.

"We don't have to go, do we?" Scot whines.

"No." Sam holds her hand out for the keys. "I can drive us back later."

Tod hesitates, but hands over the keys and permission to drive his car. "Be careful."

Sam snorts. "Yeah, whatever." She gives me a grin and a wink, then herds the younger Foxes away.

The others started filing onto the bus the second it stopped moving, so it's already nearing full by the time I make it up the stairs. I slide into the seat next to Seth, and Tod flings himself onto the empty bench in front of us, sitting with his back to the window and looking across the aisle at Aliah.

Aliah doesn't look back.

Seth and I trade raised eyebrows over that, but don't say anything on the subject as we wind our way to the school.

The bus pulls down the road by the parking garage and my eyes gravitate toward a familiar truck sitting in its usual spot. Warren stands beside it, looking up as the bus passes by him, meeting my eyes for the split second we're level.

Despite me getting off the bus almost as quickly as the sprinting Aliah does, both Warren and his truck are gone by the time I step off.

Once I realize Warren was going rather than coming, I slow down and give a sympathetic look to Tod, who looks as bewildered and cast adrift as he has all day. Putting my arm around his waist in a friendly half-hug as we walk through the rec room, I try to be optimistic. "You're going to be alright."

He sighs. "I don't know. Maybe not. This could be your last chance to make a frantic pass at me." His eyebrows do a funny wiggle, and I laugh. His smile is sad though. "I think I'm going to go lie down."

Nodding, I step away from him. "See you later?"

Miserably, he starts up the stairs as I debate whether I want to go to lunch before or after changing out of my ski things.

A loud howl, followed by a great crash, comes from one of the side study rooms. Tod spins and dashes back down the stairs, pushing past me to run through the doorway the noises came from.

"What the hell did you do to her?" he bellows.

199

I sprint the distance between me and the room, coming to a dead halt when I see Tod bending over Aliah. He partially blocks my view, but even so I can tell she's bleeding from multiple places as she leans reclined on her elbows. Lyly glares at both of them, her arms crossed. "She started it," she insists, sounding sulky and not at all upset.

"Aliah?" With the lightest of touches, Tod brushes back Aliah's hair, which, though still shockingly white, may currently be darker than her skin. "What happened?"

She shakes her head. "Nothing."

Nothing? Tod growls, thinking about as much of the answer as I do. "What did she do?" he asks, the syllables grinding their way through clinched teeth.

"She attacked me!" Lyly yells in a shrill pitch that makes me yearn to smack her. "I was just defending myself!"

Tod doesn't even glance at her. "I wasn't talking to you. I want the truth. What happened, Aliah?"

While her sister sputters, Aliah tries to sit completely upright while attempting to scoot away from Tod. Her balance is off, causing her to waver and him to put his arms around her. "What happened?" His voice is soft as he cradles her.

"I attacked her," she whispers.

Tod's start of surprise is very visible. "Why?"

With a shake of her head, Aliah looks down and refuses to answer.

Sighing, Tod looks up. "What did you do, Lyly?"

"I didn't do anything!" Lyly waves her hands in frustration. "She admitted she attacked me!"

"Yes, but I know she had a reason." His voice is firm as he goes on, "And I want to know what it was."

The idea that Aliah physically attacked her sister without provocation is preposterous. Of course, it's pretty incredible that our shy little pink-eyed introvert threw the first punch even given cause. Even more incredible than her secret identity as a park rat.

"She's psychotic!" Lyly waves her arms dramatically. "There's your reason."

"So neither of you are going to tell me?" Tod sighs as he helps Aliah to sit on her own and then moves away from her

200

with a deep frown.

Eyes on the carpet she's leaking blood onto, Aliah shakes her head, her hand pressed against the scratches across her stomach.

"You going to be alright?" Tod asks her. His annoyance is clearly etched on the lines of his face, but there's concern underneath it.

Weakly, Aliah nods.

Lyly makes an annoyed *tsk,* plants a hand on her hip, and looks considerably irked. "You're not just going to let her get away with it, are you?"

"You drew blood, Alysia."

I'm unclear if he's meaning to say Aliah is already punished because she's in a lot of pain or if there's some sort of rule he's alluding to. I do know that the use of Lyly's real name rather than her nickname has to mean something.

"But she started it!" Lyly protests. "All I did was tell her-"

"Shut up!" Aliah screams, the shriek echoing from the walls.

"Tell her..." Tod prompts after a glance at Aliah.

On the floor, Aliah starts to shake, looking like she's going to go into shock. Noticing, Tod redirects his gaze to her, eyes sharp with worry. "Aliah?" Panic lurks behind the name.

Going pale, Lyly takes a deep breath. "Nothing. I just said something stupid, and she jumped at me."

"And forced to you to grow claws and ram them into her?" Still looking at Aliah, Tod pulls himself taller and assumes a mien of responsibility. I can't say exactly how he does it, but in the space of a breath, he goes from being a confused boy to being a power to be listened to – to being our den father. "You have a choice Alysia, you can either refrain from attendance at any school social events between now and the end of the year or you can be tried by the parent den."

"Tried by the parent den?" Her eyes are huge as she stares at Tod.

"Yes." He turns his head back toward her, his eyes cold. "You performed a partial shift to aide yourself in a physical confrontation outside of an official challenge. And you did it not only to harm a den member, but to hurt your blood sister."

Shaking slightly, Lyly draws a long breath. "What about her? She admits she started the fight."

Tod looks back to Aliah and lets out a slow, saddened, breath. "Same deal."

Lyly lets out a cry of frustration. "Like anyone would take her to prom anyway! Why don't you take away something she actually cares about?"

Tod has to be well aware the punishment is worse for Lyly than for her sister. It sounds fair to me though, since Lyly's crime was the greater one.

"You can take the matter to my grandmother," Tod offers, not so much as blinking under the force of her ire.

There are honest tears in Lyly's eyes now. "I can't believe you'd do this to me because of her."

Shaking his head, Tod starts to leave the room. I stand aside to let him by and out of the corner of my eye, I catch a blur of motion. Tod spins, comprehending the situation faster than I do, and he leaps across the room to slam into Lyly, knocking her to the ground. "What was that?" he bellows at her as her body starts to shudder with huge, wracking sobs.

Aliah is staring. She had been climbing to her feet when her sister tried to take her out from behind. Lyly's hands are still shifted into claws. Smaller claws than mine, yes, but larger than those of a natural fox and capable of plenty of damage.

"Lyly!" Tod is still furious when he shouts the name, but as he looks down at her, tears marring her face and her lips quivering, something in his expression softens. When he speaks again, he is more mournful than anything. "What is going on with you, Ly? This isn't you."

Sliding back down to the ground, Aliah closes her eyes, concentrates, and then shifts in furred form. As a sleek white fox, she walks around the sofa, pausing to glance up at me before running out of the door. Blood stands out against her pale coat, but the wounds are starting to heal, their repairs accelerated by her change.

Looking back toward Tod, I see him pull himself out of a bittersweet kiss. His voice is soft, his expression tender. "I'm not taking you back."

"What?"

I notice Lyly's stopped crying completely.

Rising to his feet, Tod holds out a hand to help her up. "We're not getting back together this time."

"You're breaking up with me?" Her screech sends knives of pain through my bones. Ignoring the offer of assistance, she springs to her feet unaided. "You can't do that!"

I almost laugh.

Tod gives her a very long look. "Goodbye, Alysia."

He leaves her sputtering and hissing. He looks at me as I fall into place beside him in the corridor. Reaching out, I give his hand a quick squeeze. "Where did Aliah go?" he asks.

"I don't know," I tell him, dropping his hand and giving him a shrug. "She sprouted fur and scampered out as fast as her four little legs could carry her."

"She needs to see the nurse." His nostrils flare as he sniffs for her scent.

I sigh. "She's a big enough girl to know if she needs attention or not."

"No, she isn't," he contradicts. "In the fall, she fell when we were hiking, and she didn't say anything to anyone. Just passed out from the pain and shock of trying to walk up a mountain with a leg that was broken in three places."

That does imply a certain lack of sensibility. "Maybe she learned from that."

But her scent leads to a door, and a freshman who admits to opening it for her. Cursing, we grab our coats and go out into the cold.

Her trail leads to a thick concentration of trees, pines that are growing so closely together as to be impassable without shifting.

"It's your call," I answer Tod's questioning look. "But it looks to me like she wants to be alone. And she wasn't dripping blood or anything."

Unhappy sounds emerge from the back of his throat as he glares at where the tree branches were disturbed by Aliah's passing. He calls out her name, three times, with increasing volume and insistence.

"Aliah," he calls out again, forlorn now. "Please? I'm

worried about you." There's a rustling from inside the trees somewhere. "Did I do something wrong? Something to upset you? Because if so, whatever it was, I'm sorry. Very, very sorry."

The next rustling is from further away.

"Aliah? Please come out," he begs. "Please?"

And she starts to run.

Tod's eyes go to me, wide and hurt. "Why is she running from me?"

Taking a deep breath, I shake my head. "She needs to be alone. I doubt it's anything personal."

He frowns, but doesn't call me on the statement. Even though he had to see that it's one of the biggest lies I've ever told.

"If I change, I can go after her," he says quietly. "But I don't know if I could change back before tonight. Most people don't shift as easily as you do. And my instinct will be to keep the fox form."

I nod. I don't want to go to the meeting tonight without him, but I'm not going to tell him that holding my hand through my performance anxiety is more important than Aliah. I think she'll be fine, I really do. But if he disagrees, I'm not going to stop him from helping her.

He stares at the trees for a long time before turning with a tight expression and starting back to the school. "Do you know what's wrong with her?" he asks me as I trudge through the snow after him.

"No." That one's not a lie. Not entirely. I don't know what's wrong with her; I've merely formed a highly probable theory. There's no way I'd ever talk to Tod about it without permission though. "But I think it will work itself out."

"And how do you know that if you don't know what the problem is?" He catches on to all the wrong things, doesn't he?

I shrug. "Call it an optimistic hunch."

Snorting, he shakes his head. "Optimism," he mutters in a dark voice.

The truth is, I just can't be the one to tell him why Aliah's acting like she is. I mean, being wrong would be pretty embarrassing. But, if I'm right... Well, then it's Aliah's place to tell him. Not mine. She's the one in love with a guy who will

204

never, ever notice.

He doesn't even seem to notice he's far more upset about Aliah being out there in the woods than he would be about anyone else. But as he rushes around commanding people to keep an eye out for her while we're gone, it's pretty obvious to the rest of us.

"We'll find her," Seth assures us with calm sympathy, even though there's no way a leopard could fit in the holes she was using any more than a human could.

"You look nervous too," Seth observes as Tod goes off to spread the word to keep an eye open for Aliah further. Leaning into a loose hug, I sigh.

"That would be because I am." I wish Seth would be coming with me, but he hasn't mastered his changes enough to be allowed, even if we could get permission to take a leopard with us. "I never liked public speaking."

"You'll be fine." He plants a light kiss on the top of my head. "And when you get back, you can tell me all about everything."

"I could tell you now, but I'm not sure you'd believe me."

He makes a sound of interest. "So it really is that weird?"

Nodding, I let out a slow breath. "This meeting is so I can demonstrate. Because there's absolutely no way they'd all buy it without seeing it."

That tidbit widens his perfect eyes. "As soon as I'm human, I'm knocking on your door."

"Yeah, well, if you do it before six, there's no way I'm telling you anything." I grin up at my friend.

"Okay. See you at six-oh-one, then." He gives me a teasing wink as Tod swoops in to take me away, escorting me to his car with none of his usual banter.

We don't speak much as we drive, spending the hour long trip in virtual silence broken only by the music on the radio.

The venue for my demonstration is just as devoid of excitement as the ride to it was. I suppose I had expected to be taken to a glen deep into the forest, or possibly into a cavern secreted dramatically in the midst of a mountain, or even to a trendy nightclub closed on nights of the full moon. But, no. The meeting is in Tod's aunt's backyard.

It's a nice backyard, roomy and opening into the forest, and, most importantly, out of sight of the neighbors. But it's still just a backyard. There's even a swing set in it, half buried under the snow.

A cold wind rips through me as Tod leads me around the side of the house. Nausea grips my stomach. There are at least sixty people milling about the yard, most of whom are strangers. I saw a few of them at my introduction to the den, and I remember Tod explaining that not only are they members of his den family, the majority of them are members of his extended biological family, as well. That has something to do with the rules on who is allowed to breed. Apparently one half of any breeding pair has to come from one of a select number of genealogical lines, but it's more complicated than that. I haven't felt compelled to ask for details, being fairly certain I wouldn't like them. Catching sight of a pair of familiar faces, I approach Emma Fox to say hello to her and to be re-introduced to her youngest daughter. While I'm talking to them, a pair of wolves come over, Warren's parents. In looks, my friend takes after his mother, but he has his father's scent.

The den matriarch tells me the moon will rise in about ten minutes and urges me to have something to eat first. Nodding, I agree and go over to a buffet table filled with smoked meats and cheeses. I nibble on some jerky, but it feels like lead when I swallow it.

"You'll be fine," Tod tells me, putting a supportive smile on his face, even though the pinched skin around his eyes tells me he's still upset about Aliah.

I whimper softly in mild argument and lean toward him, into a warm and friendly hug. After a few moments, he whispers, "I think Warren could use some help."

Pulling back with a puzzled mew, I move my head around to look for the wolf. I spot him near the corner of the house, somehow giving off the impression of pacing despite standing still, his eyes on the horizon even though he won't be able to see the moon crest over the land because of all the trees.

I excuse myself from Tod and walk toward the wolf. Unlike usual, he doesn't act at all aware of my approach until I'm within a few feet of him.

"Hey, Warren."

His eyes flicker to me, but are pulled almost instantly back to the forest. "Michaela."

Why do so many of our exchanges start this way?

"You doing alright?" I ask, easing to a stop near him, letting his body block the wind a little.

"Yeah. You?"

I snort. "Nervous as hell."

The faintest trace of a smile appears on his face. "You and every fox here. But we're not going to start eating you all."

Chuckling, I shake my head. "Not what I'm afraid of. I'm more worried I'll get a bad review and ruin my performance career."

"Well, that's possible." The smile gets bigger. "Critics are the scariest monsters of them all, and we have several here tonight."

Warren's jaw tenses, and his body trembles. His attention goes back to the horizon.

"Stop fighting it," I say gently.

"If I don't fight it, I'll have to leave." His gaze forces itself to me, pain in his eyes.

"I don't want you to leave." My hand goes, of its own accord, to his arm. "What I meant was, don't deny you're a wolf. Just be a wolf in human form."

"That's really... mystic."

The statement makes me laugh. "No. I just... I realized when I watched Tod last night that he didn't change what he was when he shifted, he just changed what he looked like."

Storm clouds brew in Warren's eyes and his teeth grind together with audible menace.

"What?" I ask.

The wind blasts into me again, rushing from behind me and flinging my hair into my face. I curse and pull my hood up.

Warren, his nostrils flaring and his eyes full of hurt and anger, glowers down at me with a growl that shakes my bones. A surge of panic knifes its way into my chest. "You are not helping," the wolf grumbles at me.

Every piece of my body trembles as he stomps away. "Warren!" I yell, finding myself more frightened for him than of him. Repeating his name, I trot after him.

The look he gives me when I catch up to him is feral. He is more the wolf this second than he has ever been with me before, and I realize in a sudden blast of clarity exactly why it is harder to contain the wolf than to contain a fox. Both are wild, but the wolf... It's *wild*.

The fear rises up again, but it's still not for me. Warren, the wolf or the human, isn't going to hurt me. But he's capable of ripping himself apart.

"How can I help?" I whisper.

"How can you help?" he sneers. "You can..." A rough breath breaks into the words. "You can stop..." There's a heart wrenching growl of frustration, and he gives up trying to speak all together.

Instead, he grabs me by the shoulders, slams me into the wall, and brings his mouth down over mine with a furious passion that rips through me, tearing apart my entire world to rebuild it again with Warren stamped on every single atom of it.

I moan in displeasure when he pulls away.

"You," he places a languid kiss on my cheek, "--can," lands another kiss a millimeter away, "stop–"continues the pattern of alternating kiss with words, "smelling... like... other... people." He moves to the other cheek. "You... can... stop... doing... intimate things... with them." His lips go again to mine, brushing them ever so lightly. "You... can... stop..." Giving up on talking again, he kisses me firmly, his tongue swirling into my mouth, possessing, dominating. "Just..." He pulls away again, eyes fevered and breath catching with every syllable as he says, "Just stop reminding me you aren't mine."

His hands release me, and he walks briskly away. As his long strides steal him from me, I stare after him, my body too shocked to do anything other than lean against the building and hope it doesn't collapse.

Stop reminding him I'm not his?

My fingers go to my lips, tracing them as I think about the way he kissed me, and the way I kissed him back.

"But what if I am yours?" I whisper to him even though he's not even in sight anymore.

Chapter Twenty-Three

"There you are." Tod smiles at me as I approach him, my thoughts a swirl and my mouth still tasting of Warren. My friend's eyebrows go up at my expression, but he doesn't say anything about it. "I was starting to wonder if you'd bailed."

"Wouldn't dream of it." Okay, there's a part of me that's still considering running away. But it's tremendously important people realize what sort of creature has invaded our territory, and there's a chance I'll be able to talk to a certain wolf afterwards, conceivably even get him to kiss me again.

It amazes me to realize exactly how much I want him to kiss me again. I don't think I've ever wanted anything quite as much.

A large circle has been formed, and Emma is busy giving an introduction for me, telling the others about how I'm a new were from a previously unknown strain. "We're hunting someone who is the same species as Michaela. She hopes her demonstration today will help us understand what we're fighting against."

Insecure, nervous, and cold, I could really use another hug right about now. But thinking about Warren, I refrain from requesting one as I wait for the pressure of the moon to hit and then recede. "Show time," I whisper in a voice I somehow keep from trembling, leaving Tod's side to go stand in the middle of the circle.

With all the eyes on me, it's hard just staying upright and breathing. Knowing they can all smell my fear, I try to dampen it, but the best I can do is ignore it. It hasn't gone away as I stop in the middle of the gathering and take a deep breath. Tod, his arms folded and posture relaxed, gives me nod. I nod back, but then my eyes go to Warren. Everyone here has to notice I'm looking at him. Unlike Tod, he's not directly in front of me, but off to the side so I have to turn my head most of the way sideways to see him. Leaning nonchalantly against one of the swing set's supports, he gives me a faint, understanding, smile. It settles the fluttering in my stomach, gives me the strength to keep going.

Still looking at him, I picture in my mind the image of a fox, then focus on drawing power from the moon. Slowly, as the now familiar fog settles in, I start to tingle, then to shrink and change shape into a fox. Warren's shoulders slump a little, his smile becomes a shade sadder. Then his face stills as I start to shift again, taking on the form of a wolf. He straightens, staring at me. People around the circle start to talk.

I become a leopard. And a guinea pig, a boar, a bear, a mouse, and a woolly mammoth. I try not to spend too long as any of them, particularly the animals a wolf could describe as bite-sized.

The quiet murmuring of the crowd has become an avalanche of sound. And Warren's look has shifted to one of appalled horror.

Oh, God. My stomach plunges downward in despair, and something inside me curls up to die. I shift back to human, wrap my arms around myself, and stare at the ground. Warren thinks I'm disgusting. The pain from the thought nearly knocks me to the ground.

"Clarification, please." Emma walks up to me. "You have implied you can take any form."

I swallow. "Anything I can fully visualize. I tried to be a Tasmanian devil last night, but that didn't work because I don't know what one looks like."

"You just need to know what it looks like?" asks Warren's father. "Not how it's built or how it behaves or any real details? Just how it appears?"

Miserable, I nod.

His hand falls onto my shoulder, and he gives it a gentle squeeze. "Thank you, Michaela. You're a very brave young woman with a very impressive gift."

It takes effort to accept that with a nod rather than a derisive snort. Some gift. Warren isn't impressed by it; he's repulsed. He isn't going to want to touch me again. He's probably not even going to want to talk to me again.

210

There are a few more questions from others, which I answer numbly and without any real thought. Several people stop by just to tell me the display was amazing, but most people don't look too happy with what I showed them. And there are a lot more people refusing to even look at me than people who want to talk.

There's much whispering about the implications of an all-were. And about whether we're too dangerous to allow.

All-were. I suppose that's as good a name for me as anything.

It should upset me there are people discussing, in earshot, whether I should be executed just for existing. But it doesn't. The look on Warren's face when he realized what I am refuses to release me from its grip, playing over and over in my mind, stealing my attention and any ability I have to care about anything other than the dark acidic hole eating away at my insides.

A familiar pair of boots comes between me and my view of the ground. Heart fluttering, I move my gaze up to Warren's face. Horror still lurks in the back of his eyes, and I feel my heart shatter at the sight of it.

"Michaela..."

"Warren?"I whimper, bracing myself for being told what happened earlier was a complete mistake, that he could never be interested in a creature as hideous as I am. This preparation leaves me completely unguarded for his actual attack. My balance stands no chance against him as he grabs hold of me, pressing me against him with so much force my bones creak.

"How am I supposed to protect you from something that can be whatever it wants to be?" he growls into my hair.

A realization slams down on me. His horror isn't disgust at my condition, it's fear of the male of my species.

Wanting to howl with gleeful laughter, I wrap my arms around Warren as he holds me virtually immobile. My face safely hidden from his view, I grin at his worry. "Silly wolf. What makes you think a girl who can change into whatever she wants needs protecting?"

His arms get even tighter. "Don't talk like that, Michaela.

211

You don't know how to fight." He takes a long breath. "Do you even know how to walk as any of those animals?"

Um... " I moved around as a fox for a while..."

This is met with a massive sigh. "You moved around for a while. And you think that means you can fight this guy?"

I'm not sure the male all-were has any intention of coming near me. But if he did, it's a fairly safe bet I wouldn't want to go along with whatever he wanted. Although that probably wouldn't be fighting..."You have a point."

Loosening his grip, Warren moves back enough to look down at me, even taking an arm away from grasping me in order to grip my chin and point my face upwards. "Please don't try to fight him." The words, like his eyes, are filled with pleading.

"I won't." It hadn't occurred to me to seek him out. Although, now the thought is there... No, the wolf is right. I wouldn't know what to do if I did find him.

Nodding with a sad smile, Warren runs a hand through my hair and then takes a step backwards, releasing me completely. The temperature plummets. I was comfortable a minute ago, but now I can tell it's under zero out here. "You'll take her straight back to the school?" he asks a point over my shoulder.

"Of course," Tod answers.

He nods again. "Be careful, Michaela." His voice is thick with things unspoken, but he turns and sprints off around the house, to where the sound of motors revving testify that the wolves are leaving.

My hand goes after him, grabbing at the air, but it's several seconds too late.

Dammit.

Swallowing, I remind myself Warren will be back at school by morning. I can talk to him then, when there won't be so many strange people hovering around.

Hoping that in the dim lighting he'll mistake the redness of my face as something wind produced, I turn to Tod. "Is it time to go?"

He's grinning as he shakes his head. His eyes sparkle with what could be amusement, although it could also be tears from the wind. "Almost." He starts to walk toward the house, and I fall into step beside him. "We have to tell Grandma good night," he lets me know as he yanks open a door into blissful warmth.

Emma smiles graciously as we approach her in her daughter's kitchen. She gives us both hugs, but doesn't let us escape quite so easily. "I hoped to see your mother," she tells Tod.

He sticks his hands deep into his pockets and looks downward. "Mom isn't feeling too well."

"Yes, that's what she said on the phone." Emma sighs. "It's apparently code for that louse she broke her life mate's heart over finally going too far."

Tod doesn't bother to point out that the louse in question is his father, nor to defend him. Instead, he stares at his grandmother with dim annoyance for another reason. "You knew about her and Atherton?"

"Of course I did." Her hand swishes through the air. "Everyone did."

He leans his head back and sighs at the ceiling. "Apparently."

"Not you, dear?" Emma gives him a fond look. "Well, she wouldn't have wanted you to know, I suppose."

"Why?" Tiredly, he collapses onto one of the stools lining the breakfast bar and unzips his jacket. I go ahead and take mine off completely.

Tod's grandmother looks at him for a long time in silence before she sighs, folds her arms, and starts to answer. "Michael graduated from North Sky the year before Vivianne arrived, and he went to college in Washington. Things might have been different if he'd gone to school in Alaska, because then he may have found her sooner. Not that I can wish for that." She smiles sadly. "You know I love you kids, don't you? I realized after your grandfather died I'd given your mother the worst advice for her, but none of us would trade you for anything. Not me, not your mom, not even Micheal."

Expression pinched, Tod nods. "Of course."

"They didn't cross paths until after she had her master's degree and was interviewing for jobs. She was bound to your father already. Pure politics." Emma's gaze drifts towards the past.

"Binding the northwest together," Tod mumbles thickly, for my benefit I assume. "Dad's the first born of the British Columbia den. Mom's the heir of ours."

Emma nods, then continues her story without more elaboration. "Michael knew instantly, of course. Wolves always do. But Vivianne..." Emma shakes her head. "Everyone could tell she loved him right back, but she wouldn't be swayed by it. She picked up and moved to the lower forty eight. Claimed we needed more presence down there. And there were rumors of Washington seceding."

Tod is silent, trying to process all of this. I'm not sure why I'm even part of the conversation, much less how I should be adding to it.

"I should have beaten her with a switch and dragged her back here," Emma states, a frown deepening her wrinkles and making her seem only half her age rather than a quarter of it. "But I didn't realize it at the time. It wasn't until I lost my Bobby."

Her voice chokes, and she tries to cover it with a cough that completely fails to hide the tears swimming in her eyes. "We were a political union too. Alaska and Washington. And for so long I thought I'd been trapped into it, but it was what a noble was supposed to do." She laughs suddenly, a bitter and harsh sound. "It wasn't until he died that I realized how deeply I'd been in love with the stupid fox."

Tears roll freely now. "He always said he knew the second he saw me that we were meant to be together. Said it ran in his family, like somewhere back in history someone had gotten up to things with a wolf that they shouldn't have been doing, and now they all have the instinct of knowing when they find their mates." She's still crying, but she's smiling now too. "I don't know about all that, but I can tell both of you something."

In her pause, she switches her gaze back and forth between me and Tod. I'm the one who meets her eyes, her grandson being too preoccupied with peering at the floor as if he's trying to decipher a foreign language off of it.

"Forget politics. Forget who would and wouldn't be allowed to breed with you. Forget your pride and your history. Forget absolutely everything except love."

All you need is love.... I would sing the Beatles lyrics or make a joke or think of something derisive to do, but Emma's expression wouldn't allow any of that. The words were corny, but they were uttered with solemn belief, having an air of gospel or, my throat clinches to think of it, a death bed confession.

"Forget politics," Tod mutters under his breath. "Thanks for the permission."

Emma takes a breath at the sarcasm. "I never pushed you toward Lyly."

"Oh, really?" The caustic laugh hits my ears like nails on a chalkboard. "So you're happy to hear I broke up with her?"

Looking like she's been given a potion of youth, Emma starts to grin. "It's a good start."

Tod doesn't comment, glaring at her for a few moments before he grabs his coat and storms from the room. The door bangs behind him.

Uncomfortable in the extreme, I give Emma a tiny smile and another hug.

"I knew he wasn't ready for any of that before, but I hope he is now. You make sure his head doesn't explode on the ride home, alright?"

Laughing softly, I shake my head. "I'll try."

"Thank you for tonight." The elder fox pats my hair like I'm a little kid. "Don't let your head explode either, huh?"

She leaves me in the vacant room, going into the living room, where the rest of the den is socializing. I scramble to grab my coat and thrust it on before I have to face the freezing winter air again. I'd take my time and let Tod calm down, but I'm afraid he's angry enough to drive off without me.

But he's a better friend than that. He's at the car, leaning against the roof and staring up at the sky.

"Tod?" I ask, beyond uncertain of what I should say. I don't understand why he's so upset, so I don't know where to start trying to get him to talk about it.

With a growl, he shakes his head, then jerks open the car door and flings himself into the driver's seat.

I'm not at all convinced letting him drive is a good idea, but he isn't in a mood to be argued with. All trying to take over for him would do is make his temper even more foul.

215

The radio DJ and his callers are the only ones talking on the way back home. Their babble isn't terribly comforting. They're focusing on a recent surge in missing and mutilated domestic animals in an unnamed small town in Alaska. So far, no missing children. Thank God. But the livestock vanishing from their enclosures are starting to attract attention. Apparently national attention, since this is satellite radio. And one caller mentions the word *werewolf*. Not good. Even if the host does laugh at the guy.

Snowflakes drift lazily into our windshield and Tod flips on the wipers, which swish gently, completely out of rhythm with the song that comes on in the wake of the human speculation. It's a quiet, old country song, about pain and loss and a love that would have been the stuff of legends if our singer hadn't screwed everything up with his blind stupidity.

Tod's finger jams into one of the tuner buttons, and the numbers shift to a station offering a screaming heavy metal tune. He turns it up, and I can no longer hear the wipers. Or my own thoughts.

The bass thumps against me, making my body throb in unfamiliar ways. I cling to the door handle, holding onto it as if that will somehow make this ride safer as Tod slams us around corners and rushes into the night at speeds I didn't think this car could hit.

It's a small miracle we make it to the school both unharmed by accident and unharassed by the police.

The poor car shudders to a stop as Tod kills the engine by stalling it, leaving the keys in the ignition in his haste to get out of the vehicle. My fingers sting from lack of circulation as I reach over and switch off the headlights.

As I get out of the car, I find Tod pacing about the parking lot rather than going inside.

"Do you think..." His eyes squeeze shut although he continues to pace. "Do you think I could have inherited the ability to recognize my life mate?"

"I don't know." I edge cautiously toward him, feeling the cold to the center of my bones and selfishly wishing my friend could have started this conversation somewhere heated. "It's possible, I guess. Assuming your granddad wasn't just making things up. Mine is the lord of tall tales."

A large plume of condensation flows from him as he lets out a deep breath."I believe him." There's another cloud to obscure the air as I wait for him to go on. "Because I think I did."

He leans against one of the ceiling support columns and looks at me, level and serious. "I think..." He looks off into the distance, his eyes going toward the far wall, though he doesn't seem to see it. "Two and half years ago, there was this second when the world sort of rearranged itself and I had this... This knowledge.Some part of me that had been missing walked in and said, 'Hello, you need me.'" He takes a long pause. "And then I turned around and saw Lyly walk through the doorway." His mouth twists into a pained smile. "She was the most beautiful thing I'd ever seen."

"Yeah?" I try not to let the illness overwhelming me at the thought of Tod and Lyly as predestined life mates shine through, so I stare at the ground and keep my comment to a minimum.

"I think maybe that's why I was willing to go through so much for her. That it wasn't that I cared about allying with the east, but because deep down, I thought we were meant to be together."

"Uh-huh."

"But, Mike..." I look up at the intensity behind my name. "The feeling started before Lyly entered the room."

"It did?" Hope buoys to the surface of my mind. "So it wasn't for her?"

"No. It couldn't have been." His eyes fall to the concrete as he shakes his head. "I just let myself get distracted. It was for Aliah."

"Aliah?" I repeat, a grin breaking through.

His eyes are tightly shut again and his breath shaky."Aliah."

"That's wonderful!" I very nearly clap with glee.

"Wonderful?" His eyes spring open to stare at me with incredulity. "I spent the last two years with her sister!"

"It doesn't matter."

"How can it not matter?" he yells at me. "She was my life

217

mate, and I ignored her all this time because I thought her sister was hotter? That matters!"

"Not *was*," I correct softly."*Is*. She *is* your life mate."

He shakes his head."She'd have to be an idiot to have anything to do with me now."

"Maybe." I put my hand on his arm. I hate to betray a confidence, even if it's one I gained from observation rather than from confession. Tod is three steps past desperate though, and I just can't stand to watch him suffer more than he needs to. "But she'll do it. Because she loves you."

His eyes rove over my face, as if looking for a trace of lie. "She won't even talk to me."

I sigh. "Not this afternoon. Not since Lyly started acting like you'd gotten back together."

He lets out an anguished groan as his head bangs back against the cement support. The look he gives me bleeds misery. "If she can't forgive me for possibly taking Lyly to a dance, how is she ever going to forgive me for the rest of it?"

"She was just upset today." I try to look reassuring. "If you'd been paying attention, you'd probably have seen she got upset every time you and Lyly got back together. You were just too happy to notice it the other times."

His skin has turned a sickly shade, a color that stands in rather nasty contrast to his hair. His face twists in a decisively nauseated way.

I sigh. "I didn't say that to make you feel worse. I just meant to say you still have a chance. Because you've hurt her in the past, but she loves you anyway. Even though you've never given her an ounce of encouragement."

A long, quiet look later, he asks, "And she's told you that?"

"No." I'm reluctant to make the admission, but I'm not going to lie to him. "It's pretty obvious, though."

He doesn't say anything in response, even after contemplating the ceiling for several moments.

"Tod, if you don't ask for her forgiveness, you'll never know if she can give it or not."

More silence...

"You owe her the apology at least, don't you think?"

"Yeah." He takes a deep breath. "And you honestly think there's a chance she'll forgive me?"

"More than a chance." I smile softly as he gathers his courage and starts toward the door.

"You weren't supposed to agree with me about the idiot thing, you know."

I laugh. "I wouldn't want you to think too much of yourself."

Chapter Twenty-Four

I frown as Tod stops in his tracks and turns abruptly, facing toward the exit to the parking structure – the exit to outside, not the one that leads into the nice, warm rec room. "She'll be in fox form," I point out. "You can wait until morning, can't you?"

He grunts. "She can hear me just as well with furry ears as with hairless ones."

"Yeah, but..." Shaking my head, I realize I'm not going to get anywhere arguing with him.

"If I stop," he whispers, "I'm going to lose my courage."

"No, you won't. Don't underestimate yourself."

Then again, looking into his eyes is like peering into a vortex of fear. He's absolutely terrified.

"But, come on." I give him a gentle smile and take the lead. "We'll find her."

The wind hits us when we step from the parking garage, and I can only hope Tod realizes how good a friend I'm being going along for moral support like this when all I want to do is run up to my room and hide under the comforter for a few days.

Approaching the building the foxes use as their base during the full moon, we slow to a stop as a suspicious shape far too large to be a fox breaks away and rushes to us. Tod hisses at the leopard as it comes to rest at our feet. "What are you doing here?"

It's a snow leopard, a gorgeous animal with silky fur of black and white, a lithe body, and the most beautiful eyes I have ever seen. I shush Tod. "Seth isn't here to hunt, you idiot."

Despite the subzero temperature, I slide my glove off, unable to resist seeing if Seth's fur is really as soft as it looks. Running my fingers briefly through it proves that, yes, it is. As I soak in the warmth of him, he closes his eyes and purrs.

Tod lets out an annoyed grumble. "It's alright. He's here to flirt with you. Fine." He starts to walk around us, but Seth leaps away from me, blocking him. His eyes dart about frantically.

"I think he's trying to tell us something."

Tod gives me a droll look as I slip my glove back on. "Think it has anything to do with Timmy or wells?"

Seth snarls. Even recognizing that he's my friend and highly unlikely to eat me, the sight of it sends my fight or flight instincts into hyperdrive. It's all I can do to stand here, and I'm bouncing from side to side as I do it.

Closing his eyes again, the massive cat takes a deep breath.

He starts to shimmer, shifting back into his human form despite the fact that it is obviously causing him pain. Hunched over, he directs his fevered gaze to Tod. "Aliah. Not back. Lost the trail the same place you did. Couldn't find another."

Tod doesn't even bother to curse before he sprints into the woods. So I let out a stream of expletives long enough for the both of us. Not just repeating the word *expletive* over and over, either.

Shaking and having difficulty breathing, Seth forces his head to move to me. "News gets worse. The male you. He was there."

Oh, God. My stomach plummets sickly. I was sure before that she was just sulking, just needed time to herself. But if there's another all-were out there, she could well be in danger.

Seth is starting to shimmer. "What are—" he gets out before the change takes him and steals his ability to speak. He growls in frustration.

"I'm whatever I want to be," I whisper. At his look of feline confusion, I take a breath of the frozen air, feeling it lance into my lungs and using the pain of it to focus myself.

Fox. Leopard. Mammoth. Wolf.

I leave out the truly tiny animals of my usual demonstration, not feeling any particular need to force Seth to control his hunting urges. I leave myself as a wolf and start to unsteadily trot toward the woods. I see what Warren was getting at in telling me that turning into something is different than being able to effectively be that thing. But I'm warmer with fur, and I have to get used to it some time.

Seth bounds in front of me, pulling his lips back in warning. Guess he's a member of the Michaela-can't-take-care-of-herself camp.

Huffy, I move my eyes from Seth to the trees. This is silly. If Aliah actually is in trouble, I can help her a lot better than Tod can. There's no proof beyond my fear that she's in danger, but I can't just pretend it isn't possible. Until I lay eyes on her and see she's alright, I'm going to assume she needs me.

I could try to debate this with Seth, but Aliah may not have the time for me to waste. My solution is heavy handed, but I don't have time to think of anything subtle. I change into a dragon and leap over the leopard.

My blood starts to freeze before I can even bunch my muscles together. I don't know what to do with the wings, and the tail throws me all off balance. But I make it past Seth, even if I don't do it gracefully.

As soon as my feet touch the ground, I shift back to lupine form. The wolf's body suddenly seems a lot more familiar than it did. At least it's warm blooded. That alone makes it less alien than the dragon.

I catch up to Tod as he stares at the place we lost Aliah's trail earlier. "She's hurt," he tells me when I come to a stop. Seth's right behind me, glowering.

Nodding, I sniff at the ground. It doesn't do any good though; the fresh snowfall has taken away any hint of scent. I turn human so I can talk. "How do you know she's hurt?"

"I just do."

I agree with him, even though I admit it could just be our fear that lends us certainty.

"I can get through," I tell him. "Then be something big enough to help her. I'll bring her to you."

"I'm coming."

"No!" I yell, halting the shimmer around him as he starts to shift. "I need you human when I get back."

His mouth opens to argue, but I don't hang around for it.

Becoming a ferret, I dart into the trees. Seth's jaws snap shut behind me, although whether he's making a statement or honestly trying to stop me by whatever means necessary, I don't know. I suppose it's even dimly possible he's decided he's hungry.

Wiggling along in my weasel form, I get through the dense trees and find myself in a little gulch. There doesn't seem to be any way into it except for the way I came.

The clouds shift, and the moon shines brightly across the landscape.

Make that, I amend, two ways in: through the trees, and from that cave over there.

I stay little as I approach the hole in the rock face. If the male version of me is watching, there's no reason to make sighting me easier than it has to be. Although, I don't know why he would be watching for me. If he'd sent some sort of ransom note to the school telling me to come here, there would have been more people waiting on me when I got home.

Timidly, I creep from the sparse protection of the gulch into the cave. A small fire is lit well inside of it, far enough in that it wasn't visible from outside. Unless Aliah managed to shift her way back into her human body while injured and distressed on a full moon, someone else has been here recently.

Heart hammering, I urge myself forward and nearly gag when I get a whiff of the hole in the rock face. The cave absolutely reeks of the male all-were. The smell is strong enough I can't even begin to guess when the last time he passed through here was. He could be here now for all my nose knows.

But my eyes know he isn't.

There's a fire, and there's a tiny bundle of white fur. Tied to a stake, Aliah lays on the on the ground looking more like a discarded winter hat than a living fox.

Shifting human, I run to kneel beside her. "Aliah?" I ask, trying to tell if she's breathing. Please, God, let her be breathing!

Her dirty white body jerks just before the vixen's eyes slit open. A small whimper answers me, and I struggle not to cheer. "It's okay," I whisper, taking my coat off to lay it on the ground. While I'm thanking God for things, I should toss in some gratitude that my changes leave me clothed when I resume human form. I have no idea how I'd handle this situation naked. "I have you."

Aliah hisses and squeezes her eyes shut as I lift her, then place her gently on the coat. Tucking the jacket around her like the blankets I used to wrap around my toy dolls, I whisper to her that everything's fine now and that Tod's waiting for her. "In fact, if I don't get you back soon, he's probably going to start ripping apart the forest trying to find you."

Gently, wincing at her hiss of pain, I lift the bundle and start to walk toward the cave exit. The only way back to school is the same way I got in here, and I don't know how I am going to carry Aliah through. Perhaps I can rig some sort of sling and drag the coat behind me? Would that hurt her too much?

It hits me along with the blast of arctic wind that attacks me at the cave entrance that there has to be another way to get out of here. The trees were disturbed by Aliah, but no one else had passed through them in a long time.

Silently thanking Warren's tutoring, I look around for signs of passage from the cave. It's hard to see with the clouds passing over the moon at random intervals, and my eyes, while better in the dark than a normal human's, aren't as good at night as most animals'. The snow looks flat, and the trees blend into the sky.

I spot a broken branch hanging limply from a tree a short way from us, and I inch toward it on unsure feet. The clouds between me and the moon get thicker, diminishing my vision further. Dammit.

Hoping I can pull this off, I put Aliah down. "I can't see," I explain, taking off my scarf and tying it around her to form a sort of carry strap. I shift to wolf and gently take the scarf into my mouth.

I can't say the wool tastes good, but it holds.

Slowly, trying not to jostle the injured fox more than absolutely necessary, I edge along the floor of the gulch, the snow tickling coldly at my legs. Past the broken limb, I find enough other clues to lead me to a pass that winds gently upward.

Sadly, the pass is filled with huge boulders.

I stop to think for a few minutes. The other all-were comes this way, so I can do it. If I can just figure out how.

What form does he use?

If he flies, then I'm out of luck. I don't think I can learn to fly while carrying my friend. But there could be another way... I just need an animal known for leaping about on giant rocks.

I shimmy into the shape of a mountain goat, hoping I can get its balance right. In unfamiliar form and carrying a very important package, I start timidly onto the rocks.

It takes a long time, and I nearly lose my balance on a patch of ice and thus almost send us crashing down the incline to break all of our bones on more than one occasion. But with a lot of forethought and careful planning, I manage to summit the rocky pass. As I leap from the top of the last rock down onto a familiar path, I have to resist the urge to open my mouth and bleat in triumph.

I know exactly where I am now. I've passed this place several times in my walks with Warren. But since the rock behind me is taller than I am by several feet, I never knew there was anything interesting behind it.

Once again a human, I gather Aliah in my arms. Holding her tightly, I jog back to the school as fast and smoothly as I can. Well before I think he has a hope of hearing me, I start to yell for Tod. Seconds later, he breaks out of the woods, running toward us in a heated sprint.

He beats Seth. And leopards are not sloths.

"Aliah?" he rasps, moving aside my coat enough to reveal her face. Her eyes slit open, and when he puts his hand against her cheek she leans into it. "Oh, God, Aliah," he whispers, reaching to take her from me. "How bad is she hurt?"

I swallow. "Several gashes. Some broken ribs I think. And he was keeping her by a fire, but she was pretty cold even before we left the cave."

Holding her against him, stroking her fur gently, he walks toward the house, murmuring to her about antibiotics and painkillers. It's a sign of his anxiety that he doesn't even bother to ask me where she was or who it was that had her. Right this second, he honestly doesn't care.

Mr. Atherton cares plenty when he finds out though. He practically froths with how much he cares.

"One of my students was missing and nobody bothered to report it? Do we have to institute a roll call?"

Tod and I don't say anything.

225

"And what were you thinking going after her yourselves? The creature out there is dangerous! And you just waltzed into his lair without weapons or backup or even common sense!"

"He is dangerous," I reply, fighting to keep my voice level. "And he had one of my best friends. I'm the only person here who could have gone in and saved her."

I've told everyone the whole story, recited it while we were watching Aliah get her stitches. She's sleeping now, knocked out by the promised pain meds. It's a miracle Mr. Atherton managed to drag Tod away from her long enough to be yelled at.

"You are not the only person who could have gotten her," Mr. Atherton corrects, his teeth grinding against each other as he forces the words out. "Any fully matured fox could have done it." He punctuates this with a glare at Tod that clearly conveys belief that my den father does not fall anywhere near this category. "They could have taken flashlights and climbing gear and gotten out just fine."

"If they knew what to expect," I agree. "But, you were there when we got her inside. You heard the nurse as clearly as I did. Aliah was sliding deeper into shock. A half hour's delay would have killed her."

His look is not swayed. "You didn't know that, Michaela."

"I knew she was in danger."

"No," he argues. "You feared she was."

"And you?" He turns his head to Tod. "You're Michaela's den father, you're supposed to protect her. Part of that is keeping her from doing stupid things to put her life in danger."

Tod nods. "You're right. And I don't have an excuse. I'll tell my grandmother to appoint a new den leader."

"That's not fair," I blurt. "And you do too have an excuse!"

He smiles faintly. "I had a motive. That's different. And I had no right to risk your life to save her."

"Like you could have stopped me!" I stand, angry and fed up with all of this. My glare turns to Mr. Atherton. "Tod didn't endanger me. I endangered me. And I'd do it again in a heartbeat."

The wolf watches me for several seconds, not saying anything. "Go to bed, Michaela."

"What?"

He repeats himself, very slowly. "Go... to... bed... Michaela."

"Fine. I'm exhausted anyway."

"And Michaela?"

I stop with my hand on the office door, but refuse to turn around. "What," I growl through clenched teeth.

"You're not to leave this building until further notice."

My jaw drops and my head snaps to look behind me.

Mr. Atherton's gaze is firm and tense. Something dangerous lurks behind it, leading me to choose stomping away before I say something that will help me determine what it is.

Grounded! He grounded me! I can't believe it. I haven't been grounded since I was nine. The closest I've come was when my dad wouldn't let me go to homecoming freshman year because I cut class to go to the mall, and I told him I was looking for a dress instead of admitting I just couldn't stand to stay in school that day after I broke up with my boyfriend at lunch. I didn't even want to go to the stupid dance because I wouldn't have had a date.

Not that I have anywhere I want to go tonight either, but it's the principle of the thing.

Fuming, I sit down at my computer and open my email. I would love to write to someone about this, but what would I say? Even leaving out the shape changing, reporting that I am now locked away because I rescued my friend from the clutches of an evil killer would probably raise eyebrows, and possibly questions regarding my sanity.

There's something from Warren.

Smiling and suddenly feeling a world better, I click on it.

Reading, I stop smiling.

"Michaela.

"Weres have an interesting relationship to the moon. We love it. It's beautiful. It's part of us. The joy of the change is a high that humans can only imagine. But we also hate it because it robs us of so much, of inhibitions and sense and of our own personalities. We can't think straight. I guess you could say the moon is a drug and we're all addicts.

"Sorry to be boring you with my philosophy. I'm just trying to explain what happened tonight. I would never have treated you like that any other time. I'm sorry. Forgive me?"

227

He's apologizing for kissing me. Blaming it all on the moon.

Disgusted by the tears pricking at my eyes, I turn off the machine without replying and go to take a shower, letting myself sob as I stand in the stream of steaming water.

How could he possibly kiss me like that and then say he didn't mean it?

The moon made him do it? Because in his right mind he'd never want anything to do with me?

"Damn you, Warren. Damn you for making me feel this way."

I shudder. "And damn me for letting you."

Chapter Twenty-Five

I wake up as exhausted as when I passed out last night and drag my weary body out of bed about an hour after the start of classes. Before going downstairs to see if I can get some breakfast, I stop by Aliah's, not sure if she's up here or if she's still down in the nurse's office. Tod opens the door, huge circles under his eyes and his hair looking wind ravaged. "Hey." He steps aside for me to enter and closes the door after me again.

The room is lit by sunlight drifting through the windows. Decorated all in whites, it feels open an airy. Sitting on various surfaces, there's an endearing collection of plush arctic animals, mostly foxes. Even the paintings are predominately white, being oil renditions of local landscapes in winter. The exception is a vibrant portrait of a red fox placed prominently in sight from the bed. I have to smile at it. The painting looks just like him.

"How is she?" I ask softly, mindful of her sleep.

"Healing." He sits beside her on the bed, in a spot already rumpled. "She hasn't been awake much. I haven't been able to get her to eat anything, so she might need an IV later."

"And how are you?" I narrow my eyes at him.

"I slept."

Very little from the looks of him.

"Did you eat?"

He shakes his head. "I'm not hungry."

I sigh. "I'll be back in a few minutes with breakfast."

"I'm really not-"

"This is me leaving." I slip out the door, letting it click shut behind me.

The student kitchen doesn't have anything more nutritious than bagels this morning, so I go over to the main kitchen to see if there's a chance of getting something there.

The kitchen staff sits at a table, cups of coffee in front of all three of them. They smile when they see me and two of them clap. "The hero awakens," the lone male says cheerfully.

Hero? I nearly look over my shoulder.

"You must be hungry, what can we get you?"

Shrugging, I finish walking over to them. "Actually, I'm here to get something for Tod."

The women trade glances. "For Tod?"

"He's keeping watch over Aliah," I explain. "The poor guy hardly slept. He keeps saying he's not hungry, but I don't know when the last time he ate was." I'm not sure if he had lunch yesterday or not, but I'm certain he skipped dinner. And he only picked at breakfast. He may have had something at the coffee shop, I can't remember.

"I didn't see him yesterday," the younger of the women, a wolf, says, and the others shake their heads as they get up from their seats.

"We'll get him fixed up," the female bear assures me. "And you need to eat, too."

"What about Aliah?" the man wants to know as he takes a stack of beef from the fridge.

I sigh. "She's not awake yet."

Worried frowns appear at the news. The wolf girl sighs. "Well, at least Tod's finally come to his senses, right?"

"About time," the bear chimes agreeably.

I blink, startled the staff cares so much about student love lives. Beef sizzles as it hits a pan on the stove.

Ten minutes later, I'm heading up the stairs lugging an unbelievably heavy tray piled with rare steaks, broth, potatoes, bread, milk, ginger ale, apples, and chocolate cake. My arms ache from the weight. I could never be an old-fashioned, serving maid... or even a waitress.

"Here, let me help." Vivianne Fox rushes up a few stairs to grab one side of the tray. "How is she?"

Paused, I watch Viv for a few seconds before starting up the stairs again. "Sleeping mostly, but Tod says she's healing. She needs to eat though."

"And how's a sick person supposed to eat all of this?" She smiles at the plethora of food, which is, indeed, way too much for Aliah. Even if she'd been well, it would be too much for Aliah.

"I'm feeding Tod, too," I admit.

"How is he?" The look that accompanies the question is fearful.

"All things considered, he's doing alright." I stop and knock on Aliah's door.

The door swings open, and Tod's eyes narrow on his mother. He turns his back without saying anything to her, cleaning a space on Aliah's desk for the food.

"Tod..." Tears lurk in Vivianne's voice. "I'm sorry I didn't tell you about Micheal."

"You should be." He hands me one of the plates I brought up and motions towards the food. "That's not why I'm mad at you though."

Her shoulders slump. "What else have I done?"

Tod sits on the edge of the bed, giving her a long look. "It is about Mike, but not about you not telling me you were his life mate."

The older, masculine Mike. Not me. The conversation has absolutely nothing to do with me.... Trying not to stare at the action, I move a few pieces of beef and a potato onto my plate while I contemplate fleeing the room.

"I never did anything with him, Tod. I never betrayed your father."

"Betrayed my father?" he sputters, aghast. "My father? You don't owe him anything. You betrayed Michael Atherton!"

"Betrayed Mike? What-"

Tod's on his feet now, glaring down at his mother. "You are his life mate, Mother. You mean more to him than anything else in this universe, and you abandoned him because you were too immature to accept that the easier choice, the political choice, was the wrong choice." He takes a step closer to her. "And to make things worse, you run to him every time something goes wrong. You let him pick up the pieces for you, and then you leave again, breaking his heart all over. And he has to let you, because you're his life mate."

Her breath quivers when he's done, her lips tremble as the words sink in. Then she whispers in a voice chaotic with emotion, "What makes you think you know so much about it?"

His reply is deceptively soft. "Because like your father, I'm

231

wolf enough to know my life mate. And I nearly lost her last night. And don't think for half a second I wouldn't have lost myself, too."

Vivianne's expression softens. "You..."

"Yeah." Tod nods, and then they stand staring at each other until tears start to run down Vivianne's face.

"I..." She chokes and has to start over. "I..."

"Have no respect for the concept? Yeah, I know."

"No! That's not what I meant!" She grabs at his arm, but he jerks it away, leaving her finger to brush through the fabric of his sleeve. "I-"

"Mom, save it."

"No. Tod..." She's sobbing so hard now I can't make out what she says after that.

"There are words for what you are," Tod tells her coldly. "But they aren't words you say to your mother. So I'd appreciate it if you would leave and let me take care of my mate."

"Tod!"

"Later, Mom."

She sniffles, rubbing her hands against her face. "Later?"

"I'm not disowning you." He sighs loudly. "I'm just pissed off."

Still sobbing, but doing so less nosily now, she nods and makes a quick retreat.

Tod looks to me, his eyes tired, but I move my gaze significantly to the bed. He turns, going still when he sees Aliah looking up at him.

"Hi," he whispers. I can almost hear his thoughts demand to know what she just heard when he thought she was sleeping.

"Is that true?" Aliah asks, her voice weak.

With a little cough to clear his throat, he shifts from foot to foot. "Is what true?"

"That you think you found your life mate?"

"There's no thinking," he skirts the question. "It's a matter of knowing."

"Really?"

"Yeah." He inches around the edge of the bed. "Yeah, but I doubt she wants anything to do with me."

Her eyes locked on his, she raises her brows. "And why

232

wouldn't she want you?"

"Because I'm an idiot," he whispers. "I spent the last two years chasing her sister."

"Did you?"

"Yeah." He kneels down beside her, taking her hand in his. "And I have absolutely no idea how I could ever make that up to her."

She smiles softly. "You could try telling her you love her. She might like that."

He takes a deep breath. "I love you, Aliah." Her smile widens. "I am so sorry, and I don't– "

Her fingers lay against his lips, cutting off his words. "You can grovel later." She moves her hand. "I love you, too."

My heart flutters, and I find myself grinning inanely.

He leans over, kissing her. Slowly and gently, but with very serious intent.

I grab one of the milks, the chocolate one, and take my breakfast back to my own room, somehow holding off on the jubilant laughter until after I've closed my door.

My computer screen shows half an email to Warren before I even realize I'm typing to him, filling him in on last night and this morning.

I stop and stare at the computer.

Why am I bothering? It's not like he cares. It's not like we're friends. It's not like he meant to kiss me. It would have changed everything if he had, but he hadn't....

Besides, it's after the full moon. He's back at school now. He'll be there at lunch, brooding at his table under the window.

I finish the email anyway and hit send.

He's not in the dining room when I get there, but it isn't until the room starts to fill most of the way up that I start to worry maybe he won't show up.

While I'm staring at the empty spot that Warren's supposed to be in, the chair beside me slides out and Sam sits down, her tray landing with a dull thump. Despondently, she jabs her fork into a salad, mixing the greens around without giving off any indication she's planning on eating them.

"What's wrong?"

"Nothing."

Uh huh. I don't press the issue though because Seth and Bryce are sitting down with us.

The boys say hi, but then go back to conversing about hockey. It's not a subject I know much about. Sam, on the other hand, would be avidly contributing right now if there were nothing wrong.

At some point while I'm engrossed in eating my stew, worrying about Sam, and wondering where the heck Warren is, the conversation shifts. Dimly, I realize Bryce is talking about the dance tomorrow. And, more specifically, he's talking about the bear he's taking to it. Frozen, I stare at my food.

"Mike!" Seth says urgently, jerking my attention to him. "How's Aliah?"

Aliah? Oh, right. They went to class. No one else here knows what happened this morning.

"And why are you grinning like the Cheshire cat?" the leopard continues, a smile teasing his lips.

"Aliah's fine." I fold my hands primly on the table, struggling without success to stop grinning. "She's healing quickly and receiving excellent care."

"And..." Seth leans forward, his gorgeous eyes dancing. "Where is your illustrious den father?"

If I was grinning madly before, I must look deranged by now. "Dutifully watching over his little kit, of course."

"So the rumors in the staff room have some amount of truth in them?"

I blink. "Rumors in the staff room?"

Seth shrugs. "I had to use the photocopier. People were talking."

I doubt very much that Aliah realizes how many people care about her. And she will die of embarrassment if she ever finds out that even the faculty is gossiping about her romantic entanglements.

"Um..." Sam, pale and gloomy, finally joins the discussion. "Are you guys saying what I think you're saying?"

"That your brother and your best friend are the official It Couple of the year?" I ask. "Yep."

"Since when?" she demands.

I give an easy shrug. "Since the obvious hit Tod hard

enough in the head that he started paying attention to it?"

Despite her mood, she smiles. "Good."

"More than good," says Bryce.

He looks confused when Sam gets up and wanders off without further comment. "What's her problem?" he asks me. I don't have the heart to tell him, so I just shrug and eat my food.

The rest of lunch is strained, and Warren never does show up.

My afternoon class is held outside of the building I have been ordered not to leave, but that unfortunately doesn't get me out of attending it today as it's been moved inside for everyone's safety. I wind up not only having to attend it, but I find myself giving the lecture.

In the dining hall, where class has convened today, I tell the freshman about my experiences last night, about how I knew where to go and what to do at various places. I'm not sure how useful the information will be to them since Kim is the only other person in the room who will ever have the option to change into whatever she can think of, but everyone acts interested in it.

Everyone except Warren. He's so disinterested he doesn't even show up.

Warren's not around at dinner either. Not that he's expected at this point, although that doesn't stop my eyes from locking onto his table and refusing to leave it for more than a few seconds.

There's an email from the wolf when I get back to my computer though. My heart beat speeds up when I see it. I'm smiling as I move the mouse over the message, but there's fear in me, too. The last time he wrote to me, it wasn't exactly something I wanted to read.

Why do I care so much?

The message is simple. "Way to go. How did you manage to pull that off?"

That's in response to a quote about Tod and Aliah. He doesn't say anything about why he wasn't at school today. Maybe when he told me 'after the moon' what he meant was Monday.

He doesn't say anything about me going after Aliah last

night either, even though I told him that part of the story. I suppose he figures his disapproval is a given that doesn't need expanding on. Possibly because I actually used the phrase "your disapproval is a given" in my email.

And he, thankfully, fails to point out how I never said anything in response to the message he sent me after the gathering. Even though he knows I had to have read it because the address I wrote to was the one I got off of that and not his school account.

I opt not to answer this email and go over to Sam's room to watch a movie with her. Neither of us broach the subject of Bryce. Or of Warren, even though I'm thinking about the wolf all evening, and I'm sure her thoughts are with the bear.

On waking the next morning, I stretch and wonder how I should spend the day. I check my email, but there's nothing new from Warren. There is something from my dad, who says he's accepted an offer on the house. The news that he's that much closer to moving up here should make me happier than it does. All I can think is how much I hope it's safe for him.

There's also something new from Amanda Heathly, a friend of mine from my increasingly distant Seattle days. She asks me to call her because Alaska isn't covered by her free long-distance plan, and she's not sure what the time difference is anyway. She doesn't say what she needs to talk about, but I'm free all day and can spare a few minutes for her.

I run downstairs to grab some cereal, and then I sit down to call Washington.

"Hello?"

"Hi, Amanda!"

There's an uncomfortable humming from her end.

"It's Mike. You asked me to call you."

"Oh! Mike! I couldn't for the life of me figure out that area code!"

I've been gone long enough for people to forget my voice? If she saw me, would she still recognize me, or have I been completely erased already?

That's not fair. She did email me, after all.

"I was just wondering if you know where Troy is."

"Where Troy is?" I squint at myself in the mirror and start

to tap my fingers. "I broke up with him and moved to another state."

"Well, yeah, but he was going on and on about you after you left. He was totally devastated. And then he started talking about finding you and getting you back just before he disappeared, so I thought maybe... You know, maybe he found you."

"No." My fingers still against the cold surface of the desk. "How long has he been missing?"

A dark foreboding shadows my heart when she answers. "Almost two weeks."

My breakfast rolls unhappily in my stomach as I end the call and dash down the hallway to Aliah's room. I rap hastily on the door, my heart racing and my thoughts begging to be wrong.

Tod, showered and in clean clothes, answers my banging almost instantly, the alarm on his face escalating at the sight of me. "What's wrong?"

He moves aside to let me in the room as I shake my head at him. "Maybe nothing. I don't know."

Aliah is reclined against a stack of pillows. A checkerboard sits on a chair beside her. It looks like she's winning. "What is it?"

"The guy who captured you..." She pales at the mention of him, but nods me onward while Tod sits down and grabs her hand. "Did you see him in human form at all?"

Reluctantly, she nods. "Yeah. He wasn't very nice. I think he's going sort of crazy from being out there."

Not surprising. "What did he look like?"

"Look like?" She tilts her head to the side, her breathing losing its steady cadence. "Teenager. Tall. Medium build. Dark, spiky, hair. I couldn't tell what color his eyes were, just that they were scary. His nose was pierced."

Expletive.

"Him?" I hold up a picture of my ex-boyfriend, sighing when she nods a wide-eyed confirmation.

Chapter Twenty-Six

My stomach tries to rebel against me as I grit my teeth and toss Troy's picture to the ground. Tod bends over to pick it up as I start to pace the room, shaking my head and fighting against the feeling of my fingers shifting into claws.

"Who is he?" Tod asks quietly.

"Troy." The name bubbles up through the hatred to be spat out at my friends. "My ex-boyfriend."

I wish he was here right now. I'd rip his throat out.

"It's like a movie," Aliah says. "He wanted a mate, so he attacked his girlfriend."

"A bad B movie," Tod agrees, staring at the photograph in his hand.

"Only you didn't change when he thought you should," Aliah goes on. "So he thought it hadn't worked."

Tod nods. "So he changed Kim too."

"Stop that," I snap.

"Stop what?" Tod asks.

Folding my arms tight across my body, I glare at him. "Finishing each other's thoughts. There's only so much cute I can take right now."

"Sorry," they respond. In unison. They both struggle to hide grins.

Besides, there's a flaw in the idea he changed Kim just because nothing happened to me. "Couldn't he have smelled the difference in me?"

"It can take a while," Tod replies with a shrug. "If you'd smelled different right away, then Mom would have gotten you up here sooner. He'd probably already given up on you before your scent shifted."

Right... "I didn't feel human anymore," I mutter. All the blood lust and the restlessness and the dreams of running in the wilderness, it was pretty obvious to me that something had changed.

Aliah gives me a sympathetic look, but Tod ignores the comment. "Does this help us catch him?"

"Maybe."

"We're not using for you bait," he clarifies. "Is there any other way this could help?"

"We could use her clothes," Aliah suggests.

I snort. "I think he'd guess something was up if he found a trail of loose clothing leading him somewhere. But I may have something else."

"What?" Tod demands swiftly.

"Perfume. There's this one I wore most of the time we were going out. He really loved it. Enough that I haven't worn it once since I've been here."

"What's its name? Is it hard to find?"

"No need, I have some with me. There was a travel bottle in my toiletry bag. It came with me because I didn't notice it was there." I nearly threw it out when I found it. Glad I didn't.

Tod's on his feet. "We need to tell Atherton."

Aliah starts trying to get out of bed, her eyes latched onto Tod with a fanatic desperation. She doesn't want to be left. But she's having trouble getting up, so she needs to stay put.

"You guys wait here," I tell Tod, jerking my head significantly toward his beloved. "Take care of Aliah. I'll be back."

He doesn't look too pleased, but he goes to sit beside Aliah, holding her hand while I leave.

Taking a few seconds to grab the bottle first, I run downstairs to find Mr. Atherton. He's not in his office, but in his living quarters. Vivianne is there too, sitting on a sofa in front of darkened TV. She looks like she might have been crying recently.

"What is it, Michaela?" she asks, her voice raspy but kind.

"I think this will help catch the male all-were."

I wave the little bottle through the air. The others trade a look. "And that is?" Mr. Atherton prompts.

"My ex-boyfriend's favorite perfume."

Neither of them look startled, shocked, or even curious

about the revelation that I know who's out there. They do look guilty though.

"You knew." My knees give way, dumping me into the nearest chair. "You knew it was Troy, but you didn't tell me?"

Mr. Atherton sighs. "I thought knowing would make it harder for you just to sit here and wait."

The wolf has a point. It is hard not to run outside, screaming Troy's name. He came all the way to Alaska to live outside in the cold for me; he'll come to talk to me if I call for him.

And then I can kick his ass.

Except he's a lot tougher than I am. I've never been in a fight in my life. Troy has. And, to my knowledge, he's won all of them.

Vivianne reaches out and places her hand on mine, tentatively, as though she thinks I'm going to jerk away. "We know he wants one of you girls, but we didn't want to scare you. And we certainly didn't want you running off to handle things yourself."

"Not one of us," I correct her, telling her about my conversation with Amanda. "She's certain I'm the one he's obsessing over. Even when I pointed out that Kim has wound up in the same school as me, she was sure that if he showed up it would be on my account, because I was all he talked about for days before he vanished. Of course," I smile faintly, "she was probably also sure he wouldn't have four legs and a tail."

Lifting the bottle, Mr. Atherton turns it in his hand, studying it. "This is something he would associate with you?"

I nod. "I wore it most of the time we were going out. He bought me a bottle for my birthday and stuff." I shrug. "That's why I haven't worn it since I came here. It reminds me too much of him."

Nodding slowly, he starts to smile. "So you think we could trap him with it?"

"I think so. Unless he's gotten a lot smarter than he used to be."

He thanks me, then sends me away under renewed orders not to step outside of the building unless it's on fire.

I try to just chill, but the urge to go out and do something is nearly overwhelming.

Back in my room, I pick up my phone and dial a number from the local phone book. I think I know at least one person who will relate to how I'm feeling.

"Denali's," comes a voice. It has the same professional tone as Warren's, but is nowhere near deep enough.

"Is Warren there?" I ask. "It's Michaela."

I regret volunteering my name when she repeats it and then starts go, "Um..." and "Uh..." Clearly, she's stalling. "No," she finally recovers. "He's not home. I think he went with his dad. They're trying to figure out what this all-were does all day."

"Well, when you see him..." And why do I get the feeling she can see him right now? She can't be the one keeping him from talking to me, though. He would hear what she's doing, and he'd object if she was doing it without his permission. So, he just doesn't want to talk to me then. And he's too chicken to say so. "Just tell him I said hi, and that I hope he's alright, and that..." That I miss him more than I want to admit? That the fact he won't speak me to me makes me feel as though I'm shattering into a thousand fragments, each one throbbing in pain? "Tell him I know who the male all-were is."

"What?" she hisses. I can hear footsteps, then a door closing.

"I know who he is. He's my ex-boyfriend. He turned me. Then he turned the girl he replaced me with. And then he came up here to stalk me. I gave Mr. Atherton some perfume that should help lure him out from wherever he is."

"You cannot tell that to my son." The words are frighteningly firm and full of threat, even though they're whispered.

"Why not?" I ask, genuinely perplexed.

"Because-" She cuts off her exclamation, returning to her steady whisper. "You just can't tell him, Michaela. Please?"

The please is so heartfelt I would have to be a complete bitch not to agree.

But I wish she'd explain why not.

I'm still obsessing over this hours later, when someone knocks on my door around five and sends my heartbeat to warp speed even though I know the knock isn't one Warren would use.

It was far too timid.

Plus, there's the fact that the guy won't even talk to me on the phone. He's not exactly likely to be visiting anyway.

Expecting one of the foxes telling me it's time for the *Lord of the Rings* marathon they've planned to start, I open the door with a smile. The smile doesn't falter because I find out I'm wrong, although I'm certain my expression changes.

"Are you ogling me?" Seth asks. "And is that a good thing?" He assumes a look of puzzlement. "I'm not sure if I've ever been ogled before..."

"Oh, you've been ogled plenty, baby," I assure him with a lascivious leer. Laughing at his expression, I let my face take on a more natural countenance. "Sorry." I lean against the door frame. "You look good, Seth." This is an understatement. I don't usually ogle people who merely look good. In a black suit with blue shirt and tie, the leopard looks at least a hundred different kinds of hot. And his eyes...

Actually, his eyes aren't nearly as gorgeous as they should be considering how well the clothes set them off. They're too worried.

"What's wrong? You're not nervous about Sarah, are you?" I don't know his date, but I can't imagine her being in any way displeased with him.

"No," he responds quickly, sounding absolutely certain of the truth of the denial.

His eyes move into my room, then to the hallway, where people are running around frantically trying to finish last minute preparations, then back inside. I take the hint, scoot out of the doorway, and wave him inside, closing the door behind him.

Patiently, I wait.

He leans against my desk, picks up Wolfgang from beside my computer, staring at the plush wolf dully. He puts him down again and looks at me. "I'm worried about Sam."

Worried about Sam?

"Why?" I sit down on the edge of my bed and peer at him. "I mean, other than the whole Bryce thing."

His hands grip the edge of the desk. "Do I need something

other than the whole Bryce thing?"

"Well, yeah." I watch him closely, but his body isn't betraying much and his face is hidden. "She's hurt, but she's not going to fling herself off a glacier over it. She'll cry, she'll mope, she'll eat too much cheesecake, and then she'll get over it."

He lets out a long breath. "But she will get over it?"

"It's just a crush, Seth."

"Are you sure?" He asks this with a slow measure that makes me think he's placing a great deal of value in my answer.

"Pretty sure."

Standing so still he looks like a statue, he takes a few long moments to think about this.

"Alright," he breathes eventually. His eyes finally leave the floor and meet mine. "But you'll watch after her? Just in case she needs it?"

"Of course." My smile is small, but hopefully reassuring. "Although, Samantha Fox isn't nearly as fragile as you're implying."

"I know. It's just..." His head shakes, letting his unbound hair swish with the movement. "When Bryce started on about that bear yesterday morning, and I saw how much it hurt her... I don't know how I got out of there without trying to kill him." He falls silent for several heartbeats, then glances reluctantly at his watch. "I have to go. Commitments, you know."

"Yeah. Commitments." I don't have any idea what else to say.

I watch the door for a while after he leaves, wondering what just happened. There's never been any evidence of anything between Seth and Sam before, but that certainly came across like more than friendly concern.

When the sounds of people in the hallway die down and I'm pretty sure everyone who's leaving has left already, I slink from my room to go down the rec room, where I find the two younger Foxes at the foosball table.

"What are you doing here?" Scot asks, sounding affronted.

I shrug. "I've never been into dances. It would have been a bother, going all the way to Anchorage to hunt for a dress, then having to wear it and do makeup, then having to force myself to get through a dance...."

"Is that girl code for no one asked you?" he interrupts as his sister shoots a goal. "Because if no one asked you, then the boys here are just plain stupid."

Smiling at the kid, I shake my head. "Thanks for the sentiment, but several people did ask me." Like half of the freshman class. They seem to think I'm heroic. "I honestly didn't want to go."

Toni drops the ball in. "Besides, there's no reason to tie yourself to one person for the whole night. It's better to go stag anyway."

She tried to sell this to her sister earlier. Sam didn't buy it. Unlike me, she had a dress and had been looking forward to going before Bryce's little bomb dropped. I don't know that he needs to die for it, but I wouldn't mind it if Seth roughed the bear up a little.

I wasn't going to tell Sam about the leopard's visit to my room, but she looks so forlorn cuddled up in an armchair with a tub of Ben and Jerry's clutched in her little hands that I find myself spilling the news within minutes of the opening credits.

"You're kidding," Sam hisses when I'm done.

Holding my hand over my heart, I pledge, "May God strike me dead if I'm lying." I grin and lower my hand. "I tell you, he was really worried about you. He wouldn't go until I promised him, like, a million times not to let you wander out onto the tundra and die."

Sam stares at me by the flickering light of the television. "Seth?" she hisses. "We are still talking about Seth?"

"Yes! Seth!"

"Seth who goes to school here? The leopard? The one with the luxurious if bizarre hair and gorgeous eyes that delve into your soul and a body that's to die for? The Seth who could have any girl in this school, except for Amber and possibly - stress on the possibly - Aliah? That Seth?"

"What do you mean possibly Aliah?" Tod asks from where he lays on the sofa, his arm draping possessively over his mate, who promptly pinches him and then draws the arm tighter.

"Yes," I say, ignoring the interruption. "That Seth."

"You people are talking over the movie," Scot complains.

Toni smacks at her brother. "But, what they're saying is

244

more interesting than hobbits."

"You'd make them shut up if they were talking over elves."

"Hello! Only because Legolas is almost – *almost* – as gorgeous as the guy they're talking about. I mean, have you met Seth?"

"Hello! Not gay!"

Sam is still curled up in a pitiful way, she's still got her ice cream in a death grip, and the puffy redness has not fled from her face. But as her siblings start punching each other over a very mature argument of, "Be quiet!" verses, "No, you be quiet!" she is smiling.

My good deed accomplished, I slide over to lean against the edge of the couch. Tod reaches down to ruffle my hair. "Good work," Aliah whispers.

Too bad I'm having so much trouble ignoring my own pit of despair. I try to get caught up in the fantasy and not dwell on why Warren won't talk to me, but it's like trying to ignore starving to death. It can't be done.

We take an intermission after The *Fellowship of the Ring* and before *The Two Towers*. Volunteering for popcorn detail, I run into the mini-kitchen and start the first bag in the microwave, then rummage through the lower cabinets for large bowls.

I'm halfway into one of them, reaching way into the back, when a sudden realization I'm no longer alone causes me to jerk up, smacking my head into a shelf with a clunk I'm sure was audible throughout the entire state.

The laughter behind me, I recognize.

"Jesus Christ, Warren, what is it with you freaking me out in kitchens?"

He stops laughing. "Sorry."

He turns to go.

"Whoa! Not so fast!" I scamper to my feet.

Stopping with his back to me, he looks over his shoulder with deadened eyes. "What?"

Good question.

I feel as though I should be demanding explanations from him, but I'm not quite sure which ones.

The look in his eyes bothers me.

"What's wrong, Warren?"

"Nothing." He turns away again, although his feet don't move. "I'm just here to pick up some stuff." Another step.

"You're in the kitchen to pick up some stuff?"

"No." His shoulders move under the power of a massive sigh, settling into an uncharacteristic slump. "I'm in the building to pick up some stuff. I'm in the kitchen because I smelled your scent coming in here and wanted to make sure you were alright. You seem to be." He takes another three steps before I stop him again.

"Warren! What kind of stuff?"

"Just stuff from my room I don't want to leave here."

"Don't want to leave?" I cross the space between us in some of the longest, quickest strides of my life. "You say that like you won't be here to use them."

His face turns towards me, but his eyes refuse to meet mine. "I won't be."

I don't know the name of the emotion that grips me, but it's cold and it hurts. My heart isn't breaking, it's freezing.

"Warren..."

He looks completely away, shifts his body, but doesn't leave. "It's better, Michaela."

Then he does move away. One step... two... three. The tears make my vision blurry, but I can still see him approach the door, ready to leave, ready to walk right out of my life.

I shouldn't care, not this much. But I've never felt a pain this intense.

"Am I really that disgusting?"

He stops. "What?"

Sniffling, I run my hand along my nose, not caring how gross that is. "You find me so appalling you have to move? Kissing me was that revolting?"

"Michaela!" His hands wrap around my shoulders, and his eyes bore into mine. "Did I seem revolted to you?" he growls.

No, he didn't... not at the time. At the time, he seemed at least as attracted to me as I was to him. But then there was the email, and the refusing to talk to me, and now the leaving.

My eyes squeeze shut, and I struggle to draw enough

breath to whimper. "You said you only did it because the moon drove you crazy. You said you were sorry. You regretted it. You're never going to do it again."

There's an audible sigh, and the hands fall away, leaving my shoulders cold. "It wouldn't be very nice to Seth for me to keep doing things like that, would it?"

I open my eyes far enough to give him a confused squint.

"Seth?" My brain struggles through my agony to try to think.

"Seth?" I repeat again. Warren's looking at me like I'm an idiot. "You're not allowed to kiss me because of Seth?"

His face is close. "Your boyfriend?"

"He's not my boyfriend." My tears have stopped. The faintest of glimmers of hope starts to shine. I almost, almost, manage to laugh. "I don't know where you are getting your gossip from, but it's not a reliable source."

He scowls at me, the look dashing my newborn hope against the wall and drawing tears back to my eyes. His words are uttered in a guttural growl. "It's not gossip."

"What do you mean?"

With a deep breath, he jams his hands into his hair, leaving his fingers tangled up in it. "I've seen you."

"Seen us?" What the hell is he talking about?

His hands jerk forward. "Why are acting dumb?"

"It's not an act." I shake my head. "I don't know what you think you picked up on, but you're wrong. We flirt some, but that's the extent of it."

"Stop lying to me!" he roars.

"Warren." It's a whimper, whispered as tears start to cascade and as my whole body begins to shake with emotion. I back up, stopping when I hit the counter. "I'm not lying."

"I saw you. You were kissing him. And you meant it, Michaela. I could see you meant it." The words are dragged from somewhere deep and dark and hidden. Hearing them, I slide down the side of the cabinet to the floor. "It hurt so much," he whispers. "I jammed my claws full force into my leg and couldn't feel it."

Jammed his claws... I stop shaking, traveling to the point where I am so upset as to appear calm.

"Blood." My lips form the word, but I'm not sure it was audible. "It was your blood in the hallway outside of the music room."

"Yes."

That was the same day he left Wolfgang at my door, the plush wolf that I've clung to every night since. Bile rises in the back of my throat. That was the last day Warren was at school. He left, thinking I had chosen someone else.

"Warren..." I look up at him. His pain is raw in his eyes. "I'm sorry."

Pausing for a tearful breath, I try to let him see how much I mean it.

"Sorry?" he asks in a dull voice.

"I..." I don't know what to say, what I should be explaining. "I never meant to hurt you."

God, say something less trite! "It..." Struggling to breathe, I take half a second to try to think. It doesn't work. "I didn't even know it would have hurt you..."

Why won't he say anything? Why is he just standing there, looking at me with an expression I can't translate and a tension that feeds my tears?

"And he was so sad..." I sniffle again, an ugly sound I'm sure comes with an ugly wince. "And I didn't know I shouldn't have done it. And that's all there was, one kiss. And then we laughed about it because the idea of us being anything other than friends is just ridiculous. And I swear that's all we are, all we ever were or ever will be."

The sudden surge of words collides with a series of sobs that still only when I realize Warren has edged closer to me.

Expression guarded, his head leans to the side. He takes a long breath, and his eyes narrow. "You smell like him."

He's not exactly accusing me of anything. He's just doesn't appear certain he can let himself believe me.

I sigh. "I told you, we're friends. You probably smell Sam on me too, and, I assure you, I'm not dating her either."

His stance doesn't alter.

"I last saw Seth several hours ago," I tell him, although I don't know why I'm going to these lengths to explain myself. If he doesn't trust me, do I want him to stay? "He was on his way

248

to the dance. Without me. And he was worried about Sam. He just wanted me to tell him she'd be fine and he was doing the right thing to run off to take the girl he'd promised to go with to the dance. I gave him a very chaste hug on the way out because he is my friend, and he seemed to need it."

Abruptly, Warren sits. "He's your friend."

"Yes."

He looks down at the denim stretched over his knees, then pulls his gaze up to mine. "Am I your friend?"

My eyes drop. "Sometimes."

"When I'm not being an idiot?"

"I don't mind you being an idiot." Looking at him, I start to feel everything might be okay. "Just don't be a jerk about it."

Every so slightly, his mouth curves, and his eyes start to crinkle. "I'll try."

We sit, looking at each other and not saying anything, for what feels like years, before he takes a long, very shaky, breath as asks, "So, does that mean you are currently unattached?"

Currently unattached? I smile at the phrasing. "I don't know."

His eyes narrow. "You don't know?"

"No." I shake my head, my eyes staying with Warren's. "You see, there's this one guy I'm really, insanely, interested in... I even broke into his room once and stole a dirty shirt so I could wrap it around my pillow at night." His eyebrows go up. "And he gave me this stuffed animal I not only can't sleep without, but would carry around to class if people wouldn't make fun of me for it. And he disappeared for a few days, and I've nearly gone crazy looking for him pretty much everywhere I go, up to and including the ladies' room."

I was fine when I started speaking, but the words are getting harder to form, my breath harder to draw. My earlier panic grabs hold of me again, shaking me like a rag doll. "But he's stopped answering my email, and he won't take my phone calls, and now he says he's leaving school."

The tears are back in force, spilling down my face in an avalanche of watery grime. "And I know it's crazy when I've only known him for a month, but..." I have to fight to have enough air to go on. "I don't know how I'll stand it if you leave, Warren."

Leaning over my knees, I stop talking and allow myself to cry in earnest.

"Michaela." He moves to wrap me in his arms, pulling me onto his lap, placing me sideways to rest my head on his shoulder. Hands pushing me into him and stroking down my hair, he makes soothing sounds. "Shh... It's alright. I'm not going anywhere."

"You said," I gasp.

"That was before what you said." He arms tighten for a brief moment. "How could I leave after all of that?"

"How could you leave before it?"

There's a gentle sigh. "I didn't know you wanted me... to stay."

"Of course I want you."

He squeezes me tighter.

"God, I love you, Michaela. So much."

He loves me.

Loves me...

Love...

I love him too, don't I? That's what I was saying before, in a much more roundabout way.

I am in love with Warren Denali.

I am in love with a wolf.

My heart is cheering, and I grin as I pull back, even though the tears haven't stopped. I put my arms around his neck, bring his head down for a kiss, trying to put everything I feel into it so he will know, beyond a doubt, that I do value him... want him... love him.

"Mike!"

I go still at the sound of my name pounding against me from outdoors.

"I know you're in there, Mike!"

Oh, expletively expletiving expletive! My head turns, my eyes going in horror to the windows.

"Come out, come out, wherever you are!"

"Who is that?" Warren half-growls, half-breathes into my ear.

I look back to him, a new level of fear surging inside of me. I understand now why his mother didn't want me to tell him

250

what's going on. The fear of Warren doing something stupid and getting himself hurt is crippling.

"Come on, just one dance?" the voice comes again. "For old time's sake?"

Warren's teeth grind together. "Who is that?" The question, slowly ground out, is a deep, ominous, rumble.

"It's Troy," I admit, clinging to Warren for dear life when he tries to spring to his feet.

Chapter Twenty-Seven

Warren and I are arguing over whether he gets to go outside or not when Tod comes into the kitchen and wins it for me. "Warren, if you go, she's following you."

The wolf shuts up instantly, glowering but no longer vocal in his disapproval of the situation.

There's some more yelling for me. I try to ignore it.

Tod's eyes examine the windows. "I don't think he can see you from here. So he might not know for sure you're here. Go into the dining room." He glares when I don't move. Warren grabs my elbow and tugs me toward the doorway.

"Mike..." Troy's voice has a playful tilt to it when he says my name, but then it turns cold and brittle. "Who's touching you? Tell him to stop."

"So much for not being seen," I mutter, continuing into the hall anyway.

"Where are you going? Come outside!"

Odd, I honestly don't remember him being this insane. Or insane at all.

"Please, Mike!"

Tuning Troy out again, I look to Tod. "Is Mr. Atherton here?"

"No." He shakes his head. "And no response to his cell. I did get word to your mom, though, Warren. So I expect several pack members to be here before too long."

Warren's breath hisses inward. "They're hunting pretty far from here tonight. We didn't think he'd come back again so soon since it was obvious his lair was found."

The fox accepts that with a mild grunt.

"Tod?" Aliah, pale and vulnerable and all the prettier for it, sneaks into the room. "Think we should get the tranquilizers?"

"Sure. How?"

She dangles something in front of her. It looks like a knife until she pulls it open and a reveals a series of long, slender sticks. "Same way I got them last time."

Tod starts to grin. "You can pick locks?"

Nodding, she closes the picks with a fluid motion, laughing as Tod swoops her into his arms and spins her around asking, "Have I mentioned I absolutely adore you?"

"Not in the last five minutes." She places a playful kiss on his nose. "And you can elaborate later. We need to stop the psychopath."

He grins. "Yes, dear."

It takes Aliah all of ten seconds to get into the room off of Mr. Atherton's office where the guns are stored. It takes her a lot longer to get into the weapons cabinet itself. Nearly a minute.

Warren stands very silent through all this, scowling at nothing in particular. He keeps humming in a low, menacing tone. My hand squeezes his whenever the humming starts to get too loud. That seems to help.

He tries to move to the front when the lock snaps and Aliah swings the door open, but I hold him back. "Let the calm people be in charge of the weapons. Please?"

Looking down at me, he seems torn between anger and something else, something softer. I can't tell if it's a good something or a bad something.

"I'm not questioning your competence," I whisper. "But you've been trembling since this started."

His eyes still filled with mysterious emotions and hidden thoughts, he shuffles his feet. He opens his mouth to say something, but closes it again as Tod slaps a rifle into his hand.

The boys stare at each other for a long second. Then Warren nods, some sort of male understanding achieved. Tod goes back to the other guns as Warren removes his hand from mine, backs into the far corner, and examines his piece. I go to stand beside him, leaning against the wall.

My eyes close in a dispirited sigh as Lyly surges into the room. It didn't seem crowded a second ago, but now I feel like a sardine. "You're stealing," she proclaims.

"What are you doing here?" Tod asks her, sitting on the

253

edge of a table pressed against a wall. He opens a box of cartridges, removes some, and tosses the rest of the box to Warren.

Her hand plunks down on an upraised hip in one of Lyly's infamous dramatic poses. "You grounded me," she grits out.

"No," Tod starts to load his weapon, "I told you to stay away from school functions. I assumed you were out somewhere else."

"With whom?"

He shrugs. "With any number of people." Holding out the gun towards Aliah, he gives her smile. "You're a better shot than I am."

She mumbles something, accepting the gun while staring at the floor. His fingers linger on hers, and her lips curl almost imperceptibly, although her eyes don't lift.

"I'm not going to let you take these weapons." Lyly glares at her sister, a look more hostile than any I'd want to receive.

Warren takes a step toward her. "Then I'll shoot you."

"What?" Her jaw drops in disbelief. She says nothing as Warren and I walk around her. When Tod and Aliah try to pass though, her hand lashes out to grab his arm. "Tod, you can't shoot this guy. He's a friend of Kim's. He's harmless."

Aliah keeps walking.

Warren growls, turning to show his teeth to Lyly, who looses several shades of color when she takes in his expression.

Tod gives his arm a sharp jerk and continues onward. "Kim can call him a friend all she wants to, but half the state is looking for him."

"There's no evidence he's the one they want!" She falls in with our group as we go up the stairs. I'm not sure where we're going, but everyone else seems to know. "All you know is some people smelled a similar creature."

My steps falter. She has a point. Just because Troy is up here and acting kind of weird doesn't mean he's the horrible beast that's been terrorizing the local livestock.

"He'll have a trial," Warren growls.

"After you've shot him!" Lyly snaps.

The wolf shrugs, not at all bothered. "Non-lethal injection."

"Still! You can't just inject people who haven't done anything!"

254

"He's trespassing," Tod points out. "And disturbing the peace."

Nearing the back of the building again, we can hear his voice belting out an incredibly off-key rendition of "Buffalo Girl". "Buffalo Girl, won't you come out tonight, come out tonight..."

It's almost enough to make me laugh despite everything.

Warren makes a sound I can only call a huff. "Please tell me he is not referencing *It's A Wonderful Life*."

"Sorry, no can do." I reach out for his hand, squeezing it lightly.

"I used to like that movie."

"Yeah, me too." Enough to force Troy to sit through it about a dozen times during December. Although it didn't occur to me that he was actually paying attention to the film while learning the intricacies of my bra clasp.

"Uh, hello!" blurts Lyly. "Back to relevant conversation?" No one says anything else, which she takes as a cue to go on rather than as a sign she's being ignored. "You can't shoot someone, even non-lethally, over bad singing. You haven't even tried asking him to leave."

Dang it. Another point. We all stop walking.

"You're acting like an idiot because she has you so brainwashed!"

What? Who has who brainwashed?

"Everything was fine before she showed up!"

"Stop shrieking," Aliah snaps. "Are you trying to give away our position?"

"Give away our position? Do you think this is a spy movie or something?" Even in the present situation, Lyly finds time for a melodramatic stance, her hand gluing itself to her hip. "I know you're in league with her. I even know what your payoff was." She looks directly at Tod.

"We don't have time for this," Warren grumbles, leading me down the hall.

"Ly..." Tod's voice holds little sympathy. "You need to get over yourself." His footsteps fall behind me, Aliah's beside them.

Sputtering sounds are the only retort Lyly's able to come up with.

We find Tod's siblings in the library, near the windows. Toni's looking down thoughtfully. "You know, he's pretty cute for a deranged lunatic."

"We don't know he's a deranged lunatic," insists Lyly, coming into the room well behind the rest of us. I had sort of expected her to run off somewhere, but she's determined to inflict herself upon us for longer.

Sam sneers at her. "Aliah recognized his picture."

His arm around Aliah's shoulders, Tod glares at Lyly as she speaks her next words. "She's just saying that because it's part of their plot."

Sam snorts. "And what plot would that be?"

"I don't know exactly." Lyly sits in the middle of a sofa and gives me an arched look. "But I'm going to find out."

"Good luck with that." Sam's response is dismissive. Turning her gaze to her brother, she asks, "So, you're going to pick him off from up here?"

"That's the plan." He guides Aliah to the windows, and they look down.

"He's too far," Aliah proclaims sadly.

Lyly makes an ugly sound highly reminiscent of a pig.

Warren and I go to stand beside them.

The lights under the library window should be blocking us from Troy's view, which I assume is why we're in this room. Below, Troy paces. He's stopped singing now and is just peering anxiously in the lower windows as passes by them.

He's not nearly as close to us as the volume of his voice had led me to assume, and I gather the dart guns don't have very long range.

"I can get him closer."

"No." Warren doesn't even bother to think about the answer.

"Then I can stall him. Get him to stay longer so the pack has time to get over here. Although, I'd rather we put him to sleep before they show up. I don't want to see any of them hurt."

"No." Warren didn't think about that one either.

No one contradicts him.

"I'm not wanting to go outside," I tell the others in exasperation. "Just talk to him from a window. Give him just enough hope he doesn't give up and leave."

"No." My wolf's jaw is set firm.

I give him an inpatient look. "Warren, you're being unreasonable."

His eyes narrow, flashing like silver. "It isn't unreasonable to protect my mate."

My mouth gapes open.

Warren's mouth snaps shut.

His body stills, and his eyes swell into huge orbs.

I smile gently, laying a hand on his arm. "It's okay, mate. I'm not going to endanger myself. I'm just going to go yell out a window at some idiot I used to know."

He's still not saying anything, and everyone else is looking at us in silence, most of them shocked, but Tod and Aliah with knowing little half smiles. I pry the gun from Warren's fingers and hand it over to Tod. "We'll go next room over."

The foxes nod, and I pull Warren after me.

"Michaela..." he whispers as I lead him down the hallway.

"Yes, mate?"

"You're... I... I mean..."

"We'll talk about it later, mate."

"Okay."

His grip is tight on my hand as we go into the room. We go up to one of the windows, and Warren slides down to sit beneath it, his fingers still clutching mine and making it harder to open the window. Not that I'm complaining. If he never lets go, that's just fine by me.

I call down to get my stalker's attention.

"Mike!" Troy leaps into the air in his excitement when I stick myself halfway out the window. "There you are!"

He looks so normal grinning up at me that I almost wonder if Lyly is right about him being innocent. Maybe what happened with Aliah was just a big misunderstanding. Maybe he didn't realize she was a were and thought she was just a fox lost from her den. Maybe the other creature attacked her, and he was trying to help her. Maybe he only tied her up by the fire to make sure she stayed warm.

He bounces along the building, getting closer to me, but not quite close enough to Aliah for her to have a shot. "God, I've missed you." Too far away for me to see them, I nevertheless can vividly picture the way his deep hazel eyes must be sparkling.

"Hey, Troy," I chat. "What brings you up here?"

His arms spread wide as he grins at me. "You, babe! Surprised?"

"You could say that."

"Really?" His arms fall, and he takes an eager step forward. "So you didn't give your perfume to those disgusting wolves that are trying to murder me?"

"Of course not." They aren't trying to murder him, nor are they are disgusting. I try to smile in a beguiling, trustworthy way.

"Thank God. I couldn't stand the thought of you doing that to me."

There's a lot of anguish in the statement. Enough to make me want to feel bad, even though I don't.

"So, you're like me?" I try to sound excited. "You're the one I've been smelling?"

"Yes!" He grins, proud of himself. "I'm the one who turned you. So we could be together."

"With Kim?" I can't help but ask.

"Oh, baby!" His head shakes. "I never cared about Kim. She was a mistake. I'd never have touched her if I'd known it had worked on you. I thought you must be immune. It never occurred to me there's just a delay."

"Why should it have mattered?"

His posture angles in confusion. "What do you mean?"

I sigh. "Why should it have mattered so much? So what if I stayed human?"

Warren's thumb rubs against mine, comforting me. There's more hurt behind my question than I'd like to admit, and I guess he senses that.

"I'm a were." Troy's declaration is made with a noticeable implication that he thinks I'm an idiot for asking.

Not much point in continuing with that, is there?

"How long have you been here?" I ask, trying to verify he is, in fact, behind the missing animals without having to ask him outright and risk offending him.

"I don't know. A while. I've been trying to get up the

258

courage to come talk to you. You were so mad at me on the phone. I came up here right after that. It was like I couldn't stay away anymore when I realized how upset you were. But then I got here and, I don't know... You were never alone and... Could you come out here, I don't like shouting all of this."

I shake my head. "Sorry, I'm grounded."

"Grounded?"

"Yeah." I'm not sure if I should say what for, so I hold off on that. "I'm not allowed outside of the building at all."

"Well, can I come in?"

"I don't think that's a good idea. We're not supposed to have visitors."

He curses. "Mike! Why are you being like this?"

"Like what?"

His hands flail about in the air. "Aren't you at least a little bit happy to see me?"

"Of course I am." Seeing him means he'll be in custody soon. "But you can't expect too much from me. I mean, I did break up with you. You remember that, right?"

"Yes, I remember," he snaps. "That's why I'm up here trying to beg you to forgive me. Mike, I spent all my money getting to Anchorage. I walked – *walked* – here from there. I've been living in a cave! You do not even want to know what I've been eating."

"Like goats and sheep?" I guess.

"What? I wish! Try hibernating rats."

"Rats don't hibernate," I point out, my brain on autopilot.

He growls. "God, Mike, I don't know what they are! They're little and furry and gross, and if I couldn't change into wild animals, there's no way I'd be able to make myself eat them."

"You've been living off rodents?" I ask very slowly, narrowing my eyes at him. Could he be telling the truth?

"That and the occasional stuff stolen from town."

My head tilts to the side. "What kind of stuff?"

There's some more cursing. "What's your obsession with my diet?"

"It's important, Troy," I tell him, trying to be calm. "What have you stolen?"

259

"Christ, Mike! There was some beef jerky and candy bars from the general store. A bag of pretzels from someone's car. I did manage to get some ground beef out a truck at that bar. A couple other small things. Nothing much."

"Hold on one second!" I hold up an index finger before ducking back into the building. Sitting below the window, I look over to Warren.

"There was a box of beef missing last weekend," he admits in a low whisper, not looking happy about it. "We assumed it was lost during loading or something."

Expletive. "I don't think he's lying."

He looks even less happy than he did a second ago. "Are you sure?"

I shrug. "No, but... He's a horrible actor."

"He managed to fool you into thinking he was human."

Alright, that's a valid argument.

"Not to mention the whole second girlfriend thing." I shrug. "Except he never lied about that. He just starting avoiding me."

Troy bellows up again. "What are you doing, Mike? Is someone in there with you? It's not the guy from the kitchen is it?"

There's a shout and a long string of profanity. "What the hell? Did you just shoot me? You just shot me!"

Quickly, I lean out the window again. "What happened?"

He's not looking at me, he's looking at the dart sticking out of his arm. With a jerk, he yanks it out. "Someone shot me!"

"That looks like a tranquilizer." Not a lie. Not even an evasion, really. I have not claimed I don't know for sure what it is. "Hold on! I'll be right down!"

"Michaela..." Warren follows me, tight on my heels since my hand is still in his.

"You'd rather he ran into the woods? Give us the fun of tracking him?"

Tod's in the doorway of the library. "What are you doing?"

"I don't think he's lying," I respond. "And if he isn't the nasty bad-thing everyone's looking for, then it would be rude to leave him outside to freeze to death after we knocked him unconscious."

"He's still stalking you," my den father points out, not

exactly charitably.

I shrug. "Plenty of exes do that. Doesn't mean they deserve hypothermia."

Neither of the boys are pleased with me, but neither continues to argue. They do continue to follow me, though, making it obvious I'm not going to be allowed to go out on my own. Which isn't something I'd argue about anyway.

With my hand on the doorknob, I pause to take a steadying breath. "Warren?"

He finally drops my hand, looking down at his shoes. "I won't attack him."

Turning, I brush a finger along my wolf's jaw. "That's not what I was going to say."

"Oh?" One corner of his mouth sneaks up in a sardonic half-smile. I fight the urge to kiss it.

"I was going to ask you if you thought you could stop growling now."

The rogue corner of his mouth juts further up. "Nope."

It's disconcerting to see someone smile and growl at the same time. I'm not quite sure how he's managing it.

"Fair enough." I open the door, shivering as soon as the air hits me.

Damn, I should have taken the time to find a coat. It wasn't so bad when I was mostly in the building and yelling out, but walking outside has me instantly chilled to the core.

"Mike!" Troy rushes forward, clearly thinking to make a grab at me. He finds himself standing within an inch of Tod instead. "Who are you?"

"This is Tod Fox. He's my friend and my den father."

"Your what?"

I smile sweetly, standing behind Tod, but to the side where Troy can see me. "He's the leader of the den I joined."

Troy scowls. He tries to edge around Tod, but the fox merely repositions himself. "Is that some sort of cult?"

"No."

Troy's edging continues, but gets him closer to Warren than to me. He moves his eyes from Tod to me, urging me to do something to bring us together. Guess it doesn't occur to him I'm perfectly happy with Tod staying between us.

261

"Come inside," I invite, turning and pushing Warren through the door in front of me. "You're doing great," I whisper to him. His growling falters for a full second. Until Troy speaks again.

"Who's the other one. Is he a friend too?"

"This is Warren. And he's my boyfriend."

The growling stops dead as Warren casts a disbelieving glance over his shoulder. I hiss quickly, "Don't argue," and he raises his eyebrows at me, pivoting in order to better stare in my direction.

"Your what?" Troy's stopped moving.

Sighing, I turn back to him, letting Tod in and then leaning on the doorway. "Troy, you're going pass out soon. Do you want to do it inside or out in the snow?"

He moves forward, reaching for me, but I slide out of his way. His movements are already groggy.

"Tod?" I ask.

He makes a sound of acknowledgment, watching Troy with a displeased frown.

"How long do these darts take to kick in?"

Shrugging, he looks to Warren, who is still staring at me. "Five minutes or so?"

"Five minutes?" My arms fold tightly beneath my breasts. "So what good was having a dart gun with you the night I first changed?"

Smiling softly, Tod looks to the floor. "It wouldn't have done me any good." His eyes slide up to me. "It was just to minimize what you did after mauling me."

Shaking my head, I move to the rec room, going to stand in front of the fire, still shivering in belated response to the cold.

Troy's eyes are glazed as he stumbles after me. With a disgusted sigh, Tod reaches out to support him, keeping him from falling on his face. "Sit down." He guides him to the sofa, where Troy sits, watching me blearily.

"I don't feel too good, Mike."

Nodding, I rub my arms. "You'll feel better after you sleep."

"Promise?"

I smile. "Could you feel worse?"

Looking at Warren, he says, "Probably not."

262

Then he takes a shaky breath and promptly falls over to the side.

Chapter Twenty-Eight

With all the animation and strain suddenly drained from him, I realize exactly how tense Troy was before. Relaxed now, he looks more pitiful, easier to sympathize with. He looks like hell: filthy, exhausted, and with two weeks worth of growth on his face. Of course, to his dismay, he's never been capable of growing a full goatee, struggle though he did last summer, so what is there now can't really, in all honesty, be dubbed a beard. But something about the scraggly patchiness of what hair he does sport makes him all the more tragic to behold.

I've moved towards him before I realize it.

Leaning over him, my hand goes to his forehead, but snaps back instantly. "He's burning up."

I lean further with a thought to at least unzipping his coat, but jerk back as I catch a good whiff of him. Hand to mouth, I stagger backwards while I try not to gag.

"What's wrong?" Tod frowns with concern.

"The smell."

Puzzled, the fox sniffs the air around Troy. "He's obviously been living in a cave for the last two weeks, but he's not that ripe, considering."

I shake my head. "It's not that. It's... I felt ill when I smelled him in the woods too."

Tod's eyes widen as he remembers. "I'll take his coat off." He sets about doing that as I try to draw a clean breath, but the whole room is permeated with stench now.

Backing, my eyes go to Warren. He stands near where I was at the fire, watching it with a complete lack of interest. The firelight highlights his hair with streaks of rosy gold, makes him seem more a creature of magic than a part of the mundane world. Changing course, I rush to him, flinging my arms around him and burying my face against him.

My stomach instantly settles as the welcome scent of wolf mingled with the ashy scent of the fire drown out the unwelcome smell of male all-were.

Stiffly, Warren puts one arm around me and uses the other to draw a hand through my hair.

A group of people rush into the room, but I don't bother to look at them, assuming them to be the foxes we left upstairs. Their voices back me up in this as they start to talk about our slumbering visitor.

"He doesn't look frightening at all anymore," Aliah observes after the newcomers establish his identity and that he's sleeping, not dead.

Sam laughs softly. "Well, you're both human now. And he's out cold."

I had managed to forget for a few minutes about what Troy did to Aliah. I was too busy feeling sorry for him. Feeling tired, I shake my head at my stupidity.

"What is it?" Warren murmurs into my hair. I pull back some, looking up at the lights flickering in his eyes. The effect makes him wild, should probably make him frightening. Smiling tenderly, I reach a hand to brush through his hair.

"What's up with his smell?" Sam's question shifts our attentions to her.

"He's been living in a cave," Tod tells her, same as he told me a few minutes ago. "You expect to him to smell freshly showered?"

"It's not that," Aliah answers. "There's this... Strange undertone. An edge of..." She shakes her head helplessly.

"Does it make you nauseous?" I ask.

"No..." Aliah answers slowly, narrowing her eyes at Troy as she thinks about it.

"It doesn't make me sick either," Sam tells me. "I just don't like it much."

"It's probably pheromones," Tod says softly, letting out a sigh and sitting down in one of the armchairs. "They affect Mike more because she's of his species."

Toni clicks her tongue. "I thought pheromones were supposed to attract potential mates, not make them vomit."

Her brother shrugs. "Too many of them can probably be

overwhelming."

Lyly smirks. "Or her body could be upset with her for fighting against them," she offers with malicious sweetness oozing from her voice. "Maybe she should stop doing that."

Warren's arms tighten as if he thinks I'm actually going to act on that advice at any point.

"I'm going to try calling Mr. Atherton again." Tod pushes out of the chair with more violence than absolutely necessary and heads swiftly to the edge of the room as he pulls his cell from his pocket.

I sit on the edge of the fireplace, pulling Warren down beside me. Closing my eyes, I lean against him and let myself drift off into a world comprised only of warmth.

I wouldn't have thought I was tired enough to fall asleep, but between the heat of the fire and comfort of Warren, I get lulled into a slumber. One minute, I'm listening to the gentle flow of the foxes' conversation, focusing on the familiar and reassuring patterns rather than their words, and the next instant Seth is in the room asking questions about our guest.

Groggy, I squint at the clock on the wall. It's still shy of eleven at night, so Seth must have left the dance incredibly early.

The leopard sits down between Sam's chair and the fire, looking at Troy with an expression I can't read in the dim lighting. We still haven't turned on any of the artificial lights and have only the fire.

"So..." he says softly. "We got a call shortly after we left-"

"We?" asks Sam, a bit too eagerly.

"Well, Raja." He shrugs. "I rode back with her. Some of the chaperons from the other schools, and even a lot of the students, were pretty upset about her being there with Amber."

One of the changes in the post-Simone leopard world was that Amber decided that since she was no longer Simone's flunky, there was no longer any reason to stay in the closet.

This upset a fairly large percentage of the student body. A very large fraction of the males, to be precise. Not because they're homophobic, of course. The boys were upset because not only is Amber now lost to them, but she managed to snag a date with the incredibly gorgeous and exotic tigress Raja, something a lot of them had been trying to do for years. Losing any shot at either of the girls in one swoop was a bit too much for some of the poor things to handle.

"And you just left your date?" Sam quires.

Seth shrugs again, looking neither thrilled nor terribly unhappy. "She was one of the upset ones."

Ah. Yes, even under the best of circumstances, you aren't going to get very far with Seth if you can't accept his sister. Not after all the guilt he's been going through over Simone.

He goes back to his story. "A few minutes after we left, there was a call from Atherton. None of our students are being allowed to leave."

"Why not?" Tod leans forward, frowning.

"They're not being told. But they have been warned there's a decent chance they'll have to stay all night."

Weary looks are traded about the room.

"Mike!"

My name is shouted with gusty panic as Raja sprints into the room, her Kohl-lined eyes wide with horror. "She has Amber!"

Seth's on his feet instantly. "Who has Amber?"

"Kim."

"Kim?" Lyly repeats.

Raja nods quickly, tendrils of inky black hair falling around her face. "She was outside the kitchen and called that she needed help with something. Amber went to help her while I was pouring some drinks. Then I heard screaming, and I looked out." She pauses to gasp for breath. "I don't know what Kim turned into, but she's huge and freaky, and she says if Mike doesn't go out there right now, she's going to kill Amber."

Kill Amber?

I sprint down the hall, Warren at my heels and the others close behind him.

Noises come from outside, scuffling and howling.

Great, the calvary is here at last. If they've endangered Amber, I'm killing them all.

As we run toward the door, it crashes open and the leopardess in question virtually tumbles into the room. Her flapper-inspired evening wear is ripped in several places, but

267

otherwise she looks fine as she falls into her brother's arms.

The rest of us rush to the windows.

Outside, a pack of wolves snarl in a circle around a massive creature, some sort of demon. It's at least eight feet tall and wide as a small car. Covered in scales, its hide looks like custom-made armor. Its nails are as long as scythe blades. Its eyes glow a wicked red.

"That's Kim?" Sam asks, incredulous.

"Yes," Amber assures her.

Several wolves leap as one. It's an orchestrated attack that should have granted at least one of them a decent hit, but Kim blurs into motion, knocking them all back. One lands with its neck at a sickening angle.

The Kim Monster presses forward, sending wolves flying through the air, many with bloody swaths torn down their bodies. Most of them don't get up again.

She's decimating them.

"I have to fight her," I realize.

I don't say the words with relish.

"Like hell you do," Tod snaps. "We still have guns, you know."

"Yeah? Well, they still take five minutes to work, don't they? And that was on someone in human form, who knows how long it would take to knock out that thing."

"Michaela..." Warren's anguish does reach me, but I can't stay in here just because he'll be worried about me if I don't.

"Aliah," I look to the vixen, "can you get a shot on her?"

She nods, takes up her gun, and goes straight to crack the door and fire three rapid shots into the night. Slamming the door shut again, she takes a deep breath. "At least two of them hit. And I think they broke through the scales."

I don't know what the repercussions of an overdose of these sedatives are. I hope the list doesn't include hyperactivity. "Thanks."

Warren is between me and the door, showing no signs of budging. "If you go, I'm going," he tells me.

My eyebrows rise. "You do realize if I'm worrying about whether she's hurt you, I'm going to be paying less attention to whether she's about to hurt me?"

268

"Michaela..."

"I love that you want to protect me." I put my hand on his cheek. "But, Warren, look at how she's tossing those wolves around. You know them. They're hunters and warriors. And she's treating them like a bunch of toys. Please stay here?"

"I..."

"I know it's hard. I know. But what hope does one wolf stand against a demon?"

His eyes are hooded, his jaw clinched. He knows I'm right, but admitting it has got to be a tougher battle than the one I'm facing. It staggers me to think about the amount of strength it must take to face the facts that not only do I have to be the one to do this, but that there's not a thing he can do to help me.

My thumb strokes his skin. "I couldn't stand to see you slashed open," I whisper. "It would kill me."

With a swallow, he jerks away from me, stalking into the dining room without a backward glance.

"Alright then." My eyes move around the room. "Same to the rest of you?"

Several of them won't meet my eyes and only Tod nods, but no one says anything to stop me as I open the door and step, once again, into the bitterly cold Alaskan night.

"Back off, guys," I call to the wolves who remain able to stand. "This is a personal challenge."

I expect there to be resistance, but they all move away from Kim, literally backing from her.

"What's up, Kim?"

She snarls at me.

"Very scary."

"Where is Troy," she asks, retaining her demonic form. Her voice is gravely, sounding like it's being dredged from Hell.

I shrug. "Inside. Sleeping."

If she's noticed the darts hanging out of her hide, she's given no sign. Three of them, two nestled beside each other and one about a foot off, line up along her collarbone. At least, I think that's a collarbone.

"Did you hurt him?" she growls.

"Of course not."

She pulls her lips back, revealing sharp black teeth and

way more drool than I wanted to see. "If you're lying-"

"Hey," I interrupt. "What gave you the idea to try shifting into a demon, anyway? Were you just trying to reflect your inner personality?"

Growling, she leaps toward me, just like I knew she would. Changing quickly, I take the form of a fox and dart between her legs. She flounders comically, struggling to retain her balance.

"Not a very flexible form," I taunt after becoming human again. "Why are you so worried about Troy, anyway? He's a wanted criminal, you know."

"He didn't do those things!" Her feet stomp in a series of clunks as she turns slowly. "And even if he had, I would still love him."

Love him? She thinks she's in love with him? I try not to laugh.

"You just can't stand for me to be happy, can you, Mike? You always ruin everything! And now you've framed him for things you know he didn't do!" She swings an arm at me, but I shift into a mouse and avoid it easily.

Out of her reach again, I shift back to having vocal chords. "I don't know he didn't do them."

"Of course you do. Because you did them!"

I almost forget to evade the next attack.

Kim goes on, "They all know it was you. I heard them talking about it. They've known for ages it was a female all-were they were looking for. It was a big mistake to kill so many poor little sheep Thursday. You left your scent all over the place."

Watching my attacker closely, I wonder how long I'm going to have to keep her talking before the drugs kick in. "I was busy saving Aliah Thursday night. Get your facts straight."

She smirks. "A nice alibi, but not one that will stand up. It's obvious she only went along with you because Tod was willing to hook up with her if she did."

Pretty similar to what Lyly said earlier. I wonder what they think Tod's getting out of being pimped out? Probably shouldn't ask.

"The wolves are pissed at you," she tells me. None of the wolves do anything to back the statement up. "Not only have you been endangering their precious secret, but you've managed to brainwash their prince."

One of the wolves growls, a low and menacing sound. I look over, seeing Warren's mother behind lupine eyes. Her growl isn't for me, though; it's aimed at Kim. Apparently using her son in mad rantings isn't something she looks kindly on.

Kim growls back, bringing her arm across in a fierce swoop that Mrs. Denali can't possibly evade. Howling, I launch myself on Kim. My body lengthens, bulks up, and grows stronger as I become demon myself in order to pound her into the icy ground.

I land with a crash and move instantly to slam her head back against the ground.

Howling, she grabs at my shoulders, rolls me. She tries to take the top now, but I force the roll to continue and land several punches against the side of her head before she can move me off.

She manages to buck me with an enraged twist so she can scramble a few feet away, where she crouches and plans her next move.

Both defensively poised, we stare at each other. We're both breathing heavily, and both have broken scales, but she's the only one bleeding.

I bend when she runs at me, and send her flying over my shoulder. She staggers to her feet before I can turn and reach her, but she loses her footing and has to grab a tree to keep upright.

Leaping at her, I grab her arms to wrench them behind her back. I pin her wrists to her back with one of my hands, then use my remaining hand to grab her neck and slam her head into the tree trunk – again and again.

Slowly, she shifts into human form.

I follow in suit, but I don't stop bashing her against the tree until Warren grabs my arms and pulls me away from her.

She slumps to the ground, unconscious.

Chapter Twenty-Nine

"Get her inside, sweetie."

It's Warren's mother, speaking from somewhere behind me. Her voice is soft, compassionate. Warren obeys it without question.

Mr. Atherton seems to be with us, talking to Warren around me. I can't really focus on what they're saying. My thoughts are stuck in what just happened, my ears deafened by a crackling static that has to be born of too much adrenaline. Is this what shock feels like? Isn't that supposed to be cold? I'm not cold. I'm hot. Burning.

Warren's warmth is almost too much to handle, but he's holding on tight, and I don't have the energy to fight free of him, even if I wanted to.

He draws me down onto a couch, where I open my eyes to see Mr. Atheron's sitting room.

We're alone.

I try to ask what's going on, how Kim is... if I killed her or not. But when my mouth tries to open, all I do is yawn. My eyes shut, and I can't open them again.

Warren holds me while I sleep, is still holding me when I wake at the sound of people coming into the room.

"How are they?" Warren asks, meaning his injured packmates.

There's a deep sigh. "We lost Thomas. The others will probably be alright, but we don't know for sure."

My love makes a tiny whine of mourning at the news. I don't know who Thomas was, but for Warren, he was family.

"And Kim?" he asks.

"Still heavily drugged to prevent a change, and confessing," Mr. Atherton answers smoothly. He sits in a plush chair and Vivianne perches on the arm of it.

They look good together. Right. Is that how Warren and I look? How can she keep leaving him?

Vivianne gives me a sympathetic smile. "How are you?"

"Fine," I mumble, shifting so I'm not lying on Warren anymore, but sitting beside him. He moves too, keeping an arm around my shoulder. "Confessing?"

The vixen nods, a frown making her look years older than usual. "She was the one killing the livestock."

"Kim?"

That shouldn't be a surprise. She turned into a demon and tried to kill my friend. Did kill at least one member of Warren's pack...

"She was trying to frame you." Vivianne uses a soft tone, but the words still hurt. I knew Kim hated me, but... I don't like her either, but I would never try to set her up for something that carried a death penalty. She was trying to murder me.

"How?" I want to know.

"Perfume."

"Perfume?" Warren repeats.

Vivianne nods. "The kind you haven't worn since you got here. She never noticed you stopped wearing it, just knew you used to. And she made sure it was spread all over the sites of the livestock slayings."

Warren's radiating tension. The growling is back, quiet but impossible not to hear. "The trackers thought it was Michaela?"

"Some of them," Mr. Atherton responds. "There was definitely a female all-were to blame. Her scent was stronger than the male's. But Kim used too much of the perfume. Anyone wearing that much would drive everyone near them insane. It almost drowned out the other scents."

I squint. "So Troy was there too?"

Vivianne makes a sound. "We think she was stalking him. She'd spend time watching him, then kill something close by. It probably never occurred to her she was implicating him."

Nodding, I think she's probably right about that. Kim didn't want Troy to die; she wanted him to be hers.

But Warren is thinking about something else. "Why did no one mention the female?"

Vivianne looks uneasy, but Mr. Atherton laughs. "What

273

would you have done to someone who did?"

"They told us," Vivianne says softly. "And Mike did a lot of yelling. I think they figured that if her principal reacted that vehemently, they didn't want to learn what her mate would do."

How many people knew about that? And why didn't anyone tell me? It would have saved me a lot of worry and anxiety if I had known he was acting strange because I was his mate, not because he couldn't stand me.

Something in the back of my mind pokes into my thoughts, making me blink. "Hold on. How could she have been doing that? She hasn't been turned three months yet, has she?" Were we wrong about when he turned her? No, he admitted just tonight he didn't attack her until after I failed to change.

Mr. Atherton gives me a droll look. "She didn't need to be."

"You didn't either," Warren states, a little breathlessly, as if the realization is coming to him. "That's why it was so easy for you to make partial changes. You don't have to change on the moon, and you could have changed anytime you thought to."

"Right." Vivianne nods in my direction. "You're something completely new. It's going to take a while for us to learn the rules for what you all-weres can and can't do."

"Will the other two be around for that?" I ask.

"Maybe." Mr. Atherton shrugs, as if he doesn't care too much one way or the other. "They'll be tried by the pack."

"They'll kill Kim." Warren doesn't sound sorry about it. He also sounds distant, as if he isn't part of the group that would be doing the killing.

"And Troy?"

My wolf gives me a long, probing look. "He didn't kill the animals," he says after several moments.

"But he did turn Michaela and Kimberly," Mr. Atherton finishes.

"He didn't know the rules," Warren argues, his eyes still locked on me. "That should buy some leniency."

"Should it?" I whisper.

"We're not animals to rip people apart just because we hate them," he answers.

There's more than a hint of pride in Mr. Atherton's nod. "So what do you want to do with him?"

"North Pole."

The others murmur agreement, but I have to ask, "Huh?"

"There's a camp up there," Warren tells me. "Sort of a..."

"Prison?" I guess.

"More like rehab." He shrugs. "Similar concept."

"You should go tell your father," Mr. Atherton states. "I'd be willing to bet there's someone calling for blood by now."

"Probably," Warren agrees. Holding a hand out to pull me after him, he gets to his feet.

"Your father already asked to take Kim tonight." Mr. Atherton gets up too, Vivianne rising at his side as if their minds are linked. "Troy's going to stay here until the sedation wears off though."

Warren grunts and starts to lead me toward the door. I wobble as I follow him, causing him to stop and frown at me.

"Do you need to see the nurse?" Vivianne asks me, sounding just like a mother.

"No." I shake my head, trying to ignore how light-headed it makes me feel. "I'm just tired."

"You've had a lot of stress." She comes up and gives me a short hug. "Get some sleep, kit."

Kit... What I wouldn't give to really be a fox and not a monster.

There's a tug on my hand, and I wave goodnight as Warren guides me out. "You're not a demon," he tells me as the door closes.

"So, life mates have mind reading powers?" I start toward the stairs. "When do mine kick in?"

He lets out an amused breath. "No mind reading. You're just that obvious."

We traipse up the stairs, each one feeling like a small mountain.

"Warren?"

He gives me a lopsided smile. "Michaela?"

"I'm proud of you."

Stopping at my room, he raises his eyebrows. "For standing around while my mate risked her life?"

"Yes."

He blinks.

275

"Amongst other things," I go on. "Most noticeably, not killing Troy."

"That was pretty hard," he admits. Something flares in his eyes. "Do I get a reward?"

Wrapping my arms around his neck, I pull him close, giving him a very thorough kiss.

My knees start to weaken. And I don't think it's from exhaustion.

I whimper as he pulls away.

"Stop that," he whispers. "You might give me ideas."

My head darts forward, and my teeth nip his throat.

The responding growl is very different his earlier ones.

"Good night, Michaela."

He forces himself back, taking a huge step and plastering his back to the far wall.

If we could harness that wolf's self-control, we could power all of the state.

I grin as I reach behind me to open my door.

I'm still grinning as I crash onto my bed, falling asleep before I can even wiggle all the way under my comforter.

The grin fades sometime in the night, but I wake up laughing. I'm dancing as I get dressed, skipping while I go up the hallway. My cheer dies down as I get closer to my destination, but the flame of joy stays in my heart even as I walk up to Troy's cage.

The cage is locked, but I can only assume that's to keep people out of it rather than to keep Troy in. He could, after all, simply change into something small enough to escape if he were at all interested in leaving the warmth of the building or the food he's been given here. From the number of dishes in the cage with him, it looks like he's been making up for his weeks of near starvation.

He grins when he sees me, thinking I'm smiling at him rather than just beaming at the world in general. "Mike!"

I drag a chair over and put it just outside of his reach. He looks none the worse for his ordeals. His borrowed clothes are clean, and his hair has obviously been shampooed. He even shaved. He still smells awful, but now I know it isn't from lack of hygiene.

276

"How you feeling?"

Wrapping his hands around the bars of his cell, his gives off a dangerous rogue sort of air. A few weeks ago, it would have had my heart doing somersaults.

"My head hurts like a bitch."

Wincing in sympathy, I tell him, "I'm sorry. We probably shouldn't have shot you."

"You think?"

"Then again, maybe we should have."

He laughs. "There's my Mike." Stilling as he watches me, he turns serious. "What's going on with us?"

"Well..." I lean back and let my eyes drop to were the bars meet the floor. "I'm staying here. And you're going to the north pole."

"The north pole?" Glancing up, I see him blinking in astonishment. "Are you serious?"

"You thought we were there already, huh?"

Dropping his hands, he spreads them out. "What the hell, Mike?"

Taking pity, I stop trying to tease him. "There's a camp near North Pole. The town, not the actual pole." He nods impatiently, and I continue. "I guess you could think of it like juvie. They're going to send you there until you're rehabilitated." At least, I assume Warren's going to win that argument. From what I know of his father, the elder Denali doesn't want to kill anyone he doesn't feel he has to. And he's already had to slay one teenager this week if Kim met the fate I expect she did last night.

"Rehabilitated?" He shakes his head. "Didn't you hear, I didn't do it."

"You didn't kill those animals," I agree. "But you did turn two humans into weres. Against our wills."

"I did that because I love you."

I elect to ignore both that and the wounded expression on his face.

"It doesn't matter why you did it. It happened. And they usually kill people for it."

"But not me?"

I sigh. "They're likely to go easy on you because you didn't

277

know what you were doing."

"I knew what I was doing." His gaze is fevered. "I was turning my mate into what I am. So we could be together."

"You could have asked, you know. Permission can be given to turn a mate who wants to be turned."

He watches me closely. "What would you have said?"

"I don't know."

The answer is fully honest.

"Would I have been required to kill you for saying no?" he asks.

"What?"

He smirks. "They don't mind people telling everyone they meet that werewolves are real?"

Oh. Good point. "No, you can't tell just anyone. But a mate... A true life mate... That would be different."

"So why isn't this different?"

I sigh. "If nothing else, I'm not your mate."

"Like hell you're not."

It takes work, but I look him straight in the eye. "No, I'm Warren's."

"Right."

"I'm serious, Troy."

He laughs at that. "Sure you are," he says with several tons of sarcasm. "You're not just trying to torture me, not punishing me for what I did with Kim. This has nothing to do with vengeance."

It doesn't, but he's not going to see that yet, is he?

I get up and start to go.

"Where are you going?" he calls after me.

"I'm going to take a shower and then go find my boyfriend. I want to see if he really did manage to save your worthless ass or not."

"Save? What?"

Turning, I meet his gaze across the room. "Warren's the one trying to get you sent to North Pole."

His hands ball into fists. "I'll just bet he is."

"Everyone else wants to kill you. Like they probably killed Kim last night."

That makes him pause. He's thinking so hard it looks like

278

he's in pain from it. "And why would your precious new boyfriend help me?"

"Honestly?" I shake my head and laugh. "I have no idea."

Before he can ask me anything else, I leave him there.

Does leaving him in a cage hurt me? Yeah, I'm surprised to notice, it does. He's an idiot, a jerk, and a liar. But he's not a criminal. His crimes weren't malicious. He wasn't trying to hurt anyone. He probably thought he was doing us favors.

And in a way, he did do me a favor. If he'd never turned me, then I wouldn't have come here. I wouldn't have my wonderful new friends. I wouldn't have Warren.

Nearly weary enough to go back to bed already, I trudge into my room, head down, my thoughts turning to focus on the very long shower I intend to indulge in. I'm several steps in before I realize I'm not alone.

Warren sits on the bed, stroking Wolfgang as though he's a live pet rather than a stuffed toy. His eyes are focused on the wolf, but I have no doubt he knows I came into the room.

"Hey, Warren."

"Michaela."

I lean against my desk, watching him.

He sighs. "I was just looking to see if maybe you have this sweatshirt I'm missing," he tells Wolfgang. "But I can't find it. And I guess it doesn't matter anymore anyway."

My eyes squint and my head tilts to the side. I wish he'd look at me. "Why doesn't it matter? Did it not fit?"

"It fit fine." The words are subdued, but pained.

"What's wrong, Warren?"

I get my wish about him looking at me when he directs a quick look of confusion towards me before returning his eyes to Wolfgang. He doesn't answer me.

Something's wrong, and he's confused I'd have to ask what. It's something that would mean it no longer matters if he was the person I was talking about in the kitchen last night...

Oh.

He came into my room to find me missing first thing in the morning. And when I came in, I most likely stank of someone else. I sigh.

"Warren, please stop trying to fix me up with other people.

279

I'm only interested in them in your head."

There are several seconds of silence before he whispers, "That would be more convincing if you didn't reek of our guest."

"True," I grant. "I was about to take a shower. Would you care to join me?"

His eyes snap back to me.

I smile through the feeling of panic in my blood.

I have no idea why I just issued that invitation. It's not as though I am in the habit of inviting guys into the shower with me.

On the other hand, this isn't just some random guy.

His response is slowly measured. "I don't think that's a very good idea right now."

Shrugging, I turn away to find some clean clothes. I'll need to wash the Troy-stink off of the ones I'm in before I want to wear them again. "But you'll be here when I get out, right?"

He takes a second to answer. "Yeah."

I don't like that pause. Turning, I try to meet his eyes, but he won't look up at me. "Promise?"

"Yeah."

"You promise you'll be here when I get back?" I clarify.

There may be a hint of a smile, but it's hard to tell with his face so shadowed. "I'll be here."

Nodding, I dash into the bathroom, jumping into the water before it has a chance to warm all the way.

My shower's a lot shorter than the one I had originally planned. Despite getting his promise, part of me is honestly expecting Warren to have vanished by the time I'm done. I work up an extra lather of shampoo in my hair and use three times as much body wash as usual, although I skip the conditioning phase in favor of getting finished as soon as physically possible.

The top of several layers of clothes I pull on is the shirt Warren was looking for. He apparently didn't think to look in the box in the bathroom in which I keep my pajamas. The water running down its back from my wet hair may cause it to lose some of his scent, but I'm pretty sure I can get something to replace it.

When I open the door, I find him sitting exactly where I left him, still looking at Wolfgang. "Hey, Warren." I sit down beside him, my leg pressing against his.

"Michaela."

He doesn't say the name the way he usually does, but with a worshipful awe as he looks at me and sees what I'm wearing. You'd think I'd come out in top of the line lingerie the way he's watching me. His hand reaches out, tucking wet hair back behind my ear and then grabbing the nape of my neck. Slowly, giving me plenty of time to balk, he brings his mouth down over mine, caressing it with the same masterful grace as always. His tongue flicks across mine, making my whole body sing in approval.

I move in closer, trying to press against him, but he pulls away. "Michaela..."

"I love you, Warren."

He blinks. "You..."

"Love... you... Warren." I grin and run my fingers through his hair. "Which I think is a good thing since I'm your life mate."

Taking a shaky breath, he shies away, his eyes tightly shut.

"I know you didn't mean to blurt that out yesterday." I inch along the mattress, not letting him get away with breaking off contact. I grab his chin, turning his head toward me, and command him, "Look at me, Warren." I repeat the order, waiting to go on until he opens his eyes. My hands shift to the sides of his face. "I'm not scared away. I'm still here. I'm not going to run from you."

"Yet," he whispers.

"Silly wolf. I have no intention of ever running."

"And you aren't scared?"

I meet his scrutiny with complete openness. Maybe I should be scared, or at least doubtful, but I'm neither. "No."

His admission is scarcely louder than his breath. "I was."

Unthinking, my hands jerk away, but he launches to grab them. "Was, Michaela."

With an intense expression, as though he sees only me, he clings to my hands. "I was so scared when I first smelled you."

His eyes search mine. "Do you have any idea how terrifying it is for everything to suddenly change that fast? One second, everything was normal, and then a single breath later,

281

everything in my life had been reordered. The things I used to care about didn't matter anymore, and nothing was as important as this new scent. I didn't even know what you looked like yet. And then I did see you."

He smiles softly for a second. "You would have been the most amazing thing I had ever seen. Except for the way you looked at me. Like I was some criminal sneaking up on you."

His eyes squeeze shut again.

"Warren. I'm sorry. A stranger surprised me in the middle of the night. I was thrown off, that's all."

"You were terrified of me," he murmurs.

"Okay," I breathe. "I was scared. I didn't know you."

"I was your mate!"

I fling my arms around him, holding on tight. "I'm sorry," I repeat, my heart ripping apart at his obvious pain.

"I know it wasn't your fault. It was my fault." He starts to pet me with one hand running up and down my back. "But it hurt so much, Michaela. Hurt even worse than when I saw you with Seth. You literally screamed in terror."

"I shrieked in surprise." I squeeze as tightly as I can. "I did that last night too. And will do it next time you sneak up on me in the kitchen. Twenty years from now, you'll sneak up on me in a kitchen, I'll shriek, and our kids will laugh about it. Twenty years after that, our grandkids will think it's a riot."

He takes several long, deep breaths, while he thinks about that. "Promise?" he whispers. "Because the grandkids will be really disappointed if you don't scream."

I smile at the return of his humor. "I promise."

We cling to each other, holding tight. Silently, I make another promise, a promise never to let go.

Acknowledgements

Thanks, as always, are due to my family for putting up with having a writer in residence. This book has been a number of years in the making, a journey which crossed the width of a continent at one point, and trust me when I say that dealing with me during this time has not always been easy. Thanks to everyone who has put up with me, family or not.

Jimmy, I love you.

Eric, I know you don't think you have a choice in the matter, but thank you for all the support you give me; you really are the most wonderful son a mother could have.

Mom and Dad, thanks once again for raising me to believe in my imagination and in the value of sharing it with others.

Alaina, thanks for never killing me even if I may have deserved it a few times when we were kids. And for being an awesome creative influence. :)

Sommer, thank you for believing in this story when I would have let it die. And thank you for always believing in me.

Melody, I can't thank you enough for all the work you put into this project. Beyond being my cover artist and my editor, you've offered unflagging support and infinite sympathy even though life's been pelting you with curve balls. I consider you a blessing.

Bama, thanks for letting me ramble about a book you hardly remember so often. Even in the middle of the night.

And to everyone else I know on G+, Twitter, and in the real world: THANK YOU! You all contributed in your own ways to keeping me sane enough to publish this work. You rock!

www.ingramcontent.com/pod-product-compliance
Lightning Source LLC
Chambersburg PA
CBHW051415170626
46809CB00006B/2178